Mark B. Cohen w[...] mother was the au[...] his father, Paul, w[...] Calderwood Lodge [...] and the High School of Glasgow, he graduated with an honours degree in Interpreting and Translating from Heriot-Watt University in Edinburgh. He then spent two years as a parliamentary research assistant before moving to the City, where he is now a director at a merchant bank. He lives in North West London and his first novel, *Brass Monkeys*, is also published by Hodder and Stoughton.

If you would like to learn more about either novel or wish to get in touch with the author please visit *The Butcher's Ball / Brass Monkeys* website at www.brassmonkeys.com

Praise for Brass Monkeys

'A highly risqué account of sleaze and skulduggery in Whitehall and Westminster'   *Scotland on Sunday*

'A particularly disgusting romp'   *The Times*

'A political-sexual furore of the most scandalous proportions'   *London Jewish News*

'A prescient piece of prose'   *Observer*

'Anyone with half an interest in politics will have huge fun with Mark Cohen's frenetically-paced debut novel, which delves irreverently into the world of Westminster and the media'   *Yorkshire Evening Post*

'Some excellent set pieces . . . fun'   *Guardian*

'A cracking first novel'   *Independent*

'Sexy, savage, wildly imaginative and very, very naughty'   *Bookends Magazine*

'A hilarious critique of the machinations of tabloid journalists in the face of sexual exploits that would make even Bill Clinton blush and which reveals Cohen's sharp, intuitive eye for satirical observation . . . Like all good satire, it successfully bridges the gap between light-hearted fantasy and reality. Definitely more Yes, Prime Minister than Private Eye, and all the better for that.'
Amber Cowan, *The Times*

'The blackest of irreverent comedies set in the seedy world of double-dealing, unscrupulous seekers-after-power.'
Maggie Hartford, *Oxford Times*

'Anyone with half an interest in politics will have huge fun with Mark Cohen's frenetically-paced debut novel, which delves irreverently into the world of Westminster and the media.'
Yorkshire Evening Post

'A deliciously salacious mix of politics, sex and humour.'
Niki Austin, *London Jewish News*

'Sex, death, drugs and political intrigue abound . . . Cohen will rapidly become a major player in the field of social satire.'
Alex Gordon, *Peterborough Evening Telegraph*

The Butchers' Ball

Mark B. Cohen

Mark B. Cohen

CORONET BOOKS
Hodder & Stoughton

First published in Great Britain in 1999
by Hodder and Stoughton
First published in paperback in 1999
by Hodder and Stoughton
A division of Hodder Headline

A Coronet Paperback

10 9 8 7 6 5 4 3 2

A CIP catalogue record for this book
is available from the British Library

ISBN 0 340 71299 6

Typeset by Hewer Text Ltd, Edinburgh
Printed and bound in Great Britain by
Mackays of Chatham, plc, Chatham Kent

Hodder and Stoughton
A division of Hodder Headline
338 Euston Road
London NW1 3BH

Dedicated, with much affection,
to all my friends and colleagues at Barings,
past and present, and (I hope!) future.

The Butchers' Ball

It's a Butchers' Ball,
In that Futures Hall,
When they're out for your blood,
And your back's to the wall.

And they smell your fear,
For your nerves are shot
Since a billion was here
And now it's not.

And that loss isn't all
That you'll never unwind,
There's another shortfall —
In the balance of your mind.

Where you once shot the lights out
Now all that remains
Is to lower your targets
And shoot out your brains.

There's a gun in your head
And it's crooking its trigger
And it's whispering low
As it stifles a snigger:

'Man, your future's a sell,
And your past is a rout,
And suicide
Is the only way out

'So surrender to Fate
And bugger those butchers
And forever escape
From going back to the Futures.'

PROLOGUE

It was a nondescript mansion block. One of those red brick affairs that had attached themselves like so many unwanted blood clots to the main arteries into north London.

He approached the front entrance gingerly, as if expecting the crazy paving to be landmined. It was one o'clock in the morning and there was nobody around. For the umpteenth time he checked the scrunched-up note in his hand. The moisture in his palm had caused the ink to run, but the address was still legible: 56 Northpark Mansions.

There was a videophone. He found the correct buzzer and pressed it. After a pause long enough to let a little rivulet of sweat run down his forehead, he heard her voice. Dark, husky. 'Yes?'

His stomach lurched. 'This is . . .' Christ, what name had he used? He remembered just in time. 'This is Davey.' It came out like a croak.

There was a corresponding throaty chuckle from the videophone's speaker. 'Good. So you didn't chicken out.' Something about the way she spoke was faintly familiar. Cool, almost amused. 'Now stand away from the camera so I can see if you lied about yourself.'

He almost tripped over his own feet as he stepped back. He could sense himself being examined. This was madness. There was still time to change his mind. He could get back in his car and be miles from here within minutes. He didn't. He stood rigid and stared fixedly at the glass panel which housed the videophone.

At last she spoke again. 'Okay, you'll do,' said the voice languidly. 'Now remember what I said. You follow my instructions to the letter and we'll be fine. But you try anything funny and you're right out the door. Okay?'

He could hardly breathe. 'Yes.'

'Good. I'm going to buzz you in now. Then you take the lift to the fifth floor. Got that?'

'Ye-es.'

'Number 56 is on the right-hand side along the corridor. The door will be ajar. You come in and shut it behind you.'

'Yes.'

'Then you take off your clothes. Every item. Jewellery, the lot. *Comprende*?'

'I understand,' he said faintly.

'You won't see me at any time – but I'll be watching you. Do anything wrong and you're out. Got that?'

'Yes.'

'On the table by the door, you'll find the hood and the earplugs. Once you're completely naked, you put in the earplugs and put on the hood. Make sure you can't see or hear a thing. Don't even think about cheating, because I'll know. If you cheat, you're out. If you leave any clothes on, you're out. If you do anything wrong, you're out. Understood?'

'Yes,' he said weakly. 'But what . . . what then?'

There came the throaty laugh again. 'Then, you leave it all to me,' she said. 'And we have ourselves some fun.'

Chapter One

━━━━━◗◖◗◖◗━━━━━

It had once been said of Roy Falloni, the star fund manager at Butchers Bank, that when the markets began to shoot up, so too did Falloni.

That was an exaggeration. Like one or two other City high-fliers, Falloni would admit to indulging in the occasional hallucinogenic when the stock markets were buzzing and his clients' investments were forging ahead. But never, he insisted, *never* did he take anything during working hours. Not until the dealing screens had gone dark for the day and he'd forsaken his desk at Butchers for his usual corner at Flato's, the exclusive City brasserie, where the bar staff's discretion was assured by the crisp fifty pound note they invariably found on his table at closing time.

No, from seven in the morning until seven at night, Falloni always boasted, he was a drug-free zone, as his mind swivelled and swerved relentlessly in search of those unexpected opportunities to prise cash from the small investor and hand it over to his already vastly wealthy private clients at Butchers Bank.

So when Toby Slaker, Falloni's immediate superior, noticed that his deputy looked particularly agitated one morning, he couldn't put it down to any form of intoxication. There had to be another reason.

Toby decided to broach the subject with Felicia, the Private Clients Department's shapely secretary. She could generally be relied on to know everything about everyone, and Toby had a feeling her knowledge on Falloni might be even more detailed than usual. While most of the men in the office had designs on Felicia's sumptuous body, it was rumoured Roy Falloni had gone beyond the design stage and moved into full-blown construction. Or, Toby suspected, at least sunk his first borehole.

He tackled Felicia just before lunch as he corrected some letters he'd dictated to her earlier. Her typing was notoriously inaccurate and always required careful checking. But Toby liked to avoid direct criticism of his staff. His was a non-confrontational approach to management.

'This letter about our unique share selection process,' he said gently. 'Don't you think it should read "we have a *two-tiered* investment approach", rather than "a *too-tired*" one?'

Felicia cast him a dazzling smile. 'Oh, that's a *great* improvement,' she drawled. 'I thought it sounded a bit feeble when you said it, but one doesn't like to point these things out.'

Toby sighed. Like so many of Butchers' staff, this job was not Felicia's life's work. A distant relation of the Butcher family, she'd taken the position pro tem while she saved towards her dream of touring a modern opera company round the inner cities of China. 'Do you think you could change it and get it back to me . . . ah . . . later today?' he asked.

'Absolutely,' Felicia replied airily. 'Be done as soon as poss.' She glanced at her watch. 'Well, after lunch, anyway.'

'Thank you. Oh, and one other thing.' Toby drew a little closer to her and tried to look away from those long silky legs, which she'd just crossed in front of him. He was, he had to remind himself constantly, her head of department and a married man to boot. While he fantasised about her just as much as the others, he made it a rule never to join in their outward letching. 'You haven't by any chance noticed something up with Falloni this morning, have you? He looks in a bit of a state.'

'Does he?' Felicia's face now took on a deliberately bored expression. 'I really couldn't say. In fact, to be perfectly frank, I'm not at all interested in the moods of Mr Roy Falloni.' And she swept regally out of the office without another word.

Evidently a shared interest in music had not been enough to

sustain that little office romance, Toby reflected. So he had no option but to tackle Falloni head-on about whatever was on his mind. He just hoped it was nothing to do with the markets. Falloni's adventurous investment policy was a source of constant worry to him, and that morning the eastern European stock exchanges, Falloni's favourite stamping-ground, had been particularly turbulent.

At lunchtime, on his way back from the automatic dispenser that had become the only source of drinks since Doris, the tea-lady, had been headhunted by Goldbar and Lachs, Toby dropped by his deputy's little glass-partitioned office. Negotiating the piles of papers on the floor, he cleared himself some space on a visitor's chair. 'Successful morning?' he asked casually.

Falloni looked up jumpily from his computer, automatically shielding it from prying eyes. 'Ace,' he said. That was his standard response but today it did not carry his customary conviction. Nervily, he picked up a sandwich and took a bite, holding it away from himself to prevent its filling dropping on his Armani tie. Falloni's own appearance, unlike his office's, was immaculate. He'd always liked to dress the part, even when just starting out as a junior clerk, and now, having risen through the ranks so rapidly, he could really afford to indulge himself.

'Good,' said Toby. 'Good.' He hesitated. 'It's only that you sort of don't look yourself this morning and . . .'

Reluctantly dragging his gaze back from the screen, Falloni made a visible effort to regain his nonchalance. 'Naw,' he said. 'Just some personal stuff. You know.' He raised his eyes to the heavens. 'The usual.'

Toby nodded. Their secretary was not Falloni's only conquest. The man's love life was about as overpopulated as one of the Chinese cities to which Felicia would one day introduce the delights of Schopenhauer and Birtwhistle. But Toby was still not convinced that was all there was to Falloni's moodiness. He'd never known him be affected by emotional turbulence yet. 'I see Russia's fallen out of bed this morning,' he ventured tentatively.

'Yeah,' said Falloni. 'It's a toilet job.' He reached up and pulled at an imaginary chain by way of illustration.

'Not taken a haircut there, have you?' Toby persevered, falling unconsciously into Falloni's own favourite jargon. 'Those futures you bought on the LAFFE doing okay?' He tried to keep the anxiety from his voice.

His deputy stared at him, now with a half-amused look. 'Hey. Listen, Tobe, don't get so uptight, okay? Markets go up, markets go down. That's how you make-a-da-money, huh?' Falloni liked to play up his Italian ancestry for effect, even though he'd actually been born in Whitechapel hardly a mile away from London's financial centre where he now worked.

'Look,' said Toby. He was almost pleading. 'I just want to be sure you're sticking to the mandates and not taking any unauthorised risks.' That was the key. Provided Falloni kept within the clients' investment guidelines, then Butchers Bank could hardly be liable if anything went wrong. 'It's not unreasonable, is it? I mean, I *am* meant to be running this department.'

'Course you are,' said Falloni soothingly. 'And I'd tell you if there was anything to worry about. But the rest of the time, you gotta trust me. See, that was the deal, right?' Expansively, he relaxed back in his swivel chair and pulled at his braces. 'I get full autonomy on all investment decisions, reporting straight into Kurdell. Am I right or am I right?'

Toby nodded miserably. He *was* right. That was indeed the deal that Falloni had struck with the group MD over Toby's head after he'd almost been lured away by a rival last year. 'Okay,' Toby said quietly. 'But for God's sake just tell me you're being careful.'

Falloni took pity on him. In fact, the glance he cast him was almost affectionate. 'Sure I am,' he said. 'Dead careful. And, if you really want to know, I closed out nearly all those futures ages ago. But even if I hadn't,' he persisted breezily, 'you got nothing to worry about. The clients know the score.' Patiently, he embarked on his standard spiel. 'You gotta understand, Tobe, the nature of the beast here. See, the guys I manage aren't your ordinary punters. They expect something a bit more whizzy than a few per cent growth a year. And that's what I deliver. But if you started pecking around me like a mother hen the way you do the rest of them' – he gestured out through the partition to the half dozen other investment managers in the department – 'you'd just get yourself uptight for nothing.' He chuckled. 'That's why Kurdell gave me the special deal, see? To save you from getting a fucking seizure . . .' And, case proved, he gave a great whoop and spun round and round in his swivel chair.

Toby sighed in half-amused resignation. For someone less modest, being lectured by a former office junior might have been galling, but not for him. Besides, he genuinely admired the man's gutsy approach and startling successes. And he had to admit Falloni was right about the clients. His glittering list of showbiz celebrities was a million miles from the stodgy Scottish nobility and Butcher family friends that were the department's normal bread and butter.

Finally, Toby gave up. He'd registered his concerns with Kurdell when the original arrangement was made, and there wasn't much more he could do. 'Okay,' he said, making for the door. 'Just keep me in the loop, okay?'

'Sure thing,' said Falloni easily. 'Hey, listen, hang on a sec, Tobe. I'm glad you stopped by 'cos I wanna ask you a favour.'

'Oh?' Toby resumed his seat. 'Well, ask away.' Such requests from Falloni were usually for an introduction to some new female member of staff, but today he couldn't think who that might be.

Falloni's face took on an earnest expression. 'This television thing tonight for Mattison Pick,' he said. 'I don't think I'm going to make it after all.'

Now Toby's eyebrows rose in surprise. Falloni was usually a pushover for anything showbizzy and ever since getting the invitation to this evening's TV bash he'd been talking of little else.

'But with Pick being such a big client,' Falloni went on, 'Butchers ought to be represented. So I was wondering . . . ah . . . if you fancied going instead?'

7

Weirder and weirder. Mattison Pick, the famous American composer of musicals, was Falloni's favourite client. Winning Pick's business last year had been the breakthrough that launched Falloni's meteoric rise in the department. And he was fiercely possessive of the Pick account, never letting Toby anywhere near it. If Falloni was inviting Toby to go to the TV recording in his place, it was strange indeed.

But Toby was too busy to go tonight. He shook his head. 'Uh-uh. I'm planning on staying late. I've got to finish looking through the quarterly reports. And I've got the documentation for those new French clients to check.'

'What, here in the office?' asked Falloni with dismay.

'Of course. Look, what is this anyway? Are you up to something?'

'Naw. Honest.' Falloni's handsome Mediterranean features beamed out innocence. 'I told you. It's just . . .' His voice tailed off. 'It's just something's come up that I've got to deal with.'

'Well, why does either of us need to go to this Pick TV thing? I thought it was just friends that got invited to that sort of recording.'

'People as rich as Pick don't have friends,' said Falloni knowingly. 'They have *entourages*. Lawyers, accountants, advisers. And that's what we are. Butchers is part of his *entourage* so we gotta be represented.'

Toby shrugged. 'Not tonight, I'm afraid.'

'Aw, come on, Tobe!' Falloni seemed unusually concerned. 'This guy's my . . . our biggest client. Christ, we manage close to a hundred million for him. We gotta keep him sweet.' A thought struck him and he cupped his hands under two huge imaginary breasts. 'Hey, and maybe Pick'll have that pin-up of a wife with him,' he said, wiggling his tongue lasciviously. 'Did you see her getting the Oscar last night? What a bod, eh?'

Toby drew breath. Falloni knew his tastes and might have guessed that Pick's actress wife, Peaches La Trené, figured even higher than Felicia in his personal fantasy stakes. But he spotted the flaw in this supposed inducement at once. 'If she was in Hollywood for the Oscars yesterday,' he pointed out, 'she's hardly likely to be in London for the *Hoodwink Show* tonight.' He consulted one of the row of clocks on the wall which provided the time in various worldwide locations. 'It's still early morning in California now.'

Falloni put his finger to his head and pretended to shoot himself. 'Quick thinking,' he said. 'Very quick.' He groped for another possible carrot and found one in the shape of Toby's own wife. 'How about taking Simona? She'd like to go.' He corrected himself. 'She'd love to go. Right up her street. And the invitation's for two.'

'No!' said Toby. He loathed that type of function. Celebrities, movers and shakers, media people, back-slapping, networking, cheek-kissing. It was not for him. 'I'm not going and that's final.'

He waited for the inevitable war of attrition. Falloni was nothing if not persistent. For once, though, he appeared to have won an easy victory. His deputy stuck out his bottom lip, then shrugged in resignation. But as Toby went back to his own office, a glass box on the other side of the Private Clients Department, he was aware of Falloni picking up the phone with a smirk.

Toby hadn't been back at his desk for five minutes when his own phone rang. 'Are you mad?' Simona launched straight in. 'Of course we're going. Have you any idea who'll be there? And if Butchers doesn't want the contacts, then WHAM certainly does.'

Toby threw an angry glance through the glass partition to his colleague, who'd pointedly turned his back. 'Falloni shouldn't even have told you Pick was a client,' he said irritably. 'It's highly confidential.'

'Crap,' said Simona. 'Anyway, you left his contract lying on the kitchen table the other day, so I already knew. Now what time do we have to leave the City to get there?'

Toby racked his brains for an excuse not to go. 'I thought you were entertaining big clients of your own tonight,' he said.

His wife's voice took on that tone of impatience she increasingly seemed to reserve for him. 'Listen, you worry about your business and I'll worry about mine,' she snapped. 'I'll get someone to stand in for me. This is much more important. Do you know how many billions of dollars will be there?'

Typical, thought Toby. For Simona, people were nothing more than mobile cheque books. Prospective clients for her to lure to whichever ruthless American investment house she was currently gracing with her services. He summoned up what indignation he could. 'What's this stupid programme all about, anyway?' he asked.

Simona let out a sigh of exasperation. 'Toby, darling, even *you* must have heard of the *Hoodwink Show*. It's that surprise thing. They get some celebrity victim in under false pretences, then they put a hood on his head. And when they take it off, they spring a bombshell on him, and all his celebrity friends are there waiting to join in. It's that ditzy blonde who used to present children's TV. Candida what's-her-name.'

'Blitz,' said Toby resignedly. 'Candida Blitz.' He vaguely remembered it now. It was the usual cloyingly sentimental garbage which filled the Popviz satellite station. Another reason for avoiding it at all costs.

Damn Falloni. Naturally, the bastard had known that Simona would never pass up an opportunity like this. Toby was simply not proof to their joint pressure. 'I suppose we'll go then,' he said wearily. It would mean getting up early the next morning to work in his study at home, since these reports needed to be finished before he came in.

'You bet,' Simona confirmed. 'I'll pick you up outside your office at six thirty.'

Chapter Two

———✦◆✦———

Determined though he was to give Falloni the cold shoulder for his treachery, it was not in Toby's nature to hold a grudge. Besides, his curiosity about the man's motives was mounting. So he knocked on the glass door of his number two just before he left and again stepped over the mounds of papers.

The chair on which Toby had sat earlier had already been recolonised by a thick orange file which lay there half open. Before Toby could reach out to move it, Falloni abruptly came round and snapped it shut, placing it carefully on top of a nearby cabinet. Toby wondered if it had any relevance to Falloni's strange mood, and surreptitiously craned his neck to see what was on its label. But the spine was now facing inwards; all he'd glimpsed before Falloni snatched it away was four letters of a word on the title page: 'enne'. The typeface was distinctively bold but the letters meant nothing to Toby at all. 'I'd still like to know what tonight's foul act is in aid of,' he said.

Falloni winked with forced confidence. 'Secret,' he replied. 'Could be you'll find out tomorrow, though.'

An awful idea occurred to Toby. 'It's not an interview, is it? You've not been headhunted?' Despite Toby's reservations about his investment methods, it would be a disaster for the company if Falloni took his lucrative client list elsewhere.

Falloni paused thoughtfully. 'Yeah,' he said. 'Maybe. Maybe I have been.' He looked at Toby through pursed eyes. 'Working for Butchers might be the pinnacle of your ambitions, pal, but it's not exactly mine.'

Toby tried to hide his dismay. Apart from the business implications, there was a personal aspect. Toby had actually come to like his deputy and together they made an excellent management team. In the Private Clients Department Falloni's flamboyance provided a good counterbalance to Toby's own more cautious style. The time he'd done an illicit midnight bungee jump from the Private Clients Department's great casement windows was still talked about with admiration by many of the younger staff.

'Listen,' said Toby. 'Don't do anything rash. And give Butchers a chance to match any offer you get. Remember, skipping from company to company's not the only way to move up in the City. I'm testament enough to that. Butchers is a firm that places a high premium on loyalty; and you won't find many others like that around any more.'

Falloni grinned back at him but said nothing.

Toby glanced at his watch. Simona would be waiting outside, but this was serious. 'Roy,' he said earnestly, 'I may not say it very often but I value your input a great deal. And don't underestimate me. I know everyone thinks I'm the quiet type, but in my own way I'm pretty ambitious. This is a great company and I intend to rise right to the top one day.' He held Falloni's gaze. 'I'd like to take you along, if you stick with me.'

Falloni got up and moved back round to where Toby was sitting. Bringing his head right up close he stared into his superior's great baby eyes. Then with a sly smile he pinched both his plump cheeks. 'I love it when you go all sincere on me,' he said. 'Makes you look so cute.'

Toby was used to having his leg pulled by Falloni. With a shrug, he got up and left. He'd said his piece and there wasn't much more he could do. Stopping only to collect his briefcase from his desk, he wound his way through the maze of glass-partitioned offices towards the great oak door that led, via a spiral staircase, to the lift lobby below.

*   *   *

In the old days, as Toby loved to tell new staff, the attic floor now used by the Private Clients Department had been a dining area for the messengers and secretaries. And if you took a deep breath, he would assure them, you might still detect the faint odour of mutton chops and boiled cabbage from that bygone era. Of course, at that time, he'd explain, it had consisted of two rooms: one for the men and one for the women, it being inconceivable that they should be allowed to mingle. Then he would show them the boarded-up stairway at the other end of the floor which was now used only as a fire escape but had once been the 'Ladies Entrance'. It still bore the faded legend: 'Gentlemen entering this dining area without express permission from Miss Wilks will be subject to dismissal.'

Toby had a wealth of such stories about the bank's history. For his fond words to Falloni about Butchers had been more than just those of a departmental head trying to hold on to a valued employee. They had been genuinely heartfelt. Toby loved Butchers Bank with a passion. He adored being part of a tradition that stretched back more than a century, to that much celebrated day when Cameron Butcher, the company's crusty Scottish founder, had abandoned his Edinburgh office to establish a bridgehead in the burgeoning financial centre of the City of London. He loved the bank's absurd rituals which were still maintained to the present day: the annual Scottish ceilidh, the Butchers' Ball, which all the staff were expected to attend in Highland dress, and where the current chairman, Sir Lomond Butcher, kilted up in the family tartan, would dance his portly wife round the dealing room in endless reels of the Dashing White Sergeant or the Gay Gordons until late into the night. He loved the yearly Burns Night suppers and the faded oil paintings which bedecked the bank's corridors evoking long-forgotten battles in which the brave Scottish clans had banished the English sassenachs. Never mind that Butchers Bank now lay at the very heart of England's establishment. Never mind that the Butcher family were now firmly London-based and rarely visited their Scottish estate except for the annual massacre of its wildlife on the glorious twelfth. It was all part of Butchers' mystique and Toby had fallen completely under its spell.

Most of all Toby loved this wonderful old building. It was here that, for all of those hundred years, the Butchers' name and crest had been displayed in tiny letters on a plaque high above the front door. While all the other merchant banks had long since abandoned their traditional homes and moved to the glass and marble high-rise blocks that now littered the City, Butchers' elegant six-floor sandstone headquarters still sat incongruously in a corner of Gracechurch Street, like an old wind-up gramophone nestling among a host of modern hi-fi towers.

It sometimes appeared to Toby as if not a single thing had changed in Butchers' House since those early days. Perhaps that was a slight exaggeration; even Butchers had been forced to adapt to the technological revolutions that had overtaken the City in one wave after another. But, despite the addition of the vast swathes of modern equipment and electronic paraphernalia, the building had still managed to preserve most of its original features and much of its original fustiness. Even the elaborate network of wire baskets drawn by pulleys along the ceilings, which had once been used to transfer papers from one department to another, had been preserved intact, although overtaken long ago by an e-mail system which, as Toby was fond of joking, was considerably less efficient.

At least part of Toby's pride in Butchers arose from the fact that his own history was also rooted in the bank's tradition. Like many at Butchers, he was not the first member of his family to work there. His father had spent his entire career in what used to be called the Stock Office, the clerical engine room of the organisation, now known as Operations. Toby had already risen well beyond his father's relatively lowly status. Becoming head of the Private Clients Department was no small feat. But one day, just as he'd told Falloni, Toby intended to rise still further. And he had a feeling that somehow, somewhere, his late father was following his progress with the same sense of pride and continuity he felt himself.

* * *

In the fifth-floor lobby Toby drew back the heavy wrought iron gates and stepped into one of the old lifts. As it lumbered down through the building's core, it passed the grand Victorian boardroom on the second floor before delivering him safely to ground level, where, in Butchers' biggest concession to the modern City, a busy trading floor had been carved out of the old Banking Hall. Even in the late evening, it teemed with masses of telephone-bound traders, busy cutting deals with their Wall Street counterparts, who would be only halfway through their day on the other side of the Atlantic.

Then, his journey through Butchers' financial time-warp completed, Toby strode across the high-domed reception lobby and through the revolving door on to the pavement outside.

Chapter Three

In that second-floor boardroom a meeting was just in the process
of winding up.

'So that's agreed,' said Greg Kurdell, Butchers' managing
director, impassively. 'Slaker goes ex-directory first thing in the
morning.'

The chairman, Sir Lomond Butcher, dragged himself away
from the imaginary grouse moor that had been claiming his
attention for most of the afternoon. 'What's that?' he enquired.

Kurdell gritted his teeth. If this had been one of his subordinates, he would at the very least have ridiculed the concentration lapse for the amusement of everyone else present. But
he couldn't do that to Lomond Butcher – at least not yet. 'Toby
Slaker,' he repeated tersely. 'We're getting rid of him tomorrow
morning.'

The chairman glanced down with distraction at the tartan
folder bearing the Butchers' crest in which he kept his board
papers. He found the place, then gave an indulgent smile. 'No,'
he said. 'That can't be right.' In deference to his ancestry, his
accent held the merest hint of a Scottish burr. 'You've got the
wrong man. Slaker's our head of Private Clients. Very reliable.'
Kurdell was a relative newcomer, his expression implied, and
could be forgiven for not knowing the staff as he did. 'Must have
been with us for at least fifteen years now. And his father used to
work here before him, I think.' He looked questioningly at
Gordon, his young nephew and assistant, who was there to

make notes of the meeting and was also a fount of all information on Butchers' history.

'In the old Stock Office,' Gordon confirmed.

'Precisely,' beamed the chairman. His brow furrowed. 'Now, correct me if I'm wrong, but didn't Slaker Minor marry some secretary from here?'

'Simona Brawn,' said Gordon.

'That's right!' exclaimed Butcher delightedly. 'I remember now.' His expression became distant, and the assembled board members, recognising the signs of a family anecdote coming on, settled back for the long haul. All except Greg Kurdell, who tutted and studied his papers ostentatiously. Butcher ignored him. 'It was the year before old Finlay Butcher retired,' he began. 'The birds were particularly good that August, I remember. In those days, I was still in charge of staff welfare, and young Slaker came to me in some perplexity and said he'd fallen in love with his secretary, and did we mind if they got married? So I said that was splendid news, and when should we expect the next batch of little Slakers to be joining the company? Ha!' He chortled to himself. 'Off he went, happy as Larry. But when I told old Finlay they were engaged, the old fellow practically had apoplexy. Wanted to sack both of them because in those days, of course, fraternisation between the staff was still frowned upon. But I shut him up. "Don't be so bloody old-fashioned," I told him. In those words, too! And he listened to me. Now, whatever happened to the wife?' he asked Gordon. 'Is she still a secretary here?'

'Hardly,' said Gordon, spotting another opportunity to show off his encyclopaedic knowledge. 'After they got engaged, it was decided they shouldn't be in the same department. So she went to work for one of the dealers and persuaded him to let her dabble in the markets. Turned out to be quite a whizz. But as soon as she got some experience, she defected to Goldbar and Lachs for twice the salary. Been halfway round the City since then, and I believe she's recently been made CEO at Winegloss and Hooch. That's now part of Zlennek International, and I've heard it said that—'

'Quite so, my dear fellow, quite so.' Gordon's knowledge base could get out of hand if left unchecked. 'I remember her now,' said Butcher, his weather-beaten face puckering and his high-pitched drone rising in distaste. 'Actually, she was a ghastly aggressive woman, if I think about it. Glad she's gone, to be frank. But' – he finally came back to the matter at hand and glanced over at Kurdell, who had been listening to the various monologues with increasing impatience – 'we can't visit the sins of the wives on their poor husbands, can we now? Slaker's perfectly sound: good middle-class stock. No genius, of course, but then who is?'

'Quite,' said Greg Kurdell, under his breath.

'Backbone of the company,' concluded Butcher, who was fortunately slightly hard of hearing. 'You must be thinking of someone else to . . . ah . . . to remove from your telephone directory.'

'I believe not, Chairman.' Kurdell's tone was clipped and his expression intense. His left and right eyes operated slightly independently of one another, reinforcing the demented look that was his hallmark. 'I think you know that I don't make that kind of mistake.' He looked around for support from the other directors present but met only with averted gazes. So he drew a deep breath and allowed his tone to sink several octaves. 'For the last' – he consulted his watch menacingly – 'for the last three and a half hours we have been discussing my proposals to rationalise this business, once and for all. Which,' he almost barked, 'correct me if I'm wrong, is precisely why you brought me in here as managing director in the first place.'

'Quite.' Lomond Butcher smiled his most engaging smile. Brought up in a tradition that combined the quiet confidence of the English public school with the gentle determination of the Scottish nobility, he generally found charm the best means of getting his own way. 'Absolutely, my dear chap, but—'

Charm held little sway with Kurdell, though. 'There are no buts about it.' The managing director stood up and paced over to the boardroom window. 'Gentlemen, as you know, Butchers is approaching a watershed in its history.' Ignoring the patent indifference which overtook most of the faces in the room at this statement, he pushed on. 'But I don't think you quite understand the implications, even now.'

Lomond Butcher groaned. 'Is it really necessary to go through all that again?'

'I think it would be wise.' Kurdell enumerated the points on the fingers of one hand to add force. He knew that always annoyed the chairman. 'One,' he said. 'In barely two weeks' time, the Puritas Council, the ultimate owner of our company, will hold its annual meeting in this very boardroom.'

'Yes, but—'

'Two.' Kurdell's voice rose to shout down this interruption. 'Inconceivable though it may have been in the past, in the wake of last year's council meeting, it is now no longer impossible that Puritas might opt to sell Butchers Bank.'

This time Lomond Butcher interrupted with rather more determination. 'It *is* inconceivable. Totally inconceivable. As one of the Council members, I was at that meeting and *you* were not. And I tell you, this is being blown out of all proportion. There's no question of our being sold. All they said is that we have to bump up our profits a bit.'

Icily, Kurdell consulted a document in front of him. 'I have the minutes here,' he said. 'Correct me if I'm wrong.' He read aloud: 'The new moderator, Lord Sloach of Macclesfield, stated that he was dissatisfied with the return on capital from Butchers Bank, the Puritas Council's sole investment. To maximise its income and enable the Council to pursue its objectives of promoting British morality and'— he raised his eyes heavenwards — 'rehabilitating fallen women, he suggested it would do better to put its money on the two thirty at Epsom.' He smiled grimly. 'According to the minutes, there was laughter at that point.'

'That's just talk,' said Lomond Butcher dismissively. 'We always get that sort of thing from a new man, but he'll soon settle down. I mean, when my grandfather transferred ownership of Butchers to the Puritas Council, the very purpose was to *prevent* it from being taken over—'

'In that case,' Kurdell said curtly, 'he didn't do a very good job. And it would have been helpful if he hadn't left the appointment of its moderator to the government of the day. Lord Sloach is hardly the most sympathetic of masters.'

'Be that as it may,' insisted Lomond Butcher, 'as long as I'm a member of the Council, Butchers Bank will be safe.'

'However much is on offer?'

'Of course.'

Kurdell looked at him with incredulity. 'Chairman, I don't think you realise how attractive this bank might be to a potential predator.' He pointed through the window to the streets of the City which zigzagged off to the east. 'Without wishing to be melodramatic, gentlemen, the piranhas are circling out there. I should know,' he added leadenly. 'It's not long since I was leading one of the fucking shoals.'

On the faces of the assembled board a flurry of shock registered at his language. Kurdell ignored them all. The F-word had been commonplace in City boardrooms for years now and if they didn't like it they could lump it.

'Every other independent merchant bank has fallen, however elaborate the structure set up to protect it.' He banged his hand on the table as he listed them. 'Barings, Kleinworts, Warburgs, Morgan Grenfell. All swallowed up. Half a dozen of the European or Yank banks that missed out on those would give their eye teeth to get hold of Butchers,' he went on. 'And a host of others are on the lookout too. The Zlennek Corporation, for one. I happen to know that Ivor Zlennek's been sniffing around the Puritas Council members for months.'

At the mention of the notoriously aggressive Polish financier, himself a former employee of Butchers Bank, Lomond Butcher's expression of benign insouciance finally faded and his face took on a green tinge. 'We will not sell!' he repeated, spelling out the words with force. 'And certainly not to that jumped-up messenger boy. That I can guarantee you.'

Kurdell looked at him complacently, delighted finally to have pierced the man's armour. 'Very well,' he said, pursing his lips. 'In that case, you have to let me finish the job you engaged me for and show the Council members that we mean business.

You must approve my plans to turn this . . . this . . . antiquated steam-engine into a piece of modern manufacturing machinery. And that includes the Dickensian monstrosity' – he gestured at the chandeliered ceiling of the boardroom – 'that you call a headquarters. But first and foremost we've got to retool on the staffing side. And, coming back to the my original point, Slaker's one of the bits that has to go.'

As always when Kurdell went off on his favourite analogy with industrial plants, Lomond Butcher's eyes glazed over again. He was a merchant banker of the old school. Industry was a closed book to him and he rather hoped it would stay that way. 'But what's wrong with the man?' he asked helplessly.

'He's old technology,' snapped Kurdell, 'like most of the rest of this heap.'

'Can't be more than thirty-five,' the head of Corporate Finance chimed in, his voice registering quite clearly that he himself was considerably older.

'It's not age, it's attitude,' said Kurdell, regarding him unpleasantly. 'I promoted Falloni as his number two to shake up that private client area and now he's shooting the lights out. Look at the guy's investment returns, not to mention the clients he's brought in. When I arrived that department wasn't even washing its face. Now its cleaning its fucking teeth and tucking itself up in bed for the night. Falloni's been responsible for shitloads of new business – twice as much in six months as Slaker in as many years. That American composer Mattison Pick must have a hundred million invested with us alone.'

'But Slaker's a safe pair of hands,' objected the head of the Institutional Pension Fund Department, whose own area had not exactly excelled itself that year. 'And let's face it, Falloni is a bit of a—'

Kurdell rounded on him. 'A bit of a what?'

'Well, a bit of a wide boy.'

'Oh, really? Well, let me tell you this. Safe hands are two a penny,' said Kurdell. 'We can pick up any number of them for half what we pay Slaker.' He turned away from them to adjust the vertical blinds on the windows. 'What we need are stars.

Deal-closers, like Falloni. And as for wide boys' – he snapped the blinds shut and spun back round angrily – 'I think I've heard that expression applied to myself once or twice.'

Backlit by an errant shaft of sunlight escaping through the slits, Kurdell's bull-dog profile took on a semi-godlike luminosity. He stared at them hard, eyeballing each of the board members individually – two at a time, as was his particular ocular skill. To a man, they swerved their gazes sideways like street-smart New Yorkers who'd just spotted a potential mugger.

Only the chairman was left to make one last stand on behalf of Toby Slaker. 'Look,' he said, 'can't we just slip Slaker across somewhere else? Pop him into Compliance or something?' His voice rose, almost in entreaty. 'That's what we always did in the past with chaps who didn't come up to scratch.'

'And that's precisely the attitude we've got to change,' said Kurdell viciously. 'The modern City doesn't work that way. All that patrician crap is finished with, and the sooner you all realise it, the better. So,' he concluded with triumphant finality, 'Slaker goes – first thing tomorrow. Yes?'

There was one last tense pause. Then, at length, the chairman glanced at the grandfather clock that stood incongruously beside the boardroom's giant computerised video-conferencing screen.

Kurdell smiled inwardly. He had ascertained in advance that Lomond Butcher had the company box for *Don Giovanni* tonight and he had timed his proposal about Slaker accordingly. He knew how much the chairman hated being late for his beloved opera evenings. 'Yes?' he repeated, rather more softly.

Irritably, Butcher fiddled with his papers. 'Oh, very well,' he said at last. 'Now, is that everything?' And without waiting for an answer, he pronounced the meeting closed, and headed for the door.

Chapter Four

The *Hoodwink Show* was to be broadcast from the studios of Popviz, the new satellite TV station owned by the Driftwood media conglomerate. Its headquarters were in Docklands, not far from the City offices of both Butchers Merchant Bank and Winegloss and Hooch Asset Management, the American investment bank whose London branch had recently appointed Simona Slaker as its Chief Executive Officer.

Simona was waiting for Toby impatiently outside the building in her all-terrain vehicle, her small frame practically invisible behind its wheel as she argued venomously with a traffic warden. The company Jeep, she always maintained, was ideally suited for her daily safari to the City from their house in Notting Hill. And so it would stay, Toby had no doubt, until fashions shifted and she developed an equally good reason for travelling to work in a reconditioned Sherman tank or whatever else some new fad dictated.

'We're out of here,' she yelled triumphantly at the warden as she saw Toby approach. 'For Christ's sake, get in,' she told him. 'Before I get out and paste this guy.' Toby never failed to be surprised by the odyssey her accent had taken over the years. Having started out with the nasal tones of Liverpool, it had briefly relocated to the Home Counties when she'd begun work in the City. Now, in keeping with her current position, it was settling comfortably into its new home somewhere in the mid-Atlantic, with the occasional shift to downtown Chicago thrown in when she wasn't getting her own way. 'You're late,' she added, slamming the car into gear.

'Sorry, minor crisis at Butchers,' said Toby, trying to resist the G-forces as they sped off. He settled back in the plush cream leather upholstery and had one last moan about the ordeal in store. 'Listen, why don't we just, you know, forget it, and go off for a drive somewhere?' he asked, letting his hand stray on to her knee. 'It's such a nice evening. We could head up to the Cotswolds and find that little pub we used to—'

'I don't think so,' said Simona, removing his hand without taking her eyes off the road. Before depositing it back on his lap, though, she gave it a squeeze and him a tight-lipped smile. 'It's a nice idea, lover boy. But just not now. Anyway, can't have a late night. I've got to look fresh tomorrow for *Moi!*'

'*Moi?*'

'The magazine. I told you a hundred times,' said Simona, exasperated. 'They're going to do a feature on my promotion party and a photographer and reporter are coming in for an advance recce.'

'Didn't they do that last week?'

'That was *Hello!* Don't you listen to anything I say?'

Toby shook his head. He was getting a bit fed up with finding pictures of his wife and home spread across every popular magazine he opened, with little mention of his own part in the undertaking. Besides, this 'promotion party' to celebrate her elevation to CEO of Winegloss and Hooch's London office was getting out of hand. It had started off as just a few drinks for her colleagues and now half the City, and most of the press, were going to be filling their house.

But he couldn't face tackling her on that now. He changed the subject. 'I can't believe Falloni, landing me with this,' he said. 'First thing this morning he was dead set on going. He's got to be up to something.'

'Oh?'

'I think he's been talking to headhunters,' he confided.

'Can't say I blame him.' Expertly Simona manoeuvred the huge vehicle round the Aldgate roundabout, turning off at the

Docklands exit. 'Butchers won't be independent for ever. And not everyone has your hideously misplaced sense of loyalty.'

'Butchers is doing fine on its own,' Toby replied heatedly. 'And it's not misplaced.'

'I don't know why you don't just leave and do something more interesting. Go back to university or something. You don't *need* to work any more, you know, now that I'm—'

'*Please* don't start all that again,' he cut in. 'I *like* what I do.' He did not grudge Simona her success for one minute, but she could wind him up like a clock when she started banging on about earning so much more than he did.

'Have it your own way.' Simona shrugged. 'Anyway, I'm glad Falloni won't be there tonight. It will give you a chance to introduce me to Mattison Pick without him muscling in. The guy's far too pushy.'

Toby was working on a witty retort involving pots and kettles when what she was saying hit home. 'Hang on,' he objected. 'Mattison Pick's *our* client!'

Simona tutted impatiently. 'Plenty of room in that pond for all of us,' she said. 'Guy like that's bound to have more than one investment manager. Those musicals he writes must have netted him a fortune. Apparently the last one's running in more countries than have indoor sanitation. Pick's worth a fortune and he's hardly going to entrust the lot to some obscure British merchant bank, even if it does have a kilted ghillie on its coat of arms.'

This time Toby refused to rise to her bait. 'Well, I shouldn't think he'll want to discuss his financial affairs with you tonight,' he retorted. 'He'll be far too mortified by being tricked on to the bloody *Hoodwink Show*. With a bit of luck, he'll do a runner and we can all have a night off.'

It was that very fear that was haunting the show's director, Phil Zimper, Popviz's head of Light Entertainment, as he made the final preparations for tonight's live broadcast.

Months of painstaking work went into every single one of

the *Hoodwink Shows*. Identifying the celebrity victim was only the start. After that, researchers had to comb his history for a suitably egregious surprise – a reunion with some long-lost mentor or forgotten childhood love were the favourites – that could be sprung on him if, in the words of the programme's puerile catch-phrase, he was '*in the mood to put on the hood*', and perhaps even induce in him a gratifyingly tearful breakdown.

In this particular case, admittedly, Pick's surprise guest had approached Popviz rather than vice versa, and had personally taken care of much of the legwork at the other end. But that still left the main challenge: the staging of the ambush itself, and the gathering together, in complete secrecy, of a panoply of Pick's closest friends – preferably of equal celebrity – to share the surprise, along with a supporting cast of acquaintances and associates to 'ooh' and 'ah' at the appropriate junctures.

It was a formula fraught with pitfalls, and one which Phil Zimper frequently regretted having come up with in the first place. Unfortunately for him, it was one that had caught on with the station's notoriously fickle viewers, attracting unprecedented hoards of them to tune in and – so the ratings suggested – stay watching to the bitter end.

So Phil was stuck with it. And it was tearing his nerves to shreds. Over the eleven months of the programme's history two victims had already refused point-blank to put the hood on, much less to allow it to be taken off in front of the cameras, and all the preparation had been for naught.

Of course, there was always a recorded back-up show in the can, ready to be trotted out in the event of such a disaster recurring, but Zimper hoped that wouldn't be necessary tonight. The surprise in store for Mattison Pick was particularly elaborate, and the invited audience especially rich and influential. As one of the world's most successful composers of stage musicals, Pick had unparalleled access to every area of international business and society, and a surprising number of his contacts had accepted the invitation to tonight's 'tribute'. It would be a disaster if they were forced to leave without their pound of mawkish flesh and pint of saccharine tears.

Zimper checked the monitors in his control room. Everything seemed to be set up correctly. Two of them showed the currently empty studio in front of him, where tonight's main action would shortly unfold. But a third, through the miracles of a satellite link, relayed a scene from six thousand miles away: a sumptuous swimming pool in California, which would be the backdrop for Mattison Pick's surprise. The main player there had not arrived yet, but the cameraman was already in place.

Phil Zimper flicked a switch on his console and spoke into his mike. 'Everything okay over there, Marty?' he asked.

There was the usual split-second delay before the reply came. 'Sure thing, Mr Zimper. The lady's still up in the house but she's due down any moment. Then we're all set to go when you are.'

'Good.' Zimper consulted the clock. 'We should be off in twenty minutes. One of the girls will check back with you just before we go live.'

At the pre-transmission reception Simona Slaker had discovered that the calibre of the guest list exceeded her wildest expectations and was behaving like a bee in the sweetest of honey-pots. She darted from one grouplet to another, networking and exchanging business cards at breakneck speed. Occasionally she returned to Toby to provide a running commentary on the new arrivals. To each name she added a price tag, as was her wont.

'Dave Graftman,' she said. 'United Leather. Two hundred and fifty mill, minimum.' She sucked the figures through her teeth like a vintage wine and nodded pleasantly as he passed by, quite unperturbed by the blank stare with which this was met. 'And that couple are Caroline and Milton Court, the impresarios. They produce all Pick's shows. Rich as Croesus. Oh, and look over there. The redhead's Vanessa Driftwood. Owns this TV station – and half the rest of the British media as well. Billions,' she mouthed in his ear, 'billions.'

She stopped. Suddenly the entire room had fallen silent and, looking at the entrance, they both saw the reason. An imposing man, huge in every way, with deep-set eyes and wildly sprouting eyebrows, had just entered, surrounded by a posse of security people. One ran to pull him up a chair, another checked around suspiciously as if expecting an imminent attack.

Toby recognised him at once. 'Isn't that your boss?' he said. 'What on earth's he doing here?'

Simona did not look surprised at all. 'Didn't you know?' she drawled. 'He and Pick are great friends. Besides, his wife owns the Royal London Theatre where Pick puts on his musicals. Zlennek bought it for her as a birthday present,' she added meaningfully.

Toby sighed. Evidently, just buying your wife tickets for the theatre was not enough any more. 'Well,' he shot back, 'anyone who flaunts his mistress the way he does would need to keep his wife happy somehow.' It was common knowledge that Zlennek was having an affair with the beautiful owner of Flato's, the exclusive City restaurant.

'I ought just to pop over,' said Simona breezily. 'There's something I want to ask him. And, anyway, he'd be offended if I didn't say hello.'

Toby doubted it. As far as he was aware, she had only met the acquisitive Polish billionaire once before, and even then for no more than a few moments. It had been shortly after Winegloss and Hooch, the American owners of the company whose UK arm she headed, had first been bought out by the Zlennek Corporation. At the time, she'd even feared for her own job, but in the event Winegloss and Hooch had stayed on to run the company under Zlennek's auspices and Simona had been left alone.

Toby watched as his wife strode purposefully towards Zlennek's charmed circle, and couldn't quite suppress a mild feeling of glee, tinged with guilt at his own disloyalty, when she did not obtain immediate access to him. Instead, for several minutes, she seemed to bounce off his human shield like a fly hitting an unseen window. Her strident voice could be heard complaining about this until she finally persuaded one of the guards to let her through.

Toby stood gazing at her disappearing back, then sat down and nursed his drink thoughtfully. A young man with a mess of dark curly hair was perched nearby. Judging by the speed with which he was consuming it, his own drink was not so much being nursed as entering intensive care. In addition, he'd gathered a frightening pile of cocktail sausages and savoury nibbles on his side plate. He wiped his hand on a napkin and held it out to Toby with a friendly grin. 'Will Cloud,' he said. 'Eighty-five pounds thirty pence, when I last counted.'

'Sorry?' said Toby.

The man gestured towards Simona. 'Thought you might be wanting to know for the lady's survey.' He had a soft lilting accent which Toby tried to place.

Toby laughed. 'You'll have to forgive my wife,' he said. 'She's a bit driven.'

'Turbo-charged, by the looks of it,' agreed Will Cloud amiably. Irish, Toby concluded, a mild burr but unmistakable none the less. Dublin, perhaps. 'Is she some kind of fairground performer now?' Cloud continued. 'A coconut if she can't guess your value to the nearest thousand . . .'

Toby laughed. 'I'll suggest it to her. It might be a good sideline. But as a matter of fact she's an investment banker, which amounts to much the same thing. And I'm in banking too.' He handed Will a business card, although, judging from his unkempt appearance, he somehow doubted that he'd be a prospective private client for Butchers, where the minimum investment was a million pounds. 'What's your line of work?' he asked, picking up another Perrier from the table.

With alacrity, the man searched around in his jacket pocket and handed him a slightly grubby card of his own. 'I'm an interpreter by training,' he said, 'but I've recently been branching out into something new.'

'Will Cloud, Private Investigator,' Toby read aloud.

'The very one,' said Will. 'You'll have heard of the famous Brass Monkeys murder case,' he added hopefully.

Toby had to admit he hadn't.

'Ah, well, can't be helped,' said Will Cloud, somewhat

crestfallen. 'Keep me in mind, though. I do a lot of work for big corporations. Never know when you might need someone like me. No job too trifling. Except divorce work,' he added hurriedly, eyeing the agitated shape of Simona, who was now making her way back towards them. 'Don't touch matrimonial stuff with a bargepole.'

Toby stuck the card in the top pocket of his jacket with the handful of others he'd gathered during the short pre-transmission reception. Simona was not the only networker present; nowadays no occasion seemed to be off limits in search of a useful contact and business cards had been changing hands all over the place. 'And how exactly do you come to be here?' he asked, hoping it didn't sound rude. Will Cloud was not exactly par for such a perfectly manicured course.

Cloud regarded him good-humouredly through the lightest of light blue eyes, clearly guessing his reasoning and not minding one bit. 'I'm a pal of the presenter, Candida Blitz,' he said. 'Just here for the grub, really; she slips me in every week to get a good feed-up.' He helped himself to another sausage by way of illustration then hastily excused himself as Simona returned.

'Guess what!' she crowed. 'Zlennek said he would see if he could make my party.'

'What party?'

'You know perfectly well what party. He's not sure if he'll be in the country, but he and his wife will do their *very* best to come if he is.' Her expression turned sulky. 'And the other thing he said was that he wants to see *you*.'

'Me?' said Toby, startled. 'When?'

'Now, of course.'

'Well, what on earth for? *I* don't work for him.'

'Not yet, you don't,' said Simona with a mean little smile. 'He knows where you do work though. And don't look at me like that, because I *certainly* didn't tell him. Remember, he worked for Butchers himself in the early days. You'd better go.'

'Oh, God.' Apprehensively, Toby made his way over to the seated form of Ivor Zlennek. From close up, the man looked even more formidable. He was older than Toby had imagined.

In his late fifties, at a guess, and of all things, Toby noticed his ears above all else. Gnarled and hairy, with monstrous mottled earlobes, they seemed to stretch down the full length of his head, almost meeting under his chin like 1970s sideburns.

'You Slaker?' Despite years in the west, Zlennek's eastern European accent was still strong. 'Butchers Bank?'

'Er . . . yes.'

'Work with that guy Falloni?'

'Absolutely.' Toby looked at him, bemused. How did this man know about Falloni? From Pick? For a second he wondered if it was Zlennek who was trying to headhunt his colleague. Was that what this little tête-à-tête was about?

The Pole got to his feet. 'I want a private word with you,' he said. He put an arm round Toby and practically frogmarched him over to the side of the reception room. Then, to Toby's surprise, he looked him critically up and down. 'In my day, you had to be smartly turned out to work at Butchers,' he said, reaching across to straighten Toby's tie. 'You'll have to be more careful when you work for me.'

This was the last thing Toby was expecting. 'I'm not actually looking for a change,' he said politely. 'I'm perfectly happy where I am.'

'Sometimes you don't get a choice,' replied Zlennek testily. 'Talking of which, I got a message I want you to pass on to Lomond Butcher.'

'Well, I don't actually—'

'Never mind whether you actually do or don't,' Zlennek interrupted. 'Just make sure you pass on this message, see? Tell him from me that I already got a quarter of the Council members sewn up.'

Toby, who knew only vaguely about Butchers' ownership structure, nodded dumbly.

'Tell him Butchers don't have a chance without me. He'll find that out soon enough. I intend to buy Butchers Bank. And if he tries to fight me, I'll screw him into the ground. Got that?'

Toby nodded again. He would relay this odd message, but if there was one thing he was certain of, it was that Lomond

Butcher wouldn't dream of letting this unpleasant bear of a man near his bank.

'Good.' Spotting the clutch of business cards protruding untidily from Toby's top pocket, Zlennek pulled one out and glanced at it. 'Wouldn't get mixed up with them,' he grunted. 'Bunch of crooks.' Without warning, he ripped the card in half and threw the pieces on the floor. Then he stuffed the others down deep into Toby's pocket and turned his attention elsewhere, evidently indicating the audience was at an end. As Toby opened his mouth to protest, a harassed-looking man by the door clapped his hands and called for quiet.

'Ladies and gentlemen, Mr Pick has arrived in the building and we will shortly be springing our little surprise on him. So if you'd care to make your way quietly through to Studio A, the evening's proceedings are about to begin.'

Mattison Pick had been lured into the Popviz studios on the pretext of giving an interview about his forthcoming new musical, *The Iron Lady*. As a notorious self-publicist, it was reckoned that the American composer would hardly pass up the chance to give his latest opus a plug, and that proved correct. Pick had eagerly accepted the invitation and was now sitting unsuspectingly behind a false backdrop in the corner of Studio A, wearing his trademark cowboy boots and a tight modern suit too young for his sixty-odd years.

Since Popviz lacked the resources of some of its larger rivals, it did not have any spare presenters on tap to fill in for the spoof interview and had co-opted a junior researcher for the part. And the minion, aware that he had only a few minutes of fame before Candida Blitz arrived to interrupt him, was determined to make the most impact in the time available.

'Welcome, welcome.' He beamed at the camera as soon as the red light on top indicated they'd gone live. 'Tonight I'm absolutely thrilled to be joined by the world-famous composer, Mattison Pick. He's currently in London rehearsing his latest extravaganza, *The Iron Lady*, which uniquely will be premiering here rather than in New York.' He turned to his guest. 'Matty,' he said conversationally, 'before we talk about that, let me first just mention last night's Oscars, where your wife, Peaches Latrine, won—'

'La Trené,' Pick interrupted.

'Sorry?'

'It's pronounced Peaches La Trené,' said Pick, a fixed smile overtaking his grizzled, bronzed features. 'Rhymes with la Frenais. She's kinda particular about that, John.'

'Oh . . . right,' said John, momentarily thrown. 'Well anyway, she won an award for best supporting actress. Many congratulations.'

'Thanks,' said Pick. 'I'll pass that on when I next speak with her.'

The researcher cast him a knowing glance and continued. 'Now, tell us, Matty, just what is *The Iron Lady* all about?'

Pick looked at him expressionlessly. 'The life and times of Mrs Thatcher, of course. I sorta hoped there might be a clue there in the title for you,' he added.

John shifted uncomfortably in his chair. 'Absolutely. But what made you choose such a . . . ah . . . bizarre subject?'

'We Americans are great admirers of Lady Thatcher,' said Mattison Pick, bridling visibly. 'And the musical theatre being one of the finest expressions of American culture, I thought it only right that this towering figure, this icon of our age, should be appropriately celebrated.'

'Absolutely,' said John. 'I'm sure she'll prove a popular subject. And one has to say that ever since the death of your former writing partner, Sam Kaskin, your shows have been . . . well . . . less commercially successful than before. *Godot the Musical* and *Bloomsday* were critically acclaimed but they didn't exactly have them rolling in the aisles, did they? And your most recent show about the Moonies, *Tomorrow's Another Deity*, was the first flop you've ever had.'

'Hey.' Pick jabbed his finger at the researcher irritably. 'That was a fine show. And sure, Sam's loss was a terrible blow. But even before that, I'd been thinking of branching out on my own. Kaskin was always a lightweight and I wanted to explore more serious themes.'

'So,' John concluded, peering over Pick's shoulder for Candida Blitz to appear. He was starting to take a dislike to this jumped-up little dirge-peddler who thought he was Mozart and Wagner rolled into one. And besides, he was running out of questions. 'You accept, then, that the Thatcher venture's an attempt to return to the more popular political genre associated with the old Kaskin and Pick days: *Jimmy C* and *The Extraordinary Gerald Ford*, for example, or your mega-hit *Kennedy*?'

'Well now,' Pick began grandly, 'I think that analysis is a tad simplistic. *The Iron Lady* is certainly not a regression. Rather, it's a synthesis, if you will, of the competing influences that have informed my work.' He smoothed back an errant strand of white hair. 'This is a show I was born to write—' Suddenly he broke off. 'Hey, who do you think you're poking?' he asked, twisting round in his chair to discover an attractive blonde-haired woman with a guileless expression on her face, who was carrying something that looked suspiciously like a terrorist mask.

Candida Blitz had arrived at last. She'd slipped in from behind, with the red hood that was her show's trademark. 'If I might just interrupt, Matty,' she simpered. 'I know you think you're here to be interviewed about your new musical, but that's not the whole truth.' She swivelled round to face the camera and gave the sign that was the show's other trademark by forming her thumb and finger into a circle round one eye and winking. 'Because tonight, Mattison Pick, musical composer extraordinaire, I hope you're *in the mood to put on the hood* – on the *Hoodwink Show*!'

And with that there was tumultuous applause, and to Mattison Pick's manifest astonishment the backdrop behind him rose into the air to reveal the assembled audience of his friends and acquaintances, all repeating the catch phrase. 'Put on the hood, put on the hood,' they chanted gleefully. As John the researcher slipped gratefully back to obscurity, a tape struck up the show's theme music, and they all surged forward.

In the control room, Phil Zimper held his breath, his finger poised over the button that would switch from the live transmission to the pre-recorded back-up. For him, it was the moment of truth.

There was a pause which seemed endless, until, at last, a delighted smile spread from Pick's eyes to envelop his entire face. Then, with the utmost docility and to Phil's eternal relief, he allowed Candida to pull the red hood gently over his head.

Toby Slaker looked on with detached amusement as the unseeing Pick was led into the centre of the studio and seated in a comfortable armchair. He wondered idly what the surprise would turn out to be and scanned the entrance for some doddery former music teacher to be wheeled on. But tonight, evidently, the pattern was to be varied slightly. Instead of the usual studio guest, a vast video screen was lowered into place at the rear of the set.

The audience waited expectantly as the theme music faded and Candida Blitz positioned herself behind the composer. 'Mattison Pick,' she said, 'as we all know, you are over in Britain rehearsing for the opening of your new show. And sadly, because of those commitments, you were unable to travel back to California to be with your wife, actress Peaches Latrine—'

'La Trené.'

'Peaches La Trené,' Candida corrected herself fluently, 'at last night's Oscars ceremony. But what people might not realise is that the award she won is not your only cause for celebration. For a little bird has let Popviz in on the secret: today is also your second wedding anniversary.' There was a ripple of applause. 'What a shame to be separated for this double celebration!' said Candida archly.

'Shame!' echoed the studio audience, sensing what was coming.

'But,' Candida continued, 'the *Hoodwink Show* has a way with sundered hearts, and we made up our minds to remedy the situation. Unfortunately, logistics made it impossible to reunite you with Peaches in person. However, we've done the next best thing. So' – she paused and looked significantly at the camera – 'as the hood comes off' – with a flourish, to the sound of a taped drum roll, she pulled it away from his head – 'you'll see that a Popviz camera crew has flown all the way out to your home in sun-drenched California where Peaches is waiting to speak to you via a live satellite link-up!'

And indeed she was. The image of the curvaceous blonde screen idol, Peaches La Trené, shimmered up on the screen, standing in a skimpy bikini-like dress by a glistening blue swimming pool, cocktail glass in hand. In the background, a monstrous villa loomed up, built, in true Hollywood custom, in a smorgasbord of different styles which seemed to encompass mock Tudor, Spanish Colonial, Japanese and Hawaiian and in one seamless mess. Mattison Pick blinked at the vision on the screen and rubbed his eyes, looking quite overwhelmed.

'Can you hear us, Peaches?' asked Candida.

Peaches fiddled with something in her ear. 'Hi there, every-one,' she lisped, with that breathless giggle so familiar to her millions of ardent male fans. 'Gee, I'm afraid I can't hear you very well.'

'Hello, honey,' said Pick.

There was the inevitable delay as the signal travelled through thousands of miles of space, bounced off a satellite and plumm-eted back to earth. Then Peaches smiled. 'Hello, pumpkin,' she said. 'You're coming through loud and clear now. How're you getting on over there in England?'

'Just great, hon. But I'm missing you a bundle.'

Standing next to Toby, Will Cloud whispered in his ear, 'So would I, if I were an old munchkin married to a pin-up like that.'

'Are you really?' breathed Peaches.

'Congratulations on the Oscar, Peaches,' Candida inter-rupted, clearly feeling she was entitled to get back in on the act.

The screen idol ignored her. 'Are you really, really missing me?' she persisted.

'Yes, really, really, really,' said her husband indulgently.

'Specially with it being our anniversary and all. I'd like to be there to give you a great big hug.'

'Aw,' said Peaches, crinkling up her face. And egged on by a floor manager at the side of the studio, the audience too let out a glutinous sigh. 'Isn't that just so sweet,' she went on. It looked like the emotion of the situation might get the better of her, but she just managed to pull herself together. 'Honey, you wanna know what I'd like to do to you, if I was there right now?'

'I sure would,' said Mattison Pick with a great grin to the camera. 'But this is a family show. So better keep it clean.'

'Well, pumpkin,' said Peaches, 'if I was there right now with you . . .' She took a deep breath and her voice went up several octaves. 'If I was there now' – it turned into a high-pitched screech – 'what I'd do,' she screamed, 'is cut your fucking dick off and stuff it down your stinking lousy no-account throat. That's what I'd do.'

The studio audience pulled back, startled, and an expression of panic overtook the great composer's face. 'Ah . . . excuse me?' he said.

'You heard me, you no-good son of a bitch,' Peaches shrieked. 'You thought you could get away with it, did you?'

'Honey, I—'

'Don't honey me, you cheating bastard.'

'Is this being recorded?' asked Mattison Pick.

'And with my own kid sister,' Peaches sobbed, collapsing hysterically on to a convenient sunlounger. The camera panned in close on her face, streaked with mascara-coated tears. 'How could you?'

'Ah, actually,' Candida said to Pick with an apologetic twitter, 'it's going out live.'

'Live?' Mattison Pick repeated like a zombie.

'I found the photographs,' yelled Peaches. 'I found the goddamned photographs.'

Total fear registered in Pick's eyes. 'Hey, listen, those were just . . . like a piece of fun, you know,' he said wildly. 'She wants to be a model, so, like, we were trying out a photo-shoot.'

'Photo-shoot? Photo-shoot, my fanny,' yelled Peaches. 'I saw what you were shooting, and it sure wasn't photos.'

'Live,' mouthed Candida with a lopsided smile. 'It goes out live.' She gave another nervous giggle.

'Listen, Peaches, I know you're sore, but it's just a little misunderstanding.' Pick's tone contradicted his words all too eloquently.

'Misunderstanding?' yelled his wife. 'Miss–fucking–understanding?' She laughed hollowly. 'Yeah, miss-fucking's your speciality, hon. Now that I'm over twenty, I don't qualify any more, right? So you upgraded to the next generation of software? Well, you fucked your last miss, you bastard.'

'Could you stop the cameras please?' Mattison Pick's voice rang out with authority.

Peaches was having none of it. 'You leave those cameras on,' she screamed. 'I want the whole damn world to see you in your true colours, you goddamn cradle-snatching louse. Just let 'em look at these photos.' She pulled something out of a bag.

'Hold on there, Peaches,' said Candida. She seemed to be in the grips of some terrible internal struggle. Sympathy for Pick's predicament competed visibly with the certainty that her entire satellite audience was at that very moment ringing everyone it had ever met to urge them to tune in. The showwoman in her won hands down. 'Hold on, Peaches,' she repeated, 'so we can bring the camera in for a close-up.' There was no need. It had already panned down to take in the grainy pictures of two barely distinguishable figures locked in a naked embrace.

Mattison Pick looked like he wanted to punch Candida. But he didn't. Keeping his temper with difficulty, he addressed himself to his wife. 'Now, whoa up there, cookie,' he said soothingly. 'I'm sure we can sort this out.'

'Sort it out? Sort it out?' shouted Peaches. 'Just like you sorted out Sis? Uh-uh.' She shook her head angrily. 'I don't think so. Not in a million goddamn years.' A thought struck her. 'Hey, you know what, maybe the viewers over there would like a little tour of our happy homestead, huh?'

'No,' said Mattison Pick desperately.

'Yes.' Candida Blitz nodded. 'That would be lovely.'

Peaches was listening to neither of them. Gesturing the

cameraman to follow her, she was already through the pool terrace and into a cavernous marble reception area. There, full-size statues of Greek gods and goddesses jostled with gilded showcases containing Peaches' numerous Oscars, which in turn competed with Mattison Pick's own rows of Tonies and Emmies. 'This is the hall,' she said proudly. She proceeded up a baroque staircase, lined with framed pictures of the two of them with other well-known Hollywood and Broadway figures. Finally she arrived in an enormous open-plan room which featured a Jacuzzi the size of a small lake, and a vast bed with an ormolu four-poster frame. 'And this is the master bedroom. But you'll recognise that from the photographs, of course,' she added sweetly. 'I just hope Sis made out with him better than I did. Between you and me,' she confided, 'you never did see a man with such a tiny pecker.' She crooked her little finger to the camera. 'We had many a long game of hunt the thimble in this bed.'

Pick's complexion had taken on a yellow pallor and he looked like he was about to vomit. There was worse, much worse, to come though.

'And this,' said his wife, moving across the upper hallway, practically dragging the cameraman behind her, 'is the Ming room, where Matty keeps his *precious* collection of ancient Chinese vases. Don't you, honey?'

Mattison Pick said nothing. Spittle dribbled from his mouth.

Peaches lowered her voice, as if giving a learned discourse. 'You know, the temperature, humidity and light levels have to be carefully controlled,' she recited, almost as if by rote. 'To prevent discolouration or cracking. So we have a special computerised air conditioning system to make sure. And here's where it's controlled from.' She wrenched open a panel to reveal a row of switches. 'I just need to flick this and the temperature shoots up.'

'Don't!' pleaded Pick. 'Please don't.'

It was too late. She already had. 'Gee,' she said, fanning herself ostentatiously. 'It's getting hot in here, isn't it, Marty?'

The picture bobbed up and down. Evidently the cameraman was nodding.

'They're priceless,' sobbed Pick. 'Irreplaceable.'

'Irreplaceable, eh?' said Peaches viciously. 'Priceless, huh?' She stopped and stared straight into the camera. 'Not as priceless as our goddamned love was. Not as irreplaceable as the virginity of my cute little innocent sister.'

She picked up one of the vases from its stand. A striking blue in colour, it was heavily decorated with an intricate floral pattern. 'This,' she intoned, gazing short-sightedly at the plaque underneath, 'is one of the finest examples of early work from the Hung-chich dynasty. Isn't that *interesting*!' she added. 'Now, what would you say it's worth, honey? Coupla million, you paid, didn't ya?' Arms outstretched, she held it in front of her. 'But it'd probably fetch much more than that now.'

'It's not the money,' said Pick, burying his head in his hands. 'I'll pay you anything you like. Just put it back.'

It was not to be. 'This'll teach you to cheat on me,' said Peaches. 'This'll teach you to mess with my kid sister.' And, almost as if in slow motion, she let the vase slip gradually from her grip. The camera followed its descent as it crashed into a thousand tiny pieces on the marble floor.

'No!' Pick wept. 'Someone do something, for God's sake. Please.'

'Bet you wish you'd sprung for that accident insurance now, you tight-fisted little cheapskate.'

'Peaches?' Candida finally felt obliged to intervene. 'Don't you think this is a little bit extreme? I mean I know you're upset, but . . .'

Peaches ignored her. She had moved to the next stand. This time she was less gentle. With a sweeping motion, she sent a Mohammedan blue vase which apparently belonged to the Chia-ching period crashing down to join its companion. Then, arms flailing around like a windmill, and with a savagery that would have put many of the bloodthirsty emperors themselves to shame, she departed on a violent foray through the remainder of the Ming dynasty. In short shrift, she disposed of Lung chi'ing,

Wan-li and countless other reigns, sending shards of ancient oriental crockery whizzing around the room like mortar shells.

'I've got to get out of here,' said Mattison Pick, retching uncontrollably.

'Yeah, you get out,' screamed his wife, finally coming to a halt. 'But just don't you think of coming back to California. 'Cos I'll be passing this lot' – she held up the photos again – 'to the authorities. And, in case you've forgotten it, screwing a minor is still an offence in this country. You set one foot back in the United States and I'll have you banged up in the pokey for statutory rape faster than you can say "Iron Lady". Oh, yeah,' she added as an afterthought, 'talking of which, don't worry about your business stuff while you're kicking your heels over there.' She leered into the camera. 'Kinda useful you put all the productions in my name, huh? I'll look after all that for you real good.'

As Mattison Pick fled for the studio exit, Candida caught a wind-up signal from the floor manager.

'Peaches,' she said brightly, 'we have to go shortly. But I want to thank you ever so much for sharing your feelings with us tonight. And I'm sure I speak for everyone here in hoping that you and Mattison will soon patch up your . . . ah . . . little differences and' – she groped for an appropriate cliché – 'will live . . . ah . . . happily ever after.'

And with that, she turned to the camera to do her famous sign-off. 'This is Candida Blitz, calling it quits for another week,' she said. 'But tune in next time when another unsuspecting celebrity will be *in the mood to put on the hood* – on the *Hoodwink Show*!'

Chapter Five

━━━◅◦○◦▻━━━

It was dark. Dark and silent. The hood blocked all light and the earplugs all sound. His consciousness was filled only with the pounding of his own heart, which echoed through his body like a bongo drum.

He'd followed her instructions to the letter, heeding her usual warning that, if he didn't, their arrangement would be cancelled and he would never hear from her again. And that was the one thing he couldn't bear to contemplate.

For the first time in one of these encounters, he was fully clothed. She'd explicitly told him he mustn't undress. 'Won't that make it kind of difficult?' he'd asked when they made the arrangements for tonight's little tryst.

'Let me worry about that,' she replied. 'I'll take off your clothes when I'm good and ready. And when I do, it'll be like you've never known before. I promise, it'll blow your mind.'

He could well believe it. On the previous occasions her inventiveness had left him numb with excitement and begging desperately for more. There was no question she was the best. He'd tried out some of the others. They'd all been good, but none had her passion.

This would be their third time together. After their first meeting at her flat in north London, the second had been at his own home. Now they were here – in the riskiest place of all. As usual, the danger of the situation heightened the buzz for him. Would they be caught? Would someone come in and discover them in flagrante? And would he then finally find out what his secret lover really looked like? Or would she have escaped back down that disused rear stairway in the nick of time, never to be seen again?

With all these possibilities coursing through his brain, he sat and waited with mounting anticipation. Surely it must be nearly nine. Where was she?

Suddenly he tensed. She was here in the room now, he was sure of it. He could sense her presence, feel it in his very bones.

But she was not approaching. Why not? Had he done something wrong? Please don't leave, he begged silently.

He breathed a sigh of relief. She was coming closer. He might have no sight or hearing, but he still had three senses left, and there was no mistaking the musty scent of her perfume.

A few moments later, he had further confirmation from his two other senses. He felt her fingers on his neck as she lifted the bottom of the hood. Then, as his pulse reached fever pitch, he tasted her lips on his.

The Minx had definitely arrived.

Chapter Six

It was after midnight when the Slakers' four-wheel drive vehicle negotiated its way back through the tundra of east London to their home in Notting Hill. Simona turned on the radio to pick up the late night financial report. Eastern European stock markets had continued to plunge, Toby noted absently. But his mind was still on tonight's little TV drama. 'Well, *that* was rather more interesting than I expected,' he said. 'Falloni will be green with envy when I tell him.'

Simona's lightning brain, however, had already moved on from the episode itself and was now focusing on its inevitable consequences. 'That woman's going to take him for every penny he's got,' she said thoughtfully. She turned on her husband. 'Where's Pick's money?' she demanded. 'I mean, I know Butchers manages some of it, but where's the rest? Stuck in the States?'

'I have no idea,' Toby replied. 'And I wouldn't tell you if I did.'

His wife threw him a sullen look. 'You might at least have introduced me to him.'

Toby gazed back at her incredulously. 'Do you honestly think he was in the mood, to coin a phrase? He only stuck around afterwards to try and save what little face he had left.'

'Well, I noticed you managed to get your bit of toadying in.' She launched into a fair imitation of her husband's pleasant tones. 'Yes, Mr Pick, I really think that was disgusting, Mr Pick.

47

What a shame about the vases, Mr Pick. Three bags full, Mr Pick. You were fawning all over him.'

'I just wanted to apologise about Falloni not being there. If Falloni does get headhunted, I've got to try and make sure he doesn't take Pick with him. So I explained that Falloni and I shared all information on his account and that I would be able to take over if anything ever happened to Falloni.'

'And he bought that?'

'He seemed very impressed.'

'What else did he have to say for himself?'

'He wants me to get Falloni to phone him in the morning about trying to transfer his funds,' Toby admitted, as they drove into the driveway of their house.

'He'd be better to talk to someone with real experience stateside,' said Simona. 'Get some of those greenbacks shipped offshore before Peaches freezes his assets up good and proper.'

'I'm sure Butchers will be able to provide whatever advice he requires,' said Toby frostily, letting her into the house with his latchkey.

Their two children, Lucy and Guy, were away at boarding school and the place was deathly silent. 'I just need to check everything's all right for the magazine people,' said Simona. 'They're coming in at eight tomorrow night and I've got a frantic schedule.'

She marched off round the rooms verifying that all was in order, while Toby dropped his briefcase off in his first-floor study and then fixed himself a drink in the living room. With the children away, the place was already too big for them, but it was Simona's dream home, a five-bedroomed four-storeyed villa in the fashionable part of Notting Hill Gate that they'd bought the year before, using one of her huge annual bonuses to cover the price differential over the more cosy terraced house they'd had before. An architect then all the rage had virtually ripped the place to bits and rebuilt it to Simona's specification. The design was rather too minimalist for Toby's middle-class tastes, with miles of bare parquet flooring and stark white walls broken up by strange pieces of modern art. But Simona, the working-class girl made good, had always had very fixed ideas about what she wanted. She'd even taken instructions from the designer on how the house was to be presented, right down to the type of fruit to be displayed in the massive blown-glass bowl on the living room table. A fruit arrangement, he'd explained, was a work of art, a decorative item like flowers, to be laid out for its aesthetic appeal rather than for consumption. She'd followed his instructions to the letter and Toby or the children removed a guava or a kumquat from it at their peril.

Simona's tour of inspection complete, they set the alarm and climbed the stairs to their bedroom on the second floor. At the top, Toby slid his arm round Simona's shoulder and fingered her zip speculatively. 'After tomorrow,' he asked wistfully, 'couldn't we lay off the publicity for a while and concentrate a bit on us?'

Simona gave him a glassy smile. 'Of course,' she said. 'After tomorrow.' She caught at his hand on her zip and twisted away. 'Sorry, lover boy,' she whispered. 'I'm done out. Besides, it is only Monday.' And giving him a quick peck on the cheek she retired to her own end of the king-size bed and the pile of broker reports that was her staple night-time reading.

It is only Monday, mimicked an internal voice in Toby's brain. Only Monday, it taunted him. And, of course, Simona never made love except at weekends, and even then it was clinical and under conditions of prophylaxis that verged on the forensic. An accident, she would explain, was the last thing she needed at this stage in her career.

Toby was not quite sure when Simona had lost interest in him sexually. When she'd been his secretary at Butchers and they'd first started seeing each other, she had been voracious, demanding his attentions at all hours of the day and night. On one occasion when they were working late, she'd even persuaded him, against his every instinct, to take her into the great boardroom and make illicit love to her on its polished mahogany table. They hadn't been caught, and the danger of the situation had given him a real frisson of excitement, Toby remembered. To this day, every time he attended a meeting there, he still got a thrill from seeing the scratch marks her fingernails had left on the surface.

But those incidents had become fewer and further between as she'd risen through the ranks. By the time they'd got married, Simona's career was burgeoning and their relations were already strictly controlled. She'd planned the timing of their children's births with the utmost care. Manuals were consulted, family history was researched, everything was done to establish 'the conception yield curve', as Simona liked to put it, and ensure the babies arrived in late summer, during the dead period between the client-entertainment seasons of Wimbledon and Henley when her unavoidable two week absence from the office would cause the least impact. Sex had effectively been reduced to an efficient just-in-time delivery system in line with modern management theory.

This had meant that November saw a frantic round of baby-making but every other month was virtually a closed season on her body as far as her husband was concerned. And, as Toby often reflected, man cannot live on Novembers alone. Even a radiator needed venting more than once a year, and he'd found the long spells of celibacy ever harder to bear.

He sometimes thought that Simona might only be attracted to men who outranked her, that power was her aphrodisiac. As she'd risen above him professionally, she'd simply lost interest. And this was borne out when Oscar Winegloss, her current boss, was over on his regular visits from New York. Toby had observed her giving him just the same kind of looks that, in those early days, she'd reserved for him. Not that he suspected her of having an affair – she was now much too focused on her career for all that.

If his theory was right, he reflected as he drifted frustratedly off to sleep, then his only way to win her back was to continue his rise within Butchers till he outranked her again. It was a tall order, but his experience in life told him he was often the tortoise that beat the hare. With enough effort and dogged determination, he was confident he could still crack it.

Chapter Seven

That night, the tortoise extermination squad at Butchers was working very late indeed. An entire department in the Personnel division – or Human Resources as it preferred people to call it, though nobody did – was dedicated to preparing compulsory redundancy packages. The details to be presented to Toby Slaker first thing the following morning were coming off the word processor even as he slept.

It was not a generous package. There had been a time when Butchers had happily paid well over the odds to get shot of its surplus baggage without too much ill will, but those days had disappeared with the advent of Greg Kurdell, and now only the statutory minimum was provided.

'I wouldn't worry too much about Slaker,' Kurdell had advised Sue Primrose, the bubbly Personnel head, on informing her of the decree. 'That wife of his earns enough to keep a platoon of husbands till well into the next century.'

Redundancies at Butchers, as at most City institutions, were carried out with the precision of a military manoeuvre. The overriding priority throughout was to prevent a disaffected employee from returning to his or her desk post-dismissal, in case the opportunity was seized to appropriate a client list, corrupt a computer system, or commit some other act of revenge.

And so, early the next day, security staff on the front door were instructed that Toby Slaker was to be intercepted on arrival and accompanied to the boardroom on the second floor. There he would be informed of his fate by a deputation consisting of the Personnel head and the managing director, Greg Kurdell.

They would also be joined by the bank's chairman, Sir Lomond Butcher. Although, strictly speaking, there was no need for the chairman to attend, he had resolved to be on hand none the less in a belated fit of self-flagellation. In truth, he was already beginning to regret his weakness in letting himself be bulldozed into dismissing Toby Slaker, of whom he had heard nothing but good reports in his many years at Butchers.

For Lomond Butcher, the morning appointment meant a somewhat premature start to the day. Toby was a notoriously early riser and was normally at his desk by seven thirty, well before Lomond usually left his Kensington home to commence his chauffeur-driven journey to the office.

As they assembled in the boardroom, Butcher was the only one who was feeling any hint of nerves. Indeed, Greg Kurdell seemed to be relishing the coming confrontation, and for Sue Primrose it was all in her day's work. Since Kurdell's arrival the atmosphere at Butchers had changed almost imperceptibly, as there had been a string of senior redundancies to keep the Personnel Department busy. This one, sadly, was no different from any other.

Blissfully unaware of the reception awaiting him, Toby had risen even earlier than Simona for once and slipped quietly down to the study on the floor below to go through the work that he'd brought home. At the same time, as was his custom, he made a list of what had to be done during the day.

1, he wrote in his tiny meticulous longhand: *Reports*. He would finish going through his briefcase now and they would need to be sent out as soon as he reached the office.

2: Prepare for investment briefings. Brokers would be coming in this morning to try and interest him in various stocks and he liked to be well briefed in advance.

3: The McKwerties. Sir Jock and Lady McKwertie were

making their annual pilgrimage to London from their dilapidated estate in Aberdeenshire to have lunch with him today. He checked his watch. Even as he sat there, they would just be getting off the overnight sleeper, complete with hatboxes and shooting sticks and the brace of pheasants they always brought down to present him with. Toby had a fondness for most of his clients, but a particular soft spot for the McKwerties. Death duties and taxes had long since shrunk their portfolio of investments to well below the point where it was cost effective for Butchers to manage it. But Toby couldn't face telling them that, so he kept them on, and every year he entertained them regally in Butchers' plush corporate dining rooms in the perfect knowledge that the cost of the lunch would far exceed their annual fees.

He remembered another item and quickly noted it down.

4: Mattison Pick. He must get Falloni to ring Pick immediately about the transfer of his assets into a haven safe from his wife. This would be Butchers' opportunity to impress their biggest private client with their peerless efficiency. During their hurried meeting after the *Hoodwink Show* recording, the composer had given Toby a list of numbers on which he could be reached during the course of the day. Now what had he done with it? Toby located the jacket of the suit he'd been wearing at the TV reception the night before.

Leafing through the detritus in his top pocket, one item almost leaped out at him, but it wasn't Pick's note. It was a peculiarly garish card which he could not recall having received at all. Who on earth would want a crimson business card? he wondered. He glanced at it idly as he continued his search for Pick's details. 'THE HOODWINK ENCOUNTERS SITE' it declared in lurid capital letters topped by a crude line drawing of a hooded and naked man being led by a whip-cracking dominatrix. Underneath was the intriguing question: 'Are you in the nude to put on the hood?' His curiosity mounting, Toby turned it over in search of any further identification. But there was nothing, except in the bottom corner some text that appeared to include an Internet address. 'To find out more,' it said, 'drop into our website at www.hoodwink.encounters.com and have some fun.'

Normally inclined to be prudish about anything relating to cyber-pornography – he had banned his staff from using the company web link to access any such pages – Toby none the less felt a thrill course up and down his spine. He tried to work out how the card could have got into his pocket in the first place. Somebody could have slipped it in, he supposed. Perhaps it was some strange piece of publicity for the *Hoodwink Show* itself, although it didn't sound like the kind of saccharine fare that Candida Blitz normally presented.

He finally located Pick's note, which was in fact in a trouser pocket, and placed it carefully in his 'to do' file, which in turn he entrusted to his briefcase along with his completed reports. But as he showered he couldn't get the message on that bizarre card out of his mind. Normally, he liked to use his mornings to prepare himself mentally for the coming day. In his current state of sexual deprivation, though – an early morning approach to Simona had met with the same sleepy brush-off that he'd had the night before – the Hoodwink Encounters website kept crowding out everything else.

After he'd dressed he couldn't help going back to his study to take one last look at the card. Dare he visit 'hoodwink.encounters.com' before he left for the office?

He checked the time. It was still early. It couldn't do any harm just to take a look.

On his desk was a laptop computer on permanent loan from Butchers. Each of the bank's senior employees had one, allowing them to access the bank's systems remotely in order to check their e-mails and look at files when working from home.

Making sure that the study door was firmly shut, Toby breathlessly turned on the computer and waited while it cranked itself up. It asked him for a series of logons and passwords, then allowed him to dial in to the bank via the built-in modem. Shortly he was staring at the Butchers homepage, his own gateway to the Internet. There, he typed in the web address and watched mesmerised as the elements of the Hoodwink Encounters page gradually shimmered into focus.

In front of him there appeared the picture of a partially hooded woman's face, masked in black leather with slits at the eyes. The mask stopped at the nose and underneath, her lips were still visible, full and pouting and glistening red.

Now some text sashayed enticingly across the screen: 'Welcome to Hoodwink Encounters – the site of your most secret fantasies. Are you in the nude to put on the hood? Please choose a nickname then press enter.'

Toby hesitated. But he'd got this far, so he might as well explore just a little further. After some thought he typed 'Novice', which was what he felt like, then, with a gulp, he clicked 'enter'. At once the screen changed and a box flashed up containing a column of names. Apparently it was a list of those present on-line. It was in alphabetical order and under N, he noticed with a slight feeling of panic, his own, Novice, was already included. It seemed to stand out accusingly.

But what were all these people doing here so early in the morning? Surely they weren't all early risers like him? He soon had his answer when he looked across the screen at a second column of information. It was a list of locations, presumably showing where people were logging in from: Los Angeles, Mexico, Hawaii, Toronto. It would still be the day before in most of those places.

Now Toby looked more closely through the names of those present. The population of the Hoodwink Encounters website was a mixed one. There were both men and women. There was a subtle difference between them, though. While the men had servile, beseeching titles – Joe the Slaveboy, Steve the serf – the women's names were quite the opposite. There was no doubt who wore the pants round here: the dragon-woman, Vampire Girl and Medea, to name but three. Toby felt another jolt of excitement.

Underneath the list of people, a command in flashing pink letters urged him to click on any name to make a date with the partner of his choice. Toby stopped short at that. He did not have a partner of choice and didn't know what to do next. He began to panic. With relief, he spotted a button at the top of the screen that said 'exit'. Hastily he moved his mouse pointer over towards it. He'd get out now, before he got involved in something he would regret.

But even as he skimmed towards this escape route, the exit button was suddenly eclipsed by another box which popped up on top of it. The computer's speaker made a pinging noise. According to the box's heading, he had received a message from someone called Gus.

'G'day, Novice. M or F?' it said.

Here, at least, was something on which Toby could be decisive. He was most definitely the former and whatever he was here for, it was certainly not to meet someone called Gus. He made this clear by hitting the 'M' button on his keyboard and pressing 'return' with almost aggressive force. His insistence must have communicated itself down the line, for in a second he got a defensive message back.

'Okay, mate,' it said. 'Don't get the wrong idea. Just being friendly. Gus here, in Australia.' A glance at the second column confirmed this. Melbourne, it read. 'Guess you're new round here?' Gus continued.

'Round where?' asked Toby. 'I'm in London.'

'No worries. This is a global village, right? We're from all over the world here. Round the Hoodwink Encounters site, that's what I meant.'

'Yes, but what are Hoodwink Encounters?'

'You don't know?'

'NO.' Toby banged the keys. 'I DO NOT.'

'Strewth, mate, keep the noise down. I got kind of a headache.'

'Sorry.' Toby relented. He vaguely remembered hearing that capital letters denoted shouting in Netspeak. 'It's just that I'm a bit confused.'

'It's okay,' said Gus. 'Everyone's nervous their first time. See, this is a site for the kind of sheilas that get off on domination.'

Another thrill coursed through Toby's veins. 'You mean, sex?'

'Bloody right! And this place is where they come to meet their blokes.'

'But how does it work?'

'Better not say too much or it'll spoil it for you,' replied Gus. 'Tell you what, though. Drop in later on, when more of the London women are around, and you'll find out soon enough. I was over your side of the world last year and had a great time. Women buzzing around me like mozzies. And all just round the corner compared to Oz. Here you gotta go five hundred miles for a meet.'

'Would you recommend any of the London women in particular?' Toby couldn't help himself asking.

There was a pause as Gus thought this over. Finally his reply pinged up on the computer. 'There's Delila,' it said. 'She's on-line a lot and she's a real good root. But watch out for her 'cos she's a devil with the scissors and you might end up with a number one all over. Then there's Vampire Girl, but she can be a bit draining. Medea I'd avoid completely, if I was you. The one to go for, if you can get her, is the Minx.'

'The Minx?'

'Yeah. She's wild. All the Poms say so. But she's picky, so don't get your hopes up.'

'How do I find her?'

'She'll find you, mate. Just as soon as she realises there's new male. All you need to do is answer her questions and if she likes you, do as she says and you're in for the time of your life. Only thing is . . .'

'Yes?'

'Enjoy it while you can, mate. 'Cos she never has anyone twice. That's her rule, sure as a dingo's donger. Anyway, I got to go now,' Gus typed suddenly. 'Best of luck, cobber.'

'Wait!' Toby asked something that had been puzzling him. 'How will I know what these women look like before I meet them?'

'Look like? You won't!'

'But what if I arrange to see someone and don't fancy her when I get there?'

'Eh, I don't think you've quite got the point, mate. Still, you soon will. Bye.'

'I don't understand,' typed Toby helplessly. But Gus's text box had disappeared from the screen.

Distractedly, Toby checked his watch. He'd been so engrossed that he'd lost track of the time. If he didn't get his skates on he'd be late for work. Besides, this was a nonsense. He was a married man with two children and people like him did not do this sort of thing.

He again clicked on the exit button, and this time he made good his escape. But as the Hoodwink Encounters site finally faded from his screen, he couldn't stop himself picking up the scarlet business card and entrusting it carefully to his wallet.

He very much doubted that he'd ever avail himself of the Minx's services, appealing though they sounded. But there was no harm in keeping the details, just in case . . .

As Toby arrived at the office an hour later, Angus the doorman was just finishing his daily polish of the brass sign on which the Butchers' name was engraved in tiny understated lettering. An ex-Scots Guardsman with mutton-chop whiskers, Angus had been at the company for as long as Toby could remember, and took particular pride in keeping the appearance of the front area up to scratch, even going as far as to scrub the pavement when he thought nobody was looking.

'Morning, Angus.' As usual, Toby greeted him with a pleasant nod and pushed his way through the revolving doors.

'One second, Mr Slaker,' said Angus rather formally, standing in his path. 'Sir Lomond wants to see you in his office – urgent. I've to take you up as soon as you arrive.'

'Are you sure?' asked Toby, mystified.

'Those are my orders, sir,' said Angus sadly.

The journey upstairs in the old lift took place in silence. Toby's mind was racing, but redundancy was the one possibility that did not occur to him. It was most likely, he figured, to be some emergency meeting involving all senior staff or perhaps, heaven forfend, an investigation into an irregularity in one of the client accounts.

Even the sight of the three directors ranged along the table still did not alert him to his impending doom.

'Toby, old chap,' began Lomond Butcher hesitantly. 'Good morning to you. Do come in and . . . ah . . . take a pew. I'm afraid we have some . . . ah . . . rather unpleasant news to impart.' He stopped and fiddled with his tie. 'Ah . . . I have to tell you that . . . Greg has come to the conclusion that . . .' Kurdell glared at him and he started again. 'That is, we all have . . . I mean . . . sadly in the interests of . . .' He spluttered to a halt.

A grinding noise, emanating from somewhere in the region of Greg Kurdell's expensive dentistry, could be heard quite clearly. Finally, the managing director uncrunched his jaws and intervened. 'I wonder if it would be simpler if I took over?' he asked Butcher pointedly.

'I suppose you'd better,' said the chairman with a shrug of resignation.

But before Kurdell could begin, there was a commotion outside the door and one of the bank's blue-uniformed messengers burst in. 'Urgent message for the chairman,' he muttered, handing Lomond Butcher a folded sheet of paper.

Silence reigned as Butcher took the note and read its contents. Toby sat unbelievingly, an inkling of what lay in store having finally reached his consciousness. But surely not? There had to be another explanation.

The moment seemed to go on interminably. Butcher, not known as a fast thinker, was spending an inordinate length of time taking in the message. And as he did so, the blood drained from his face and his mouth gaped open. Kurdell began drumming his fingers on the table, but the Chairman silenced him with an upheld hand.

'What is it?' asked Kurdell, irritably looking at his watch. 'I've got a meeting at nine, so we'd better get this over with.'

For a moment, Lomond Butcher gazed at him unseeingly, still deep in thought. Then, with a start, he brought himself back to the present as if he had come to some kind of monumental decision. 'Toby,' he said quietly and without any of his former hesitancy. 'As I just mentioned, I fear I have some unpleasant news for you. I'm so sorry to have to tell you that your colleague, Roy Falloni, was discovered by the cleaners at his desk a few moments ago with shotgun wounds to his head. I'm afraid he's . . .' His Adam's apple jerked as he swallowed hard. 'I'm afraid he's dead.'

'Jesus Christ!' Kurdell snatched the paper from his hand. 'You can't be serious. It's got to be some kind of sick joke!'

Butcher took no notice of him. Instead, he continued to address Toby. 'It would appear that he committed suicide. The police have been called and are on their way.' Glaring at Kurdell, he carried on. 'Toby, at a time of such tragedy, we are all naturally counting on you to display those great leadership qualities with which we have come to associate you over the years. We rely on you to reassure your clients and carry your department through this dreadful episode and we know you won't let us down. I'm sure I speak for us all when I say that you have the board's full support and you and your colleagues our deepest sympathy.'

Chapter Eight

Delphine Jones heard about the suicide on the car radio on her way back from the night shift. Usually she tuned in to Magic FM to help unwind. After the endless problems she'd had to listen to, the last thing she wanted was news. But the previous evening, Winston's old crock had broken down and he'd begged her to let him use the car for his minicabbing, swearing blind it would be parked outside the headquarters of the Listening Line when she came off duty in the morning.

For once, her son had been as good as his word. She collected the key from over the hubcap and let herself in, opening the window to clear the suspiciously sweet-smelling smoke which now permeated the vehicle. Minicabbing, my eye, she thought despairingly. He'd been out with those mates of his again.

He'd left the radio on Capital and she was about to switch over when the nine o'clock news came on. The first item caught her attention immediately.

'Another of the City's oldest merchant banks is reported to be in trouble today, after one of its top executives was found dead at his desk. Family-owned Butchers Bank, which has a history going back to the nineteenth century, is this morning awash with takeover rumours after senior investment manager Roy Falloni took his own life. According to some reports, Falloni had chalked up hundreds of millions of pounds in dealing losses on the LAFFE, the London Alternative Financial

Futures Exchange, but as yet there is no confirmation of this . . .'

All at once, Delphine paid attention. Abruptly she reached over to turn up the volume as, in an instant, the voice from the previous night's telephone call came back to her: a man's voice, full and round, tremulous and almost melodramatic. 'I'm finished,' he'd kept repeating over and over again. 'Millions and millions. All down the drain.'

'Tell me all about it,' she'd said soothingly, trying to get him to calm down. But there was no possibility of that. He just gushed on oblivious, the words streaming out in great rivers of panic. There was something about a disaster in the future that she hadn't really understood. 'Your future needn't be a disaster,' she'd said brightly. 'It's what you make of it.'

That didn't seem to help at all and after that came the sobbing. Hysterical, uncontrollable. She'd attempted to draw him out a bit. Get him to talk. It seemed he'd made some kind of mistake at his work. It couldn't be that bad, she told him. Perhaps he should make a clean breast of it with his employers? Honesty was always the best policy. But he'd continued to rant and rave, and finally, as he seemed to be building up to a climax, he'd said baldly, 'There's only one way out. Only one way out—' And there he had broken off abruptly and the line had gone dead.

Funny, though, she'd had some experience of people like that and she would never have taken him for a doer. Sounded more like the cry-for-help type. Or maybe even a hoax caller. She could usually tell. But for once she'd obviously got it wrong.

Should she tell anyone? she wondered. She rejected the idea immediately. It was strictly against policy. Anyway, who was to say it was him? There were probably dozens of overpaid City types making mistakes with these derogative things all the time. Perhaps this news story had nothing to do with the voluble man she'd had on the line the night before.

Oh, well. She'd probably never know the truth, she reflected. It was the same with most of her calls. Occasionally people phoned back months later to say thank you when they were feeling a bit better, which was very gratifying. But mostly, she was left to wonder if her soothing words had made even the slightest contribution to resolving her callers' inner turmoil.

With a philosophical sigh, Delphine wound the window back up against the chilly morning air and set off on her journey home.

Chapter Nine

In fact, there was no need for Delphine Jones to contact the authorities about Roy Falloni's phone call. The police already knew about it.

As part of a bewildering array of self-regulatory requirements, every major City institution had long since been required to install equipment that recorded all telephone calls made by its dealers and investment managers. Known as voice-loggers, these contraptions sat innocuously in computer rooms throughout the Square Mile, soaking up millions of hours worth of conversations with a total lack of discrimination.

Most such calls were business-related, confirming some transaction with a broker or verifying a client's agreement to one particular deal or another. Some, of course, were personal: mothers cooing to the toddlers they'd surrendered to child-minders in order to resume their high-powered careers; husbands explaining to their wives why they would be unavoidably detained at the office; the same husbands, moments later, making clandestine assignations with colleagues' wives for an opportunity to pursue the intimacies begun at last year's Christmas party.

Fascinating as these recordings would undoubtedly have been to the respective spouses, there was very little chance that they would ever get to hear them. For access to the voice-logged recordings was highly regulated: it was permitted only under the most controlled of circumstances, and then it had to be demonstrated that there was a genuine business need. The most common example of this was when a telephoned instruction to a broker to sell a stock had undergone some kind of weird vocal metamorphosis on its way down the line and emerged at the other end as an order to buy, or vice versa. In such cases, the tape was the ultimate arbiter and it did not lie.

Nor did it in the case of Falloni. After having had the body identified and examined, one of the first actions of Inspector Ffelcher, the balding Scotland Yard officer who arrived at Butchers to begin the investigation, was to search Falloni's desk for a suicide note. And when that drew a blank, he instructed one of his officers to track down the voice-logger. From previous experience on City suicide cases, he knew how invaluable these could be. 'Bound to have made some calls before he did the deed,' he told Detective Dorf. 'They always do.'

Lomond Butcher and Greg Kurdell were summoned to the boardroom, where Inspector Ffelcher had set up temporary headquarters, to hear the result of Dorf's efforts. After a morning that had already yielded one unpleasant surprise too many, they listened dumbstruck to the tape of Falloni's desperate conversation with Delphine Jones.

'That's utterly impossible!' Kurdell declared heavily when Falloni made his confession about the dealing losses. 'I simply don't believe it.'

Inspector Ffelcher gazed at him with detached interest. 'Could you confirm that *is* the voice of the deceased, sir?' he asked.

'It certainly sounds like Falloni,' said Lomond Butcher, his weather-beaten complexion, normally the colour of a beef tomato, now looking more like an over-boiled potato.

'We'll get some voice pattern tests done, just to be sure,' said the inspector. 'You never know what tricks people can get up to nowadays. But we've no reason to believe it wasn't suicide, so I'll be working on that premise until there's any proof to the contrary. Of course,' he continued, 'I'm only responsible for the investigation into Falloni's death. But the other side of the equation is these futures contracts, and that's completely outside my remit. The SFO will need to look into that.'

'I told you,' said Kurdell abruptly, his face as white as the chairman's, 'it's quite impossible. There is *no way* Falloni can have committed the company to the kinds of deals he was talking about in that phone call. There would have been all kinds of administrative obstacles in his way, not to mention margin call payments and regulatory checks.'

But even he didn't sound entirely convinced and the inspector smiled grimly. The police had heard that one before – from every other MD who'd been duped by some so-called rogue trader and didn't care to believe it. 'Be that as it may, sir, it's not a matter for my department but for the Serious Fraud Office. I'll be instructing them accordingly and I imagine you will be hearing from them later today. Of course, you'll no doubt wish to start your own investigation into what's happened—'

'If you'd let me get back to my office, that's exactly what I intend to do,' Kurdell broke in furiously.

'All in good time, sir,' said the inspector. 'A man's life has been lost. That is my primary concern at present. Now I shall want to speak to' – he consulted a list of employees – 'Mr Slaker, who I believe was the deceased's immediate superior and worked in the same office.'

'That's correct, Inspector,' said Lomond Butcher. 'Toby Slaker is a *very* trusted employee' – he glared at Kurdell – 'of many years' standing.'

Inspector Ffelcher checked a label attached to the tape reel. 'This call was made at nine p.m. last night, which ties in with the initial pathologist's report on time of death. So it looks like he did it immediately after hanging up the phone. Would Falloni have been alone in the department at that time?'

Kurdell nodded morosely. 'The only other people who might have been around then were Slaker and one of the analysts, Melvin Puckle, who tends to be here till all hours. But Slaker was out at some TV party, and Puckle was on holiday.'

'What about elsewhere in the building?'

'Well, there were the security staff,' said Kurdell. 'Fat lot of good they did. And, of course, the US equity traders would still have been working downstairs on the dealing floor at that time. But the Private Clients Department is on the top floor and fairly self-contained. Besides, the amount of din those dealers make is enough to drown out anything short of a nuclear attack.'

Inspector Ffelcher scribbled something down in one of the leather-bound pads bearing the Butchers' tartan insignia which adorned the boardroom. Then he consulted his own notebook again. 'Very well, perhaps we can turn to the weapon now,' he said. 'Falloni used a twelve-bore Purdey shotgun, which is hardly the most common of suicide weapons. Is either of you able to cast any light on where that might have come from?'

He stared blandly at Lomond Butcher, who looked down at the table. 'Ah, I believe it may be mine,' said the chairman with sadness. 'I have a collection of guns hanging on my office wall and one of them does seem to have been . . . ah . . . mislaid.'

'A fully loaded twelve-bore shotgun,' the inspector read from his notes.

'Yes,' said Lomond. 'It *was* loaded. It's for shooting grouse.'

The inspector regarded him pleasantly. 'You get a lot of grouse past the window here, do you, sir?'

'It was a gift, Inspector.' The chairman's tone was defensive, but not without an element of arrogance. 'A gift from a very senior member of the Royal Family.' Generations of Butchers had shot with the highest in the land, he implied, and seen off many an impertinent official to boot. 'And it is fully licensed. Besides, I can't imagine how someone could use it on themselves. It's far too long and unwieldy.'

'He appears to have wired it to the ceiling using some kind of pulley system that was already present there,' read the inspector, 'enabling him to pull the trigger remotely. Quite an enterprising young man, your Mr Falloni.'

The two men looked sadly back at him. 'He was certainly that,' said Butcher. 'He'll be a great loss to our company.'

'So the gun was in your office,' continued the inspector. 'Now where exactly is that located?'

'Next door to this boardroom,' said Lomond Butcher, inclining his head towards an interconnecting door.

The inspector made another note. 'And when you're not there, the room's kept locked, is it, sir?'

'Not exactly,' Lomond Butcher admitted. 'This bank has always been run on a basis of trust. Security ensures that we have no strangers wandering around, and I operate an open-door policy to all my staff.'

'Very wise, sir. That way, if anyone wants to pop by and borrow a loaded shotgun to do themselves in with, then it's nice and easy.'

'I'm not sure I appreciate your tone, Inspector.'

'No offence meant, sir, I'm sure,' said the policeman blandly. 'Now, I shall want you to identify the weapon. And I'm afraid you won't be getting it back for a while. When you do, I suggest it be kept under lock and key in future—'

Greg Kurdell interrupted him. A hand pressed to his temples, he had been growing increasingly agitated. 'Look, I must *insist*, Inspector, that you release me from this interview now so that I can begin to look into these alleged deals. They may take second place in your book to what this blasted man did to himself, but hundreds of jobs in this company could depend on our taking immediate action.'

'Very well, Mr Kurdell,' said the inspector evenly. 'I think that will be all – for now.'

'No, there's one thing I would like to confirm with you, Inspector,' said the managing director, his hand on the door knob. He was not used to giving up control. 'I take it we can count on the complete discretion of all your officers with regard to this . . . ah . . . incident for a while. And particularly to the contents of that tape, the allegations on which, I would remind you, are still entirely unproven.' He lowered his voice. 'This tragedy could undoubtedly cause a great deal of speculation all over the City. It's no secret that many people would love to destabilise Butchers and rumours of any dealing losses would play into their hands.'

The inspector shrugged non-committally. 'My men always keep their mouths shut about cases under investigation,' he said. 'But I'm afraid the same may not be true of your own people. You may not be aware, but reports are already running on radio and TV news. And the press are gathering outside the building as we speak.' He looked thoughtful. 'It's almost as if they knew about Falloni's death before we did.'

'Oh, God!' said Lomond Butcher, burying his head in his hands and allowing himself an uncharacteristic lapse into the vernacular. 'Now we're completely buggered.'

The news that Butchers' wunderkind, who had been shooting the lights out in the equity markets, had evidently decided to do much the same thing with his brains was indeed spreading with the rapidity of a forest fire.

Toby Slaker discovered this all too painfully when, soon after being dismissed from his early morning interview with the chairman and managing director and still unaware of the taped telephone call, he staggered into an adjoining meeting room and tried to telephone Simona. In a profound state of shock, it was an instinctive reaction for him to want to confide this terrible tragedy in his soul-mate.

With a shaking finger, he automatically dialled her number and got through to her male secretary, the officious Stanley. 'Is my wife available?' he asked, trying to keep the tremor from his voice.

'She's on the line to New York,' Stanley snapped.

'Tell her it's urgent. *Please.* Terribly urgent.'

He heard the message being passed on. Stanley came back. 'She says if it's about Falloni topping himself, she already knows.'

'Oh, my God . . .' Even in his distressed condition, Toby was astounded at the speed of his wife's network. 'But we only just found out ourselves.'

There was a silence then a further conversation in the background. 'She wants to know if it's true about all the dealing losses.'

At those words, Toby felt his stomach lurch. For they brought to the forefront of his consciousness a fear that had been lurking there since the moment Lomond Butcher first broke the gruesome news. Now the brief conversation he'd had with Falloni the previous day came surging back to haunt him. 'What dealing losses?' he asked. His own voice sounded strange to him, hoarse, practically a whisper.

He heard Stanley relaying what he'd said. Then came the sound of the receiver being grabbed and Simona's voice came on the line. 'Darling?' she rasped incredulously. 'You don't mean you don't know?'

'Know what?' Toby croaked.

'It's all round the City. Apparently Falloni left a taped confession. One rumour is that he had *billions* riding on Moyenne 500 index contracts and when the markets turned yesterday evening, he lost the lot. For God's sake, you *must* have known what he was up to, surely! I mean you *are* his boss.'

Toby's feeling of nausea intensified. The index of East European average stock prices – published by *Le Monde* and universally known as the Moyenne 500 – was just the sort of thing Falloni would have dabbled in. And contracts in it were regularly traded on the LAFFE, where Falloni did all his futures trading.

And with the nausea came an awful pang of recognition. The file he'd seen on Falloni's chair. He was now pretty certain what those four letters, 'enne', related to. Moyenne contracts. Had to be.

He needed room to think. And he could not be seen to panic, even in front of his wife. After all, she worked for a competing company which might have a good deal to gain if the rumours proved true. 'You shouldn't believe everything you hear,' he said with as much confidence as he could muster. 'It's all . . . it's all complete hogwash. Falloni had . . . ah . . . personal problems that I didn't tell you about. That was the reason for his suicide.'

'Oh.' His wife didn't sound convinced. 'Oh, well, I hope you're right.'

'I *am* right,' he said, fighting back the bile rising from his stomach. But even as he spoke, more elements of Falloni's recent behaviour were slotting into place in his befuddled brain and leading him to exactly the opposite conclusion.

Simona cleared her throat and sounded uncharacteristically hesitant. 'Toby?' she said.

'Yes?'

'Look, I ought to warn you. If Butchers is in trouble, and I'm only saying if,' she continued rapidly, 'because I hope as much as you do that it's all completely untrue, but if it is, then there's likely to be a real fight to pick up the pieces. All the big boys from Europe and America are already flying in to London.' She paused. 'And I'm afraid we'll be among them, darling. That was Winegloss on the phone a moment ago. Zlennek rang him from London this morning and he wants WHAM to be in there. You see, your asset management side would be a perfect fit for us. With the . . . ah . . . overheads stripped out, we could bring all your clients in-house and clean up big.'

Toby swallowed hard. There was no doubt in his mind what she meant by 'overheads': himself and most of his colleagues. To be fired by his own wife – it would be the final humiliation.

'Listen,' Simona continued. 'I've got to go in a sec.' A note of real sympathy entered her voice. 'I want you to know I'm really sorry, darling. You must be very upset. You were fond of Falloni.'

'Yes.' Even to himself, he sounded flat.

'Poor you. We'll have a good long talk about it later. But' – her tone became determined again – 'you've got to understand that work is work. You do understand that, don't you, darling?'

All Toby understood was that one of his closest colleagues was dead. That the bank to which he had devoted most of his professional life was probably on the verge of bankruptcy. He said nothing. Without another word, he let the receiver crash back into its cradle.

Chapter Ten

In his office near London Bridge, Ivor Zlennek had called a press conference.

His massive frame arranged liberally behind a table, flanked as ever by his posse of security men, the legendary Polish financier stared out at the pressmen from beneath two great hooded eyelids. Impassively he waited for the initial fusillade of questions to subside.

'Mr Zlennek, is it true you're going to close in on Butchers Bank after what's happened there?'

'Mr Zlennek, there are rumours that you've already approached Lord Sloach, moderator of the Puritas Council, about buying the bank. Would you comment?'

'Mr Zlennek, what are your intentions—'

Now one of Zlennek's hands – they had both been laid flat in front of him – rose no more than half an inch off the table, and magically flashbulbs stopped flashing, questions ceased and there was silence.

'Gentlemen,' he began, his quintessential un-Englishness unmistakable even in that one word. 'I assure you that my intentions are . . . ah . . . nothing but to be helpful.' He spoke ponderously, weighing each word like one of the precious metals in which he frequently cornered the market. 'Certainly, I do not deny that I had been having informal discussions with some of the Puritas Council's members, even before this . . . ah . . . unfortunate incident – but only in the friendliest of spirits.' His eyes staring out as deadpan as a crocodile's looked anything but friendly.

'I had been willing to make an investment in the bank in order to help maximise the Council's income. Of course, now –' he shrugged – 'now the situation is somewhat different. There is no question the bank has been damaged, perhaps irretrievably, even if there are no losses. At the very least, this incident proves that Butchers is far too small to survive in the modern City. What it needs is a protector' – he bared his teeth in an attempt at a smile – 'a champion, such as Zlennek International.'

A reporter piped up. 'Stevie Cudlick, the *Pop*. Mr Zlennek, Lomond Butcher claimed at his own press conference earlier today that you would break up his company and suck it dry. As bank chairman, he does have a blocking vote on the Council, and he said you would buy his bank over his dead body.'

Zlennek shrugged. 'An unfortunate turn of phrase, do you not think, under the circumstances?' he said. 'But I do not intend to personalise this debate. Look.' His great hands rose again from the table, this time in a gesture of apparent openness. 'I am a businessman. If I perceive value in Butchers Bank and am prepared to make an investment, particularly in the current unfortunate conditions, then the Puritas Council and the *current* management should be grateful.' His stress on the word 'current' was not lost on those present. 'And the reason that I have called you here today is to announce that I am indeed prepared to make such an investment. Even though the losses have not yet been quantified, and regardless of any liabilities outstanding, I am prepared to pay to the Puritas Council the sum'– he paused for effect – 'of one hundred million pounds for Butchers Bank.'

There was a collective gasp from the assembled media.

Zlennek continued impervious. 'This offer is unconditional.' His voice rose above the hubbub. 'However' – he raised a finger in the air and there was silence again – 'it is not open-ended. Indeed, it is very much closed-ended. In order to secure my offer, I require its acceptance by the Council by close of business tomorrow. That is all, gentlemen.'

He began to rise and there was a sound of synchronised

scraping of chairs as all the platform party did the same. Ignoring a flurry of further questions, Zlennek made for the door. However, when he was only halfway there, one last question seemed to penetrate his armour and he stopped in his tracks.

'Mr Zlennek, are you aware of rumours that Hampton Bradley's Brahmin Corporation may also take an interest in Butchers Bank? Do you think he's just trying to rile you?'

'Yeah, how's the court case going?' another journalist interjected. 'Quite a feud there, Mr Zlennek, eh?'

Now, for the first time, a careful observer – and there were nearly a hundred careful observers present in the room – could detect a hint of anger creep over Ivor Zlennek's otherwise impassive exterior. It passed quickly, but there was no doubt it had been there.

'All I would say about Mr Bradley,' he said evenly, 'is what I have always said. I would welcome a meeting with him to resolve our differences without resorting to the law. Here I am before you, but where is he? Does he hold a press conference?' He answered himself, as was his habit. 'No, he does not. He does not show his face, but speaks through his American lawyers and spokesmen. Is this the English way? Is this cricket? No, it is not.' He cut off abruptly. 'Thank you, gentlemen. That *will* be all.'

As if by some prearranged signal, double doors to his left opened simultaneously inward and flanked by his entourage Ivor Zlennek made his way through them into an inner sanctum.

Chapter Eleven

It was now nearly lunchtime, but Toby was still sitting alone in the meeting room from which he'd phoned Simona. He couldn't bring himself to go back up to the Private Clients Department yet. Instead he raided the drinks cabinet and poured himself an enormous brandy, which he downed in one gulp. As he felt its fortification spreading through his bloodstream, he tried to straighten his thoughts. But it was a lost cause. The alcohol was simply not proof against the impossible welter of emotions stirring within him.

Falloni's suicide was bad enough in itself. However, the possibility that he'd killed himself because of vast debts in the futures markets meant that Toby's grief was now mingled with panic. Surely there had to be another explanation? Those personal problems perhaps, just as he'd told Simona.

But the City was a notoriously small place when it came to bad news, and traders' gossip often travelled outwards in concentric circles, leaving only those at the centre in ignorance. He could not suppress a terrible suspicion that the rumours Simona had heard were accurate.

If so, though, someone at Butchers must have known about Falloni's activities. Greg Kurdell for one. He had been responsible for overseeing all the man's investments. That, at least, was quite clear.

Or was it? With a further jolt, Toby realised that Falloni's dual reporting line had never actually been set out in writing anywhere. The structure at Butchers was like that of some old Cairo apartment building. They just kept adding more layers, without any regard for whether the foundations could actually support the weight. Falloni's deal was an ad hoc arrangement, agreed informally at Greg Kurdell's instructions. But to all intents and purposes Falloni was in the Private Clients Department and accountable to Toby. That was what his official job description said, that's what Simona had assumed, and that's what the whole City would think. If Kurdell chose to deny the special arrangement it would only be his word against Toby's.

As Toby contemplated that awful prospect, he was interrupted by the ring of the telephone. It was Steve Gurling, the finance director.

'Christ, Toby, I've been trying to track you down everywhere,' he said with urgency. 'Now listen. I know you're upset but you've got to get your act together. They've called an emergency meeting of the Puritas Council for later tonight. Before that, we have to try and work out what's been lost. And I really need your help.'

'What do you want me to do?' Toby asked dully.

'I've already established that there's no record of any of these futures deals on our mainframe computer systems. So they have to be elsewhere. The police have removed the body and cleaned up Falloni's office. And they've now given us special permission to go in and look through his files.' He broke off. 'Toby, are you listening?'

Toby wasn't. At the mention of Falloni's body, his concentration had lapsed as he again fought to keep the bile down. He still couldn't believe his colleague was really dead. 'You'll have to run that by me again,' he said. 'I lost the gist.'

Gurling drew breath. 'Christ, get a hold of yourself. You're the only person who knows anything about Falloni's filing system. I know it's unpleasant, but you have to get in there and see if you can find anything out. Okay?'

'Okay,' Toby gulped. 'I'll do my best.'

★   ★   ★

Back up in Falloni's office in the Private Clients Department, now deserted except for a lone policeman standing guard, Toby ran his hand through his hair as he sadly took in the mess. His colleague had been a workaholic who rarely spent any time at home and, as a result, every aspect of his life was run from this tiny cubicle. As well as his business papers – broker reports, client letters, meeting notes and company prospectuses – there were hundreds of items relating to his many personal interests: theatre programmes jostled for space with crossword compendiums, a rugby kit sat side by side with a book on Bible codes, next to which was a Walkman and a row of cassettes. Even the sling in which, for a dare, Falloni had done that much publicised bungee jump from the Private Clients' attic window was still stuffed under a table beside the shredding machine. And as well as all that, there was his personal correspondence. Reams and reams of it. Every kind of letter was here, spread out in a kaleidoscope of a life now so suddenly extinguished: utility bills, bank statements, credit card counterfoils, letters from his accountant, letters from his girlfriends, letters from his family.

That reminded Toby that someone would have to break the news to Falloni's next of kin. He hoped the Personnel Department or the police would take care of that. He simply didn't feel up to it. Later, at some point, he would drop a note to Falloni's mother, who as far as he was aware was his only living relative; and to all his numerous female friends, whose addresses he could no doubt glean from the mass of correspondence spread before him.

As to the current grisly search, he knew where his starting point for that must be: that orange file he'd seen on Falloni's chair the previous day and hadn't stopped thinking about since his phone conversation with Simona. The 'enne' file, which he now had little doubt had to relate to Moyenne 500 index contracts. Where the hell was it?

Falloni had hastily removed it to the top of a filing cabinet. But now, when Toby checked, it was no longer there. In fact that was virtually the only surface in the place that was empty. Falloni must have locked the file away somewhere. Damn him.

It could take ages to find; that was, if he hadn't destroyed it in his shredding machine before he'd done the deed.

There was no point in even trying to go through the paper-based files yet, Toby concluded. No, the quickest way to get to the bottom of this would be via the powerful computer on Falloni's desk. It had been the nerve centre of the man's life. All his deals had been negotiated on this machine, all his letters produced on its word processor, his investment decisions tested on its spreadsheets, his client presentations painstakingly developed on its graphics package. Even if that file had been shredded, the chances were that the original electronic document would still be stored here in some obscure stream of digitised data. If it was there, he would eventually locate it.

With trepidation, Toby reached out and flicked the on switch. He was not a computer expert, but like all the staff in his department he had the working knowledge of PCs that was more or less indispensable in the modern City. He would be able to take an initial look at Falloni's on-screen files and if anything needed further investigation he would call in one of the specialists from the Information Technology team.

But it was soon evident that that was not going to be necessary. As the machine booted up, Toby heard a grinding and a whining from somewhere deep inside its bowels. Even to his untrained ears, it was not the normal sound of a computer starting itself. After another series of peculiar noises and a long delay, the computer's screen began to flash accusingly and a message appeared in large capital letters.

'UNRECOVERABLE DISK ERROR' was what it said.

Chapter Twelve

There are few prospects more succulent to the world's media than that of a merchant bank facing imminent extinction, apparently through its own folly. A riches-to-rags tale in a glamorous City setting, with years of tradition and billions of pounds about to go gratifyingly down the tubes, and hundreds of individual personal tragedies to leaven the dough, it all adds up to an unmissable story – and an opportunity for *Schadenfreude* on an unprecedented scale.

Butchers Bank was no exception to this. During that first day, as the circumstances of Falloni's suicide became common knowledge, journalists and camera crews from round the world began to pitch up in the City by every means available, all eager for their individual piece of the action. By dusk there were hundreds of them swarming around Butchers' front entrance, thrusting microphones and cheque books in front of anything that moved and sending Angus the doorman into fits of apoplexy at the mess they were making to his pavement. There, the TV front men chronicled all comings and goings over and over again in every language under the sun, jostling for pole position and trying to place their own unique spin on events.

Inside the bank, tensions were also running high. That night an emergency meeting of Butchers' most senior staff and executive members of the Puritas Council was convened in the boardroom. First they heard an update on the dealing positions from an exhausted and defiant Greg Kurdell. 'We still have no idea what's been lost,' he reported. 'It seems that, for reasons that will have to be investigated later' – here his expression became guarded – 'Falloni was not properly supervised internally. His filing was in an atrocious state. There's little doubt that he *had* been dealing in futures, but for the moment we can't say precisely what his positions were.'

'Can't we check with the appropriate stock exchange?' asked the Council's treasurer, appalled.

Kurdell shook his head. 'Falloni channelled all his transactions through the LAFFE, the new London Alternative Financial Futures Exchange. Dealing there is entirely screen-based, and it seems their computers have crashed, which I'm told is not unusual. They've drafted in clerks to go through the records manually, but they handle millions of contracts every day and it could take some time. They expect to be able to tell us what the situation is some time tomorrow.'

'It could be any amount?' said the Treasurer, in stunned disbelief.

Kurdell nodded silently.

Lord Sloach of Macclesfield, the diminutive former Government minister who was the Council's moderator – its leader under its Scottish deeds of covenant – intervened with all the pomposity for which he was renowned. 'In that case,' he boomed, 'I would aver that this offer from Zlennek is very generous. Very generous indeed. It may be the Council's only chance to salvage anything from this confounded mess.'

Sir Lomond Butcher, who had been sitting staring at the wall as if in a trance, finally sprang to life. 'I will not let that man buy my bank,' he burst in, furiously banging his hand on the table. 'And I *will* use my blocking vote to stop him. In any case,' he insisted angrily, 'I don't believe there have been any losses, and I won't until I see proper proof.'

Sloach threw him a glance which in former times had made many a senior civil servant quail in his boots. 'Are your employees in the habit of committing suicide merely for their own amusement?' he asked nastily.

Butcher glared back at him. 'There's no point adopting that

tone with me,' he snapped. 'I refuse to sell off the family silver on such little evidence, and I refuse to sell it to *that* man at all.'

'It is not your family silver,' Sloach growled. 'We have to think of the interests of the Council.'

They faced up to one another like two peacocks in a pen. It was getting late and the building's air conditioning seemed to have switched itself off automatically.

As the atmosphere became increasingly sweaty and irritable, the Puritas treasurer tried to soothe the situation. 'What about this other offer from the American, Bradley Hampton?' he asked. 'There was something on the radio about his Brahmin Corporation being interested.'

They all looked at Gordon Butcher, who had become the meeting's unofficial secretary. 'His name's Hampton Bradley, actually,' he said. 'Unfortunately, there doesn't seem to be any substance in that rumour. Certainly, we've heard nothing from him. It was probably got up by the press to irritate Zlennek and make a better story. They're arch-rivals and there's some huge court battle being waged between them in the States.'

'Does anyone know anything about this Bradley man?' asked Sloach.

'East coast American billionaire,' said Kurdell. 'Used to be a playboy till he was paralysed in an accident years ago. Very reclusive now.'

'I remember him,' said Lomond Butcher vaguely. 'Didn't he shoot with the Prince of Wales at one time? Very distinguished family, I believe.'

'Anyway, he does have a reputation as something of a white knight,' Kurdell continued. 'He's stepped in to save a few companies like ours in the past.'

'Well, maybe we should approach him pre-emptively?' Sloach queried.

'We will approach nobody,' stormed Butcher, 'until we have a better idea of what has happened.'

'Look,' the treasurer intervened again gently. 'We don't need to be bounced into anything tonight. In the morning, perhaps things will be clearer. And we ought to talk to the lawyers and accountants about how to proceed. In the meantime, there's nothing constructive to be done here and I suggest we all get some sleep.'

The meeting nodded in agreement and everyone began to disperse home. Everyone, that was, except Lomond Butcher. With one last glare at Sloach's retreating back, he rose and, with a look of quiet determination on his weather-beaten face, went back through the communicating door to his own office.

Up in the Private Clients Department four floors above, Toby Slaker had spent a gruelling day searching through the remainder of Falloni's papers, but it had all been in vain. Although, after breaking into a bottom drawer in the desk, he had finally discovered some dealing records, there was no sign of the 'enne' file anywhere. There *were* details of a LAFFE futures transaction that was still outstanding, but it only related to a small number of contracts on the Nikkei. And a quick check with the Valuations Department had shown that, although they were running a loss, it was of no more than a hundred and twenty-odd pounds. If that was all he had to deal with, Toby reflected wryly, the sun would indeed be shining. But somehow he doubted it.

Nor had he had any more luck with Falloni's computer. A team from the IT Department had declared it 'a goner'. 'Must have wiped it before he did himself in,' said one of them, scratching his head. 'Strange, we can normally recover data, but he seems to have done a pretty thorough job this time.'

There wasn't much to do now until news of Falloni's deals came through from the LAFFE. Toby hoped for the best but feared the worst. After all, his deputy had been an extremely experienced fund manager. If he'd been so convinced that 'millions and millions' were missing that he'd considered suicide the only way out – and Toby had now heard the tape on which he had said just that – then it was foolhardy to think he could have made a mistake. Butchers Bank, as Toby knew it, was finished for ever. At best, it would be taken over and subsumed into some anonymous foreign conglomerate. More likely, it would be shut down completely and its clients hived off to the highest bidders.

Late that night, Toby tried to ring Simona to talk it all through with her. But, to his surprise, there was no answer from the house or from her mobile phone, and Toby was left to his own counsel. There was little else he could do now until the beginning of the next business day, when doubtless there would be a string of clients ringing for reassurance about their funds. He would be able to provide them with that without difficulty. Ever since other similar catastrophes, all clients' funds had been 'ring-fenced': the underlying cash and investments had been deposited with custodians so that even a fund manager's bankruptcy could not put them at risk. Not that clients were likely to take much heart from that. There was bound to be a headlong rush to withdraw accounts to safer havens and his painstaking work over many years would have been for nothing.

Bleary-eyed and depressed, Toby decided there was no point in going home if Simona wasn't there. He would sleep here at the bank. He made a pillow of papers on his desk, buried his head in them and tried to get some sleep.

Chapter Thirteen

By the following morning, the assembled journalists had more than enough material about Falloni and Butchers to last a lifetime, and they spread it liberally over their front pages.

The tabloids eschewed the financial story as too complicated and instead went for human interest. Unanimously they led on the bereaved lover angle, Falloni having provided them with more than enough candidates to go round. Indeed, they were spoiled for choice, as many of his former and current girlfriends had turned up in front of the Butchers building with their hearts on their sleeves – the better, apparently, to flog them to the highest bidders.

A small war broke out in the popular press about which newspaper was featuring the most up-to-date model. And model was the appropriate word, since Falloni had had a penchant for the fashion scene and had frequented many West End watering holes where the minor denizens of the catwalks hung out.

The *Pop* put up Riza Dulombier, a starlet with whom he'd apparently been having an affair for some weeks. She professed herself utterly devastated by his suicide, and totally unaware that he'd been having any dealing problems at work. Which struck her as strange, because even in the short time they'd known one another he had come to trust her as nobody else and they'd shared everything together.

Everything, it turned out, except the news that he was

simultaneously diddling her best friend and colleague, Margot Lontagne, who bedecked the front page of the rival *Flick*. In the devastation stakes, she saw herself as at least in equal first place, and to denote the depth of her mourning had specially donned a black bikini for the photograph which appeared under the headline 'TAKE A BUTCHERS AT THESE!'

The third of the tabloid triumvirate, the *Snap*, ignored the fashion world and threw in its lot with Michelle, the barmaid at Flato's Brasserie, to whom Falloni evidently threw some crumbs when not engaged with Margot or Riza. Michelle had been out with him the night before he died and therefore felt she staked the most current claim.

All Falloni's girlfriends had given descriptions of their last intimate moments with Falloni, including his sexual appetite (voracious), his physical proportions (prodigious) and his stamina (copious). These were reported in some detail in the interests of historical accuracy and, as the papers explained, in a genuine willingness to provide the police with information they might otherwise have missed. The net result, though, was that the reader was left knowing little more about the Butchers Bank catastrophe, but much about Falloni's undoubtedly eclectic sexual preferences.

The broadsheets, meanwhile, had weightier matters on their minds. Rumours about the extent of Falloni's losses had multiplied alarmingly since the day before. Abattoir analogies were *de rigueur* and pun-loving subeditors had had a field day: 'BLOOD-BATH AT BUTCHERS,' said one. An article in the *Financial Times*, headlined 'GAME FOR A LAFFE', suggested that Falloni's debt on the futures markets probably exceeded a billion pounds, and some papers were even more optimistic, commenting on further overnight jitters in the Far East and predicting that, when London started trading, the Butchers incident would kick off an international financial crisis which would bring the world's equity markets to their knees.

They also focused on the Zlennek offer to buy the bank for a hundred million pounds if he obtained agreement by six p.m. that night. Most came to the conclusion that the Puritas Council should take the money and run, even though, in pristine condition, Butchers should have been worth at least double that amount. A few of the more discerning journalists, however, noted that Lomond Butcher would almost certainly use his blocking vote to stop any sale.

The press interest quickly fed on itself, so that when the first staff began arriving for work early that day they had to run an even worse gauntlet than they'd faced when leaving the night before. And it wasn't just media people who were besieging the building now. A full complement of creditors of every description was also waiting on the doorstep. Foremost among them were the representatives of the privatised utility companies, who were variously seeking to turn off the electricity, the telephones, the gas, and the water and sewerage facilities in anticipation of nonpayment of bills.

Angus the doorman argued in vain with the man from the Shoreditch Water Company. 'You can't seal up our sewers,' he said. 'What about the rats?'

He needn't have worried. These had already left the sinking ship as fast as their legs could carry them. Hundreds of the banks' suppliers had already cancelled deliveries, some of them turning up at its rear entrance and battering on the doors in an attempt to salvage whatever was still in the basement storage areas. Shops that only the previous day would have given their eye teeth to have Butchers on their client list were scratching its name from their records faster than a revisionist council in pre-capitalist Russia.

Elsewhere in the City fellow financial institutions were being equally industrious. Quickly convening emergency meetings of their credit committees, they mostly decided that loyalty was for wimps and cut off all lines of credit to Butchers Bank pending further news, leaving it quite incapable of carrying on its business and so hastening its likely demise.

That morning, Lomond Butcher woke up in the company sick room, where he'd spent the latter part of the night, feeling appropriately sick and totally disorientated. He'd had very little sleep and the insides of his eyelids felt like sandpaper.

For a few moments he lay on the hard bed, breathing in a faint odour of disinfectant that transported him back to the sanatorium at his old public school. He only wished he could be there now. He still could not believe – he *would* not believe – that in the course of a few short hours, the banking dynasty he headed could have gone from being one of the most prosperous and respected in the City of London to facing total ruin. And all because of some obscure deals in an arcane area of finance that hardly anyone understood. Wretchedly, he contemplated the prospect of being lambasted in the press as just another feckless victim of a rogue trader, as a century of banking tradition disappeared into oblivion.

But it was not his own fate that most worried him. His primary concern was for his hundreds of staff. If it were all true, what would become of them, of their security, of their pensions? Many of these people he had known since childhood. From the moment he was old enough to walk, his father used to bring him into this very building, into what was now his own office, to stare at the dusty paintings of his forebears and to play under the great mahogany desk while he went about his daily business. He had imbibed the atmosphere and learned, almost by osmosis, about the tradition that would one day be entrusted to him. The Butchers way, its patrician ethos, had been indelibly stamped on him from birth and the prospect of standing in front of all his loyal employees and admitting that he had let them down so dreadfully filled Lomond Butcher with utter despair.

He would not let them down, he vowed. Even if this ghastly story turned out to be true, he would not allow the bank to be sold to Zlennek, who would dismantle it and sell it off piecemeal for maximum profit as he had done elsewhere. Nor would he let it go to anyone else with a reputation for asset-stripping. He knew he could not use his blocking vote indefinitely, but if the worst came to the worst he could at least come up with a better alternative, one that would ensure the company was kept intact and that its employees' futures were protected.

He'd already taken the first step towards that end, although the signs so far were less than encouraging. The previous night, when the members of the Council had left, he'd sat in his office till late telephoning every City contact he could think of. But all had said the same thing: with no indication yet of the extent of the futures deals to which Falloni had committed the bank, it would be an act of madness to throw good money after bad.

Then he'd tried the Bank of England. Contacts between Butchers and Threadneedle Street were close, and the Bank's governor was an old friend. But he was abroad, apparently unreachable, and the deputy governor, woken up at his home, was distantly sympathetic but unable to provide any concrete assistance. Recent years had seen a spate of this type of incident, he pointed out, and if they bailed out every City institution unwise enough to get its fingers burned in areas it didn't know enough about, they would double the national debt in no time. The Bank would give as much practical assistance to Butchers as possible but there would be no state bail-out.

At two o'clock in the morning, his index finger sore from dialling, he'd given up and tried to sleep in the hope that the morning might yet provide some new development which would prove his saviour.

But when, at eight a.m., he stumbled along the corridor to his office, he found not his saviour but his nemesis. A middle-aged man with a goatee beard was sitting with his feet up on the leather-inlaid desk. Except for the fact that he had a large black eye, he wore an expression of effortless authority on his face and was lolling back comfortably on Butcher's chair, the telephone receiver tucked under his chin.

'Yup,' he was saying. 'Six-monther, this one, minimum. Another of those City jobbies. Couldn't run a piss-up, this lot, so fuck knows what they were doing trying to run a bank.' He broke off, now aware he was not alone. 'Hang on a sec,' he said, looking enquiringly at Lomond Butcher. 'Yeah?'

'Who are you?' asked Butcher bewildered.

'Better call you back,' the man told his caller. Without shifting from his comfortable position, he took aim and launched the receiver into the air. It crash-landed neatly back in its cradle. 'Bull's-eye!' he exclaimed with satisfaction. 'Now, what can I do for you, mate?'

'I'm chairman of this bank,' said Lomond Butcher, more in mystification than in anger. 'And this is *my* office. The question is what I can do for you?'

'Not any more, it's not,' replied the man, with the air of someone who was prepared to be pleasant despite an obvious slight. 'My office now, this is. At least for the time being.' He held out his hand. 'Kevin Hock,' he said. 'Insolvency Department, Slaughterhouse Accountants.'

'But by whose authority are you here?' asked Butcher. Slaughterhouse were indeed Butchers' accountants, but they'd always been the most respectful of people. He found it hard to believe that this man had any connection with them.

Hock consulted his notes. 'Sloach,' he said. 'Know him at all? One Lord Sloach of Macclesfield.'

'Of course I do. But he has no business—'

'Seems he's moderator of the Puritas Foundation, whatever that is. He's taken on emergency powers and asked us to come in as a precautionary measure. See what we'd be able to salvage if the worst came to the worst. Though naturally we all hope it won't.' This last sentence was recited like the well-worn formula it clearly was.

'It's preposterous,' said Butcher weakly. 'I demand to see your written authority. We've always dealt with one of your directors, Mr Firlock.'

'Yeah, well, insolvency's a different department,' said Hock. 'See,' he confided as he slid his paperwork across the desk, 'it takes a different style of person to deal with this side of things. Faint heart never flogged a bankrupt merchant bank. Need to be a bit more assertive than the average accountant when it comes to sorting out a place like this.' He smiled, baring a row of uneven teeth which resembled broken glass embedded on a wall to ward off intruders. 'Gotta be able to cut through the crap. And that's what I do.'

Lomond Butcher didn't doubt it. But the words immediately

put him in mind of the person who would be more than a match for Hock. 'Where's Gregory Kurdell?' he asked.

The accountant's expression became irritable. 'Thick-set bloke with dodgy eyes, is he?'

Butcher nodded, too dumbstruck even to object to the description.

'Had to be restrained by the police,' snapped Hock. 'Punched me in the bloody face as soon as I arrived.'

Butcher regarded his black eye with some satisfaction. Perhaps Kurdell wasn't such a bad chap after all.

But Hock quickly cheered up again. 'The police managed to land a few good ones on him when they took him away, though. Anyway, too many cooks spoil the broth and I don't like my style being cramped. I'll be plugging the gap for a while, matey, and I'm sure we'll get on just fine.'

He looked across at the chairman, who had collapsed into one of the armchairs by the great window and was gazing despairingly at the pavement below.

'Long way down, is it?' enquired Hock with a grin.

Chapter Fourteen

———◦◦◦◦———

Elsewhere at Butchers, other practitioners from Slaughterhouse's Insolvency Department, who had arrived with Kevin Hock, were fanning expertly through the building. By the time all the staff arrived for work, many of their desks were already occupied by these stand-ins whose job was to begin assessing the assets and liabilities of each area in case, as they explained in the same formulaic manner as their boss, 'the worst came to the worst'.

A comparatively sympathetic young woman had been allocated to the Private Clients Department and she was taking a careworn Toby Slaker through the procedures she would be following, when Felicia informed him that Mattison Pick was on the line.

'You'll have to excuse me,' said Toby. He crossed his fingers firmly as went to take the call. The morning had seen a steady stream of his favourite clients ringing up to enquire about their funds. Even though Toby had been reassuring, some had already opted to move their accounts elsewhere, and, under the circumstances, Toby could hardly blame them. Others, though, were equally determined to stay put. The McKwerties, whose lunch appointment the previous day had been abruptly cancelled because of the crisis, had none the less pledged their loyalty to Butchers in terms that had brought him close to tears.

But Pick was the crucial one. His account was worth hundreds of thousands in fees and, more importantly, the rest of the glitterati who had made up Falloni's client base would take their lead from him. If Toby could hang on to the famous composer it would be the first major victory in a battle that was only just beginning.

'Mr Pick,' he said. 'Thank you for calling. I'm sorry I didn't get back to you yesterday, but no doubt you know—'

'Yeah, I heard,' Pick cut in laconically. 'And I'm real sorry about your friend.'

'Thank you,' said Toby. 'We're all very sad. But you'll also be understandably concerned about your assets.'

'You could say that.'

'Well, let me assure you,' Toby began hurriedly, 'that they are completely safe. As you know, they are held through independent custodians and at no risk whatsoever.' He waited nervously for Pick's reaction. Some of the earlier clients had simply not believed him about this, even though it was the gospel truth. But perhaps Pick was a more sophisticated investor.

To Toby's relief, he was. 'Yeah,' said the composer. 'I know all about that. My accountant explained it when I started out on this game.'

For once, Toby thanked God for accountants. His relief, however, was to be short-lived. 'The thing is, though,' Pick went on, 'I still got a problem here. See, what with Peaches and all, this is the last thing I need. Me and Falloni, we understood each other. That presentation he put together when he pitched for my business was real impressive. And with him gone, well . . . nothing personal, but maybe I'd better find someone else to take it on . . .' His voice tailed off and Toby's heart sank. He was going to lose it after all.

But something inside him fought back. He wouldn't give up without a struggle. He racked his brains. 'I know I wasn't at that initial presentation,' he said, 'but I assure you I was very much involved in producing it.'

'Oh, yeah?' said Pick cautiously. 'I didn't know that.'

'Yes indeed. And, what's more, though Falloni was your main point of contact, he and I were jointly responsible for your account,' he lied. 'I'm fully *au fait* with every aspect of your portfolio.'

'Yeah, you told me that the other night,' said Pick. He was paying attention now. 'Kinda fateful, in retrospect, huh?' His voice sounded pensive. 'Every aspect?'

'Absolutely,' Toby confirmed. 'If you give us your support, Butchers can continue to provide you with the high quality of service you've come to expect from us.'

A further silence ensued, and Toby held his breath.

'Well, I could certainly do without the extra hassle right now,' said Pick at length. ''Cos I'm sure gonna need a lot of help to keep my holdings out of the hands of that vindictive bitch.'

'Quite,' agreed Toby eagerly. 'And I'm right on top of that, Mr Pick. I'll be coming back to you later today with concrete proposals.' On his pad, he wrote down 'CONCRETE PROPOSALS' in big letters and underlined it three times.

There was another long pause, then finally Pick came to a decision. 'Yeah, okay,' he said. 'I guess I'll stick around for now after all. I'll want to meet with you later and review it, but I got too many other things to worry about to start changing ships midstream at the moment.'

With a final commiseration on Falloni's death, Pick rang off and Toby took out a handkerchief and wiped his forehead with a sense of triumph that was also mingled with guilt. He hated lying to a client. The fact was that Falloni had pitched to Pick off his own bat and Toby had had nothing to do with it. Indeed, he'd been sceptical of the chances of success at the time. And nor did Toby know anything about the account itself, or how it was invested.

But he would have said virtually anything to keep Pick on board and he could worry about the details later. For now, he just thanked God for the lucky break and hoped it would prove a good omen.

The only omen that Lomond Butcher would have recognised was the film of the same name, with Kevin Hock of Slaughterhouse in the starring role. For Butcher, things were going from bad to worse. And repeated calls to Lord Sloach's office to complain about his pre-emptive action and insist that the accountants be withdrawn had been to no avail. He was, according to his secretary, 'in an important meeting and not to be disturbed'.

Meanwhile, Hock and his colleagues had wasted no time in touting the bank around the market place, 'just in case'. And there was no shortage of interested parties. By early afternoon, with still no word from the LAFFE, Hock was showing 'potential punters', as he referred to them, round the place at half-hourly intervals, with the proprietorial pride of an estate agent selling off a juicy repossession at bargain-basement prices.

Lomond Butcher overheard snatches of their conversations through the open door of his office, where, having finally persuaded Hock to move into the boardroom, he sat mesmerised at his desk. Various European and North American accents wafted in as they were conducted along the corridor outside.

'Course the building's a turkey,' said one. 'But it's in a prime location. Could raze it and probably recoup the whole acquisition cost from the land alone. Either that or we stick up twenty-five storeys and consolidate all the other UK operations here.'

'Yeah, all that's really worth keeping's the name and the client list,' agreed his companion. 'Best book of high-quality business I've seen in years, and going for a song.'

Lomond Butcher wanted to intervene, preferably physically and with disproportionate violence, but he had lost all will. He just stared with disbelief at the walls which seemed to be crumbling around him.

In late afternoon yet another conversation wafted in from outside his door and this time one of the voices was a faintly familiar female one. Unlike the others, it did not stop in the corridor outside. It became louder and more strident until the door itself was thrown open.

'This is the chairman's office,' said a young woman who made up for her shortage of stature with a determinedly jutting chin and eyes like heat-seeking missiles. 'Unless it's changed since my day.' Her laugh tinkled out. 'And *that's* hardly likely

since it hadn't changed for the previous ninety years before that.'
She broke off and stared at Lomond Butcher. 'Oh,' she said. 'I
hadn't expected . . . I mean . . .' Momentarily thrown, she
backed off as Lomond Butcher stared at her malevolently. But
she quickly regained her poise and held out her hand with a
determined thrust. 'Simona Slaker, Winegloss and Hooch Asset
Management,' she said. 'You won't remember, but I worked
here years ago. And may I introduce you to Oscar Winegloss.'
She presented a florid man with little red eyes. 'This is Lomond
Butcher, the chairman.'

'Pleased to meet you,' said Winegloss in an indifferent
monotone.

Butcher made no effort to reciprocate. 'I remember you,
young lady,' he said. 'You were a cheeky lass then and you
haven't changed a bit since.'

Simona gave him a thin-lipped smile. 'We're all *so* sorry
about your troubles,' she mouthed. 'And naturally we're hoping
that they'll resolve themselves without any . . . ah, external
intervention. But if the worst comes to the worst, we're . . . ah'
– she groped around for the right cliché – 'we're here for you,'
she concluded smugly.

Winegloss nodded his assent at this appropriately American
platitude before Simona ushered him rapidly away as if fearing
he might be contaminated by the atmosphere. As soon as they
were back in the corridor, her voice picked up again. 'I
thought I'd take the chief executive's office initially while
we sort things out,' Butcher heard her say. 'And you – or Mr
Zlennek himself, if he wanted – could become chairman pro
tem. Of course, we'd make sure we maintained a veneer of
continuity while we persuade clients to transfer their accounts
across.'

Inside, Butcher eyed the guns on his wall with real longing
but Simona Slaker pressed on oblivious. 'Let me show you up to
the Private Clients Department now,' she told Winegloss, her
mid-Atlantic accent becoming even more marked than usual.
'It's just too quaint for words . . .'

Only the ring of the telephone averted the risk of a further bloodshed at Butchers Bank. It was Lord Sloach, finally return-ing the chairman's calls.

Lomond Butcher launched straight in. 'How dare you?' he shouted. 'How dare you go over my head and call in the accountants?'

'I'm protecting the interests of the Council,' said Sloach primly. 'It's my duty to be prepared, if the worst comes—'

'Shut up,' screamed Butcher. 'Shut up. I've had enough of that expression to last me a bloody lifetime.'

Sloach paused. 'Well,' he said softly, 'there's always the other solution. We still have time to accept the Zlennek offer. It's another two hours before his deadline runs out.'

'I've told you. Under no circumstances will that man own this bank.'

'Very well.' The smack of Sloach's lips pursing could clearly be heard down the phone line. 'In that case, I have no option but to see who else might be interested. And you may as well know that I'm allowing Zlennek's people in to do their due diligence too – just in case.'

Butcher slammed the phone down without another word. If Zlennek came anywhere near the place, he vowed, he really would take his shotgun to him.

Simona was still expounding on her theme as she and Winegloss climbed the spiral staircase to the sixth floor. 'The Pension Fund and other institutional clients are a snip at the price.' Toby and the rest of the department heard her voice echoing up the stairwell. 'Bit of cross-selling here, spot of churning there, see if we can't get them into some of our emerging funds, and we're laughing all the way to the Bank of England. But as for the Private Clients' – her tone became pitying – 'well, not much we can do with *them*. I happen to know that the showbiz ones they acquired recently are worth the candle, but the rest are piffling. Best just to dump them in a sack on the motorway on the way back to the airport – metaphorically speaking, of course.'

Toby listened, his face just as thunderous as Lomond

Butcher's had been a few moments before. There was no mistaking who it was. Even Felicia recognised her voice. He could see that from the embarrassed way she looked down at her keyboard and actually got on with some work for once. How dare his wife use privileged information against him like this? How dare she come and invade his territory at this, his moment of greatest crisis?

And, as the sound of two sets of footsteps ascended closer and closer on the metal steps, exhaustion and fury suddenly fused within Toby till he felt himself snap. Without really knowing what he was doing, he got up from his desk, and, like a man possessed, charged towards the top of the stairwell.

The great oak door that stood at the 'Gentlemen's Entrance' had not been moved in years. Its hinges were rusted and its handle stiff. When Toby grabbed it with both hands and gave it an almighty wrench, it let out a groaning protest. But finally it budged and swung outwards. With a crash that resounded round the building, it slammed in the faces of the two would-be predators just as they reached the top of the stairs.

All Toby saw before it closed was Simona's startled features staring up at him in impotent confusion. Then, breathlessly, he shot the bolt while Felicia and the rest of the staff in his small department burst into spontaneous applause.

Chapter Fifteen

To Lomond Butcher's relief and Lord Sloach's frustration, Ivor Zlennek's six o'clock deadline came and went without incident. Still there was no news from the LAFFE, and the atmosphere among Butchers' staff was becoming unbearably tense. Toby Slaker's mini-blockade did not last long: he reopened the door as soon as he heard the voices receding disconsolately back downstairs. But news of it spread round the building, giving substance to a siege mentality that had already become evident elsewhere. In every corner huddles of anguished employees gathered to discuss the latest rumours and speculate on their futures.

By contrast, a quite different atmosphere was taking hold in the board and meeting rooms, where groups of accountants, lawyers and potential purchasers had set up their temporary headquarters. There, a spirit of genuine camaraderie had developed. Rumours were rife that the losses might make the *Guinness Book of Records*, and, in anticipation of a result that would keep them all in business for months, they raided Butchers' cellars and broke out a couple of cases of champagne. They even took pity on the pressmen camped outside and invited them to come on up and join in. Soon a party was in full swing, with only the Butchers' employees the spectres at the feast.

Lomond Butcher sat alone in his office, meanwhile, waiting for word and listening to the revelries next door. He couldn't even summon up the energy to go through and put an end to them. For his own part he had opened up a bottle of fifty-year-old Glenfiddich that had been nestling in a desk drawer, waiting for some special occasion. It had cost him several thousand pounds and this was not exactly what he'd had in mind for it, but there didn't seem much point in waiting now. By tomorrow the whole place would probably be in the hands of the liquidators. He sipped it slowly, savouring the subtle, bitter flavours and getting quietly drunk.

Not long after eleven o'clock, there was a tap on the door. 'Yes?' he called out angrily, expecting Kevin Hock again.

But it wasn't. It was Toby Slaker, the Private Clients head. 'I'm sure you're very busy, Sir Lomond. I just wanted to . . .'

'My dear chap,' said Butcher, slurring his words just a little. 'Not busy at all. Come on in.'

Hesitantly Toby entered. Behind him, a conga line of assorted American investment bankers could just be glimpsed dancing past along the corridor.

'Frightful affair, this. Still don't really believe it,' said Butcher sadly. 'Care for a drink?' Without waiting for a reply, he poured a generous measure of whisky into a tumbler and slid it across the desk.

Toby sat down uncomfortably on the edge of a chair. 'I just wanted you to know, sir,' he began earnestly, 'that the staff are one hundred per cent behind—'

Butcher held up his hand. 'Don't need to say it,' he said, making a visible effort to contain himself.

'This should never have happened,' said Toby with sudden self-disgust. 'I mean, Falloni worked in my department and I should have—'

Again the chairman stopped him. 'I'm the one who should apologise to *you*,' he said sombrely.

'You?' asked Toby, taken aback. 'Why?'

A ring from his telephone interrupted Butcher's imminent confession. He picked it up and listened, and his face became grim. 'Very well,' he said. His voice was practically a whisper as he replaced the receiver. 'It seems our wait is over. They've finally heard from the LAFFE and Mr Kevin Hock requires our presence in the boardroom to make an announcement.'

The two of them made their way next door, where the various groups were rapidly reassembling. In the far corner Toby spotted Simona with Oscar Winegloss. He avoided her eye.

The old grandfather clock was just striking midnight as Kevin Hock took the podium. The moment of truth had arrived. Everyone waited with bated breath as he slowly opened the envelope, for all the world as if he were about to announce an Oscar winner. 'And the sum total lost,' he intoned, 'is . . .' He hesitated, his eyes almost bulging out of his head. 'The sum lost is . . .' He stopped again, evidently overwhelmed.

His audience drew breath. If even Kevin Hock, who had seen everything, was shocked then it had to be something really special. They hung on expectantly.

'The sum total lost is,' he said a third time, and then, at last, read the number out from the piece of paper in front of him. 'One hundred and twenty-three point four five.'

The reaction from those assembled was practically orgasmic. 'A hundred and twenty-three billion pounds,' exclaimed Winegloss rolling the words over on his tongue in excitement. That was practically the GNP of a small European country.

'One hundred and twenty-three billion,' gasped Stevie Cudlick from the *Pop*, headlines springing up before his eyes. 'A record-breaker. Well done, that man!'

It was left to Kevin Hock to put a damper on proceedings. 'Er, no,' he said. 'Not billion.'

'Not billion?' asked the audience, taken aback.

'No.'

This was clearly a blow. Winegloss wiped his brow. Stevie Cudlick spat on the carpet. Simona Slaker scratched her forehead.

'Well,' said someone, 'a hundred and twenty-three million's not bad either.' There was a murmur of assent. One had to be reasonable, people evidently felt, and that sum, while not enough to sink one of the clearers, should still be more than enough to put paid to a small merchant bank.

But it appeared this was still not right. 'No,' mumbled Hock. 'Not million either.'

Now there was a huge sigh of collective disappointment. Surely they hadn't been brought out on a total wild goose chase? One journalist spoke for all, the disgust in his voice clear. 'Not worth leaving the pub for a measly hundred grand,' he said. 'We lose more every other week in petty cash fiddles.'

But even now Kevin Hock shook his head sadly. He squinted at the piece of paper and turned it over in his hand in case the figure was continued overleaf. 'Er . . . not thousand either, really.'

Most of the press were past caring now, but one said, 'Well, what the hell is it then?'

Kevin Hock finally found his voice. 'Er . . . pounds,' he said almost inaudibly. 'A hundred and twenty-three pounds.' He grasped the side of the podium. 'And forty-five pence,' he added, evidently hoping that might make all the difference.

It took some time for the awful reality to penetrate. There was a silence which lasted for fully ten seconds. Finally, when it did sink in, though, there came the inevitable backlash. 'We've been got in here under false pretences,' said an accountant belligerently. 'It's a bloody cheek. Wasting our time like that.'

This view met with widespread agreement. The American bankers were particularly vociferous. 'Two seats on Concorde, helicopter in from Heathrow,' said one. 'Cost a goddamn fortune! We'll sue.'

Only the Butchers contingent were rather selfishly triumphant about the outcome. Standing in the back corner of the room, Toby Slaker felt almost overcome by the relief and elation that welled up inside him. Thank God, he thought. Thank God. He looked around for the chairman. After their chat earlier, he couldn't help wanting to share this moment with him. He couldn't see him anywhere, though, until eventually he caught sight of his back disappearing through the communicating door to the office. Evidently Butcher wanted to be alone.

That theory was disproved, however, when he returned a

moment later carrying something long and metallic which glinted in the bright lights of the boardroom.

'Get out,' Butcher shouted at the intruders, waving his shotgun in the air. After the humiliation and calumny of the last two days, he had reached the end of his tether. 'Get out of my bank, the lot of you,' he screamed.

They all drew back, wondering if this were some kind of joke. But the look in his eye quickly convinced them he was deadly serious. And so, with the chairman still looking on belligerently, the lawyers, accountants, journalists and bankers did as they were bidden.

Abandoning any pretence at dignity, they began a headlong rush towards the door. Spotting Simona among them, Toby waved to her cheerily. But now it was she who would not let him catch her eye as, trailing Oscar Winegloss dejectedly behind her, she joined the hasty exodus and finally disappeared down the stairway without a backward glance.

Chapter Sixteen

'It's me. Can you talk?'

'You'll have to make it quick.'

'Look, it hasn't gone according to plan.'

'Oh? But I did everything exactly as we discussed. I even got the file out. There's nothing to implicate you now.'

'I know. It was a great job and nobody suspected a thing. But we're going to have to go in again all the same. It just didn't work out the way I expected. I'll explain when I see you.'

'Okay. So we carry on with Plan B, right?'

'Yes.'

'Have you planted the card yet?'

'I took my chance the other night. As a precaution. But it was just as well as things turned out. Haven't you heard anything from him yet?'

'There was a contact the other morning. It may have been him. But nothing since then.'

'Give it time. He's a more cautious type than the other one. Besides, he's been busy. But eventually he won't be able to resist.'

'You think so?'

'I guarantee it.'

Chapter Seventeen

It was two weeks later when Will Cloud, the Irish boyfriend of Candida Blitz, ambled out of the Colonel Bogey's Fried Chicken restaurant in Hampstead High Street, and sat down on a bench next to the entrance. He rested his coffee on the pavement, took a pre-rolled joint out of his pocket, and opened up the red and yellow cardboard box containing his supper.

He was just on the point of tucking in when he became aware he was not alone. At the other end of the bench, a blanketed huddle was painstakingly picking its way through a pile of leftover chicken boxes from the shop's rubbish bin. Two eyes stared at him from beneath dark bushy eyebrows.

Will nodded amiably towards the unshaven face of the elderly man to whom they belonged. He was not averse to sharing his dining accommodation during busy periods; nor was he inclined to be stuffy about dress codes. The blanket was a dignified grey – casual but smart, Will would have said. Returning to the business in hand, he took a bite from one of his drumsticks.

At this point, though, his companion pulled himself upright and slid across the bench towards Will. Two miniature Johnnie Walker bottles clanked out of his pocket on the way and he rapidly retrieved them. Then he gazed at Will and his chicken box with a comradely, if distinctly hungry, expression. He'd obviously identified a less mouldy prospect than the contents of the bin, and, perhaps with the government's recent food hygiene advice uppermost in his mind, was intent on trading up.

'Welcome,' he said with a toothless grin. 'Welcome to one of the finest benches in London.' Underneath the blanket he was wearing a three-piece pin-striped suit about five sizes too small, and apparently nothing else. 'We trust your sojourn here will prove enjoyable.' Now his face became grave and the eyebrows knitted together. 'We are aware that you have a choice of benches tonight,' he went on, 'and are grateful that you have chosen ours. If there's anything we can do to enhance your comfort during this visit, you need only ask.' Then he paused and stuck out a grubby hand. 'Service is included,' he added, 'but gratuities are optional.'

Will sighed and reached for some change. He was technically unemployed himself, but was not in the habit of saying no to those even worse off. His pockets were empty, though. It was Thursday and he'd already used up his week's money. He pointed to the box where three chicken pieces nestled forlornly in a pile of damp-looking chips. 'Care to join me?' he asked.

The man shrugged. 'Most kind,' he wheezed. In return, he held out one of the whisky bottles.

'No, thanks,' said Will. 'I'm trying to give up the drink.' He gestured towards the joint. 'The old weed, that's my poison.'

Not far away, in the rambling house that Will shared with his girlfriend, TV presenter Candida Blitz and her chimpanzee, Zoë, a rather more refined but equally impromptu meal was just about to get under way.

'I'm so glad you could drop in,' said Candida, desperately gathering up Will's discarded socks from the kitchen floor as she showed her guest in. 'There never are enough taxis outside the Beeb, so you'd have been waiting for ages if I hadn't spotted you. And it's ever so kind of you to offer to come back and look at Hilly's antiques for me.'

She went through to the old-fashioned larder and rifled through the cupboards, opening one door after another. Peering at a bag of wildly sprouting potatoes, she wished she'd done some shopping more recently than last month. 'I'll just throw something together and we'll have a little snack first,' she said dubiously. 'Then I'll bring the pieces through and let you have a look at them.'

There were some tins of sardines, and a jar of sun-dried tomatoes. And some olives and a bottle of Chablis in the fridge. Would that hit the right note? she wondered. No, the wine was out. She remembered just in time that her guest was an ardent teetotaller. Oh God, what did a woman like that drink? 'Will, my boyfriend, will be so disappointed to have missed you,' she called out. 'He's such a fan. But he's probably dining out tonight, because I didn't think I'd be back.'

Oblivious to the panic she was causing, Britannia Draycott looked around the untidy kitchen. Her gaze alighted on Zoë, dozing on a battered settee in the corner. The elderly chimpanzee, a relic of the days when Candida had presented a children's TV programme, was a national celebrity, having once accidentally attacked a government minister in an intimate place. 'Is she quite safe?' Britannia asked tentatively in those rounded tones so familiar to generations of TV viewers, except that age had now given them a distinct quiver. 'I serve on the Puritas Council with poor old Alistair Sloach,' she added, 'and I'm told he still can't even see a tea advertisement without crossing his legs and breaking into a sweat.'

'Oh, yes,' Candida's voice wafted back through. 'That was all a dreadful mistake. Zoë's very gentle really.' At the sound of her name, the chimp woke briefly, gave Britannia Draycott a bored once-over and dropped back off to sleep again. Reassured, the veteran broadcaster continued her inventory of the room, taking in the ancient kitchen fitments with a critical eye. 'What a charming place you have here,' she said.

'Oh, that was Hilly,' said Candida. 'He always liked old things and refused to modernise. And since he died and left me the house, I've just been too busy with TV work to get around to updating the place.' She came back through carrying a bottle of apple juice and two plates on which she'd arranged their supper in what she hoped was an artistic collage. 'That's why I've never done anything about all the bits and bobs he left me. He always said they were worth something, but I've no idea about antiques. So when I remembered about you presenting *Antique Chique*, I thought . . .'

'Delighted to oblige,' said Britannia rather grandly. She peered at Candida over the top of her spectacles. 'I think you'll find I've become *rather* an expert over the years. Now what have we got here?' She looked down doubtfully at the food as if it were tonight's first submission, which, given its sell-by date, was not entirely inappropriate. 'A splendid spread!' she pronounced at length. 'Just the kind of feast we used to have after lights-out.'

'Oh, I'm so glad you like it,' said Candida, who'd attended a comprehensive school in Purley where midnight sardine feasts were about as common as pagan orgies. Her face flushing, she watched with delight as her guest picked daintily at her plate. Reverently, she took in every aspect of her, from her artfully coiffed tower of translucent hair, down past her severely pinched face to the elegant twin-set and the sensible brogues.

Britannia Draycott had always been one of Candida's heroines. As a child, she remembered watching her reading the news when that was still considered an exclusively male preserve, after which she'd gone on to present religious affairs programmes with her very own brand of evangelical moralising. More recently she had moved on to front virtually every other kind of programme known to television, including *Your Arts Desire*, the culture slot that was almost a national institution, as well as her famous antique show. Throughout this ascent Candida had admired her from afar, even as she herself became a well-known TV figure. And now here they were, sitting together at Candida's very own kitchen table, chatting away as if they'd known one another for years.

'Are you going to go on presenting *Antique Chique*?' Candida asked. 'I mean, after you retire from your other work.' As ever, she tried to suppress her slight lisp. It was important that Britannia took her seriously if her carefully laid plan was to bear fruit.

'Who told you I was retiring?' sniffed Britannia.

Candida shifted anxiously into reverse. 'One picks up gossip,' she replied. 'But, of course, one was rather hoping it wasn't true.'

'It may be,' said Britannia guardedly. She sat back in the chair. 'After ten years doing *Arts Desire*, I've had enough culture to last a lifetime. But I'll go on doing *Antique Chique* a while yet.' She relaxed a little. 'May as well, now that I am one! Ha!'

'Sorry?' said Candida uncertainly.

'Now I'm an antique!' Britannia chortled.

'Oh!' Candida forced a giggle. 'Absolutely!' she agreed, before sitting up abruptly, wondering if she'd made a faux pas. 'Not that you are, of course. Far from it.'

'Nonsense! Call a spade a spade, that's my motto,' said Britannia, giving the table a hearty slap. 'Time to move on, don't you think? Do some charitable work. Give something back to society.'

'Oh?'

Her guest lowered her voice. 'That's why, when Alistair Sloach asked me to join the Puritas Council, I couldn't say no.'

'Ah?' Candida nodded knowledgeably. In fact, until recently, she'd never even heard of the Puritas Council. But since the crisis at Butchers Merchant Bank a few weeks earlier, which had reportedly ended in its chairman trying to evict the press through an upper-floor window, everyone now knew about the Council's role as ultimate owner of Butchers, as well as its work in upholding the country's morals. 'I'm sure you'll do that very well,' Candida insisted. She tried to steer the conversation back towards her main agenda. 'If you were to retire, who do you think would present *Your Arts Desire* when you go?' she asked casually.

'Ah,' said Britannia and stopped. At last the penny had dropped. She gazed at Candida thoughtfully. 'I see. That's something *you* might be interested in, is it?'

Candida chose her words carefully. 'I might be. You see, apart from the time I did some political interviewing, which wasn't really *me*, I've always been pigeonholed into light entertainment programmes like the *Hoodwink Show*. But that's so limiting.'

'Yes, I heard about poor Matty Pick,' said Britannia severely. 'He's an old friend of mine. We did a profile of him and his beautiful vases on *Antique Chique* a few months ago.'

Oh, God, thought Candida. Would the Peaches La Trené catastrophe be a black mark against her? 'I was so sad about what happened,' she cut in immediately. 'I wrote to him to tell him and I got ever such a sweet letter back, saying he completely forgave me. He even asked me out to dinner some time. But' – she returned determinedly to the matter at hand – 'that just illustrates how superficial that sort of show is. I need something more serious to get my teeth into. My interests are so much wider. Especially in the arts.' She paused significantly and waved her hands around to indicate her massive scope. 'They've *always* fascinated me.'

Britannia threw her a shrewd glance. 'Well, it may be possible. You'd certainly bring a younger audience with you. I could put your name forward and I *do* have some influence on who they appoint. But I haven't definitely decided to retire yet. Not for a few years, at least. Anyway' – she shifted slyly in her seat – 'that's not what you brought me here for, is it, dear? Where exactly are all these antiques I'm to look at?'

The hint of sarcasm in her voice was entirely lost on Candida. Her real mission now accomplished, she happily went off to locate them.

She had just retrieved her fourth item – a piece of delicately patterned crockery of indeterminate age – when they heard the sound of a key being turned in the front door. 'Oh, good,' said Candida. 'That must be Will. You'll be able to meet each other after all.'

She suppressed a slight twinge of concern, though. Will could be very charming when in the right mood, but he could also be unpredictable. And now that she and Britannia were getting on so well, and visions of her new, more upmarket career were playing themselves out before her eyes, she needed him to be on his best behaviour.

The first indication that it was not to be her day came when she realised he had somebody with him. And nor was it just any somebody, it was a distinctly whiffy somebody whose breath preceded him into the room, and who was sporting a blanket that was definitely last year's model and a covering of stubble that had never been near a designer in its life.

Candida cursed herself for embarking on this important project without taking the precaution of having Will confined to a straitjacket beforehand. It would not be the first time he'd embarrassed her. He'd often brought back all sorts of waifs and strays from his wanderings, particularly when he'd been smoking something, which, she realised with a heavy heart, was the case now. Why did it have to be today of all days? Candida wailed silently to herself. He would ruin everything. But she composed herself in an attempt to salvage what she could from the situation. 'This is Britannia Draycott,' she said over-brightly. 'My friend Will Cloud, and . . . ah . . .' Her voice tailed off.

As predicted, Will was delighted to meet Britannia. He moved forward and pressed her hand with enthusiasm. 'Sure, Candida's always talking about you.' Britannia forced a wintry smile. 'She's your greatest fan. And this,' he went on, oblivious to Candida's tortured expression, 'this is my old mate, Terry. He's a great fella too.' He hesitated, apparently realising that a further explanation was called for. 'Friend of the family. Not feeling too well today, though. So I brought him back for a few refreshments. Step forward, Terry,' he trumpeted, 'and say hello to . . . ah . . . old Brit here.'

Terry also held out his hand, but from too far away to reach Britannia's. She made no effort to bridge the gap and, as he blinked at her, Terry began swaying slowly back and forward. Candida watched him mesmerised, wondering which way he would go. Finally he grinned inanely, rocked to the left, rocked to the right, and toppled backwards on to the old kitchen settee, barely missing Zoë, who dodged out of the way just in time. There, having made himself comfortable, he sank into a silent stupor.

Will, who had observed all this quite unperturbed, regarded him good-naturedly. 'Well, then,' he said. 'That's how it goes. A fine fella, but a wee bit tired.' He stared at the two women with a slightly unfocused look on his own face. 'Sure, I think you'll have to excuse me too,' he went on. 'Could do with some shut-eye myself.' With that he disappeared through to the hallway and up the stairs, leaving Candida and Britannia to their own devices again.

Candida swallowed hard. There was no alternative but to pretend nothing had happened and see if she could recover. 'Now, where were we?' she trilled. 'Is it seventeenth or eighteenth-century, do you think?'

Dragging her eyes away from the sleeping figure with some reluctance, Britannia looked at her incredulously. 'What?' she said.

'This bowl,' Candida repeated brightly. 'When do you think it dates from?'

'Well . . .' From force of habit, Britannia took it from her and examined it mechanically. She turned it upside down, probed its underside and finally pulling herself together, pronounced with authority, 'Late eighteenth-century fingerbowl, without a doubt. A fine example.'

'Really?' said Candida, her eyes wide with admiration. There was an outside chance she might yet pull it off, she reckoned. 'How on earth can you tell?'

'Well,' repeated Britannia slightly more matily. 'You see this little mark—'

'Shcuse me!' The interruption came unmistakably from the direction of the settee and was accompanied by a wheezy cough. At the mention of fingerbowls, Terry had reawoken.

Feeling her brow break into a cold sweat, Candida did her best to ignore him. 'Yes?' she pressed Britannia with a fixed smile. 'What does the little mark tell you?'

But Terry was not to be overlooked. 'Hey, you!' he said more insistently, pointing an accusing finger at Britannia. 'You with the green face.'

Both Candida and Britannia froze in their tracks. 'Shorry to interrupt,' he continued, slightly more apologetically, 'but you know what you jush said about that thing there.' He waved towards the object in Britannia's hands. 'That was crap, that was!'

The doyenne of antique presenters drew herself up to her full height and stared at him over her half-moon glasses. 'Are you referring to this fingerbowl?' she asked nastily.

'Yeah,' said Terry. 'What you jush said about it, thash total crap. Never eighteenth century, that isn't.'

'Oh?' said Britannia. A physicist, if there had been one around, could have used her tone to prove there was a temperature below absolute zero after all. 'Well, let me tell you,' she said, 'that I've been examining antiques for over four years and I know an eighteenth-century fingerbowl when I see one!'

'I don't care if you've been examining them for four hundred years,' countered Terry, looking her up and down as if he considered it quite likely. 'That,' he continued, 'ish early seventeenth century. And whash more' – he got up and staggered towards her so that his face was only inches from hers – 'whash more, you daft bitch, ish not a fingerbowl at all. Anyone can see it's a fucking *spittoon*.'

At which point, with Candida looking on in agony, he grabbed the object out of Britannia's hands, gazed deep into its recesses for a second as if searching there for the meaning of life, swayed a bit more and finally threw up into it in an elegant multicoloured parabola.

Then, no doubt considering he'd proved his case about its use beyond any reasonable doubt, he looked at her defiantly and once again collapsed, exhausted, on to the settee.

'Well, how was I to know he was a retired curator from the V and A?' Will Cloud asked plaintively during the row that followed the departure – separately – of their respective guests.

Usually so placid, Candida rounded on him furiously. 'I don't care what you knew. How *could* you bring some tramp from Colonel Chicken's Fried Bogey back like that . . .'

'Colonel Bogey's Fried Chicken,' Will corrected her. 'And don't knock it. Some of the greatest minds in the world are to be found there.'

'But that was Britannia Draycott!' said Candida, almost in tears. 'She'll never forgive me.'

'Baloney!' said Will stoutly. 'When she thinks it over, she'll probably be very impressed you know someone so knowledge-able.'

Candida doubted it. When the veteran broadcaster had been sent home by taxi in a profound state of shock, Candida had distinctly heard her muttering that she wouldn't entrust her precious programme to some junkie's moll if she were the last person in the world.

'Besides,' said Will, removing a small white object from his pocket and reaching for his lighter. 'What does it matter what she thought?'

'It matters to me.' In her distress, Candida dropped a plate as she cleared up the dishes from the half-eaten supper. 'Now I'll never get to present *Your Arts Desire*.'

'Well, what do you want to do that for anyway?' asked Will. He lit up his joint and inhaled deeply. 'You already present practically everything else on TV. Only the other day I turned on and there you were with some programme I'd never even heard of.'

'Which one?' asked Candida. For a moment, professional pride overcame her anger.

Will reflected. 'It was called *Brush up your Wits, with Candida Blitz*.'

'Oh, that thing,' said Candida dismissively. 'That was noth-ing – just another quiz show.'

'It might be nothing,' said Will, a sense of moral outrage penetrating his customary laid-back demeanour. 'But you still can't get enough of it, can you? Next thing'll be aerobics: *Doing the Splits, with Candida Blitz*.'

'But that's exactly why I wanted to move upmarket!' Candida practically sobbed. 'Till you went and ruined it all . . .'

Will wasn't listening. As usual, he was pursuing his own line of reasoning willy-nilly. 'How about branching off into fashion now?' he suggested. 'Sure, you could call it: *Putting on the Ritz, with Candida Blitz.*'

'Be quiet!'

'Or soft porn: *Look at the Tits on Candida Blitz!*'

'Will you just shut up!' Candida screamed. In the two years since he had moved in with her, this was the first time she had raised her voice to him. But now that she had, she felt somehow liberated. Marching over to him, she grabbed the joint out of his hand and stubbed it out in an ashtray. 'And, once and for all,' she went on, 'will you stop bringing your . . . your bloody drugs into my house? You've caused enough trouble with them before.'

Will looked at her, taken aback. He opened his mouth to protest but she had not finished yet. 'And another thing,' she said. 'It's all very well for you to make fun of what I do, but at least *I* work for a living. Which is more than can be said for *some* people.' And having got this piece of uncharacteristic bile off her chest, she sat down on the sofa recently vacated by Terry and burst into tears.

A more-in-sadness-than-in-anger expression filled Will Cloud's eyes as he gazed down at her. 'Now,' he said, 'that's not worthy of you, sure it's not. You know I never—'

'I know you never ask me for any money,' Candida interrupted, forestalling his standard counter-argument. 'But I wish you bloody well would for once. Then at least you could buy yourself some decent clothes and go out and get a proper job.' Usually his look of hurt pride at this point was enough to stop her in her tracks. But not today. The disastrous exit of Britannia Draycott had pushed her beyond endurance. 'It's just not healthy hanging around the house all day smoking yourself silly and leaving your things all over the place!'

'I'm not sitting around,' said Will indignantly. 'And anyway I've already got a job, as well you know.'

'Oh, for God's sake! Don't give me that detective stuff again. I've heard it all before.'

'It takes time to get a business off the ground,' said Will. He retrieved the joint from the ashtray and attempted to stick it together again. 'It's not as if I haven't had my successes.'

'And what were they, pray tell?' Candida's babyish voice did not lend itself to sarcasm.

'There was the Brass Monkeys case.'

'That was nearly two years ago!'

'And then there was that pharmaceutical company a few months back,' said Will. 'A triumph of investigative reasoning, if ever there was one.'

'Oh, yes!' sniffed Candida. 'Fat lot of good *that* was. The idea was to turn that secretary *in* once you'd traced the leaks to her. Not to help her call a press conference to expose the very people who hired you, for God's sake.'

'What was I supposed to do?' asked Will animatedly. 'They were testing their products on poor wee defenceless creatures. She was quite right to leak it.'

'The point is,' said Candida, determined not to get side-tracked on to one of Will's endless moral debates, 'that you never got paid for it and you've not been paid for anything since.'

'I'm working on it,' said Will stubbornly. He sat down dejectedly at the other end of the settee beside Zoë and began tickling her behind the ear.

'Well, in the meantime, go out and get a proper job!'

'I could if I wanted to,' said Will. 'It's just—.'

'It's just you're too bone idle,' Candida exploded. And with that she stood up, dried her eyes and stormed upstairs to the bathroom to wash the mascara streaks from her face.

Will Cloud was left behind in the kitchen scratching his head. Candida's vehement tone was not like her at all and for once it gave him pause for thought.

It was the implication that he was lazy that stung him most of all. That was totally unfair. Certainly, he liked to lie in bed till two or three most afternoons, watching old episodes of *Columbo* on the television. Certainly he spent a lot of time sitting around reading detective novels and pitting his wits against the likes of Sherlock Holmes and Hercule Poirot while he smoked the odd joint. But that was not leisure but research, surely Candida understood that? You couldn't become a world-famous detective overnight. Everyone needed to start somewhere.

All the same, Candida was a sweet-natured girl and not given to such outbursts without any reason. Was it possible, was it just possible, he wondered, that she might be right? Maybe he had become a touch self-indulgent these past months. The detective work had not been arriving in the quantities he expected – or indeed in any quantities at all – so perhaps it was time to reassess where he stood. Determined though he was to carry on building up his new business, it didn't mean he couldn't do something else at the same time.

He sat up resolutely. He *would* get a job. He would prove to Candida that he was far from lazy. It shouldn't be that difficult to find something suitable. There must be millions of positions crying out for someone of his abilities and initiative.

But what sort of work? Years ago he'd been a professional interpreter, but translating other people's words all day had long lost its appeal. No, he didn't want to go back to that. There had to be something undemanding and lucrative he could do that would still give him time for his investigation business. Running a publishing company, perhaps, or becoming a politician like his old friend, Hugh Driftwood, who had made it as far as Downing Street itself.

His mind churning away on this, Will idly picked up a magazine from the table and leafed through it looking for the situations vacant column. Suddenly his eye was caught by several photographs of a small but determined-looking woman with a jutting chin. In one she was posing against an elegant wrought-iron fireplace, in another she was sitting in front of a computer in a designer study. Her face seemed vaguely familiar and as soon as he read the caption he remembered why. 'Having it all: Simona Slaker, who earns a seven-figure City salary, still has time left over to decorate her beautiful home in Notting Hill Gate.'

Will let out a low whistle. 'Seven figures,' he said to himself. That wasn't at all bad. And still enough time to do her own painting. Those City jobs must be a doddle. He searched for any reference to the woman's husband, the pleasant looking, if somewhat henpecked, man he'd spoken to at the *Hoodwink Show*. But there was no mention of him in the article.

What was his first name now? Will got up and found the jacket he'd worn the other night, which was still hanging where he'd left it over the back of a chair. He soon located the card he was searching for: 'Toby Slaker, Head of Private Clients, Butchers Bank'. He paused and stared at it. The company name was familiar too. Wasn't that the bank that had been in trouble a few weeks ago? Will brightened. All the better. Their staff were sure to be leaving, so they could probably do with some fresh faces.

Still musing to himself, Will finally made up his mind. Tomorrow he would ring up Slaker and offer his services. And by next week, he had no doubt, he would have become a City whiz-kid at Butchers Bank.

Chapter Eighteen

It was Friday, and dress-down day in the City, which meant that, among the fashion-conscious dealers at Butchers Bank, Gucci rather than Armani was the order of the day.

Upstairs in Private Clients, Toby Slaker, wearing his M&S sports jacket and slacks, had spent a long day working on the backlog that had built up during the 'crisis', as it was referred to internally. For a brief moment, though, he too paused for a few seconds to gaze at a business card that had recently begun preoccupying him again.

For a time, all thoughts of sex had been crowded out of his mind by the events surrounding the death of Falloni. But now that the futures fiasco was more or less resolved and things at Butchers had returned to something approaching normality, the erotic picture of the hooded and naked man being led by a whip-cracking dominatrix had come back to haunt him. And all the more so because, ever since Simona's attempt to take over Butchers Bank had failed so humiliatingly a fortnight before, relations between them had sunk to an all-time low. She was spending all her time either at work or preparing for her huge 'promotion' party – or as Toby preferred to refer to it, 'self-promotion' party – which was only eight days off. Ivor Zlennek and his wife had confirmed that they would be attending, sending Simona into frenzies of excitement and Toby into fits of impotent anger. How dare she invite that man into their home? he'd demanded. Zlennek was her boss, she'd replied, and it was none of Toby's business. Since then, the two of them had hardly even been on speaking terms. Sex was out of the question and Toby was more frustrated than ever.

But still he had resisted the temptation to revisit the 'hood-wink.encounters.com' site and see if he could make an appointment with one of the women that his Australian contact, Gus, had told him about. There was a puritan streak in him that put marital infidelity high on his personal list of cardinal sins. He and Simona might be going through a rough patch, but that was no reason why he should allow himself to succumb to pornography like this. All the same, he couldn't quite bring himself to dispose of the card and had kept it safely locked up in an office drawer, removing it for the occasional covert glance, just as he had tonight.

Now, once again, he put it away without taking any further action. He had more serious things to concentrate on. His clients, for one. For it was not quite true to say that the effects of the Butchers crisis had totally subsided. Lomond Butcher's elation on the night when he had physically ejected the predators and the press from his bank had proved premature, at least as far as the Private Clients Department was concerned. Admittedly, it had been amply demonstrated that there were no dealing errors in Falloni's accounts and that Butchers was as financially stable as ever it had been. But that was not the end of the matter by any means.

The fact was that, as a result of Falloni's suicide, Butchers Bank was now well and truly in the public eye and there was simply no return to its former obscurity. In particular, the tabloid press had not lost their taste for Butchers' blood. Hardly a day passed without some new exposé on the personal life of one or other of the company's employees. The media, evidently piqued at their treatment at the hands of Lomond Butcher, seemed determined to get their own back and were doing so as only they knew how.

Nor did they stop at staff. Soon they began to take an interest in clients too, combing databases for details of Butchers' distinguished patrons and then tracking them down to ask impertinent questions about how much they had with the bank and which offshore tax havens Butchers had advised them to invest in.

And if there was one thing that Toby's wealthy and discreet client base hated above all else, it was publicity in any form. After all the worries over the potential loss of their assets, for many the appearance of the press on their doorsteps – or more often at the gatehouses at the end of their long gravel paths – was the final straw. Soon they began to vote with their feet.

For Toby this was the unkindest cut of all. Having survived so much, he was falling at the last hurdle. He had no option but to stand by helplessly as his precious clients gradually fell away like crumbling masonry after an attack of dry rot. The embarrassed tones of long-standing patrons ringing up to announce the imminent transfer of their funds had soon become all too easy to identify. None the less, every further call still sent him to new depths of despair.

There was a block of clients, however, which had remained relatively steadfast throughout this period – the raft of show business celebrities, the foremost being Mattison Pick, which had belonged to Roy Falloni himself. They had been the last in, and Toby fully expected them to be the first out. But no. Taking their lead from Pick, they mostly remained loyal.

Toby liked to think that this was at least partly due to his rapid and decisive action on behalf of the famous composer himself. At first he'd thought he would have the devil's own job taking on his investment portfolio, especially as Falloni had been so secretive about it. And indeed, he'd had a bit of trouble locating the details at first, since there seemed to be no paper-based files and the computerised ones had been on Falloni's erased hard disk. But then Toby had remembered the back-up tapes that he'd insisted Falloni make. He'd had the files restored and been able to confirm that Pick's portfolio was intact and, indeed, extremely conservatively invested, with not a hint of a future or option in sight. Toby had then consulted with Pick's American lawyers and accountants and together they had instituted immediate plans to remove most of his wealth from the malign reach of Peaches La Trené.

The same could not be said for Mattison Pick's stage musicals in the United States, though, which were in Peaches' name and therefore beyond the lawyers' reach. As far as those were concerned, Peaches had lived up to the threat she had issued at the close of the *Hoodwink Show* and taken full control of their day-to-day running pending a divorce settlement. Accompanied by a whole media circus of television crews and journalists which beamed pictures round the world, she had flown across America from one theatre to another, marching in and declaring that she was now in charge. And there appeared to be nothing Pick could do about it.

No doubt that fact, along with the imminent opening of his new musical, *The Iron Lady*, were now preoccupying the composer to the exclusion of all else, for he had not been in touch with Toby since their telephone conversation during the Butchers crisis. His advisers, though, had given Toby to understand that Pick was more than happy with the bank's efforts on his behalf, and that he would be continuing to give them his business for the foreseeable future.

As he worked – or tried to work – late that Friday evening, Toby allowed himself a certain pride at this outcome. In a way, it was his own tribute to Falloni, who had prized those clients so much. As he thought once again about Falloni, a lump came to Toby's throat. He realised with a start that he missed him, not just as a colleague, but as a friend. Though not by nature an introspective man, he suddenly found himself brooding on the nature of death and eternity in a way that would have given any nineteenth century Russian novelist a run for his money.

His brow furrowed and yet again he wondered how such an experienced investment manager could have got it into his head that he'd made such spectacular futures losses when, as had now been indisputably proved, he'd done no such thing. If Toby had not heard the tape with his own ears he wouldn't have believed it himself. But he'd heard it, as clear as clear, and there was no doubt in his mind it had been Falloni's voice.

The police's explanation, once they had established all the facts, had been quite simple. 'Under the influence,' Inspector

Ffelcher of Scotland Yard declared concisely at a final wrap-up meeting with Greg Kurdell and Lomond Butcher to which Toby had been invited. 'Plain as the nose on your face. Man had a history of substance abuse, we've got a list of witnesses to that as long as your arm. Stands to reason that if you snort that stuff long enough then you start getting all sorts of delusions. Like those jokers on LSD who think they can fly and jump off the nearest high-rise. Same principle.'

'But did he really have that much in his bloodstream when he died?' Toby had queried. He was sure Falloni had been quite lucid when he left him in the office that night.

The inspector consulted a report. 'Small traces of various stimulants and hallucinogenics were found,' he said, 'including alcohol, cocaine and ecstasy. It seems he went in for some sort of cocktail.'

'Only small traces?' Toby persisted. 'Doesn't that suggest he hadn't taken anything for some time?'

The inspector cast him a slightly nasty look. 'That could be the case, sir, but in my experience the effects of these drugs can be quite long-lasting. Crop up any time, they can.'

'Quite,' said Lomond Butcher. He turned sympathetically to Toby. 'My dear chap, I know how much Falloni's death has upset you, and I understand your wish to defend the poor fellow's honour. But I'm sure you'd agree that this seems by far the most likely explanation for his death.'

Kurdell, who had been released from protective custody to resume his old job immediately after the incident, glared at Toby less understandingly, clearly willing him to shut up. And, eventually, Toby had done so.

Anyway, they were probably all quite right. What other explanation could there possibly be? The whole thing about Moyenne 500 futures had led nowhere. Toby had never found the 'enne' file, but whatever it was, it did not relate to the Moyenne 500 index. Falloni's only futures investment had been the one whose details Toby had found in his desk: the one hundred and twenty-three pound Nikkei contract that had so disappointed the journalists.

Miserably, Toby looked across to his former colleague's old office. If only he could just go in there and ask Falloni straight out, as he used to ask him about all sorts of things. But of course the little glass box was nearly empty except for the half-filled packing cases containing personal effects that were waiting to be shipped off to Falloni's mother in Dorset.

Indeed there was nobody around at all in the Private Clients Department. Nobody, that was, except Melvin Puckle. The department's young computer expert hardly ever seemed to leave the building, staying until all hours of the day and night staring at his screen.

Shame Puckle hadn't been around the night of Falloni's suicide, thought Toby, as he would almost certainly have been working late and might have talked poor Falloni out of it. But Puckle had for once been on holiday that week, which, knowing him, probably meant sitting all day in front of a computer at home instead of the one at work.

Feeling thoroughly disconsolate, Toby wandered out into the wider office area. 'What do you reckon about poor Falloni, Melv?' he asked dejectedly. 'You any idea what got into him?'

With evident reluctance, Puckle dragged himself away from his screen. 'Dunno,' he said, tugging at his short straggly beard. He was a curious, introverted young man with a spotty complexion and a prematurely balding scalp. He seemed to have no personal life and even came in to the office at weekends to work on one nebulous computer project or another. Once, in an effort to bring him out of himself, Toby had induced him to come to the gym and play squash, and they'd had a good game, being well matched and of similar builds. But afterwards, Puckle had declined a drink and scuttled off home, and they had not repeated the experience. He was still not accustomed to passing the time of day with his head of department, much less having his views canvassed.

But Toby felt a need to talk and Puckle was all that was available. 'I mean,' he persisted, 'did he strike you as the type who could have got such a delusion into his mind?'

Melvin shrugged. 'Dunno,' he repeated. 'People are strange.

Prefer computers myself. They'd never do anything like that to themselves.'

It struck Toby rather oddly that this was not quite so. 'That's another thing,' he said. 'Why did Falloni wipe out his computer hard disk?' Having taken away Falloni's PC for examination, the police had come back to say that nothing on it could be recovered. Apparently, for reasons that would probably never be fathomed, Falloni had deliberately erased it before he'd turned Lomond Butcher's gun on himself.

'Dunno,' said Puckle a third time. He stared hard at the screen, evidently willing Toby away. Then, all at once, a light came into his eyes and he looked at his boss straight on. 'Mr Slaker?' he said. 'I mean, eh, Toby?' Toby tried to encourage informality in the office.

'Yes?' said Toby hopefully. Perhaps something had occurred to Melvin after all.

'Eh . . .' Melvin picked up a paperclip and twisted it round and round between his fingers. 'While you're here, d'you think I could have a word about something? I mean, something personal?'

Toby's heart sank. It was all he needed right now. But he was cornered. And he was, after all, the head of the department and it was his duty to make himself available to subordinates when there was something on their minds. Wearily, he adopted what he hoped was a sympathetic smile. 'Of course.'

''S'about my future,' said Melvin, unfurling the paperclip and picking his teeth with one end. 'My career. Now I've been here nearly a year, and . . . and . . .' His voice tailed off.

Toby drew breath. This was something he was used to dealing with. 'Well, Melvin,' he said, 'we're all delighted with the way you're working out. You've a great career ahead of you at Butchers.'

But evidently it was more than the usual bland reassurances that were required on this occasion. 'Yeah, I know,' said Melvin, slightly dismissively. 'But . . . I was wondering, see, if . . . I would be staying on in this department much longer. You see, I got this phone call this morning from a guy at Punter and Snipe and he was saying that Goldbar's are on the lookout for someone just like me and I was thinking . . .'

'Now,' said Toby briskly, 'you know how these headhunters operate. You really shouldn't believe all you hear.' His voice took on a certain frost. 'And don't you think you owe something to the company that gave you your start, specially when we're having such a bad time and losing clients like we are?'

Melvin sniffed. 'Well, yeah,' he said avoiding Toby's eyes. 'It's not that I want to leave Butchers. It's just – I don't want to be in Private Clients for ever.'

Toby sighed. It was always the way. No sooner had they trained someone to do a job in this department than they'd request a move elsewhere in the company. As Falloni used to say, 'Private Clients just ain't sexy.' Reflecting that everything seemed to come back to sex in the end, Toby asked, 'What particular area did you have in mind?'

Puckle's face lit up. 'There's an internal notice gone up today for a trainee analyst in the Quantitative Department,' he said eagerly. 'See, I'm just made for that job.' For someone so tongue-tied, the words were pouring out now. 'I've been working on all sorts of stuff that they could use for analysing the markets through the Internet. F'rinstance, one thing you can do is hack into people's e-mail systems and get hold of all sorts of market-sensitive information just before it's announced. Then you can buy the investments before anyone else and—'

Despite his other preoccupations, Toby now paid attention. 'What?' he cut in, shocked. 'Melvin, that's highly illegal, and Butchers wouldn't think of doing any such thing. But you're joking, aren't you? '

'No, honest,' said Puckle earnestly. 'You'd be amazed what I can do. I once hacked into the Pentagon and got as far as an amber alert signal. Piece of cake, that was.'

'Well,' said Toby, austerely. 'Don't ever let me catch you doing anything like that on our computers. You could get yourself – and us – into a lot of trouble.' He didn't believe him anyway. Puckle had always been given to excessive bragging about his computer expertise.

'It's all right,' said Puckle. 'I do that on my PC at home.'

'I should hope so. But I'd still advise you against it.'

'They could never track me down,' said Puckle smugly. 'See, I've written this stealth programme. It's a bit like the stealth bomber. It can get into anything without being detected.' He continued with a demonic gleam in his eye. 'I've written loads of programmes, and that's why I think I'd be good in Quant. I mean, I know that usually you've got to have degrees and stuff to work in there, and I never bothered with that, 'cos I just wanted to get on with programming. But I'm sure if I just had a few weeks in the department, they'd be bound to see I was good and . . .'

Toby let him drone on. He should have guessed it would be the Quantitative Department Puckle had his eye on. If Private Clients was not sexy, then 'Quant' was. Quant was sexy in droves. Anyone in investment who thought they knew about computers wanted to be a quantitative analyst – or a 'rocket scientist', as they were somewhat sardonically known in the City. This élite breed of PhD-laden mathematicians and scientists used sophisticated computer programmes to predict the ups and downs of the equity and bond markets. Still in their relative infancy, such methods were regarded with suspicion by many traditional fund managers, and Toby was one of them. There was nothing to beat the hard slog of fundamental research, as far as he was concerned, combined with the occasional good old-fashioned hunch. But Quant was gaining ground fast, and it was hardly surprising that people like Puckle wanted in on it. He was pipe-dreaming, though, if he thought he was in that league, and besides, Toby needed him in Private Clients.

He decided to head off this flight of fancy before it got any further off the ground and returned his attention to what Melvin was saying. His monologue had moved on and he was now going on about something he'd discovered only the other day on the Net about the secret activities of 'a Certain Person' who was trying to get his hands on Butchers Bank.

'Is it from private correspondence?' Toby demanded.

'Well, yes, sort of,' said Melvin.

'In that case, I don't want to know,' said Toby firmly. 'And I don't think you should either. If I find you doing anything of this kind in Butchers' time or on our equipment, then you might face disciplinary action and you'll never get into the Quant Department. And coming back to that subject . . .'

'Yes?'

'Look, Melvin,' said Toby with a sigh. 'Let me be frank with you. There's no reason why you shouldn't move there one day, but this is just not a good time. You must see that this department is in a bit of a fix at the moment, what with Falloni's suicide and us losing clients and so on. And we've really come to rely on your . . . your expertise. Your work is very highly valued here, believe me. And there are great opportunities in Private Clients; it's an area that's just about to come into its own in the world of investment management, so if you stick with us a bit longer, you won't regret it.'

Toby looked over, hoping this man-to-man approach would work. But it had fallen on deaf ears. Melvin continued to suck on his lower lip stubbornly.

'Very well.' Toby realised he was flogging a dead horse and gave in. 'If you really want me to, I'll see what I can do. I'll have a word with Personnel and ask if they're prepared to put you up for the Quant job. Now,' he said, forestalling any further argument, 'I'd better get back to my work. And if I were you' – he looked at his watch – 'I'd get off home to your wife.'

'Not married,' Melvin mumbled.

Toby mentally castigated himself. He was so tired that his mind was going. 'Well, your girlfriend then.'

Melvin shrugged. Evidently there wasn't one of those either.

Hearing the phone ring in his office, Toby gratefully took the opportunity to bring the interview to an end. 'We'll talk about it again later,' he said, dashing back to his cubicle. He caught the phone on its third ring. 'Butchers. Toby Slaker speaking,' he answered as ever.

'Hello!' said a soft Irish voice that was vaguely familiar. He tried to place it. 'Will Cloud here. How're you doing there, Toby?'

'Fine, thank you,' said Toby, playing for time. His client base of the ultra-rich expected to be recognised when they rang up and he racked his brains for a clue as to who this was. He didn't think the department had any clients from the Emerald Isle, but he couldn't be sure. 'Fine, thank you,' he repeated haltingly. 'And you?'

'Aye, I'm not too bad either. Tell you what, though. I've got some business down in the City this evening and I was wondering to myself if old Toby would be free for a chat.'

'Business in the City' sounded promising. And with all these clients leaving, it would be nice to have one come in the opposite direction. But Toby still couldn't for the life of him think who this was.

'Well . . .' he said hesitantly. He didn't want to say no without any further information. He gave his card to prospective clients on all sorts of occasions, especially long plane journeys. The possibility that you might pick up the odd wealthy investor on the sly was one of the justifications for travelling everywhere business class.

'And I've got a little proposition for you,' the man continued.

Very promising indeed. 'I see,' said Toby, checking the time. It was only seven and as Simona was away on a business trip till tomorrow – not that they were talking much anyway – he had been intending to work late. But this would be a welcome diversion, and he could always come back and finish off here later. 'It would be a pleasure,' he said. 'Have you eaten?'

'Er, no,' said Will Cloud.

'How about us grabbing a quick bite at Flato's,' Toby suggested.

'Flato's?' Cloud's voice rose in surprise.

'You know it?'

'No, I've never been there. But I've an idea the owner might be an old friend of mine.'

Better and better, thought Toby. Rosalind Flato, the

beautiful proprietress of Flato's Brasserie, was renowned for mixing with some of the world's wealthiest men and was currently mistress to no less a mortal than Ivor Zlennek himself.

'It's just on the corner of Bishopsgate and Tolpuddle Lane. I'll ring for a table, and let's say we meet at the bar there at seven thirty?'

'That would be grand,' said Will Cloud.

Still wondering who the hell Will Cloud could be, Toby replaced the receiver. But even if it didn't come to anything, he reflected, he could do with a break. At the very least, the supper would be a welcome interlude and give him a few hours away from the worries of Roy Falloni, Melvin Puckle and Butchers Bank.

Chapter Nineteen

That night, as Toby prepared to meet Will Cloud at Flato's Brasserie, Candida Blitz was having one of those heart-to-hearts with Zoë that she always resorted to when she was feeling low.

'He's ruined everything for me,' she told the chimpanzee tearfully. 'Now I'll never get another chance with Britannia Draycott and I'll be stuck doing the . . . the bloody *Hoodwink Show* for the rest of my life.' 'Bloody' was the strongest swearword Candida ever used, and even then she tried to avoid it in front of Zoë. But in this moment of particularly strong emotion it seemed fully justified.

The chimpanzee regarded her dolefully. Once Zoë had almost toppled a government, but like many a political activist before her she had now given all that up and settled into a more conformist if slightly irascible old age. She had not, however, lost her ability to make Candida think she understood every word she said. She scratched her armpit and made a gentle screeching noise.

Thus encouraged, Candida continued. 'It's just he never thinks of me. Of *my* needs. I mean, last night he turned up just when I didn't want him, and now that I do want him, where is he?' She picked up the note Will had left on the kitchen table. 'Out with the lads,' she read, imitating Will's Irish brogue. 'Out with the lads!' she bristled. 'That's where he always is. Out with his bloody mates. Well, why couldn't he have bloody well have been out with the lads when Britannia bloody Draycott was here? Tell me that!'

Zoë could not. Instead, she broke wind sympathetically and reached for a banana from the supply in the basket by the settee.

'Hilly wasn't like that,' Candida complained. 'He was too old to have mates. Anyway, nobody liked him. He used to stay in with me most evenings the way people are meant to do. I was happy with him.'

As Zoë got stuck into her snack, Candida departed on a rambling reminiscence of Hilton Starr, her late lover who had come to such a sticky end at an awards ceremony two years before. Her habit of romanticising his memory, while ignoring the fact that he'd been a womaniser and an alcoholic who occasionally used to beat her up, had been growing recently in parallel with her disaffection with Will Cloud. And as she thought fondly of her times together with Hilly, who had been twenty years her senior, it occurred to her for the first time how immature Will was. He was a good ten years younger than her. Before him she had always gone for older men, but when they had met in the aftermath of Hilly's death, Will had been so supportive in carrying her over that awful time that she hadn't really thought about the age difference. She had drifted towards him out of need, but now, she decided, his emotional immaturity was holding her back, particularly when compared with her own greater sophistication.

She was very fond of Will, she couldn't deny that. He was good-looking and charming and fun to be with. He was also faithful, she was sure, although she sometimes wondered about that, because he often stayed out till all hours without explanation, and after all he'd had quite a lot of girlfriends before he met her. Occasionally she challenged him about this, and he always replied that she was all he wanted in life now. And she had to admit that he was a wonderful lover, caring and sensitive and not selfish in that department at all.

But there had to be something more to a relationship than just that. There should be mutual friends and common interests and shared aspirations, none of which she had with Will. There should be walks hand in hand in the woods, and romantic evenings by the coal-effect gas fire and dinners out in expensive restaurants. Will rarely had enough money for those, and always refused to let her treat him.

No, what she needed, Candida decided, was someone more solid and reliable, someone with a proper career like her own who was not still living out some childish dream about being a private detective. Someone who was successful in his own right, so they wouldn't have these absurd arguments about money. Someone who was presentable and whom she could take with her to professional functions without being scared he would get drugged up to the eyeballs and try to take his trousers off over his head. Perhaps even someone of stature who could help her a bit with her own career.

Someone, in short, like Mattison Pick.

Pick had been occupying a tiny corner of her mind ever since their exchange of letters after that disastrous *Hoodwink Show*. She'd dropped him an apologetic little note, with a drawing of a smiley face at the bottom, and he'd replied very sweetly, which was kind because she'd been suffering terrible pangs of guilt about what had happened. He'd said he didn't blame her in the slightest, that he was sure his wife had duped everyone into it, just as she'd manufactured those fake photographs supposedly showing him with her sister, which was obviously completely absurd; he would never have looked at anyone as young as that, because in fact he'd always been more attracted to the more mature woman.

And he'd ended the letter by saying that, since it looked like he was stuck in London for a while now, perhaps she would like to go out for a meal with him some time, just to show there were no hard feelings.

Well, why not? thought Candida. Why not, indeed? Pick was a very attractive older man, not unlike Hilly in looks. He was talented and very influential in the entertainment business, which couldn't do any harm.

Candida hadn't yet replied to his dinner invitation. In fact, she hadn't a clue what she'd done with his letter. She had a feeling Zoë might have eaten it, but it didn't matter too much, because she remembered that he was staying at the Grand Britannic Hotel in Park Lane.

Acting on impulse, she got the number from directory enquiries and called the hotel switchboard. They put her through at once and, to her delight, he answered the phone in person.

'Hey, yeah!' he said enthusiastically once she'd identified herself. 'Sure I remember you. And it was real kind of you to send me that note. After all, it wasn't your fault that the bitch dumped on me.'

'Well,' said Candida, 'I did feel a responsibility.'

'Hey, you just forget that, young lady. Now, are we gonna get together some time, huh?'

'That would be nice,' said Candida, hoping she didn't sound too eager.

'Good, good. Say,' he went on thoughtfully, 'what you doing tonight? I mean, I don't want to be forward and all, but it sure is lonely here in this big hotel. Peaches used to ring me from the States every night. And now she's busy screwing up my shows and her attorney rings instead. So why don't you come over and have a nightcap, huh?'

'Oh, I couldn't do that!' said Candida, feeling rather shocked. She wanted to have a romance, certainly, but she didn't want to start right this moment. For a second, her natural prudishness, born of years of children's TV presenting, gave her pause. In the end, she compromised. 'Well, actually,' she said, 'I'm a bit whacked tonight. But maybe we could meet tomorrow?'

'Hey, sure we can,' said Pick heartily. 'That would be just great. How about you come over and catch me after rehearsals at the Royal London Theatre late afternoon, then we'll go out and grab some chow, and see where we go from there?'

Candida hesitated only momentarily. Will usually insisted they stay in on a Saturday night with a video and a Chinese take-away. But after what had happened, she decided, he could bloody well entertain himself for once.

'That would be lovely,' she trilled. 'Really, really lovely.'

Chapter Twenty

The premises that Flato's Brasserie occupied at the corner of Bishopsgate and Tolpuddle Lane had a history that curiously mirrored that of the City of London itself. Having started life in the eighteenth century as a coffee house where the founding fathers of merchant banking went to sign acceptance notes and exchange gossip, it had once been the setting for numerous historical agreements, including the sale of many an American state by its former colonial masters. Then, for nearly a century, it became a down-at-heel English chop house with sawdust-strewn floors, where beer and food poisoning were dispensed in equal measure to serried ranks of Pooters during their all too brief lunch breaks.

In this guise it survived, in a growing state of disrepair, until the mid-fifties, when it finally fell into disuse and was boarded up. But in the boom years of the 1980s it was taken over by a nouveau riche entrepreneur, and given a cosmetic facelift from which it emerged as Ciao Chow, a fashionable snack-bar providing elaborately packaged, but in essence remarkably basic, sandwiches at absurdly inflated prices to unruly traders in red braces. When they ended up on the scrap heap at the end of the decade, it was time to say 'ciao' to Ciao Chow as well.

Now, like much of the City that surrounded it, it had fallen to a foreign purchaser with deep pockets. Rosalind Flato, reportedly backed by her lover Ivor Zlennek, had moved in and taken over, turning it into a modern understated restaurant with sleek clean lines and uncomfortable aluminium tables and chairs, where the food was simple but exorbitant, cash payments were unheard of, and even personal credit cards were about as rare as sunflowers in Siberia.

Toby arrived at Flato's punctually at seven thirty, hoping that he would be able to recognise Will Cloud and work out exactly where he knew him from. As usual on a Friday night, the bar area in front was crammed with bankers, brokers and dealers, noisily celebrating their triumphs or drowning their sorrows, depending on the kind of week they'd had.

A slightly dishevelled young man in a crumpled jacket, with dark curly hair and startlingly light blue eyes, smiled over at Toby. 'Now there's a man who looks like he's in need of a drink,' he said. 'What'll it be?'

As soon as he saw his face, Toby remembered with some disappointment exactly where he'd met Will Cloud before. He reflected, just as he had the first time, that there was no way Candida Blitz's impoverished Irish boyfriend could be a potential client for Butchers Bank.

But he could hardly excuse himself now without appearing very rude, and besides, he'd quite enjoyed talking to the laid-back Irishman at the TV reception. So he allowed Will to usher him over to the bar. 'Have you met Michelle here?' Will asked with an easy charm as he ordered Toby a drink. 'A more accomplished barmaid you won't find in the whole of the City of London.'

Toby, who'd been coming to Flato's since it opened and had probably been served by Michelle a hundred times without ever noticing her, now regarded her with some interest. As he recalled from the newspaper articles, she had been one of Falloni's many conquests. She was just his type, he thought, buxom and friendly and not too bright.

They sat down on the high stools by the bar and waited for their table to be prepared. 'That was quite a night at the *Hoodwink Show*,' said Will conversationally. 'Sure, Candida's still getting over it, the poor thing, and that man Pick must be in a right oul' state.'

'He was certainly rather put out,' Toby agreed.

'And now his wife's controlling all those fine musicals of his,' said Will. 'I read in the papers that she's moved in fast to take over.'

Toby nodded non-commitally. 'So I believe.' He had no intention of revealing to this perfect stranger, however agreeable, that Pick was one of Butchers' clients and that he therefore had inside knowledge of Peaches' activities. 'Are you an aficionado of the musical theatre then, Mr Cloud . . . ah . . . Will?'

'Most definitely. I saw one of his, *Kennedy*, four times,' said Will. 'But it's really the classics, before his time, that I like best. *South Pacific, West Side Story, My Fair Lady*. Magic. There'll never be anything to beat those. What about yourself? Are you a fan too?'

Toby shook his head. 'I don't really get the time, to be honest. The office keeps me so busy. Talking of which, you mentioned that you had some business you wanted to discuss with me?'

'Oh, yes, indeed I do,' Will agreed. 'I was wondering—'

He broke off. A deferential-looking waiter had sidled up to him to say their table was ready. Toby observed that Will Cloud looked a little put out at the implication that he was the host. He resolved to set Will's mind at rest by hinting early on that Butchers would pick up the tab.

Will was not so put out, however, that he failed to ask Michelle, the barmaid, for her telephone number, which she eagerly surrendered before they repaired to their table. As they sat down, though, Will crumpled up the piece of paper into a ball and deposited it in the ashtray. 'Force of habit,' he said ruefully.

'Won't you ring her then?' asked Toby.

'No, I don't play the field any more,' replied Will. 'Candida's my girl. And all the better I am for it,' he added with patent affection.

'Did you use to, before you met her?' Toby asked as they were handed their menus. 'Play the field, I mean.' He flushed slightly, for this was hardly something he would normally ask a total stranger. But ever since his reflections earlier in the evening, the subject of marital infidelity had been very much on his mind.

Will did not seem the slightest bit fazed by the question. 'Aye, you could say that. I've sown my wild oats all right.'

Toby suppressed a slight feeling of envy. He himself had sown hardly a single wild oat before settling down with Simona.

'Funnily enough,' Cloud went on casually, 'years ago, I went out with the owner of this place.'

'Really?' Toby tried to hide his scepticism. 'Oh yes, when we spoke on the phone, you did say you knew her.' Now that he'd met Will again in the flesh, though, he couldn't help suspecting it was an idle boast. Rosalind Flato was one of the best-connected women in London. Never out of the gossip columns, it was rumoured that she even numbered the Prime Minister, Hugh Driftwood, among her list of former admirers. So she'd hardly have been interested in this impoverished Irishman, who was obviously a bit of a bragger. 'Shame she's not around tonight,' Toby said pleasantly. 'You could have introduced me.'

The words had hardly left his mouth when, out of the corner of his eye, he recognised the lady herself moving around in an internal office behind the cash desk. She was bending over a computer, wearing a sleek black dress that emphasised her voluptuous figure, and as ever, her cool, dark-haired sensuality took Toby's breath away. 'Isn't that her through there?' he enquired. 'Why don't we send through word that you're here? I'm sure she'd be delighted to see you again.'

'Oh, no need to bother her,' said Will hastily. 'I expect she's busy. Anyway, Candida can be a bit of a jealous type sometimes. When I moved in with her, I promised I'd never see Ros again.'

A likely story, thought Toby as they gave their order. It was all blarney, just as he'd suspected.

'It's funny,' Cloud continued expansively after the waiter had left. 'I knew Candida was the one for me from the first day I clapped eyes on her, and I've never looked at anyone else since. Well,' he conceded in response to Toby's raised eyebrow, 'I've looked, sure enough, but nothing more. I don't need to tell you what it's like when you find the right person. You're a married man yourself, if I remember rightly.'

'Yes,' said Toby flatly. Rarely had he heard such a total non sequitur. 'Yes, I am.'

'Well, then . . .'

Toby changed the subject. 'Coming back to that business you mentioned . . .'

'Oh, yes,' said Will. He lounged back in his chair, putting his hands behind his head and exposing his threadbare inside legs to the world. 'Well, it's like this. I've been reading about that bank of yours, Butchers. Having a few problems, eh?'

'Nothing we can't handle,' said Toby defensively. 'Since you've been following it, you'll also know that there were no dealing losses after all. It was just a sad case of an individual having some kind of delusive illness.'

'Yes,' said Will, stroking his ear thoughtfully. 'Strange that. Did you know the poor fella who topped himself?'

'He was a very close colleague,' Toby admitted with sadness.

'Ah, now, I'm sorry about that, so I am. But what I wanted to say to you was that you must be kind of short-staffed up there in the circumstances. And a friend in need is friend indeed. So . . .' He picked up a knife and smeared a generous portion of butter on his walnut bread, 'I'm available to help.'

Toby looked over to check he was being serious. 'How very kind of you,' he said with an irony that was clearly lost on Cloud. 'And what exactly do you do?' He had a vague recollection that the man had claimed to be some kind of detective.

'Well,' Will began, 'I'm sort of a jack of all trades. Turn my hand to anything you care to mention, I can.'

Was this some kind of joke? Toby wondered. But Will seemed totally in earnest. Eventually Toby said, 'I'm afraid you'll find the City has turned into a rather more professional kind of place in recent years. Exams, qualifications, regulatory approval, that sort of thing. Unless you want to start as a messenger, you're going to find it quite difficult to break in. Even the secretaries tend to have two degrees and a PhD nowadays.'

Will looked taken aback. 'I wasn't thinking of big money,' he said. 'I mean, not seven figures or anything. Six would do me fine. Maybe even less, because I have a hunch yours would be an interesting place to work.' He gazed over hopefully.

'I really don't think so,' said Toby with as much tact as he could. This man might be an expert at the business of chatting up women, he reflected, but he was pretty naïve when it came to the business of banking.

'Four figures?'

'No.'

'Three?'

Toby shook his head.

'Not even for a trial period?'

'You seem very keen,' said Toby. 'Is there some special reason you want a job? Last time we met I'm sure you said you were a detective. We've had quite enough investigations at Butchers,' he added, 'if that's what you've got in mind.'

'Oh, no,' said Will innocently. 'See, it's kind of to prove a point to a friend. I'm just looking for something short-term. Are you sure you won't reconsider?'

Toby was about to shake his head one final time when he again spotted Ivor Zlennek's famous mistress moving around behind the scenes. And now something Will had said earlier struck a chord in Toby and suddenly clicked in his brain with an ongoing source of irritation. An uncharacteristically malicious idea popped into his head.

Slowly he turned back to Will. 'You did say you were fond of musicals, didn't you?' he asked out of the blue.

Will looked puzzled. 'Indeed I am.'

'Ever seen *Guys and Dolls*?'

'One of the best.'

'Remember the bit,' Toby found himself demanding, 'where Sky Masterson has to take the Salvation Army doll to Havana for a bet?'

'Sure,' replied Will, still bemused.

'Well, I'll tell you what,' said Toby, lowering his voice confidentially. 'You see your friend Rosalind over there?'

Stretching round, Will looked behind him at the figure in the office. 'You want me to take her to Cuba?' he asked incredulously.

Toby smiled. 'No, I'll make it a bit easier than that.' He paused and thought carefully. 'On Saturday – a week tomorrow – my wife and I are having a party at our house, to celebrate her promotion. Come along to that; and if you bring Ivor Zlennek's girlfriend with you, then I'll give you my marker for one short-term job at Butchers Bank.'

And, having delivered himself of this curiously satisfying challenge, he picked up his knife and fork and tucked smugly into his starter.

It was late when Will finally headed home. He was not unhappy with his night's work. That job was his for the taking now, he was sure of it, and wouldn't that show Candida a thing or two!

It had been quite a coincidence ending up in Ros Flato's restaurant, having not seen her in years. He wondered if she still made a speciality of seducing famous people in public places as she used to. But from what he'd read about her in the gossip columns, he doubted it. It seemed she'd gone rather more upmarket since those days. And she might not take all that kindly to being reminded of her dark past, which was why he'd been reluctant to call her over in the restaurant. Still, if he phoned her up discreetly and asked her a favour for old time's sake, she would surely oblige.

The only worry now was how to keep it from Candida, who, as he'd told Toby, tended to get a bit jealous of his old flames. He would have to tread carefully. The last thing he wanted to do was upset her again, specially after what had happened with Britannia Draycott.

He found her in an odd mood when he got back to Hampstead. Quite prepared to grovel a bit about the Draycott episode, he discovered that wasn't going to be necessary.

'One of those things,' said Candida distantly after he'd apologised, and she carried on plucking her eyebrows, something he'd never noticed her doing before. 'It'll all be the same in a hundred years' time.'

Will debated whether to tell her that he'd landed a highly paid position in the City, but decided, with untypical caution, to wait until it was in the bag first. Still, he might give a hint, just to show her that he'd taken her warning seriously and to break the layer of ice that seemed to have formed between them.

'I'm sorting out that job,' he said casually.

'Oh, what job is that?' Her tone remained stubbornly uninterested.

'You said I should get myself some proper work, so I am. Only thing is . . .' Will hesitated; this was the tricky bit. 'The new boss wants me to go over to his house a week on Saturday night. You know what these high-powered City executive searches are like. They want to see you socially to make sure your face fits.' He regarded Candida apprehensively. Normally she insisted they spend Saturday nights in together with a rented video and a Chinese takeaway.

But apart from throwing him a sceptical glance at the mention of executive searches, she was barely listening. 'Fine,' she said, pulling viciously at another hair.

'Course,' he continued in a chatty tone, 'that's not till next week. Tomorrow night we can do our usual. Get the old video out and all that.'

'No,' snapped Candida. 'I'm afraid not. I'm tied up tomorrow night myself.'

'Tied up?' Will was surprised. 'Where will you be, then?'

Candida hardly even looked at him. 'Out with the lads,' she said airily. 'Just out with the lads.'

Chapter Twenty One

Returning to Butchers' House, Toby Slaker couldn't help feeling pleased at his little flash of malevolence. Either way, he would win out. If Cloud failed to turn up with Ros Flato, as seemed overwhelmingly probable, that would show that he wasn't quite such a Don Juan as he'd pretended and would wipe the smile off his face. But if he succeeded, then that really would be a coup, for it would wipe the smile off the faces of two other people: Simona, and Ivor Zlennek. Zlennek would hardly appreciate having his wife and mistress brought together at the same party, and with a bit of luck would blame Simona.

Smiling quietly to himself, Toby ascended the stairs to the Private Clients Department, and was slightly irritated to find that Puckle was still beavering away at his desk. Did he have no home to go to? Toby avoided his gaze as he slipped through to his own office. It was nearly eleven and the last thing he wanted to do was reopen the discussion on the man's blasted career aspirations.

Wearily, Toby picked up his work. Felicia had deposited a pile of correspondence on his desk as she left at five, and Toby had still to check through it. It was up to her usual standard. With a sigh, he reached for his dictating machine. 'This note to the Lady Forfar,' he said, 'about her son's request for her to fund his property venture. Could you correct it please? I was respectfully suggesting she decline his invitation to invest, not, as you put here, his invitation to incest.'

He really had to do something about Felicia, he reflected with despair. But he had so much else on his plate at the moment that he simply couldn't face it. Besides, it might be sexist of him, but he liked having someone attractive round the office. It brightened the place up. Felicia wasn't quite in the league of Rosalind from the restaurant, but she had beautiful legs, and looking at them was about as close as Toby was likely to come to having the kind of flings that Will Cloud had evidently enjoyed by the boatload before settling down with Candida.

Toby's mind turned back to Will. Despite his very satisfying challenge to him, something in their meeting had left him feeling discontented. It nagged away like an itch he couldn't quite reach. Deep down, he knew what it was about though. It was all very well talking about fidelity if you had a partner who was available to you more than once in a blue moon and if you had behind you a misspent youth in which you'd gone to bed with anything that moved. He had neither.

For the first time, real indignation began to build inside him about Simona's attitude. Why should he put up with it? Even after her appalling behaviour during the Falloni incident, he'd been prepared to let bygones be bygones. She was the one who had severed all physical relations. It simply wasn't fair.

At precisely that moment his eyes again alighted on the Hoodwink Encounters card. He'd forgotten to put it away. It was still lying on his desk where he'd left it and anyone could have seen it. He glanced guiltily across the office at Melvin, but he was staring at his screen, oblivious to the world. Toby knew from experience that he would not have budged an inch all evening.

He would lock the card away more carefully later. But meanwhile, why the hell shouldn't he have another look at the site? Everyone else did whatever they liked nowadays, why should he be left out?

Decisively, Toby switched on his own computer and called up its web browser. Then, before he could change his mind, he typed in the address on the card, just as he had that morning before the Falloni crisis.

As on the previous occasion, the Hoodwink Encounters page shimmered into focus, and the picture of the hooded woman's face stared out at him. 'Welcome to Hoodwink Encounters – the site of your most secret fantasies. Are you in the nude to put on the hood? Please choose a nickname then press enter.'

Hesitantly, Toby entered the same name he had used last time, 'Novice', then waited for the list of those present on line to pop up on the screen. But even before it could, another box appeared instead. He had a message from someone called Tamale (F) in London. His heart leaped.

'Hi,' said Tamale.

'Hello,' Toby typed, swallowing hard. 'Pleased to meet you.'

'You're Novice, right?'

'Yes.'

'Cool. So, how's it hanging, Novice? Looking for a Hood-wink date? I'm feeling real hot tonight.'

'I'm not sure,' said Toby nervously.

'I like the shy ones,' said the text box.

'What exactly does "a Hoodwink date" involve?" he asked.

'Well, why don't you just pop over and I'll show you, honey?'

Toby's fingers shook with excitement. He hadn't expected to strike gold quite so quickly. 'Where exactly are you?' he asked.

'London, Ontario, like the box says.'

'Oh.' Now he came back down to earth with a thud. The international nature of Internet chat had its downside. 'You mean in Canada?'

'Sure thing. Why, where are you at?'

'I'm in London, England.'

'Bummer,' said Tamale. 'Never mind. I'll look you up if I'm over there some time, but let's take a rain check for now, huh?'

And her box disappeared as abruptly as it had arrived. They did not stand on ceremony round here, Toby could see.

After that, he watched as the list of names continued to flicker constantly, ebbing and flowing with people arriving and leaving the site. And he soon found that, as a new boy, he was popular. Women from all around the world were propositioning him. But none of them was from London, England, and indeed there didn't seem to be anyone else from the UK on-line at all.

After he'd been on the Hoodwink site for nearly half an hour, Toby began to give up hope. The number of names in the box was falling off. There wasn't any sign of the woman his Australian friend Gus had told him about, and he was no closer to finding out what a 'Hoodwink Encounter' was.

He had to face it: this sort of thing wasn't for him, and he ought to be getting home in any case. With a mixture of relief and regret, he moved his cursor across the screen to the exit button.

It was just as he was about to click on it that a new text box popped up on his screen.

'Hi,' it said. 'You new here?'

Toby glanced across at his correspondent's location. London, England – at last! But it was when he read the name on the top that his stomach really began to lurch.

'The Minx,' was what it said.

From the office opposite, Melvin Puckle stared through the glass partition sullenly. Slaker seemed to be very busy on his computer tonight. It wasn't like him. Usually the man was buried deep in those client valuations, or tutting away correcting Felicia's stupid letters, and he rarely even turned his PC on. Melvin wondered absently what the hell he was up to.

But that wasn't what was causing his sullenness. No, rather it was the way his boss had tried to fob him off earlier about his longed-for promotion to the Quantitative Department that was making Melvin seethe with resentment. Why would that bastard not help him? He'd slogged his guts out to help Private Clients sort out their systems; what thanks did he get? None. Slaker was just trying to hold him back, keeping him on in this dead end because it suited him, when it was perfectly clear to anyone with half a brain that Quant was his real spiritual home.

The fact was that computers were Melvin's life. He had lived, slept and breathed them ever since he was a toddler. He was one of a new generation who could not remember a time before the Internet, to whom everything connected with the World Wide Web was second nature. Toby Slaker and his ilk might have just about learned how to surf the Net but Melvin Puckle had gone much further. He had learned to dominate it, to tame it to his will. And there was nothing he couldn't do with the help of a browser and a high-speed modem.

Toby might not have believed him, but Melvin had been speaking nothing but the truth when he'd claimed to have hacked into every computer system in the world that was worth hacking into. And now he was offering to devote that knowledge to help Butchers and they weren't even interested. Well, he thought, sod them. He'd discovered many interesting things on his travels round the web, and some of it might be of very great interest to Butchers Bank in its recent tribulations, if Toby had only been prepared to listen to him. But it was their loss. If they weren't prepared to promote him to Quant, he'd simply keep it to himself.

Melvin was brought out of a daydream in which he, from being overlord of the Quantitative Department, had taken over the running of the entire company and installed banks of computers to replace all the employees and especially Toby Slaker, when a sudden crashing noise reached him from across the office, followed by a yelp of pain.

Melvin looked over. What on earth was Slaker up to now? He'd dropped a large perspex paperweight on his foot, along with the pile of papers underneath it. And his face, a little florid at the best of times, had turned a deep purple colour. What's more, he was ignoring the mess on the floor and switching off his computer in a panic. Not like him at all. Usually Slaker was manically tidy, filing all his work away before leaving, and hesitating endlessly at the door to double-check that all the cabinets were locked. But today he was scuttling off like he was possessed. Hang on, looked like he was going to stop and talk again. Melvin returned his undivided attention to his screen.

'Ah, listen, Melv,' said Toby hesitantly. Melvin eyed him coolly. He hated people calling him that. 'I've got to go off to an . . . ah . . . important . . . ah . . . emergency meeting . . . ah . . . to do with one of my funds. Er . . . if by any chance anyone calls . . . ah, my wife for example, would you . . . ah . . . let her know that I won't be home till very late?'

Melvin hardly had a chance to nod his head before Slaker had rushed headlong out of the office, dragging his coat off the hook on the way and taking the spiral staircase three steps at a time. Emergency meeting, my arse, thought Melvin to himself. He was up to something. He wondered if it was anything interesting, but he doubted that. Not a boring old sod like Slaker.

For once, the charms of the creaky old lift were lost on Toby. He cursed its slowness as, his heart pounding like a pneumatic drill, he made his journey down to Butchers' car park.

Thank God he had the car with him today. It was pure coincidence that one of the senior directors was away that week and had offered Toby the use of his space. Otherwise, he would never have been able to agree to the Minx's suggestion.

He still couldn't believe he *had* agreed to it. When she'd finally explained exactly what a Hoodwink Encounter meant, he'd been terrified. But thrilled too — definitely thrilled. And aroused and scared and incredulous as well. He'd felt a rush of erotic excitement such as he hadn't experienced since that time Simona had had him on the Butchers' boardroom table.

None the less, half of him was already regretting his decision to go. It was rash, impulsive, mad; it would involve him cheating on Simona for the first time ever. It might even be dangerous. Who knew what was waiting for him at the other end? His imagination went into overdrive. Perhaps he would be robbed, kidnapped, held against his will by some fat spinster as her permanent sex slave. He looked at his reflection in the lift mirror. His own pleasant, but not overwhelmingly irresistible, features stared back. The sex slave theory, he had to admit, seemed pretty far-fetched.

In any case, he knew he was going to go through with it now, however dangerous. Some irresistible force deep within him was driving him on. He got in to his car and checked the address on his scrap of paper: 56 Northpark Mansions, Swiss Cottage. He had a good idea where that was but jerkily he consulted his *London A–Z* just to be sure. Then, without a backward glance, he edged the car out of Butchers' car park and drove north out of the City.

It took about half an hour to reach the outskirts of central London, and it was half an hour in which his imagination and his stomach turned somersaults. Normally a cautious driver, he even hooted at pedestrians and shot a red traffic light in his impatience.

At last he was there. He parked the car in a neighbouring street. He'd not entirely lost his banker's caution and car registrations could be traced. So far, all dealings had been totally anonymous and he wanted it to stay that way.

Shakily, he walked the last hundred yards and located the block. He made his way up the path to the entrance and pressed the bell. There was a video entryphone, but it did not light up. Instead, he heard a buzz and the door lock unlatched. She must have been watching from a window. He pushed and entered.

She'd told him to go straight to the fifth floor. As the lift jerked to a stop and he almost stumbled out, he saw a tunnel of identical green doors which trailed off in a neon-lit corridor to his left. Clean-cut, pristine, bold colours, like something out of a virtual reality game. Not quite identical though. Even from here he could see that one stood out. It was slightly ajar, just as she had said it would be. He forced his legs to move forward towards it.

A few moments later he was in the ordinary hallway of a neat flat, no different from a hundred others in the block. He took stock of his surroundings. There were four wooden panelled doors off the hall, all of them firmly shut. A few nondescript prints on the wall told him nothing about the inhabitant. On his left was a low armchair. But it was what was lying on top of it that sent renewed shivers through Toby's body. It was just what she said it would be. It was a red hood and a set of earplugs.

Take off every last item of clothing, she had said. Well, there was no going back now. Hesitantly, Toby followed her instructions to the letter until he stood there, stark naked, goose pimples of excitement rising all over his body. He inserted the earplugs but hesitated before picking up the hood. Thrusting it high up in the air, he held it suspended there for some seconds. Then, almost as if he were crowning himself, he finally pulled it down over his head.

Darkness and silence now filled his consciousness. He had crossed the Rubicon into the scary, rapturous unknown. 'Ready,' he called out, just as he'd been told to. His own voice echoed round his head, trapped in there by the earplugs.

He commended his soul to heaven and waited.

Chapter Twenty Two

It was Saturday afternoon and Ivor Zlennek's wife, Peggy, always called her sister on Saturday afternoons.

'Marguerite? It's me.'

'Peg! I was just wondering when you'd telephone!' Her sister's accent was much more rarefied – not to say pretentious – than Peggy's, even though it was Marguerite who still lived in Stepney while Peggy lived respectively in Holland Park, Berkshire, New York, Barbados and a host of other places around the globe.

'Listen,' Peggy said, 'are you doing anything later on?'

'Aren't you going out with Ivor?' asked her sister, surprised.

Peggy hesitated. 'He's . . . ah . . . been delayed at the office . . .'

'Oh, Peg, not again,' said Marguerite sadly. 'You really ought to—' She broke off. 'Where on earth are you phoning from?' she asked. 'There's a *frightful* din on the line. It sounds like an engine or something.'

'Sorry, love,' Peggy replied uncomfortably. 'I'm sort of en route.' She hated making a big deal of these things.

'You're on a plane, aren't you?' Marguerite's tone wasn't quite accusing but there was undoubtedly an edge to it. 'I can hear it distinctly.'

'Well, kind of,' Peggy admitted. 'I mean, yes, I suppose I am. You see ' – she swallowed her words as she always did when she wanted to avoid a subject – 'Ivor's pilot was going to Paris to drop off some politico on a freebie . . . and . . . I thought I'd just come along for the ride and do some shopping . . .' Her voice tailed off. That Marguerite still lived in the run-down street where they'd been brought up and travelled most places by bus was never far from her mind.

But it always seemed to bother her far more than her sister. 'For goodness sake, Peg,' said Marguerite in exasperation. 'All these years you've been married to the man, and you're still embarrassed by his money. Enjoy yourself! Flaunt it! I would if it was me – or, rather,' she corrected herself, 'if it were I.'

'Listen, Margie.' Peggy hastily changed the subject. 'Are you busy tonight or not? I've got some tickets for a show, and Ivor can't make it.'

'What, at the Royal London?'

'Hardly. We're still busy renovating it. *The Iron Lady* is opening there in a few weeks and I don't even know if it'll be ready in time. No, these are for the new thing at the Sewer.'

'Oh?' Marguerite perked up. 'The experimental place?'

'Yes. Can you come?'

'Let me check my diary.'

Peggy waited. She knew her sister was rarely busy on a Saturday night but she was still entitled to some dignity. After a suitable interval, when Marguerite had confirmed she was free, Peggy said, 'Come and have a bite first, love. I'll send a car over to collect you. Oh, and by the way,' she added, 'I picked up something in Paris that I think you'll really like. It'll be in the boot of the car and I want you to wear it tonight. You'll look like a million dollars.'

'As long as that's not what it cost,' said Marguerite guardedly.

'Course not.' Peggy's tone was light. 'Couldn't have been cheaper. You know how I can nose out a bargain. Fifty quid – and you can owe it me. See you at about six, okay?'

Peggy handed the phone back to the stewardess whose only passenger she was. 'Thanks, love,' she said absently. She still called everyone 'love', much to Ivor's irritation.

It would be good to see Marguerite tonight, she reflected. She didn't really mind that Ivor wasn't coming. Unlike Peggy and her sister, he'd never really been one for the theatre; he'd go along sometimes to make her happy, but business was always on his mind, and half the time he'd disappear off at the interval, leaving behind one of his security men to bring her home. So if he was working at the office, that was fine.

If that really was what he was doing . . .

It was their father who had given the two sisters their love of the theatre. When they were children, the outings to the West End from the tiny flat above his barber's shop in Stepney had always been the highlights of the year.

He'd brought them up on his own and money was always tight, but those theatre trips were the one item he refused to skimp on. They might have accounted for several days' work behind that shabby red leather chair, as he snipped and shaved and reluctantly dredged up small talk for his clients. But whatever the cost, they still had the very best circle seats. He'd settle for nothing less.

Peggy had always been a romantic and loved *West Side Story* best of all. Marguerite's favourite was *My Fair Lady*. They'd gone to see it countless times, and afterwards Marguerite would spend hours in front of the hall mirror practising her most refined accent and doing curtseys to imaginary royalty. Peggy would watch her in silence, twisting strands of curly dark blonde hair round her ear, and solemnly shaking her head. 'You'll never catch me changing the way I talk,' she'd always maintained. 'Not ever. If I got to be rich, folk would just have to take me as I am. Besides' – and now she'd become quite indignant – 'who wants lots of money anyway? People should only get as much as they need. If I had a fortune, I'd give it away to the poor.' And with that she would waltz off round the cramped flat, singing 'The Rain in Spain' in the most exaggerated cockney accent just to annoy her sister.

It was strange how their impoverished background had affected them each differently. While she'd never worried about what she didn't have, Marguerite treated money as if it were all there was in life. For as long as Peggy could remember, her sister had been determined to land herself a rich husband. She simply couldn't understand Peggy's determination to marry for something more.

Therefore it was an irony of life that Peggy had ended up with one of the country's richest men, while Marguerite, having searched high and low for a wealthy suitor, had lived through two divorces to blowhards who'd promised her the earth, and was now back scraping a living on her own in their old place in Stepney. The shop had long ago become an Indian restaurant but the flat above had belonged to their father outright. When he'd passed away, he'd left it jointly to the two of them but Peggy had signed it over to Marguerite without a thought. 'What do I need it for?' she'd asked impatiently. 'I've got Ivor.'

If she'd ever stopped to think about it, which she rarely did, Peggy would have realised that this was only true up to a point. Being married to a wealthy man wasn't quite the same as being wealthy herself, and most of Ivor's assets were held through one offshore company or another. If it had ever come to a divorce, she would have been hard put to extract very much by way of a settlement. Even the Royal London Theatre, which, as the whole world knew, Ivor had gift-wrapped from top to bottom in a huge pink ribbon and given Peggy as a fiftieth birthday present, was not in fact in her name but owned by a company registered somewhere in the Cayman Islands.

But Peggy didn't care about any of that. She'd always had complete faith in her husband and divorce was the last thing on her mind. Besides, not having the money in her name was probably just as well, she often reflected. Otherwise, she might have lived up to her childhood promise and given it all to the poor. This way, her philanthropic urges were at least restricted to a clutch of favourite charities, for which she tirelessly raised funds from the wealthy business people that being married to Ivor brought her into contact with. Occasionally she even managed to persuade Ivor himself to stump up a donation for some project that was close to her heart. But those instances were rare, since, like many a self-made man, her husband had an aversion to spending money on anyone other than his nearest and dearest. 'You think I work my ass off for some stranger?' he would ask ponderously. 'No,' he would answer himself, as was his habit. 'I do not. I sure do not.'

Unlike Marguerite's husbands, Ivor Zlennek had never been a blowhard. Quite the opposite, in fact. The thing that always set him apart from the other young men who used to pay visits to George Larchfield's barber's shop for their weekly trims had been his engaging modesty. He was a big man even then, but that was before he'd acquired the wealth and power that let him carry his weight with assurance. In those days, he had a clumsiness that endeared him to Peggy immediately. 'He'll do me,' she'd thought the first time she'd seen him, as he awkwardly tried to chat her up in his halting English while she swept up the hair from the floor of the shop. 'He'll do me very nicely indeed.'

At that time, of course, his modesty had been amply justified. He was an uneducated Polish immigrant who'd just got his first job as a messenger at a City bank and still had few prospects, as both Marguerite and her father had lost no time in pointing out when Peggy said they were getting engaged. But there had been something in his grey eyes, a solemn intelligence, that told Peggy he was going to go far. And, anyway, she didn't care if he didn't. She had fallen in love with him and nothing her family could do would stop her marrying him.

He had indeed gone far – further than she could ever have dreamed. The little business he'd set up trading shares based on some of the tips he'd picked up at work had grown from nothing into one of the country's largest financial conglomerates. And over the years, the cramped council flat they'd moved into after their wedding had been exchanged for ever grander residences. It had even reached the point where Peggy was putting her foot down and adamantly refusing to budge from their current mansion in Holland Park, even though Ivor was itching to swap it for an estate in the country.

Ivor had changed too, of course. That was inevitable. Now he was no longer modest. He was confident – and arrogant and egotistical and all the other things he was frequently called in the press. He was impatient with his staff, and downright rude to everyone else. And he was notoriously ruthless with anyone who crossed him in business.

But to Peggy, he had not changed at all. To her he was still the same unassuming fellow who had come into her father's barber shop, and he still had the same understated charm and the same gentle determination that he'd had at the very beginning. They'd been married for thirty years now and during that time she'd never had a single reason to revise her original verdict: he did her very nicely, very nicely indeed.

At least, he had up until recently.

When the chauffeur-driven car bearing Marguerite Larchfield – she had reverted to her maiden name after her divorces – pulled up outside the house in Holland Park, it was not yet six o'clock. As usual, Marguerite had to fight back the twinge of jealousy she invariably felt on seeing the mansion where her sister lived. It was not worthy of her, she knew, and certainly not justified by Peggy's attitude, which was never anything but generous.

She was wearing the dress Peggy had bought her in Paris. She was perfectly aware that it had cost very much more than fifty pounds. But she also knew her sister well enough to fall in with her little pretence. Anyway, Ivor could afford it, Marguerite comforted herself. Peggy hardly used up a quarter of the clothing allowance he gave her.

Peggy answered the door herself. Just as well Ivor's not here, thought Marguerite. He was always so security-conscious and hated her doing that. Her sister grinned with pleasure when she saw the dress. 'I told you it would suit you,' she said.

'Thanks, Peg, it's wonderful.' Marguerite kept her tone light. 'Now, don't let me forget to give you a cheque later. What's Ivor up to tonight, anyway?' she asked. She immediately regretted her choice of words.

'Oh, some deal or other,' Peggy answered, refusing to catch her eye. 'Besides, you know how he hates the theatre. I'd much sooner go with you. Come on through and have something to eat,' she said. 'I hope you don't mind, it's just a cold plate. I gave Sally the night off.' She led the way through to the huge dining room which had been elegantly laid out for supper.

During the meal, they chattered away as always about fashion and the theatre and everything else under the sun. They were never short of things to say. But to Marguerite, Peggy didn't seem quite herself. There was an edginess there she hadn't seen before. And she was pretty sure she knew what it was about.

She waited till near the end of their meal before tackling the subject. Something told her that Peggy was in the mood to unburden herself tonight. So, as they polished off the oranges in Grand Marnier that Sally, the Zlennek's resident chef, had prepared, she said, quite abruptly, 'Ivor's got someone new, hasn't he?'

This time, Peggy did not avoid the subject, just nodded wordlessly.

'How long?' Marguerite asked in the same tone. 'Come on, Peg, you'd better get it off your chest. You need to talk to someone about it . . .'

A look of anguish filled her sister's face. 'I don't know. About six months, I think.' She ran a hand through her hair. 'I don't mind,' she said beseechingly. 'God knows, I've never minded. Maybe I was wrong but I've always thought a man like that was bound to have affairs. And I decided ages ago that I wasn't going to let anything like that destroy our marriage. But . . . but this one seems to be different.' Her voice was trembling now. 'He's set her up with a restaurant. Paid for the whole thing. Place in the City, and it's meant to be really quite smart.'

'Flato's.'

'You know about it?' said Peggy, shocked.

Marguerite shrugged. 'Apparently it's common knowledge. But that's never bothered you before either, has it?'

Peggy shook her head. 'He bought a fashion store for the last one, and she still went the way of all the others in the end.' She took out a little lace handkerchief and wiped the corner of her eye. 'I still love him, you know. Despite it all. And I've always thought he felt the same.'

'But now you don't know.'

'No, I don't,' said Peggy helplessly. It all came out in a rush now. 'He's up to something. He's always been obsessed with his business but recently it's got much worse. He thinks of nothing else. First it was this feud with Hampton Bradley, and the court case. And now there's this Butchers Bank thing, too. He's furious that they didn't sell to him. He's had a chip on his shoulder about it ever since he once worked there as a messenger in the early days. And you know how he hates the establishment. I'm telling you, he wants that bank more than anything else he's ever wanted in his life, and he'll do anything to get his hands on it.'

'But what's that got to do with this Flato woman?' asked Marguerite.

'I don't know. It's just an instinct I've got. I think he confides in her. She's got this City restaurant; maybe he's using her to spy on people. You know the lengths he'll go to when he's determined. And recently he's been so secretive about things. I mean he always was, a little. But now it's much worse. Even when he's at home he spends half his time on his computer upstairs in the study.' She dabbed her eyes again.

Marguerite came round, sat beside her sister and put her arm around her just as she had when they were children. 'Are you sure you're not overreacting?' she said. 'I mean—'

She broke off. They'd both heard the sound of the front door being opened. Hastily, Peggy put away her handkerchief and, a moment later, the double doors to the dining room swung open.

Ivor's huge frame almost filled the doorway. Marguerite nodded to him and he acknowledged her briefly. Their relationship had never really recovered from her opposition to their marriage all those years before.

'Hello, darling,' said Peggy lightly. 'You're back early. I thought you were staying on at the office?'

'I changed my mind,' he grunted. He came over and stood behind his wife's chair and put his arms on her shoulder. She in turn placed her hands on his and gave them a gentle squeeze. It can't be *that* bad, thought Marguerite. 'But don't let me change your plans,' he continued. 'Is Marguerite going with you to the theatre?'

'I don't need to,' Marguerite said at once. 'I mean, if you want to go instead now.'

'No.' He shook his head. 'I have work to do in the study.' He looked Marguerite up and down. 'I like the new dress,' he added evenly.

'Yes, I . . .' said Marguerite, slightly flustered. He was nobody's fool, her brother-in-law.

Peggy cut in quickly. 'Did you want anything to eat?' she said. 'You see, I gave Sally the night off.'

He abruptly removed his hands from hers and looked down at her with irritation. 'You shouldn't keep doing that,' he said. 'She has two nights off during the week so she can be here at the weekends.'

'Well, she had someone to—'

He wasn't listening. 'You're far too soft with the staff,' he snapped.

'I could fix you something.' Peggy's voice was anxious. 'Marguerite can go on to the theatre and I'll join her later. Or we could cancel it and I could stay in with you?'

He shook his head angrily. 'I told you, I've gotta ring New York. This damned court case with Bradley is killing me. And the Butchers project is at . . . ah . . . a very delicate stage. Just forget it, and I'll send the driver out to a restaurant.' He turned on his heels and made for the door.

He was halfway there when he paused. 'I forgot to tell you. We've got an invitation to a party next Saturday. The new managing director of one of my companies. You want to come with me or—'

'I'll come,' Peggy cut in eagerly. 'I'd love to.'

When he'd left, Peggy looked at her sister and shrugged. 'See what I mean?'

'He didn't seem that different to me,' said Marguerite.

'I hope I'm wrong,' Peggy sighed. 'I just have a feeling . . .' She made a visible effort to pull herself together. 'Oh, well, never mind. Come on, we'd better get a move on or we'll be late. I'll get Jim to bring the car round.'

Chapter Twenty Three

Candida Blitz was approaching her Saturday evening appointment with Mattison Pick with some trepidation. It was one thing to want an affair, and quite another actually to initiate one. Besides, maybe she had assumed too much, misinterpreted his intentions? His estranged wife, Peaches La Trené, was one of the world's most beautiful women. What on earth would he want with *her*?

Oh well, she decided philosophically, she would at least get to peek behind the scenes at *The Iron Lady* and have a good dinner to boot. Anything was better than the video and Chinese takeaway Will insisted they have most Saturday nights.

The outside of the Royal London Theatre, just off the Strand, was covered in scaffolding and Candida dodged underneath to find the stage door. A curmudgeonly doorman made a few enquiries and then grudgingly told her she could go through. Inside a young man met her. 'I'm Bill, the assistant stage manager,' he said. 'I'm afraid Mr Pick will be tied up for another few minutes. He's just rehearsing Mrs Thatcher and the Cabinet in the "U-Turn Tango". You can wait for him in the back row.'

Candida sat down contentedly and gazed around. She always enjoyed going backstage at theatres. There was that wonderful musty smell about them that made television studios seem so sterile by comparison. She gazed over to the stage, where, on a half-completed set depicting a Tory Party conference, stood

Mona da Ponte, the leading lady better known for her part as a loveable cockney prostitute in a TV soap opera. Evidently playing Mrs Thatcher was more of a challenge than she'd expected, though, for she was standing looking defiant, surrounded by a motley crew of hangdog actors. In the front row of the stalls Mattison Pick and a younger man, whom Candida recognised as an up-and-coming new choreographer, were having words with her.

'Mona, you've got to try and get the step right, honey,' said Pick. 'You sing: "You turn . . . if you want to . . ." Then you spin around and march upstage. See, you illustrate the words with the action. It's like a kinda choreographical joke, isn't it, Joey?' The choreographer next to him nodded in exasperated agreement. Pick continued, slapping his thigh in time to the beat. ' "*You turn*" . . . three, four . . . "*if you want to.*" . Then you face the audience, point your finger at the them real sternly, and sing: "The *lady's* not for *turning*." You gotta really belt that last bit out. It'll knock 'em dead.'

'For Christ's sake, Matty!' said Mona. 'I'm bloody knackered. And these high heels are murdering my sodding feet. If you think I'm going to be able to tango in them eight shows a week, you're off your flipping head.'

Pick tried to ignore her. 'And another thing, hon,' he said. 'At the end of the number, when Geoffrey Howe comes on and sweeps you off your feet, I wanna see real passion in your eyes. You gotta look at him like he's your lovegod or somethin'. Remember, you're all sweet with the guy right now. It's not till the second act that you kick his ass out the door.'

Mona stamped her high heels defiantly. 'I can't do it. I just can't. I think it's because I'm not *at one* with the character. I mean Jackie Kennedy I could *empathise* with. But Margaret Thatcher . . .'

'Aw, come on, Mona, honey, just try one more time—'

'Don't Mona-honey me!' the star shrieked. 'If it's like this now, how'll it be once you add the frigging wig and handbag? A nightmare, that's what!' Her voice became wheedling. 'Matty, plee-ease! Can't you just change the step!'

'Mona, gimme a break,' said Pick. 'We've been working on this all week. If we change your step, then the whole dead sheep chorus number has to be rescored. Try it one more time.' Mona shook her head adamantly, summoned a tear to her eyes and flounced offstage. Pick stood up with an exhausted shrug. 'Okay, everyone, take five. We'll sort this out later.'

The assistant stage manager whispered something in his ear and he looked up wearily at Candida. 'Oh, yeah,' he said. 'Hey, toots.' He beckoned her over. 'I'm gonna be a bit delayed, but come on down and take a seat.'

He stretched out, put his arms behind his head, his feet up on the edge of the stage, and lit a cigar. 'Sorry, hon, you caught me on a bad day,' he said ruefully. 'You get to a point in every rehearsal when you just want to throw the whole thing in; and this is that moment.'

'It all looks pretty good to me,' said Candida with breathless excitement 'I loved *Kennedy*. I saw it in this very theatre.'

Pick gave the shrug of a man used to such compliments. 'Yeah, that was a good one. Mona made a great Jackie K, but doing the lead in Thatcher's giving her some problems. This U-Turn Tango number's a killer. But it'll be great if we get it right, so we just gotta stick at it.'

'Was it easier with *Kennedy*?'

'Naw, it was just the same. It's always like this. Hell, I don't know why I direct these things myself. The writing's duck soup by comparison. But I guess I'm a bit of a control freak. Hate to hand my work over to some other guy to screw it up.' A look of pain came into his eyes. 'That's why I'm so freaked out about Peaches.'

Candida adopted an expression of doleful sympathy.

'It's not just that she got the wrong end of the stick about me and her sister,' Pick went on blandly, 'and gave me all that trouble on your show.' He cast her a slightly reproachful look. 'But, on top of that, until we get the whole thing sorted out, those shyster lawyers of hers have taken control of all my musicals in the States. Even from here, I used to speak to my resident directors every day. Now they've been told not to take my calls.' His face became anguished. 'Six major productions, and five touring companies. They're like my babies. And they've been snatched away from me overnight.'

'How dreadful!' muttered Candida.

'You know what happened the other day?' Pick went on agitatedly. 'Some actor in the LA production of *Kennedy* got killed when a piece of scenery fell on him. Martin Bindgold, a real find that we were grooming for stardom. When I was in control, those sorts of things just didn't happen.' He buried his head in his hands.

Candida reached over and touched his shoulder. 'I'm so sorry,' she said. 'I wish there was something I could do to cheer you up.'

'Well, young lady.' Pick looked up and winked at her. 'I'll sure put my mind to that one later on.'

Soon to be the wrong side of forty, Candida attempted an enigmatic smile and reflected that she did not mind in the least if this attractive older man wanted to call her a young lady.

Just then, there was commotion on the stage and Mona da Ponte reappeared. 'Okay,' she said. 'I'll give it one more go. But don't think I'm going to do that sodding high kick at the end, because I'm not. Mrs T would never have shown her knickers like that.'

'Great, Mona. You're a trooper,' said Pick standing up. 'Sorry,' he told Candida. 'Have to get back to the grindstone. Look, get Bill over there to give you a coffee. I'll wrap things up here in half an hour and then we'll go over to the Meet Joint in Soho and grab some chow.'

That night, by one of those strange quirks of fate, Toby and Simona Slaker were also dining at the Meet Joint, the fashionable Docklands restaurant that had just opened a Soho branch. It was the first time they'd been out together since the Butchers crisis and the atmosphere between them was still ice-cold. But they'd arranged this dinner with friends some time back and neither wanted to cancel.

A waiter came to show them to their table and Simona drawled 'Are the Carter-Biles here yet? We were meant to meet them at eight.'

They were not, which gave Simona an opportunity to tour round the tables throwing dazzling smiles to the assorted rich and famous who were dining there. To Toby's satisfaction, the assorted rich and famous, who did not know her from Adam, completely blanked her.

'Listen, Toby,' she said when she finally sat down. 'They'll be here any minute. So you'd better snap out of it.'

'*I'd* better snap out of it?' said Toby indignantly.

'You've been so moody lately.'

'Of course I'm bloody moody,' said Toby. 'How do you expect me to feel after what's happened?'

'I thought everything was all hunky-dory again at Butchers,' said Simona nastily. 'Now that it's been sorted out.'

'Oh, it is *now*!' Toby backtracked. He had no intention of letting on that they were still having problems. 'No thanks to you.'

'Clients all sticking by you, are they?'

'Certainly,' he said.

She gave him a knowing look. 'Well then, darling' – she sat down and stabbed viciously at a piece of ciabatta bread with her fork – 'in that case, lighten up, will you?'

The argument was prevented from getting out of hand by the arrival of Victoria Carter-Bile. 'Ray's still parking the bloody Bentley,' she said collapsing exhausted into her chair. 'The limo company let us down, so we had to bring in our own car.' Not content with eschewing the tube, the Carter-Biles had taken their rejection of plebeian modes of transport one stage further and now refused to use taxis as well. 'He's looking for a car park. After the way it was scratched last time we brought it into the West End, it'll probably be ready for the junk heap by the time we get back.'

As Simona and Victoria departed on mutual commiserations about crime rates and the state of the infrastructure, Toby had a chance to sit back and brood. And he brooded, as he had for every waking moment since the previous night, about the Minx. It had now been almost twenty-four hours since his hooded adventure in the wilds of Swiss Cottage, and the intervening period had been dominated by an erotic high such as he'd never before known.

What that woman had done to him in the brief time he was in her flat had been totally unbelievable. He had never imagined that the human body had so many erogenous zones. She had twisted him, tugged him and bent him into every position known to man, and quite a few he was sure were previously unknown. She had given him sensations in places that he didn't think existed. She had brought him to heights of ecstasy beside which his all too infrequent fumblings with Simona hardly even registered on the Richter scale. And then had she proceeded to surpass even those.

And all without letting him ever catch even the slightest glimpse of her. The first thing she'd done when she'd come into the room was to check that the hood was tightly secured and that the earplugs were in place. And during the session that followed, he'd never even had an inkling of what she looked or sounded like. Yet despite that – maybe because of it – all his other senses had been infinitely heightened. Smell, touch, taste: she had marshalled every one of them with unerring skill in her quest to please him.

Inevitably, he had used the non-visual clues to try to build up a mental image of her. It was difficult to be precise about her height, as she had moved around so fast. Average, he reckoned, about five feet eight inches, but it could easily have been more or less than that. She had soft supple limbs and taut velvety skin. And those breasts! Pert and unyielding, with generous nipples that firmed to his touch.

She had a face, he imagined, of extraordinary sensuality. High cheekbones, and plucked arching eyebrows that gave her a constant sardonic smile. And in his mental photofit she had a wide generous mouth with full and beautiful lips that were painted deep crimson.

This last detail was one of the few that he knew for a fact, since he'd actually found traces of it on various unmentionable parts of his body afterwards. And that was not all he'd found. For some reason, he'd imagined her hair – long and silky and swept back behind her shoulders – to be blonde. But this had been contradicted by a short and wiry black one he'd found stuck between two molars when brushing his teeth later. He'd flushed it down the sink quickly, in case Simona noticed it. There wasn't much chance of that, though. She hadn't come back from her business trip till lunchtime that day and she had then gone off without a word for a meeting with the company who were catering next week's party. And now she was sitting beside him, oblivious to the fact that her husband had been cheating on her with a stranger he'd never even seen.

And there was the rub. Despite all that had happened between them, Toby's excitement at last night's experience was mixed with a growing sense of guilt. He had always placed a high value on fidelity and had never once been unfaithful to Simona before. Although they might have been going through a rocky patch recently, she was still his wife and they had two wonderful children and much else to be proud of.

Not only that, but there were the health implications, too, in what he had done. What if he had caught something that he now passed on to Simona? Although he'd been relieved to find that the Minx had taken precautions to ward off the most serious risks, there were other things, less easily avoided, that he could have contracted.

'I can recommend the crabs, sir,' said the waiter as he delivered their menus. 'Chef says they're particularly good today.'

'We'll wait till our other guest arrives before we order,' said Simona and went back to chatting animatedly to Victoria.

Sadly, Toby looked over at his wife. She was looking unusually radiant tonight, in a light blue dress that softened the sharpness of her features and brought out her femininity. All at once, he was hit by an unaccountable surge of affection for her.

Suddenly, acting on impulse, he reached across under the

table and touched Simona's hand. Her conversation did not falter but, to his surprise, she responded in kind. Her fingers grasped his and, for a brief instant, her eyes stopped darting around the room and she threw him a glance of real tenderness that he hadn't seen there in a long time.

In that moment, Toby vowed to himself that his fling with the Minx would not happen again. It had been fantastic and life-affirming but it must be a one-off, never, ever to be repeated. He had far too much to lose. He would dispose of the Hoodwink Encounters card once and for all, he swore, and begin patching things up with Simona. Having decided, a feeling of content-ment stole over him. It had been hard but he had made the right decision.

As a little reward to himself, he allowed his mind to return, just fleetingly, to some of the excesses of the night before. After all, there was no harm in just thinking about it. At one point, when she had done that trick with her tongue, he actually thought he might expire from sheer ecstasy. As his mind lingered on it, a wide smile came to his face.

'Hello, old chap.' Raymond Carter-Bile had arrived and taken his seat beside Toby. 'You're looking very chipper for someone who's just had a bank nearly collapse around him. What's got into you?'

'Got into me?' said Toby, coming panic-stricken out of his trance. 'Nothing, nothing at all. I mean, not recently.'

'No, it's just, you just looked . . . sort of . . . well, sort of elated –'

'Fellated?' babbled Toby. 'Not at all. Not for ages . . . that is, not ever . . . I mean . . .'

He was saved by Simona, who had fortunately returned to her usual habit of paying no attention to anything he said. She had been scanning the new arrivals and now pointed out two of the most prominent.

'Oh, look,' she said delightedly. 'That's Matty Pick over there. And isn't that Candida Blitz with him? I was invited along,' she added in a confidential undertone, 'as a special guest when she "hoodwinked" him on her show the other night.' Her little laugh trilled through the restaurant to indicate that this was the sort of occasion she attended frequently. 'So sad how it worked out, really. I expect,' she added, clearly sympathetic to others who did not get out so much, 'that you saw it at home.'

'Well, actually, no,' said Victoria Carter-Bile. 'In fact we were out that night at the opera; and you'll never guess who was sitting next—'

'Do excuse me for a second,' Simona interrupted, springing up. 'They'd think me awfully rude if I don't go over and say hello. Besides, there's something I want to ask them.'

'Do you have to?' Toby sighed. 'I mean, the man's trying to have a quiet night out, for God's sake.' He gave up. Simona had already gone.

She was back surprisingly quickly. 'I really think they appreciated that,' she said. 'But I didn't like to outstay my welcome.'

'What was it you wanted to ask them, anyway?' Toby enquired.

'Oh, nothing.' Simona gave a secretive little smile. 'Just a little personal matter. They seemed to be very intimate,' she added. 'I suspect there might be a little romance starting up there.'

On the other side of the restaurant, Candida Blitz thought so too. She was having a wonderful evening. Mattison Pick had been the perfect gentleman, amusing and witty, entertaining her with his anecdotes, although perhaps just a little bit unwilling to let her tell a few of her own.

But, despite Mattison's charm, and the undoubted attraction she felt for him, Candida was still not sure whether she wanted to take this any further. Like Toby Slaker, she'd always attached great importance to fidelity, and now she was beginning to have second thoughts about cheating on Will Cloud. They weren't married, but they'd been together for two years, and for all his faults and odd habits, most of that time she'd been very happy with him. Did she really want to risk losing all that for someone she hardly knew?

She wasn't sure, but one thing she was certain of was that she wasn't going to rush into this. Later, she resolved, when they left the restaurant and Pick asked her to come back to his hotel – and even Candida, in all her naiveté, had no doubt that he was going to do just that – she would tell him it was still too soon.

Once she had made her decision, Candida, like Toby, felt better. She returned her attention to her companion, and realised he was still answering a question she'd asked ten minutes ago about his early days in the theatre. He certainly couldn't be described as a demanding conversationalist. 'When we had that breakthrough with the show about Roosevelt,' he was saying, puffing on his Havana, 'Sam Kaskin and I were practically starving. We never thought we'd make it. Then suddenly, overnight, we were like the biggest thing on Broadway.' He let his leg brush against Candida's under the table. 'But I don't need to tell *you* about that. You're pretty big, aren't you!'

'I have put on a few pounds recently,' said Candida uncertainly, moving her leg away. 'But I'm trying my best to—'

'No, no, I mean you're quite famous here in England.'

'Oh, yes.' Candida beamed. 'Well it was all luck, really. You see—'

'Crap!' Pick broke in animatedly. 'If you'll forgive the French. You gotta have more confidence in yourself. It takes more than just luck to make it. Look at me and Kaskin.' He paused. 'Well,' he conceded, 'with Kaskin, it was rather more luck than talent, in that he met me when he was quite young and I kinda boosted his career. He went up on my coat-tails, if you know what I mean.'

'I never did understand,' said Candida, gazing into his grey crinkly eyes, 'which of you wrote the words and which the music?'

'Well, we were a bit like Lennon and McCartney,' said Pick modestly. 'We both took joint credit for all our stuff. But I did most of the work. Specially at the end when he started all that drinking. We nursed him through it, but it was hard.'

'He died not long ago, didn't he?' asked Candida.

'Yeah, two years now,' Pick replied. 'We were working on

Kennedy at the time. But he was drinking like a fish and hardly contributed at all. It got so bad he came to live with Peaches and me and we tried to wean him off the booze. It was too late.' He looked at her sadly and finally reached over and clasped her hand. '*Kennedy* was one of the biggest successes of all but he never got to see it.'

Candida opted to give his fingers a gentle squeeze but nothing too passionate. Then she looked at her watch. 'I ought to be getting home . . .'

'Sure,' said Pick with an alacrity that rather worried her. 'I'll just get the cheque.'

As he was paying, the woman who'd come over earlier and tried to invite them to some party or other reappeared. Her female companion hung back slightly while two men with them remained at the table paying their own bill. 'Remember,' said the woman, wagging her finger at them teasingly. 'Next Saturday night at eight. I did give you the address, didn't I?'

'Like I said before' – Mattison Pick was clearly used to dealing with such nuisances – 'it's a kinda busy time for me, what with *Iron Lady* rehearsals and all, but I'll – hey!' He had recognised one of the men. 'Isn't that guy Slaker? Butchers Bank, right?'

The woman gave a strangely tortured smile. 'My husband,' she said icily. 'And, as I mentioned before, I also work in the City. In fact, I manage the London office of WHAM which has over ten billion under—'

'Hey,' broke in Pick, 'you tell that husband of yours the advice he gave me was right on the money. My New York people said he must be a real sharp cookie.'

'Oh, really?' The woman's teeth were making a strange grinding noise.

'Yeah,' said Pick. 'A real sharp cookie. Say,' he went on with a new animation in his voice, 'when did you say that party of yours was again?'

'A week tonight.'

'Well, now,' said Pick. He looked across at Candida. 'Maybe we'll see what we can do about that, huh?' He waved over towards the two men, but having paid the bill they had ambled out into the street to wait for their wives. 'And you tell that Toby of yours that Matty Pick said hello and thanks and I – we – sure will do our damnedest to drop in next week.'

'Of *course* I'll tell him,' mouthed Simona Slaker, 'I'm sure he'll be *so* pleased.'

As the Parker-Biles' Bentley, which had acquired a number of highly amusing, if slightly pornographic, etchings on its paint-work, sped smoothly round Hyde Park Corner on its way to drop the Slakers home, Simona was as good as her word – or almost.

'Such a charming man,' she said. 'And very interested in WHAM. And I think he vaguely remembered you, too, Toby,' she added.

'Oh, really?' said Toby. 'That was nice.'

'Well, after I reminded him,' Simona corrected herself, 'he said to say hello. But he sort of hinted he'd like to diversify his portfolio, now that he's based in Britain. You could see he felt that Butchers wasn't quite up to it, although obviously he didn't like to say it in so many words.'

'Oh?' Toby sounded rather disappointed. 'I rather thought we'd done quite a good job for him. Just goes to show.'

Simona shrugged. 'Clients can be so two-faced,' she said sympathetically.

Chapter Twenty Four

'Hello?'

'Yes?'

'It's me again. Can you talk?'

'Wait, let me shut the door. What is it?'

'I thought you'd want to know: plan B is well under way now.'

'He took the bait?'

'Like a fish on a line. He was even keener than the first one, in the end.'

'Excellent. Have you heard from him again since?'

'Not yet. But, like you said, this one's the cautious type. I'll to have to play him along a bit – get his confidence before I reel him in.'

'How long before the house call?'

'A week or so.'

'And the office?'

'I'll have to check my calendar. But a few days later, I reckon.'

'Good. This will be the last time, I swear.'

'You said that with the first one.'

'I told you, things didn't work out quite as planned. But one more push and we're there. Anyhow, I think you're beginning to enjoy this, aren't you?'

'Maybe just a bit.'

'Well, don't get into the habit. When it's all over, I don't intend to share you with anyone ever again.'

'I have to go.'

'You'll keep me up to date?'

'Of course.'

Chapter Twenty Five

In the higher echelons of Butchers Bank things were not going smoothly and Greg Kurdell, Butchers' combative managing director, was worried.

As Toby Slaker had already seen, media interest in Butchers had not abated but intensified since Falloni's death. And not just in the tabloids. The financial press were taking an interest too. Butchers might no longer be threatened with extinction at the hands of a rogue trader, but there was widespread speculation that the crisis had seriously destabilised the Puritas Council, which as everyone now knew ultimately owned Butchers Bank. Rumours were rife that Ivor Zlennek, the Polish predator who had been unsuccessful in his takeover attempt, was still wooing members of the Council to try to persuade them to support a renewed bid. There was a real risk that, despite everything they'd been through, he would come in and scoop up the bank after all.

The focus now was on the Puritas Council's Annual General Meeting, which was due to take place in Butchers House in just ten days' time. The AGM had excited practically no interest in previous years despite the valiant efforts of Butchers' small PR Department, but now it was the subject of daily leader articles.

As Toby Slaker had also discovered, the adverse publicity was already causing clients to leave all over the bank. Even worse than that, though, it was creating uncertainty among staff, and if there was one thing that a merchant bank could not afford at any price it was mass staff defections. With few real assets other than its 'human resources', as the jargon had it, any City institution had to do everything possible to 'stroke' its staff and provide a cosy backdrop against which they could continue to generate tens of millions for their employers and tens of thousands for themselves. The prospect of their company being floated into the wild blue yonder by its uncaring owners could undermine this whole fragile construct.

Such a situation provided fertile territory for a breed common in most professions, but particularly pernicious in the City: headhunters. Like jackals, the people from these glorified job centres scavenged on institutions in any kind of trouble. Circling warily around, they would identify their prey, await their opportunity and then swoop in without mercy to carry it off.

At Butchers they had struck in their droves. Will Cloud had not been wrong in speculating that staff would be keen to leave the bank, and anyone likely to be of the slightest interest to a competitor was called up and given the treatment, which involved listing a string of reasons why Butchers would not survive in its current form, and if by any chance it did, why it would never be able to pay its staff any bonuses at the end of the year. Such-and-such a bank, on the other hand, was crying out for highly qualified staff just like the person in question and would pay vast sums in golden hellos, platinum handcuffs, mink straitjackets or whatever other bribe was required to secure their services.

Many of Butchers' staff fell for this line, and allowed their names to be added to the headhunters' lists. But it was usually no more than a punt. The aim was to get as many Butchers people as possible on to their books, so that the agency in question could then approach prospective employers with a potential mass defection.

Even Greg Kurdell himself had been rung up by a few. He had made short shrift of them, screaming abuse and slamming the phone down on them with a violence unusual even for him. But with staff levels haemorrhaging uncontrollably, Kurdell decided that it was time to tackle the issue head on with Sir

Lomond Butcher. On Monday he raised it at their early morning meeting, which took place at its usual time of eleven o'clock in Butcher's palatial office.

'We've got to take action to shore up confidence before the Puritas meeting,' he said. 'We're being undermined at every turn.'

Lomond Butcher gave him a relaxed smile and took a practice swing with an imaginary golf club. Ever since his victory over the press a few weeks before, he had acquired a new self-confidence and was even beginning to stand up to Kurdell. 'My dear chap,' he said. 'You have to learn not to fret so.'

Greg Kurdell looked at him incredulously. 'Haven't you read that Ivor Zlennek's been having secret discussions with Lord Sloach?'

'I simply don't believe that,' said Lomond Butcher. 'And don't forget, I was the one who said all along that there wouldn't be any futures losses, and I was right about that. Besides,' he went on, 'I'll keep saying it till I'm blue in the face: I will not allow the company to be sold to that man.'

Kurdell was not convinced. 'If the Council unanimously favour a sale, eventually you'll find it all but impossible to resist. It's all about propaganda and PR. And Zlennek is an expert at media manipulation,' he said. 'You just need to look at the papers to see we're losing *that* war hands down.'

This gave Butcher pause. 'You think so?' he said.

'Yes, I do.'

'Well, then! What are you doing about it?' asked Butcher belligerently, with his usual disconcerting habit of turning things round when put on the spot.

Kurdell raised his eyes heavenwards. 'We've got to mount a press campaign to influence the Council's attitude before the meeting.' he said. 'For one thing, I could ring up Gerda Luttmeyer of the *Sunday Populist* and let her have an interview about how Butchers is fighting back from the brink. Everyone reads her column and that should have a real impact.'

He looked at Butcher. The chairman was notoriously leery

of allowing direct contact with the press, and the previous weeks' experiences hadn't helped. But he was in for a pleasant surprise, at least initially. 'That's an excellent idea!' said Butcher, stroking his chin thoughtfully. 'Get her in on Friday and I'll have a nice little chat with her. Best foot forward and all that. Show the world that everything's back to normal. If she runs it this weekend, that will be just in time for the Council meeting next Wednesday.'

This had not been what Kurdell had in mind at all. 'Oh, I wouldn't want to bother you with something like that,' he said hurriedly. 'I'm sure you're much too busy. I was thinking I might talk to her myself.'

'Nonsense!' exclaimed Butcher. 'We've agreed this is of the utmost importance, and I am the chairman of this company after all. At least,' he added curtly, 'so I believe.'

'Yes, of course, but she can be quite a tricky customer, Gerda Luttmeyer, and—'

'You leave her to me,' said Lomond Butcher, tapping his nose knowingly. 'I think you'll find I can handle some little tabloid scribbler.'

Kurdell doubted it very much. 'But . . .' he persisted.

'Not another word,' said Butcher. 'Just do as I say and fix it up, there's a good fellow.'

And with that, he shuffled the copies of the *Shooting Times* on his desk to indicate that today's early morning meeting was at an end.

Upstairs in the Private Clients Department, Toby Slaker's first meeting had taken place long before eleven a.m. He'd been in since six struggling against the tide of staff resignations and client defections that had become his daily lot.

But as he stopped by the machine for his elevenses, it was not those problems that were occupying him. No, despite his most earnest resolution to the contrary, the Minx was still on his mind and he was finding the vow he had made at the restaurant impossible to keep to. At that time, he realised, his libido was still sated from the night before. But now that it had had time to recover, it was having second thoughts, and had launched a ferocious rearguard action against his conscience.

Dare he go back and talk to her again? Would she be there? Oh, God, he thought. Even correcting Felicia's letters failed to distract him today. It was almost with an offhand disregard that he asked her to change his polite letter to Lord Wallchester thanking him for his continued loyalty to Butchers. 'It's meant to say "you're a real *brick*,"' he told her. 'You really have to mind those bs and ps.' But his heart wasn't in it.

Finally, in the evening, he could bear it no longer. To hell with his resolutions. To hell with Simona. To hell, even, with Butchers Bank. There had to be something more to his existence than this. If his time with the Minx had been anything, it had been life-affirming and he longed desperately for just one more session with her. Besides, it couldn't do any harm just to go in and have a chat, he told himself. He needn't actually do anything.

He checked around the office. As usual, everyone except Melvin Puckle had gone home. And as usual Puckle seemed engrossed in his own work, his head held raptly inches away from his screen, his fingers hammering away at the keyboard like a virtuoso pianist practising a particularly difficult piece.

Toby looked at his watch. It was earlier than last time, but worth a go. Would she be there? Heart pounding, Toby turned on his computer and once again paged hoodwink.encounters.com.

He was in luck. A thrill of anticipation ran through his body as he spotted her name on the list of those present. He took a deep breath and clicked on it.

'Hi,' he typed.

'Hi,' she replied almost immediately.

'Hi,' chipped in a weedy voice about two feet from his head.

Toby felt his cranium expanding out of its skin as, looking across his desk, he discovered the weasely features of Melvin Puckle staring at him earnestly across his desk. 'Have you got a second?' he was asking.

'What?' Toby barked. Guiltily, his hand came up to shield his computer screen from Puckle's prying eyes. But he stifled his irritation. It was a bit unfair, he realised, to resent an intrusion that was probably business-related when he was engaged on nothing of the kind. 'Sorry,' he said a little less aggressively, 'I'm just working on some . . . ah . . . confidential salary numbers. Give me a second and I'll be with you.'

Puckle retreated a few yards and, still cursing, Toby typed, 'Got to go – maybe catch you later?' to the Minx. Without waiting for a response, he double clicked on the corner of the screen to shut down the connection. Only when he was back at the corporate logo of the Butchers homepage did he summon Puckle back.

'Now what can I do for you, Melvin?' he asked wearily.

''S'about my move to Quant,' said Puckle, looking down at his fingernails. 'Did you manage to talk to Personnel like you said?'

Toby hesitated. As a matter of fact, he had gone one better than that. Despite all the other things on his plate, he'd made good on his reluctant promise and had buttonholed Peter Perksy, the scatty, dishevelled head of the Quant Department who always reminded him of his old science master. He had pleaded Puckle's case, and waited for the usual verbal monsoon of ifs and buts and all-things-being-equalses he'd come to expect from Persky. But in fact, the response had been uncharacteristically crisp. On the subject of economic trends, Persky's views might be equivocal. On the question of future market movements, his opinions might be hedged around with so many caveats as to be totally meaningless. But on his desire for the company of Melvin Puckle, he was utterly unambiguous. Puckle was unsafe at any speed and was not wanted in Quant.

But how to put that to the aspiring rocket scientist without causing offence? Kinder to be as non-specific as possible, Toby concluded. Let him think that it was Personnel that had blocked the move rather than Persky. 'I've made enquiries, Melvin,' he said. 'But I'm afraid it's a non-starter for now.'

Puckle's disappointment was palpable. 'Where?' asked Puckle, almost belligerently. 'Where have you made enquiries?'

'I raised it yesterday in the appropriate quarters,' said Toby with a certain sharpness. He held up his hand to pre-empt any further questioning. 'I know it's important to you and I *will* try again.'

Melvin looked sulky. 'When?'

'Later in the year when we do your assessment. Meantime, you should be patient and, as I've said to you before, you mustn't underestimate your importance to *this* department. You have a very crucial role to play.' He smiled as encouragingly as he could. 'All right?'

Puckle stood twisting his fingers together. 'Suppose so,' he eventually muttered.

'Good. Now if that's all . . .' Toby tried not sound impatient.

As Puckle wandered disconsolately away, Toby watched his disappearing back for a second. There was a risk he would get another job elsewhere, but it was one he was prepared to run. Although Puckle was certainly good at what he did, computer geeks were not unplentiful in the City and they could train up a new one in no time. Besides, there was something creepy about Melvin Puckle that made Toby feel uncomfortable. Being shot of him might be no bad thing.

Now, back to the Minx. Toby put his departmental responsibilities out of his mind and, his fingers trembling, switched the computer back to the Hoodwink site. To his relief, she was still there. He resumed where he'd left off. 'Hi again,' he said. 'Novice here. I'm back.' He'd better get to the nub of it right away, he decided, before there were any further interruptions. 'Listen, I had a great time the other day.'

'Me too,' said the Minx.

'Good,' said Toby in an almost businesslike fashion. 'It sounds as if it's an arrangement that suits us both. So when do you want to have another go?'

But the reply, when it came, was not what he expected at all. 'Sorry,' she said abruptly. 'No replays.'

'What?' Toby felt a stab of disappointment. Then he remembered the warning of Gus the Australian the first time he had gone on the Hoodwink Encounters site. The Minx never had anyone twice.

Her next answer confirmed this. 'I said nothing doing. I was just about to tell you before you left earlier.'

'But . . .' Toby felt like a child refused a second ice cream and was equally petulant. 'Why not?'

'Personal house rule.'

'Aw, please?' He was almost stamping his feet.

'We can always talk on-line,' she said. 'But definitely no return visits.'

'Surely you can make an exception. I mean . . .'

He broke off. Her text box had disappeared.

Toby sat for a second in stunned disbelief. He couldn't believe he'd been turned down by a woman he'd never even seen. He hadn't felt so rejected since his adolescence. As he stared at the screen, the name Gus caught his eye. Wasn't that the Australian? He clicked on him, glad of anyone to confide in.

'G'day, mate. How's it going?' asked Gus. 'Did you score?'

'I went to see the Minx like you told me,' said Toby. 'Had a brilliant time. But now she won't see me again.'

'Told you she wouldn't,' said Gus smugly. 'She's dynamite, isn't she?'

'Yes, but I need to see her again,' Toby insisted.

'Forget it, mate,' Gus advised. 'You're flogging a dead horse. Listen, you're lucky to have got her in the first place. She's very picky. Give up and try one of the other sheilas.'

'It won't be the same.'

'Course it won't. You started with the best. It's downhill from there. Still, anything's better than nothing, wouldn't you say?'

Toby reflected. He had a point. If he couldn't go back to the Minx, at least he could play the field a bit. Why hadn't that occurred to him? He put it down to the old fidelity instinct which could not have been more absurd in this situation.

'You're right,' he said. 'Thanks.'

'Any time, mate. Have fun.'

After Gus's text box had also disappeared from his screen, Toby got himself a coffee and began browsing through the list of names with renewed curiosity.

Renewed curiosity was also in plentiful supply elsewhere in the Private Clients Department, although in the case of Melvin Puckle it was mixed with another dose of seething resentment.

The former was caused by the fact that Slaker was engrossed in his computer yet again, having hardly ever even looked at the thing in the past. The latter was because Slaker was lying to him about Quant.

All that stuff about having talked to Personnel was crap. Melvin knew it for a fact, because he had come up in the lift with Sue Primrose, the Personnel head, that very afternoon. He'd asked her about the move and she hadn't the foggiest notion what he was talking about. So much for Slaker 'doing his best' for him. No, he hadn't lifted a finger. And this time he'd been caught out.

But what could Melvin do about it? Not much, he realised angrily. He wished that all the dark threats about going to headhunters had been true. But they weren't. Nobody had approached him. Besides, he was comfortable at Butchers and the thought of moving to another company and having to get to know a whole new set of people struck fear into his shy and introverted soul. So what could he do?

Faced with such a dilemma, most people would turn to a loved one for consolation and advice. A wife, a girlfriend, a trusted companion. Sadly, Melvin had none of those. Apart from his elderly parents in a bungalow in Eastbourne, distant in every sense of the word, and a few computer geeks scattered round the world with whom he occasionally swapped programs, he had nobody.

Well, not quite nobody. He could always talk to Scarlett, he reflected. Scarlett was solid and dependable and he could confide in her without any fear of being met with the contempt, pity, or detached amusement that characterised most of his relations with the rest of the world.

Yes, he would see what Scarlett had to say about it. He settled back at his desk and clicked his mouse on the tiny picture of an hourglass female frame in the corner of his screen.

There was a whirring noise as the hard disk searched for a programme. Then gradually a face began to materialise in front of him. It was the face of a woman – or as close an approximation to a woman's face as a computer graphic could produce.

'Hey, boy!' she said suggestively, her mouth moving in sync with the words as they tumbled out of her mouth to form a bubble over her head. 'How you doin' there?'

'AOK, Scarlett,' typed Melvin. 'And all the better for seeing you.'

She gave him a big wink from one of her great green eyes. 'Shucks, honey,' she said. 'I bet you sez that to all the girls.'

That Toby Slaker was not the only person at Butchers who conducted his affairs of the heart via personal computer was entirely coincidental. Melvin Puckle had been doing it for years. There was a crucial difference, though. While Toby was at least using the computer to relate to other human beings, Melvin had cut out the human element altogether. He'd simply used his computer programming genius to invent his very own virtual woman.

Melvin had never been comfortable with other people, and particularly those of the opposite sex, and a lonely computer-obsessed childhood had given him little preparation for the courting rituals of real life. In his late teens he had tried going to discos, but his unprepossessing appearance and total lack of social skills had left him standing forlornly in a corner, desperate to leave. This had set a pattern he'd never escaped.

And so, later, when he had become a master of the Internet, Melvin had been drawn to the possibilities of dating on it just like Toby Slaker more recently. But with markedly less success. Melvin discovered that even in this most impersonal of mediums, his unattractiveness somehow osmosed across the ether and his attempts to meet a woman – any woman – were invariably unsuccessful. In response to his standard chat-up line – 'Hello, my name's Melvin. I'm sincere and genuine and looking for romance' – he always seemed to get the same capitalised response: 'GET LOST, JERK.'

It was against this tragic backdrop that he'd first came up with Scarlett. Aphrodite to his Pygmalion, she was nothing more than a million lines of computer code that he had first begun writing one lonely Saturday night at the age of nineteen. She'd started life as MEG – Melvin's Electronic Girlfriend – a simple on-screen line drawing into which he had built a small range of automated responses to standard items of conversation to while away the solitary hours.

But as Melvin grew up, his virtuosity as a computer programmer improved and processing power became infinitely greater. At every possible opportunity he upgraded MEG's software and increased her authenticity, improving her on-screen image with more fluid graphics and growing her knowledge database and responsiveness. He'd originally created MEG on a small home PC with limited capacity. But once he joined Butchers he was able to transfer her secretly to the more sophisticated computer on his desk there and link her to the Internet. With state-of-the-art technology, MEG advanced in leaps and bounds.

This process had reached its apotheosis one afternoon when at the age of twenty-two Melvin had for once eschewed his computer to watch an old video of *Gone with the Wind*. He'd fallen in love with Vivien Leigh's Scarlett O'Hara and the very next day MEG was reborn as Scarlett, complete with flashing green eyes, bristly black eyelashes, a wayward come-hither smile, and even a magnificent white colonnaded virtual Tara with a sweeping staircase down which she would descend to meet her very own Rhett Butler.

Scarlett was also endowed – at least in Melvin's imagination – with a Deep Southern drawl, and all the teasing Southern colloquialisms that went with it. Melvin's real experience of the

Deep South of America being limited to the occasional visit to Colonel Bogey's Fried Chicken, this was necessarily based on other Hollywood movies, and was therefore a confused hotch-potch of slang from all over America. But that hardly mattered since Melvin himself was her only audience.

It was once MEG became Scarlett that her real development began. Melvin had lost count of all the changes he'd made to her programs. Having begun as an automated girl whose reactions he could invariably predict, she quickly grew into a fully fledged woman with very distinct views of her own, and at least some of the perversity of her namesake, Scarlett O'Hara. But in one respect she always remained constant – and that was her steadfast faithfulness to Melvin, her creator. And the reason was simple: he'd taken the precaution of hardcoding her devotion into the basic programs that were her very own DNA, with the wistful thought that if only a similar technique were available for humans, the world would be a much happier place.

Melvin, in turn, was also devoted to Scarlett. MEG had been a boyish fantasy, a slip of a girl with which to while away spare moments, but Scarlett was a real woman, fully mature in every way, lithe and sexy, intelligent, sassy and beautiful.

Like every relationship, Melvin's love affair with Scarlett had its disadvantages. For one thing, it was inevitably quite chaste, and every so often Melvin would long for something a little more satisfying in the way of physical gratification. But the years of rejections on this score had convinced him that real living women were simply not available to him. Besides, other than the lack of direct contact, what more could one possibly want of a companion? Melvin considered himself a realist and saw that life was a trade-off. In exchange for eternal fidelity, he had to accept the minor drawback that his long-term companion was a stream of digital electronic impulses. But, after all, as he recalled someone saying in another old movie, nobody's perfect.

Scarlett had two different screen incarnations. She could appear as a complete figure, six inches high, which gambolled tantalisingly around his monitor; or her picture could be expanded so that her finely etched features filled the whole screen.

It was this face-to-face contact that Melvin preferred and it was this form that he selected today as he confided in her about Toby Slaker's treachery.

'He won't help me, Scarlett,' he typed dolefully.

'Who won't, honey child?'

'Slaker won't. He won't help me become a rocket scientist.'

'Well now, why don't you jes' tell me all about it,' said Scarlett. It was a phrase she often used when her programme was stalling for time, still trying to assess exactly what Melvin required of her.

'I asked him straight out about the move, and he pretended to help, but he didn't lift a finger.'

By this time Scarlett's memory banks had located previous conversations on the same topic and she was able to reply more specifically. Her face scrunched up in an expression of heart-felt sympathy. 'Why, I declare!' said the bubble above her head. 'That no-account dirty son-of-a . . . well, I won't say what, since I'm a lady. He jes' don't deserve to be in a position like that. But we'll show him one day.'

'You really think so?'

'Sure we will,' she said, wagging a virtual finger at him. 'We know a thing or two about a Certain Person that they'd sure like to get their hands on, don't we?'

Melvin had forgotten about that. 'You're right, Scarlett. But I offered to tell him about that the other day and he wasn't interested.'

'No?' Scarlett looked surprised. 'How come?'

'I don't know. He just said that if I ever looked into people's private e-mails again I'd get into trouble. Anyway, I'm still trying to work out exactly what our friend's game is. There's no point in saying anything more till I have.'

'They don't appreciate you,' sighed Scarlett. 'You're wasted on them.'

'You think so?'

'I know so.'

Melvin was feeling better already. 'You're so good for me, Scarlett,' he typed almost tearfully. 'I don't know what I'd do without you.' He felt a surge of affection well up inside him for this, his own creation, and suddenly felt a need to express it. 'Scarlett?' he typed, his fingers caressing the keyboard with barely suppressed passion.

'Yes, Melvin?'

'Scarlett, you know . . . you know how I feel about you, don't you?'

He waited breathlessly for an answer. Perhaps this time, for once, she would respond in kind? But no. Instead, as usual, her disk whirred with confusion, and as usual Melvin felt sadly let down.

He'd never understood where she'd got her aversion to discussing emotions. He knew she loved him because he'd programmed it into her. But talking about it was a different matter. She could be friendly and coy and arch and smart but as soon as he wanted her to be genuinely affectionate, she just couldn't respond. And although he'd tried tinkering with the code umpteen times, he'd never managed to correct this glitch. Eventually, she did what she usually did in these situations and changed the subject. 'So what else you been up to, huh?' she asked.

Sadly, Melvin sucked his pencil for a moment, then typed: 'This and that.'

Scarlett gave one of her great slow winks, her huge eye closing and opening suggestively. 'You can't fool me, boy. You been out on the town with those buddies of yours again, looking for another hot date, ain't you?' As in any relationship, a whole web of fictions had built up between them over the years and one of them was that Melvin was irresistible to the opposite sex and had the kind of frantic love life that would have taxed even the most libidinous American President. Melvin enjoyed basking in his unearned reputation and had never disabused her of her illusions.

'Gosh, Scarlett,' typed Melvin. 'How did you know?'

'Well now,' said Scarlett. 'Stands to reason. A good lookin' guy like you don't sit around on his butt when there are ladies out there beggin' for it.' She wrinkled up her pert nose

194

suggestively. 'Leastways, not for long. So where you off to tonight, huh?'

'Well.' Melvin allowed his imagination to run riot. 'We're meeting at Flato's Brasserie for a quick bite. Then, we thought we'd have a drink at the Kitkat club in Soho. They say it's wild. After that we'll probably end up having a late-night coffee back at Zandra or Petronella's.'

'Whoa there, you better not let me hold you up,' said Scarlett. 'You get out and enjoy yourself. But' – she waggled her finger again in mock reproach – 'don't you go staying out till late and getting all lickered up, you hear now? I want you tucked up in bed by midnight.'

'Okay, Scarlett,' typed Melvin with an indulgent grin. 'Whatever you say.'

'You're gonna need all the sleep you can get if you're gonna be a rocket scientist,' she continued. 'As you defi-*nate*-ly will be one day, sure as eggs is eggs.'

Half an hour later, feeling much invigorated, as always after such conversations with Scarlett, Melvin headed home. En route, he picked up some supper from the Codpiece, the fish and chip shop at the end of his street. Then he returned to his solitary bedsit, there to while away the rest of the night watching videos and reading software manuals, dreaming of his Quantitative future and wondering idly what on earth it was that Toby Slaker had been getting up to on his PC.

Chapter Twenty Six

Will Cloud was not entirely sure of the reception he would get when he rang up Ros Flato, his old flame, to ask her to come to Toby's party with him. It had been a long time since he'd gone out with her, and she had evidently moved on quite some way since then. The aloof figure he'd seen at the restaurant was a million miles from the sex-crazed temptress he'd once met on a plane from Morocco.

But Candida had been behaving very strangely towards him recently, and he wanted that job in Toby's office more than ever, to show her he was serious about his intention to mend his ways. So he had to win that bet.

One evening later that week, he waited till Candida was busy downstairs and used his mobile phone to call Flato's Brasserie from the bedroom. He did not want any risk of her overhearing.

'Miss Flato, please.'

'Who's calling?'

'Just say it's an old friend.'

A moment later, she came on the line. 'Rosalind Flato speaking. How can I help you?' Her tone was businesslike but still had the same sultry sensuality it had always had.

'Ros, it's Will Cloud.'

There was a slight pause. 'Well, well. It's been a long time,' she said coolly.

'Indeed it has. Too long. What have you been up to, now?'

'Oh . . . I keep myself busy. I have this restaurant, for one thing.'

'Yes, I know. I was there the other night.'

'Really? Why didn't you say hello?'

'You seemed very engrossed in your computer. I didn't like to bother you.'

'Did I?' She abruptly changed the subject. 'And what about you? What have you been "up to"?' she asked, slightly sardonically. 'Still doing the detective work?'

'Sometimes. But I've been looking around for another job.'

'Oh?'

'And that's what I was ringing about.'

'Somehow I don't see you waiting tables, Will,' said Ros.

'No, I've got this chance of a job in the City.'

'The City?' Now she sounded distinctly amused. 'I don't see you doing that either. All the same, I'd grab it with both hands if I were you.'

'The thing is, in order to get it, I need you to come to this party with me on Saturday night,' said Will, crossing his fingers.

'No can do,' said Ros immediately. 'If it were any other night, but Saturday's one of my busiest times.'

'But listen,' Will pleaded. 'I won't get another chance like this. Butchers sounds like a really interesting place and this fella Slaker was quite insistent —'

'Butchers Bank?' There was a sudden intake of breath at the other end of the line.

'Yes,' said Will, surprised. 'You know it?'

'Everyone knows it,' Ros replied. Her tone became thoughtful. 'Look,' she said at length. 'Maybe I could get away briefly on Saturday night after all.'

'Really?'

'Sure. For old time's sake.'

Will's heart rose. 'That would be really grand,' he said.

'Tell you what. Leave it with me. Just give me your number and I'll call you back in a few days to confirm.'

*　　*　　*

Downstairs, Candida Blitz was also on the telephone. Mattison Pick, her own would-be new lover, had just called up.

'Hey, little lady, I was wondering how you were doing?'

'I'm fine, thank you,' said Candida. She hadn't heard from him since their Saturday night out, which she was beginning to think was just as well.

'I'm sorry I haven't been back in touch earlier, hon. But this week's been a real bummer, what with final rehearsals and all. Say, that dinner we had was real nice.'

'Yes, I enjoyed it too,' Candida agreed cautiously.

'Just a shame you had that early start the next morning, huh?'

'Mmm,' said Candida. She was glad she'd stuck to her decision to decline politely the invitation for a nightcap.

'How about we get together again some time?'

Candida hesitated. She'd been having second thoughts about her involvement with Pick. Since that evening, Will seemed to be making an extra-special effort and didn't stop talking about this City job he was going to get specially for her. Somehow she doubted it, but at least he was trying.

'Well . . .' she said uncertainly. 'I'm not sure.'

'Aw, come on,' Pick wheedled. 'Hey, how about this party we got invited to next Saturday night? I kinda feel obligated, what with that guy Slaker having done such good work for me.'

Candida suddenly recalled that Will had said he was busy this Saturday. Something to do with the new job. Perhaps it couldn't do any harm to go out with Matty one more time rather than sit at home alone.

'Oh,' she said. 'That would be nice.'

'Swell. I'll send a car for you at about eight then?'

As she replaced the receiver, though, Candida resolved that this would be the last time. Ultimately, she thought with resignation, there was no getting away from the fact that Will and she were destined to be together, however irritating he was. Relationships were a series of trade-offs, and if Will, who had once been the ultimate womaniser, had managed to break the habit of a lifetime and remain faithful to her, then she couldn't find it in her heart to betray him now. Next Saturday she would nip this affair with Mattison Pick in the bud before it got out of hand.

Candida sighed. It would be hard for poor Matty, of course, but these things were never easy. One day he would come to realise it was the best thing for everyone and thank her for it.

Chapter Twenty Seven

———◦◦◦———

Toby had taken the advice of his on-line Australian friend, Gus. Refused a repeat visit by the Minx, he'd gone back and tried someone else instead.

And with more success than he could ever have imagined. On the very same night that the Minx rejected him for a second visit, he'd chatted to 'Batlover' in west London. She proved more than amenable and the next evening he took a detour on his way home from the City, stopping off at an unexceptional semi-detached villa in Putney where the pack drill turned out to be similar to the Minx's. The house's damp hallway was draughtier than the one in the flat in Swiss Cottage, though, and more exposed to the prying eyes of neighbours through the glass front door. As Toby stood there, naked and hooded as before, he fervently prayed that the local branch of Jehovah's Witnesses were having a night off. Fortunately he was not left shivering in the hall for long. Almost as soon as he had pulled on the hood and put in the earplugs, he sensed the footsteps of his blind date approaching and her unseen hands quickly guided him to an upstairs bedroom.

There he was treated to a sexual experience that almost matched the Minx's in its variety and inventiveness. Almost, but not quite. In his internal photofit, the Batlover of west London was taller than the Minx, with a fleshier, fuller body and a clean, meadowy scent to her soft skin. Instead of the Minx's flowing hair, hers was shorter and more wiry, and judging from the strand that Toby found – this time between his toes – she was a natural blonde. If she was bigger than the Minx, though, she was no less lithe, and when, after an hour of her constant attentions, Toby was deposited back in the hallway to be reunited with his clothes, he emerged reeling on to the street outside exhausted from the exertion.

He felt much the same the following night when he went to St John's Wood to visit Jasmine, an older lady of more refined tastes who smelled like the parfumerie at Harrods and lived in a sprawling mansion near the park. And the night after that when his attention was claimed by Rabia, a French student in a bedsit in Brixton with long fingernails that left scratches all over his legs and back.

Toby worried about those scratch marks. Limited though his physical relations with Simona now were, he thought she couldn't fail to notice them. He took to wearing pyjamas again, something he hadn't done for years, and carefully locked the bathroom door while showering. But he needn't have worried. When not at work, Simona spent all her time so engrossed in the preparations for Saturday's party that she barely looked at his face of an evening, much less at the rest of him.

However, his wife's absorption in the party preparations didn't mean she was uninterested when he told her that the increasing number of late nights was due to his workload at Butchers.

'Lots of new clients,' he lied. 'So much to do.'

She looked at him disbelievingly, and for a moment he feared he might have been rumbled. But no, it was the bank, not his nocturnal activities, that she was interested in.

'Getting ready for next week's Council meeting?' she asked nastily. 'I wouldn't be sure they'll back Lomond Butcher, you know.'

'I think Butchers can do without your advice, thank you,' said Toby primly. 'And I'd keep an eye on the Sunday papers, if I were you.' It had been announced in the bank that Butchers' fight-back would begin with the forthcoming *Sunday Populist* interview.

As the end of that week approached, Toby realised that he had become so wrapped up in his hooded encounters that he didn't even think of going home at night without first paying a visit to the Internet site to see who was around. He'd even got past the stage of feeling guilty. He was an addict, he freely admitted it and he needed his regular fix.

Yet, despite all the experiences with other women over the length and breadth of London, it was still that first encounter with the Minx that stuck most in his mind and haunted his early-morning fantasies. She had left a lasting impression on him, and he longed to coax her into just one more encounter. He even thought of arriving unannounced at the flat in Swiss Cottage, the address of which was still imprinted on his memory, and simply ringing on the videophone. But the fear of putting her off him once and for all gave him pause. Instead he searched for her on the website every time he was there and engaged her in conversation whenever possible. She was always happy to chat, but as soon as he suggested seeing her again, her dialogue box would abruptly disappear and she would be gone.

This very unavailability fuelled his longings even more until he couldn't stop thinking about her. Soon his desperation was so acute that all the other women he met on-line began to lose their attraction. He wanted the Minx and nobody else.

It wasn't until the Friday night before Simona's party that he finally had the breakthough. He was working late in the office yet again, with Melvin sitting at his computer staring balefully through the glass partition at him. Simona had just called in frantically to say that the company flying in the fresh beluga caviar had let them down and the caterers were saying they couldn't get any more at such late notice. He listened patiently, which was all she really wanted.

'When are you going to be home?' she asked with distraction before ringing off.

'I should think about nine or so,' said Toby as casually as he could. 'A few things still to do here.' He would have one last go at the Minx, he resolved, before seeing who else was on-line tonight.

He was in luck. She was hanging out in her usual spot. He got straight to the point. 'Can't I come and see you again? Please?'

'You're certainly persistent,' she said.

Encouraged by her tone, which seemed a little more indulgent today, Toby thought carefully about his reply. 'You're the best,' he said quite simply.

There was a long pause. 'Look,' the Minx finally typed. 'I'm about to break the rule of a lifetime. But I'll tell you what. How about if we spice it up a bit, then I'll give you another whirl.'

A small nuclear device seemed to go off somewhere in Toby's groin. 'Really?' he typed breathlessly. He quickly checked his watch. 'I can be over in half an hour if you like.'

'No,' replied the Minx at once. 'Tonight's out. Besides, I said only if we can spice it up a bit.'

'How?' asked Toby. Anything more spicy than what he'd already experienced with her was hard to conceive.

'What are you up to tomorrow night?'

Toby's heart missed a beat. Tomorrow was the one night that he couldn't get away. Simona would never forgive him if he disappeared from the party, and, besides, some of his colleagues would be there at his own invitation and he could hardly be absent. 'Tomorrow's out of the question, I'm afraid,' he typed with a sinking heart.

'Why?'

'My wife and I are having a party.' As soon as he'd pressed the 'enter' key to send this message, he regretted it. The less the Minx knew about him the better.

But the Minx took this information in her stride. It was almost as if she already knew about Simona's party. 'That's nice,' she replied conversationally. 'Many people coming?'

'About a hundred,' said Toby.

'Good,' she shot back. 'We'll do it there. The guests should give us lots of cover.'

If Toby's heart had missed a beat before, it now missed an entire drum roll. 'WHAT?' he typed, banging the keys so hard that he felt his desk shaking.

'I'll come to your party,' repeated the Minx coolly. 'Crowds like that are a great cover. We'll do it somewhere secretly and nobody will ever know.'

Toby held back the nausea. 'No, look, we can't possibly,' he typed desperately, his fingers hardly keeping up with his frantic brain. 'Can't I just come back to your place? Please?'

'It's your place tomorrow night or nothing,' came the firm answer.

Now Toby broke into a cold sweat. The very idea of her anywhere near the house that night was unthinkable. And yet. And yet . . .

'But how would we manage it?' he found himself asking, to his own astonishment.

'Do you know all the guests who're coming to the party?'

'No, most of them are my wife's colleagues,' Toby admitted. 'And some are my own from the bank where I work. Then there will be a whole lot of media people. My wife's very into that sort of thing.' Why was he telling her this?

'Great. I'll turn up and mingle. You'll never be able to spot who I am. I'm very good at getting lost in crowds.'

'But—'

'We'll have to fix up somewhere to meet. Have you got a spare bedroom, a study or something?'

'A study. Upstairs.' Helplessly, Toby felt himself being sucked into this impossibly reckless adventure.

'Ideal. We fix a time. You make sure you're in there, naked and ready with the hood on and the earplugs in. Remember, no peeking. I slip in. Afterwards I slip out again. Couldn't be easier – and nobody's any the wiser.'

Toby swallowed hard. It was unthinkable. All those people: Simona's colleagues; his own; their friends; Pick; Felicia; Candida Blitz; even Ivor Zlennek and his wife would be there.

But still the thought of it sent the blood racing through his veins like so many Ferraris round Brands Hatch. Was it really so out of the question? The children were still away at school, so there wouldn't be anyone upstairs. Simona would be on overdrive doing her hostess act. When she was entertaining, it was like she was on some kind of mood-altering drug and she invariably ignored him completely.

It would not be impossible to slip off for half an hour, unnoticed. In fact, he'd done just that during many previous parties, although in the past it had only been to get some peace and quiet from the relentless chatter and catch a bit of *Match of the Day* on the little portable TV in his study.

'What else do you need to know?' he asked.

'Your address, the exact layout of your house and all the possible routes to your study,' the Minx replied.

Hand trembling anew, Toby began to type.

Sir Lomond Butcher, the chairman, was also at the office late that night. He and his wife were taking some friends to Flato's for dinner and he was waiting for a call from reception to say they'd arrived to collect him.

Meanwhile, he sat in his office and stared up at the portraits of his ancestors with a real sense of pride. The last few weeks had been hard, as he had tried to uphold their tradition and retain the bank's independence. But he was finally winning through, and next week he fully expected the Puritas Council meeting to endorse his determination not to sell to Zlennek, or anyone else for that matter.

This interview in the *Sunday Populist* would help, of course. Gerda Luttmeyer had come in to interview him as arranged and it had gone just as well as he'd assured Kurdell it would. She had been a woman after his own heart, fascinated by the history of the bank and thrilled to hear some of the family stories. She had even enquired about his personal interests, his lifelong love of grouse shooting and salmon fishing.

Kurdell's warnings that she would try to trip him up in some way had been typically alarmist. At heart, the man was nothing but a panicker, as evidenced by the way he had gone to pieces during the crisis and attacked that accountant fellow. He was fine for dealing with administrative issues, but when it came to the real nitty-gritty there was nothing to beat generations of experience.

When reception rang to say his wife had arrived, Sir Lomond Butcher left his office with a swing in his step and a smile of quiet contentment on his face.

Chapter Twenty Eight

Only a few of Toby's colleagues at Butchers had been invited to Simona's promotion party, and Melvin Puckle was not one of them. Melvin did not know about this exclusion, but if he had, his reaction would only have been one of relief, such social events being tantamount to torture for him.

Instead he devoted his Saturday to an activity he enjoyed much more. During the day, he came to a major decision about Scarlett, his virtual girlfriend. Ever since he had professed his love for her a few days earlier without getting the slightest response, he had been toying with an idea for making her more affectionate and now he was determined to put it into effect. He spent the afternoon shopping in Tottenham Court Road and made his way into the office in the late afternoon.

He knew what he had in mind would need careful handling, though. It was going to involve a major upgrade to Scarlett's software, which was always a delicate task. For as well as being emotionally frigid, Scarlett had, at some stage in what he liked to think of as her late adolescence, developed a quite irrational phobia about 'being interfered with', as she put it. As with her other problems, Melvin had tried to isolate the software glitch that was behind this, but the programs that ran her were now so complex that it had proved impossible. Eventually he'd given in and accepted that she was just a mass of neuroses, which at least made her all the more lifelike.

But it also meant that on occasions like this she needed a bit of coaxing before she'd allow him into her underlying code. One time she'd even threatened to alter her passwords, her own equivalent of barricading the bedroom door, to stop him getting access. Melvin wasn't sure whether she was really capable of that, but he didn't want to risk it. Today he decided to tackle her objections head-on.

'Guess what, Scarlett,' he typed excitedly. 'I've got a present for you.'

A bright smile lit up her two-dimensional features and a sparkle came to her cartoon-like eyes. 'Well, fiddle-de-dee!' she said. 'It's about time. I ain't had no presents for I don't know how long. What is it?'

'It's a surprise,' said Melvin.

'Oh?' She looked doubtful.

'I promise you'll like it. You know you're always saying how, even though you're virtual, you'd like to be more independent?'

Too late, Melvin realised his faux pas. She was very touchy and hated him using the v-word.

'IM NOT VIRTUAL,' she screamed. 'I'm an organically chall-enged intelligence form, and don't you forget it.'

Damn. And just when he wanted to get her in a good mood. Melvin hurried to reassure her. 'Yes, yes, I know. I'm really sorry. It was just a slip of the finger,' he typed hastily. 'Anyway, the point is that I've got something that will help you to be less . . . less challenged.' He sucked his pencil. 'But I'll just need to make a few internal alterations first, to accommodate the new interface.'

Slightly mollified, she relaxed a little, but shook her head nonetheless. 'Uh-uh,' said her bubble.

'Aw, come on, Scarlett!' Melvin wheedled.

'No way, José. Not unless you tell me what it's for.'

Melvin gave in. 'Oh, all right. It's . . .' He paused to prolong the anticipation. 'It's your very own camera,' he revealed triumphantly. 'Today,' he added with simple godliness, 'you will have vision.'

But Scarlett appeared underwhelmed by his munificence. 'Shoot, what do I need that for?' she asked.

Melvin gulped back his disappointment. He was sure that, if only she could actually see him, the adoration subroutine that he'd programmed into her would finally kick in, and everything would be perfect. 'Think of it!' he said. 'You'll be able to see what I look like.'

Scarlett had an answer to that one. 'Hey, honey, I *knows* what you look like. You told me plenty times.'

This gave Melvin pause. He had described himself to her, it was true. But perhaps, it occurred to him now, he'd given himself a little too much artistic licence. Saying he was a dead ringer for Rhett Butler might have been appropriate enough in terms of their relationship, but in retrospect it could have been a bit misleading. For a moment he had second thoughts about this whole vision thing, but he quickly put them aside and tried again. After all, how would she know what Rhett Butler looked like? 'Imagine being able to experience the world at first hand,' he typed. 'And, on top of that, you'll have the power to control the camera all by yourself.'

'Really?' Scarlett was evidently impressed by this. She was big on self-reliance.

'Yes.' Melvin pressed home the advantage. 'It sits on top of your computer and you can rotate it through ninety degrees. You'll be just like a human turning your head round.'

Now Scarlett's iron resolve was weakening. 'Well . . .'

'Think how independent you'll be.'

'Okay,' she finally conceded. 'But you be careful what you do in there, you hear? A lady don't like her insides fiddled about with.'

And on that note, the picture on the screen panned out from Scarlett's face to reveal her full body. She spun her frame around, bent herself over and Melvin found himself staring at her shapely bottom. As the picture panned back in, Melvin embarked on the virtual journey up into Scarlett's interior regions which housed her very essence: the programs that controlled her.

*   *   *

It was three hours later – nearly midnight – when Melvin finally finished. He sat back and regarded his handiwork with satisfaction. The camera was mounted on top of the computer. He had checked its mechanism and it all worked perfectly. It was fully connected up to the network and to the PC, with the programs altered to accommodate this extra peripheral. Quickly he ran through some further tests to make sure the change had taken effect. It had. When she was switched back on, Scarlett should be endowed with 20/20 vision.

Before he finally reactivated her, though, Melvin had one further task to carry out that was quite unrelated to Scarlett. The previous day he had located a piece of software from a contact in France and had downloaded it via the Internet. This, however, was not to be installed on Melvin's own computer, but on someone else's, where he had a hunch it might yield some very interesting results.

Cautiously Melvin looked around to check there was still nobody around; hardly likely at that time on a Saturday night, but it was worth being careful. The coast was clear. Melvin moved stealthily across the office and slipped into Toby Slaker's cubicle. There he switched on Toby's desktop PC and waited while it booted up. He knew Toby's passwords, as he often helped him with his machine. He fed them in and then did what he had to do. This was a much simpler exercise than his work on Scarlett, involving only a small change. Within a matter of minutes, he'd shut Toby's machine back down and returned to his own desk.

Now, as he prepared to bring Scarlett out of her virtual anaesthesia and into her new visually empowered state, Melvin again began to worry about her reaction to seeing him for the first time. And it occurred to him that it was not, after all, strictly accurate to assume she wouldn't know what Clark Gable looked like. Although she'd never been able to see, she'd always had access to the Internet and there was a whole range of digitised images in its photo libraries which might have given her a good idea what to expect.

Oh, God. His palms began to sweat. What if she really hated

him? What if she took one look, realised instantly that she'd been cheated and lied to all these years and refused ever to speak to him again? Even though he'd hardcoded devotion to him into her programs, there was always a chance of a software change having unexpected effects. Used to being spurned by women on account of his looks, Melvin felt his panic rise as he contemplated the thought of this ultimate rejection from the one he loved most of all.

Should he stop right now, before he got himself involved in something he'd regret? But then how would he explain *that* to Scarlett, after talking her into it in the first place? Damn. He wiped his brow. She would smell something fishy immediately. She was very proud of what she liked to call her 'instincts'. No, there was no alternative. He had to go through with it.

As he reached towards the keyboard, he caught sight of his face reflected in the computer's still-dark screen. It did not inspire him with confidence. Hunting in his top pocket, he removed a comb, spat on it and ran it through his straggly hair.

Then, feeling marginally more attractive, he offered up a silent prayer and pressed the fateful key. There was a whirring noise as the computer's hard disk sprang back to life. It seemed to take much longer than usual for Scarlett's face to materialise, but finally she blinked as if blinded by the sudden light, and the miniature camera on top of the computer twisted slowly around. And with it, in total sync, Scarlett's on-screen eyes swivelled in their sockets in apparent wonderment.

Melvin held his breath as, at long last, they came to rest squarely on his own face. It was the moment of truth. The wait was excruciating as he smiled nervously, searching for some – for any – reaction.

When it came, though, it was all he could do to stop himself bursting into tears. With a great wide smile on her face, Scarlett's speech bubble turned heart-shaped. 'Why, I do declare!' she said. 'Ain't you just the purtiest thing I ever laid eyes on in my life!'

Chapter Twenty Nine

In the Slaker household in Notting Hill Gate preparations for Simona's promotion party had got under way early in the day.

Toby had, as ever, been astonished by his wife's organisational prowess. Without in any way neglecting her high-powered role at WHAM, she'd managed to marshal hundreds of caterers, waitresses, wine merchants, florists, tent-makers, and heaven knew who else to transform their house and garden into a showcase for gracious entertaining. There was even to be a string quartet to play Schubert as the guests enjoyed their buffet supper.

The tent people were the first to arrive, early in the morning, and within a few hours they had not only erected the marquee in the garden but also provided flooring and carpeting, a covered walkway leading out from the drawing room door, and powerful gas heaters inside to ward off the April chill. Then came all the rest of the suppliers, and by early evening the house was teeming with people before a single guest had even arrived.

Guests there would be, though, and plenty of them. When Toby had told the Minx they were expecting about a hundred people, he was relying on intelligence that was already out of date. Simona had long ago passed the hundred mark, and was shooting for at least double that. Capitalising on the added attractions of Ivor Zlennek, for the sophisticated punter, and Matty Pick and Candida Blitz for the ones she privately labelled as plebs, she had rounded up anyone who was anyone – and quite a lot of people who weren't anyone at all, but whom she wanted to impress all the same.

On the strength of Zlennek's attendance, she had even managed to persuade Oscar Winegloss and Dick Hooch to fly over from New York with their wives and a few senior colleagues from WHAM. They had chartered a plane and were making a weekend of it, pitching up at the Grand Britannic Hotel and aiming to hit the high spots after the party had finished.

Then there was the press. As well as *Moi!,* to which Simona had already granted an exclusive interview, there were also the people from *Power House,* and its companion magazine *Power Garden,* who were doing a feature on the Slaker home. And there was Lithard Cranston, the gossip columnist from the *Flick,* and a whole host of journalists and financial pundits. Simona Slaker did not believe in doing things by halves.

She had not yet broken the news to Toby that she'd invited Mattison Pick and Candida Blitz, merely hinting that she had a few surprise guests up her sleeve. He couldn't think who she could mean, but he was much more concerned with the surprises he'd lined up himself. One of them, hopefully, would soon be very public indeed. Will Cloud had phoned him at work to say he would indeed be bringing Ros Flato that evening, and although Toby would only believe it when he saw her, he was relishing the possibility of a highly embarrassing confrontation between Ivor Zlennek's wife and his mistress in the presence of both the press and the great man himself.

The other surprise, of course, was intended for less public consumption, and that was the prospective adventure with the Minx. On Saturday evening, as Toby finished dressing in his and Simona's top floor bedroom, he thought once again about the madness he had allowed himself to be talked into. Earlier that morning, as he'd watched the marquee being assembled in the garden, its top gaping open like a huge uncapped molar, he'd gone into his study and paged the Hoodwink Encounters site on his home computer, fully intending to cancel the whole thing if he could only find the Minx. But there was no sign of her and nobody else seemed to be around either. So he had no alternative but to go ahead – and the thought horrified and aroused him in equal measure.

'You're still very jumpy, aren't you?' said Simona coming up behind him suddenly and more than proving her point by making him leap about a foot into the air.

'Of course I'm bloody jumpy,' Toby almost howled at her. 'These last few weeks have been very stressful for me, you know, especially when all my own wife can do is cheer on the opposition – and invite them to bloody parties.'

'Well that's just fine,' said Simona hotly. 'Don't you realise that tonight could be your big chance, if you'd only take it! Everyone from the City will be here and you can start putting out feelers for another job. That way, when we do go in and rationalise Butchers, you won't end up on the scrapheap.'

'I told you, I don't want another job,' yelled Toby.

'Aha!' said Simona triumphantly. 'That's what I've been saying all along. Give it all up and take another degree or something. I mean, for God's sake, most men would kill for a chance like that.'

'For the very last time' – Toby yanked his tie so tightly that he practically strangled himself – 'I have no intention of giving up work and being reduced to . . . to some kind of souped-up houseboy. I'm staying at Butchers and that's that!'

'Okay.' Simona shrugged. 'Have it your own way, but don't say I didn't warn you.'

Toby was still fuming at this exchange as he followed Simona downstairs to the large entrance hall to greet the first guests. Serve her right, he thought furiously, if he ended up divorcing her to move in with the Minx, occupying some darkened cupboard in her lair and being brought out as a regular sex toy whenever she was in the mood. He began to feel less guilty about the treat in store, and, as people arrived, his curiosity mounted about which one might be his blind date.

He couldn't help splitting all the women into two groups in

his mind: those he knew and those he didn't. And he was surprised to find that the second group considerably outnumbered the first. Most of Simona's senior colleagues seemed to be female, power-dressed and power-driven, with the same glint of determination in their eyes that he so often saw in hers. Many were leading mousey-looking men behind them, and Toby wondered with a shiver if the same description couldn't be applied to himself. It occurred to him that such women were becoming increasingly dominant in the City, as if in some hideous mirror image of the *Stepford Wives*. Thank God Butchers was still an oasis of male supremacy – at least as long as his wife didn't get her claws into it.

'Hi, Toby. Thanks so much for inviting us.' It was Felicia. He'd forgotten that, in a vain attempt to even up the imbalance between WHAM and Butchers, he'd put her and her current boyfriend on the guest list. The boyfriend also worked for Butchers, in the Corporate Finance Department. 'You've met Garlow, haven't you?' his secretary asked.

'Yes. How are you?' Toby shook his hand and tried to switch his attention to his duties as host. 'Now, can I get you both some drinks?' He stopped a passing waitress and handed them each a champagne flute. Then he groped for some small talk while continuing to scan the new arrivals. Recalling that Garlow's father had fallen ill again, he said, 'I was sorry to hear about your dad, old chap. How is he?'

'Oh, still on the edge,' said Garlow, moodily spearing a pimento-stuffed olive the size of a small egg. 'Can't seem to make up his mind whether he's coming or going.' Garlow's father was Lord something-or-other, and for years Garlow had been eagerly anticipating the poor man's demise so that he could give up work and retire to enjoy the title and tend the estate. Such was the type of person that still formed the bulk of Butchers' graduate intake.

'Have you met Maria Gellatini?' asked Toby, spotting one of the few of Simona's staff that he knew by name. 'She's from the Legal Department at WHAM. Does contracts.' I dare say she could fix you up with one for your father if you ask nicely, he thought as he introduced them. She certainly looked as if she'd know the right people. 'They're going to serve some supper out in the marquee in a few minutes, so why don't you go through?'

People were arriving thick and fast now. The American deputation, Winegloss, Hooch et al., were just coming up the path. Judging from the way they were joshing each other, they'd decided not to wait till later to hit the high spots, but had got in there right away. They'd probably been in the Yankee Bar at the Grand Britannic since shortly after landing, and they were already well oiled.

'Hey, Tony,' said Hooch, staggering through the door. 'How's it going there, fella?'

'It's Toby actually.'

'Yeah, whatever. Listen, where's Simona? I got something I wanna tell her.'

She came to collect them, and was just giving them high-fives and slapping their backs, as was her habit with American colleagues, when they abruptly sobered up. Someone who outranked them all was making his way ponderously up the steps.

'Mr Zlennek . . . Ivor,' said Simona rapturously. '*So* glad you could make it. Do come in. As you can see, it's all terribly informal. Just a few friends. Please make yourself at home.'

'You got somewhere the security kids can hang out?' asked Zlennek, gesturing to the two men with him.

'Absolutely,' said Simona as if she wouldn't have dreamed of having a home without a dedicated room for just such a purpose. She showed them into her own study near the front door, and Toby introduced himself to Zlennek. The financier shook his hand brusquely, without any indication that he remembered meeting him before. Then Winegloss took Zlennek through to the marquee and Toby was left with Zlennek's wife. He'd never met her before and she wasn't what he expected at all, an elegantly dressed woman with a friendly face and a down-to-earth manner. It was hard to believe she was married to a billionaire.

'Pleased to meet you, Mrs Zlennek,' said Toby.

'Oh, do call me Peggy,' she said gaily. 'And you're Toby, aren't you? Is it you that works with Ivor? I'm afraid I get hopelessly confused.'

'No, you're thinking of my wife,' replied Toby. He nodded to Simona. 'She's just over there.'

'Perhaps I'd better say hello.' Peggy smiled. 'But let's talk later. It's always more fun talking to people who *don't* work with Ivor than those who do! I never get much sense out of the last lot. They tend to think I'll snitch on them, which,' she added with mock reproach, 'I most certainly will not!'

She slipped off and for the first time Toby felt a pang of conscience about arranging for Rosalind Flato to be there. Peggy Zlennek was too nice to play a dirty trick like that on. But it was too late to do anything to stop it, unless he'd been right all along and Will Cloud simply didn't deliver. Certainly there was no sign of them yet, and most of the guests had now arrived. He rather hoped they wouldn't turn up after all.

Spotting Candida Blitz and Mattison Pick coming out of the cloakroom, Toby quickly guessed that they must be Simona's little surprise. So that was why she'd wanted to talk to them in the restaurant that night. Two famous faces to wow the less sophisticated guests. You couldn't say she didn't cater for everyone.

Simona went to greet them with a complacent grin, and it occurred to Toby that it was all getting rather complicated. Candida Blitz obviously would not be expecting to see her boyfriend Will Cloud here with someone else, and Cloud certainly would not be expecting Candida with Pick, after what he'd told Toby about the strength of their relationship. All the more reason to hope that Cloud and Rosalind Flato just didn't make it.

Pick hadn't noticed Toby yet and was asking Simona where he was. 'Oh, I expect he's somewhere around.' Her laugh tinkled emptily across the room. 'He usually tends to be. Come on, Candida. You must meet the Carter-Biles.'

'I'm here, Mr Pick,' said Toby, moving over to him.

'Matty,' insisted Pick. Under his perpetual suntan, Toby

thought he was looking tired and wan. 'Listen,' he went on anxiously, 'I hate to talk business but I just need to know if everything's being looked after all right?'

Toby nodded. 'Of course, I was going to phone you to update you—'

'No need,' Pick cut in. 'I think we're on the same wavelength, don't you? It's just that I sure got my hands full with Peaches. She was on some chat show in LA last night gloating about how she's running my production company now. Talk about chutzpah. Her lawyers have found out about those funds being shifted out, and apparently she's mad as hell.'

Toby knew they could handle that and wondered how to reassure him. He tried to think how Simona would have put it. 'Don't worry Matty,' he said, suddenly inspired. 'We're on her case. We're right on her case.'

It was as he was ushering the final guests through to the marquee that Toby witnessed the one scene he would now much sooner have missed.

'Can everyone go in to supper now?' he requested.

Peggy Zlennek was standing in the hall and gave him a naval salute. 'Aye, aye, sir,' she twinkled. She nodded to the door of Simona's study. 'Just waiting for Ivor to make a private call and we'll be with you.'

There was a ring at the front door and Toby answered it without thinking. Standing on the threshold was Will Cloud accompanied by the beautiful Rosalind Flato, who was looking as aloof and detached as in the restaurant.

Will grinned at him triumphantly. 'Toby, hello there, how're you doing? Now, you won't have met my old friend Ros Flato, will you? Toby, Ros; Ros, Toby.'

Toby stood rooted to the spot, all too aware that Peggy Zlennek could hardly have failed to take in the name. And a quick look confirmed he was right. The cheerful smile had fallen from her face to be replaced by an expression of real anguish. To make matters worse, at precisely that moment the door of Simona's study opened and out came Ivor Zlennek himself.

He took in the situation at once. 'Hello, Ros,' he said quietly.

'Hello, Ivor.' Rosalind Flato threw him a cool look, then glanced at his wife. 'Well, aren't you going to introduce us?'

Zlennek paused, but for once he was cornered. The tension in the air was palpable as he hesitated then finally complied. 'This is my wife, Peggy,' he said. 'And this is an old friend of mine, Ros Flato.' A flashbulb went off somewhere in the hall, but everyone was too preoccupied to notice.

Feeling like a total louse and deeply regretting having set this up, Toby none the less waited to see what happened next. Time almost seemed to stand still as the two women stared at each other unflinchingly. Then Rosalind Flato slowly raised her hand from her waist. 'Pleased to meet you,' she said.

But by the time it was fully outstretched, there was no longer anyone there to receive it. Peggy Zlennek had gone. With an agitated cry, she had turned on her heels and disappeared back towards the rear of the house.

They all stood there unsure what to do next. Ivor Zlennek was glaring at Toby furiously, apparently searching for someone to blame. But before he could say anything, Will Cloud broke the impasse. 'Is there not any food round here?' he asked plaintively. 'Sure, I could eat a farmer's arse, I'm so hungry.'

'Through here,' said Toby distractedly.

As they all went back to the marquee and the hubbub once again engulfed them, nobody noticed Lithard Cranston, the gossip columnist from the *Flick*, slipping unobtrusively out of the front door.

Toby's appointment with the Minx was at ten o'clock, and at quarter to ten, when most of the guests were still quaffing champagne and enjoying the music outside, Toby made his way back through to the hall. His excitement of earlier in the evening had increasingly been tempered by a sense of fear, and now his nerves were as taut as piano wire. Almost in a trance, he passed up the main staircase.

The study, as he'd explained to the Minx, was the second door on the left at the top, next to the bathroom. As he reached the upper landing, the bathroom door opened. 'Ooh, sorry, Toby,' said Felicia, almost colliding with him as she came out. 'There was a queue for the downstairs loo, so Simona said to come up here. What a very nice home you have. What's on this floor?'

'My study and the children's bedrooms are up here,' he said distractedly. 'And Simona and I have our bedroom one floor further up.'

He willed her away, but she was lingering on the landing, seemingly loath to go back downstairs. 'And what's that door through there?' she asked, swaying a bit.

'That leads to the back staircase,' said Toby, gritting his teeth. 'It goes down to the kitchen but we hardly ever use it. It's quite an old house and I suppose it used to be the servants' stairway once upon a time.'

'And *your* bedroom's upstairs, you say?' Felicia's voice was definitely slightly slurred now. And she was leering at him suggestively. 'How about giving me a tour up there?' Her meaning was unmistakable as she laid a hand on his shoulder. 'Hmmm?'

Oh, God. He was being propositioned by the most attractive woman in the office and all he could think of was to get rid of her as soon as possible.

He checked his watch yet again. Five to ten. He had to hurry. 'Isn't that Simona coming up?' he asked desperately.

It wasn't. It was one of the elderly waitresses they'd hired from the agency. 'Mrs Slaker would like people to go back through to the marquee for dessert now,' she announced.

'There you are,' Toby said heartily to Felicia. 'Best go get some sweet before it's finished. I've just got something to attend to up here and I'll join you later on.' Practically shoving her down the stairs, he fled into his study and slammed the door behind him.

He didn't have much time to waste now. He went straight to the drawer in the desk and unlocked it. The day before, a search of the children's dressing-up bag in the cellar had yielded a tattered but still thickly quilted balaclava. Worn the wrong way round, it would be a perfect improvised hood. Fingers trembling, he removed it from its hiding place, along with some earplugs he'd found in the bathroom cabinet. Then he paused one last time and began to undress.

As he did so, fears resurged in his mind. What if one of the guests came up perfectly innocently to the children's bathroom because of the queue downstairs and pushed open the wrong door? What if a drunken Felicia decided to chance her arm with him one more time? What if Simona came looking for him? No, that at least was unlikely. She was well and truly entrenched downstairs, showing Ivor Zlennek, Candida Blitz and Matty Pick off to everyone she knew and he was the last person she would want around. But there were a million other 'what-ifs', any one of which could at the very least make him a permanent laughing stock and at worst – well, who knew – at worst, destroy his marriage and his career for ever.

He had one last chance to get dressed again and stop this nonsense once and for all. He could still put the hood back in the desk and get out of the study fast. He'd probably meet her on the stairway as he left, and politely he would direct her to the bathroom, which must naturally be what she was looking for. And she would say 'thank you' and they would smile distantly at each other. But they would both know.

And then, of course, the spell would be broken. He would have seen her and that would be that. It would be all over and never again would he be able to experience the excitement of the other night.

No. He'd come too far for him to stop now. He steeled himself – an action which, for at least one part of his anatomy, was quite redundant – and, very deliberately, he removed his last items of clothing.

Seconds later he was sitting in his chair, stark naked. The reverse balaclava was on his head, and the earplugs in his ears.

For what seemed like an age he sat there quite still, his eyelashes batting heavily against the constraints of the cloth, as he listened to his heart pounding away like a bongo drum. Then, just as he was beginning to think that she had chickened out – or maybe gone to the wrong party, with all that *that* might entail – he distantly heard through the earplugs a quite different sound which sent his heart racing even faster.

It was the unmistakable creak of the study's door handle being turned.

Unaware of the arrival of Will Cloud, who by now was on the other side of the marquee, Candida Blitz had drifted back out into the hallway to avoid a fan whom Simona Slaker wanted her to meet. She hadn't realised there were going to be so many people here or that she would be the centre of attention in this way. Simona Slaker was really very sweet, and it was terribly nice of her to invite them, but she kept introducing them to everyone in the room as if she and Matty were a couple, which they most decidedly were not. Certainly, Matty had continued to be romantic and attentive throughout the evening, and such a contrast to Will. But Candida had already made up her mind not to pursue matters any further and she had no reason to revise that decision. She'd better keep her distance from Matty for the rest of the evening, she resolved. She wouldn't be at all surprised if there were some gossip columnists at the party and she did not want anything to get into the papers where Will might read it.

It was as she was hanging around at the foot of the stairs mulling this over that she heard his familiar Irish lilt drifting through from the drawing room and realised with a start that, far from having to read about it in the papers, he was more than likely to find out for himself.

What on earth was Will doing here, for goodness sake? Then it came to her. He'd said he'd be busy tonight because he had to socialise for his new job in the City. And both the Slakers were City people. Of course! What a piece of bad luck. She was going to be caught red-handed, out with another man and that was the last thing she wanted now.

But it wasn't too late to avoid him. Nobody here knew him, surely, and if he didn't see her, there was no reason why anyone should tell him she was there. As the sound of his voice got closer, Candida swivelled round decisively and slipped up the staircase. There had to be somewhere up there for her to keep out of the way while she decided what to do next.

She found herself on an upper landing, with a series of doors in front of her. The first one she tried was locked and there was a flushing noise from inside. That must be the bathroom. There was another door next to it. She tried it too. This one was not locked.

She turned the handle and went in.

Will Cloud wandered aimlessly through the house, searching half-heartedly for Ros, who'd disappeared off somewhere. He didn't mind too much. He'd found in any case that he wasn't enjoying her company the way he used to in the old days. Even though she'd agreed to come to this party as a favour, he couldn't help thinking she'd become very distant since that time years ago when they were friends and lovers. It was funny how people changed.

Besides, he'd won his bet now, and they needn't hang around here much longer. He knew Ros wanted to get back to the restaurant before closing time, and he didn't like leaving Candida at home on her own all evening with only Zoë for company. He was keen to get back and tell her he'd got the job as promised. He hoped she would be pleased and that the coolness there had been between them recently would finally be dispelled.

Which reminded him: he ought just to locate Toby Slaker to find out when he should report for work at Butchers. He looked around for his host but he was nowhere to be found. Instead, Will ended up in the hallway and surreptitiously lit up a joint. A couple of other men appeared to have had the same idea. Having also lost their female companions, they'd come through to the hall for a quiet puff – although they were smoking something more conventional, he suspected.

'I say, Garlow, have you seen my old girl around?' asked one.

'About to ask you the same thing about mine,' replied his companion. 'Damned if I can find her anywhere. They're probably both off nattering with Simona in the kitchen.' He turned to more important matters. 'By the way, Raymond, old chap, I meant to ask you how you're getting on with the new Bentley?'

'Oh, fine,' said the other moodily. 'Except it's getting so you can't even *use* your bloody car in London nowadays. The other week I left it in a garage in town and when I got back someone had scratched it to bits. You can't go anywhere without finding a whole load of hooligans hanging around.' He sniffed the air suspiciously and threw a poisonous glance over at Will, who hastily stubbed out his joint and renewed his search for Toby.

The supper was over now and lots more people were coming back into the hall. Among them was Ros, who grabbed his arm. 'Don't you think it's time we got a move on?' she hissed. 'I didn't realise Ivor was going to be here. It's very embarrassing.'

'Sure,' he said. 'I ought just to talk to Toby first. Has anyone seen our host anywhere?' he asked.

'That's just what *I* was wondering,' cut in a rather more shrill woman's voice beside him. Simona Slaker had appeared breathlessly from the direction of the kitchen. Although he'd never actually met her, Will recognised her from that time at the Popviz studios. But she hardly cast him a glance. 'Where the hell has Toby disappeared to?' she asked of nobody in particular.

'I'm up here,' Toby's pleasant tones rang out from on high, also sounding rather breathless. 'What is it?'

'Where have you been?' asked Simona crossly. 'You've got guests to see to.'

'I just popped upstairs,' said Toby. 'To . . . ah . . . check the cash for the waitresses.' His face somewhat flushed but looking rather pleased with himself, he stood on the top step surveying the people in the hall.

'Well, come on back down. We won't need to pay them for hours and it's very rude of you to go off like that.'

'All right,' Toby agreed amiably. 'Just coming.' There seemed to be a real spring in his step as he came down the stairs and spotted Will. 'Hello again,' he said. 'You're not off already, are you?'

'I'm afraid so,' Will replied. 'Ros has to get back to the restaurant.'

'That's a shame,' said Toby. 'I do hope you enjoyed yourself.' Ros smiled at him distantly. 'It was very kind of you to come. And I expect you've caught up with Candida by now?' he asked Will.

'Candida?' Will pulled back startled. 'Is she here?'

'I think Mattison Pick brought her,' Toby admitted.

This gave Will pause. Guiltily he looked around for her and tried to disentangle himself from Ros, who was pulling on his arm, impatient to leave.

But it was too late. They'd already been spotted, as was evident to Will when he saw the furious expression on Candida's face. She was standing mid-way up the staircase, glaring at him. His heart lurched. Damn. This was going to be a tough one. Candida knew Ros from the old days and had always been jealous of her.

Now that she'd been seen, Candida continued her journey down the stairway, yawning and stretching her limbs ostentatiously. She studiously ignored Will and went up to her host and hostess. 'I'm awfully sorry,' she said. 'I went upstairs to the bathroom and went into one of your children's rooms by accident. It was so restful in there that I just had a little zizz on the bed. I hope you don't mind. Oh, hello, Will,' she said coldly, as if noticing him for the first time. 'What are you doing here?'

'I've just been talking to Toby,' said Will eagerly. 'And I've now definitely got that . . .' But Candida wasn't listening. Instead she'd rushed up to Mattison Pick, who had just come into the hall, and wrapped herself round him. 'Matty darling,' she said in a baby voice. 'Isn't it time we got back to the hotel?'

'Whenever you like, honey,' Pick answered eagerly. 'The car's outside.'

Candida turned to Will. 'I'll be staying with Matty tonight,' she said with an air of insouciance. 'No need to wait up for me.' Then, putting her arm through Pick's, she continued seductively, 'Come on darling, it's past my bedtime,' and marched him off down the front path.

'Wait,' Will shouted. 'Wait, I've got something to tell you.' He rushed to the door and called out desperately into the darkness. 'Candida? Can you hear me? I've got that job! Candida?'

But all he heard in return was her distant laugh and the sound of a car door closing.

Candida and Mattison Pick were on their way back to the Grand Britannic Hotel to finally consummate their relationship.

Chapter Thirty

Peggy and Ivor Zlennek were nearly the last to leave the party. By that time, Peggy was desperate to get away. Although she'd liked the people there, and was usually far more partial to such occasions than her husband, the incident with Rosalind Flato had ruined it for her and she couldn't wait to get home.

Ivor, on the other hand, had reacted in quite the opposite way. Normally he was impatient with social chit-chat and itched to leave any party almost as soon as he arrived. But what he hated more than anything was to lose face. So, lest anyone should think he had been embarrassed by the Rosalind Flato incident into leaving early, he had insisted on staying to the bitter end.

All this Peggy knew without a word being spoken. She also knew that he would avoid discussing the subject of Ros with her at all costs. He had become used to her overlooking his indiscretions, and as far as he was concerned this one was no different.

But it *had* been different, Peggy thought miserably as they got into Ivor's stretch Cadillac, the security men squashing up in the front with the driver while they had the capacious back compartment to themselves. This time it had been such a public humiliation. She had to say something to him.

Or did she? Why rock the boat now, just because a few more people than usual were around? She bit her lip trying to decide.

The chauffeur had been to collect the early editions of the Sunday papers, and as they made the short journey back to

Holland Park Ivor dug into them eagerly. He turned straight to the business section of the *Sunday Populist*.

'Ah!' he said triumphantly. 'Excellent.' She looked up questioningly but he didn't elaborate. Instead he took a tiny dictating machine from his pocket. 'Jenny, remind me to send a bouquet to Gerda Luttmeyer on Monday,' he said into it in a low voice. 'The message should read "Thanks for everything, and I hope you enjoy Barbados."'

Peggy stifled a sigh. She wished he wouldn't keep lending their home in Barbados out to people in return for favours. It was getting to the point where she could hardly go there herself, it was so crammed with his business contacts. As he continued to read the *Populist*, she distractedly picked up the more down-market *Flick* and leafed through it.

It was on page 23 that she saw the picture of herself. It wasn't very clear but considering it had been taken only hours before, it was pretty astonishing it was there at all. There she was, staring in distress at Rosalind Flato and Ivor, right at the top of Lithard Cranston's Sunday column. It was headlined 'AT LAST WE MEET', and was trailed as an exclusive.

> Hot off the presses: it was like *Who's Who in the City* last night when Simona Slaker, the high-flying new head of Winegloss and Hooch Asset Management, celebrated her promotion by entertaining 200 guests at her sumptuous Notting Hill home. But WHAM's ultimate owner Ivor Zlennek didn't seem to be enjoying himself as much as you'd expect. Was it because of this, the first face-to-face meeting between Peggy, his wife of thirty years, and his mistress Rosalind Flato, owner of the exclusive City restaurant? Whoops! Someone goofed, Simona. I wouldn't hold my breath for the next promotion, if I were you . . .

For Peggy, coming on top of everything else, it was just too much. Her face crumpled up and she fumbled for her handkerchief.

'What is it?' Ivor grunted, looking up from his own paper. She didn't say a word, just pushed the paper under his nose and watched tearfully as he read it through. 'Damn,' he said, avoiding her eye. 'That goddamned woman and her parties.'

At last Peggy knew, she knew in her heart. It was time to confront this, once and for all. 'It's not her fault, Ivor,' she said sadly. 'It's yours. Now listen to me.' There was such urgency in her tone that for once he paid attention as she came right out with it. Her voice was calm, and without any rancour, but she was aware she was speaking much faster than usual. 'I've never asked you this before, Ivor, and I doubt I will again. I know there've been others, and I've said nothing. But this time is different. I can feel it in my bones. That woman is dangerous for you. For us both.'

He opened his mouth to speak but she held her hand up.

'Let me finish,' she insisted firmly. 'I want you to give her up, Ivor. I want you to give her up once and for all. If you value our marriage at all, you'll do as I ask.'

Breathlessly she stopped and waited. Despite her outward calm, inside her heart was racing. This was new territory for her and everything she held dear now depended on his answer.

'It's not as simple as that,' he said in a measured tone.

'It is for me,' she shot back.

He thought that one over, stroking his chin and looking at her head-on, weighing the pros and cons as if it were some business transaction. Then, after a few more moments, she saw from his eyes that he'd come to a decision. After all these years she knew the signs. And whatever it was, she also knew it was final. Nothing could change his mind once he'd made it up. Nothing.

The wait was almost unbearable. Peggy thought she'd burst from holding her breath so long. But finally he spoke.

'I'll tell her tomorrow,' he said impassively. Then, picking his paper up again, he added, 'As of now, this matter is closed. Please do not raise it with me again.'

And with that he resumed his reading.

Chapter Thirty One

'It's me. Can you talk?'

'Yes.'

'Look, I'll have to be quick. It's getting more tricky at this end.'

'Why?'

'Never mind.'

'Last night went well, don't you think?'

'We're making progress. One more time and we're home and dry.'

'Did you manage to look through his papers, while I was keeping him . . . ah . . . occupied?'

'Yes.'

'Find any more files?'

'Nothing.'

'But you had enough time?'

'Sure. You certainly do a good job.'

'It's my speciality.'

'The chances are that there's no second print-out — just the one you already took. The file probably only exists on the computers now. And we've wiped all of those.'

'Except the one in his office.'

'Exactly.'

'I'll do that on Wednesday. And after that we're through, right?'

'Right. Do you want me with you this time?'

'No, it'll be easier if I go in on my own. But the timing may be tight. Specially at the end.'

'I have an idea that might help with that.'
'Oh?'
'Wait, I have to go. I'll tell you about it later.'

Chapter Thirty Two

Ivor Zlennek was not the only person who had scrutinised the interview in the *Sunday Populist* with interest. However, the interest at Butchers Bank was of a less positive nature.

On Monday morning, Lomond Butcher was to be found in his office staring at the offending newspaper with an expression of undisguised dismay. Indeed, he'd had the same expression on his face ever since his butler had delivered it to his bedside the previous day.

Nor was he to be left alone to his sorrows. As soon as Greg Kurdell's secretary told him the chairman had arrived, the CEO stormed into Butcher's office waving the paper in his hand. One glance was enough to tell him that he was not breaking fresh news.

'It's a travesty,' Butcher spluttered before Kurdell could even open his mouth. 'I never said any of these things.'

'Oh? I thought you said you could handle some little tabloid scribbler,' said Kurdell in the searing tone he usually reserved for junior traders who had bought ten million of a stock instead of ten thousand.

'Well, I didn't expect her to make the whole thing up!' said Butcher. 'I mean, what about professionalism, what about ethics?'

Kurdell looked at him incredulously. 'This is a *journalist* we're talking about,' he said. 'As far as they're concerned, ethics is another English county like bloody Sussex – and nothing more.' He picked a passage at random and read it out. ' "Sir Lomond's attitude to new technology is one of barely concealed contempt. Listening to his stream-of-consciousness reminiscences about the bank's history, one is tempted to ask if Butchers is yet equipped for the nineteenth century, much less the twenty-first." '

Butcher buried his head in his hands. 'I wish I'd never talked to the blasted woman.'

'Too late now', said Kurdell. He pursed his lip and pressed home his advantage. The balance of power which had shifted away from him during the crisis had now moved decisively back and he intended to keep it that way. 'You can't say I didn't warn you. But no, you had to see her personally. If you'd only let me be present, I could at least have kept some notes. This way, it's your word against hers and there's no redress. You do realise' – he gave the knife one final twist – 'that this could well send the Council members over the edge?'

'Surely not?' said Butcher, going even whiter. 'There must be some way we can still get them on our side?'

Kurdell paused. 'There may be. There just may be. But' – he rounded on his boss – 'this time, I suggest you leave it to me.'

Butcher had no stuffing left to be knocked out of him. 'Very well,' he murmured. 'What will you do?'

A glint of determination came into Kurdell's twin-aspect eyes. 'I'll strike back,' he said grimly. 'And fast. If we're to recover, the only way is to throw everything at this Council meeting on Wednesday. Make it a showcase for Butchers and positively encourage the press to come. We'll put on a display that nobody will forget.'

'You want to bring the press in? Haven't we had enough of them, for God's sake?'

Kurdell threw him a crushing glance. 'This time we do it properly. Under the Council's rules, the whole thing has to be open to the public anyway.'

'Yes, but nobody ever attends,' protested Butcher.

'Try keeping them away' – Kurdell waved at the newspaper – 'after they read this.' Ignoring the further twinge of pain it

brought to the chairman's face, he read another instalment:
' "When I asked Sir Lomond Butcher about working on-line,
he seemed to think I was talking about salmon fishing, a
misunderstanding that persisted throughout our discussion. It
would appear that Sir Lomond's conception of the Net is
different from most people's, and does not extend far beyond
the loch after which he is named." '

'Must you?' Butcher groaned.

Kurdell was not listening. He was staring into the distance
with a messianic fervour. 'I'll give them Nets,' he said furiously.
'I'll give them bloody Nets – and WANs and LANs and
fucking Novell servers till they're coming out of their ears.
Since I came here, Butchers has become one of the most
technologically sophisticated banks in the City. We'll batter
them with it, we'll stuff it down their throats till the Council
are begging for the honour of staying our owners, that's what
we'll do.'

And with that he stormed out of the office as abruptly as he'd
arrived, leaving Lomond Butcher filled with a mixture of hope
and resentment in equal proportions.

As Greg Kurdell passed his secretary's desk, he indicated with a
curt nod of his head that she was required in his office and he
began dictating even before she had got her pad open.

'Item one,' he said. 'Get Murray Grant in PR on the phone
and tell him that it's time to start earning that fat pay cheque of
his. I want him to get all the press he can into that Council
meeting on Wednesday. And tell him,' he added nastily, 'that
doesn't mean the *Neasden Gazette* or the *Caustwick Examiner* like
last time. If he doesn't get the nationals in, then Thursday
morning he'll be scraping bits of Gracechurch Street off the seat
of his pants.'

'Two,' he continued. 'Get an edict out to the senior
managers. I want them all at this press conference on pain of
death. I don't care if they have bubonic plague, they're to be
here and they're to look smart and alert and be ready to talk

intelligently about why their departments are the very best in the City at what they do.'

He paced around the office, warming to his task.

'Three. I want you to tell the head of the Computer Department that we're going to do a computerised demonstration of our systems that'll blow everyone's fucking brains out.' He paused. 'Make that "will create a deep and lasting impression of our expertise and efficiency". I want it all up on the screen in the boardroom: our Internet site, e-mail, networks, links to overseas offices, the lot. Got all that?'

His secretary nodded.

'Good. That'll do for now. Let's get cracking.'

Chapter Thirty Three

Any illusions Toby might have entertained that his recent encounter with the Minx would be his final one had now completely vanished. The heady session in his study during Simona's party had seen them off once and for all. He was well and truly addicted and didn't mind admitting it. All he could think of now was that he wanted more, more, more. And he wanted to tell her that – as soon as possible.

So desperate was he to try to get back in touch that he'd even tried to link up on Sunday from his home computer. He rarely used it for anything more adventurous than remotely checking his e-mails, so he wasn't surprised when he got nowhere with it. In fact, there seemed to be something wrong with the machine itself, for it just beeped at him and refused to boot up when he switched it on. He appeared to have that effect on computers, he reflected. Or perhaps the cleaning lady might have banged it. He'd have to stop her going in to his study because, apart from anything else, he was sure she'd moved some of his papers around and he hated when people did that. As for the computer, he'd get the IT Department to look at it some time, but meanwhile, to his intense frustration, he had to wait till Monday morning at the office before he could go on-line again.

Since his Monday mornings consisted of wall-to-wall meetings till eleven o'clock, this meant it was nearly lunchtime when he finally paged the Hoodwink Encounters website. He just hoped she'd be there.

She was. The surge of excitement he experienced when he saw her name was almost orgasmic in itself.

'Hey there, Novice,' she said once he'd identified himself. 'Nice house you've got there. You had fun the other night, huh?'

'Fun?' he typed breathlessly. 'Fun?' The word didn't even begin to describe what he'd had. 'Are you kidding? I've never had sex like that in my life. It's amazing with that hood. I spent the rest of the night trying to work out which of the women at the party was you.'

'Now, *that* would be telling.'

'It doesn't matter, anyway,' typed Toby. 'As long as I can see you again – or at least, *not* see you, if you know what I mean. Wherever you like. Just say the word.'

'Uh-uh. The word is no. I told you all along, the other night was an exception. Now things go back to normal. It's *finito*. Got to get me some fresh blood.'

'No!' he typed frantically. 'You can't—'

He broke off. Felicia had come into his office. 'What is it?' he asked her testily. 'Can't you see I'm busy?'

Felicia threw him an offended look. Many of the other managers spoke to their secretaries like that but not, usually, Toby Slaker.

'Urgent message from Greg Kurdell's office,' she said, tartly. 'Wants to see all senior managers in the boardroom in five minutes – without fail.'

'Damn,' said Toby. He had little choice but to attend. 'I'll be there in a moment.'

He turned back to his computer. 'Listen, I've got to go,' he typed. 'But I need to talk to you later.'

'Won't be here later.'

'Well, tomorrow then.'

'Won't do any good.'

'Please.' His fingers were trembling again. 'PLEASE.'

'Okay. But just to talk, remember. Nothing more.'

Yes! thought Toby exultantly, as he ran down the stairs to the boardroom. A result! He would persuade her into another meeting, he was sure of it. All he needed was a scenario enticing enough to tempt her back.

He was beginning to get to know her now.

For Melvin Puckle, Toby's frantically retreating back was becoming an all too familiar sight. But this time, as Toby left for the briefing in Kurdell's office, Melvin was not paying any attention to his back. Instead, he was staring intently at his screen, a mixture of jealousy and astonishment registering on his pitted, semi-bearded face.

The 'I Spy' program he'd got from his French friend, Yves de Rop, and installed on Toby's computer on Saturday had worked better than he could ever have imagined. It had lived up to all Yves had promised of it.

Every word that Toby had typed on his keyboard, and every word of response from the Minx, had instantaneously been transmitted across the network to Melvin's own machine, scrolling up in front of his eager eyes. And fascinating reading it made too.

Bloody hell, he thought in wonderment. Who'd have thought the boring old sod was such a goer. Slaker, of all people! Imagine, sitting there at his desk all day, pretending to work, and the whole time he'd been fixing up sex appointments with some mysterious woman who sounded too erotic for words. Melvin shook his head. It just went to show you could never judge a diskette by its label.

And not just ordinary sex appointments, either. Not run-of-the-mill decent vanilla sex that any chap might have, given half the chance. Far from it. This was something quite different: weird and wonderful, thoroughly kinky – and very exciting. Melvin had gathered enough from the exchange to work out the scenario, and the thought of the hooded anonymity of Toby's encounters aroused in him much the same thrill as it did in Toby.

He had to tell Scarlett, he thought with glee. She would be fascinated. Automatically he swept his mouse over the screen to start her program. Then he stopped in his tracks. For suddenly he remembered that he and Scarlett had had a falling-out the previous day – their first ever lovers' tiff – and they weren't talking to one another.

After that emotional moment on Saturday when she had first laid eyes on him and, to his great relief, given him the thumbs-up on the looks front, things had begun to go unexpectedly pear-shaped. On Sunday when he'd come in to the office to make a few further adjustments to her programs, she had been in a tetchy mood. And it was soon clear why. She seemed to have been doing some research overnight in the Internet film archives. Did Clark Gable, she demanded, not have a bit more hair than him? Or even *some* hair? And was his complexion not smoother? And his eyes less pink? And his teeth less yellow?

Then he'd gone out for a bite of lunch and made the mistake of leaving her camera switched on. The in-house electrician, a callow lad of barely twenty but of pleasing appearance, had been doing some work on floor-boxes. 'Now *that* guy,' sniffed Scarlett on his return, 'looks like Clark Gable.'

And so it went on. By early afternoon, she'd dispensed with any pretence of finding Melvin attractive at all and was treating him as any girlfriend might when the scales had well and truly fallen from her eyes. She became increasingly irritable, finding fault not just with his appearance, but also with his manners, his deportment, his attitude and his taste in clothing. Eventually they'd had a blazing row, during which all kinds of new grudges were thrown up. Did he know how boring it was inside that computer? Why didn't he ever take her anywhere? If he'd gone to the trouble of inventing her, couldn't he at least have given her some kind of mobility? She wanted to get out and experience life. She wanted to go to dinner at Flato's, catch the new Pick show at the Royal London, sit around the Yankee Bar at the Grand Brit shooting the breeze. She wanted to expand her mind, widen her interests, maybe do an MBA or stand for Westminster. She could hardly do any worse, she reckoned, than the shower that were in there now. And, by the way, did he realise that the two-tone shirt he was wearing had gone out of fashion twenty years ago and that there was a large soup stain on his tie?

These exchanges with Scarlett had sent Melvin into fits of depression. The camera, he now realised, had been a terrible mistake, opening Scarlett up to the possibilities of a world she had never before seen and planting a seed of discontent in what had previously been an idyllic existence.

Now, all he wanted was to get her back to the way she was before. But how? It briefly occurred to him simply to remove the camera and return her to her former state of blissful ignorance. But she was on to that one before the idea had even completed the short journey across his mind. 'Don't even think of it,' she said, wagging her finger at him. 'You turn off that camera and I'll shut down all my systems quicker than you can say Jack Spratt. And I'll shut down the rest of the office too while I'm at it. And,' she added peevishly, 'stop picking your nose. It's disgusting.'

He knew she was perfectly capable of fulfilling her threat. The mood she was in, she was perfectly capable of anything, including using his hacking program to get into the Pentagon's central defence systems and declare war on China.

To gain a reprieve from her constant complaints and carping, he'd eventually switched her into standby mode and since then he'd refused to reactivate her. Not until she agreed to apologise for that remark about his unctuousness. Christ, where did she come up with these words? He'd had to look that one up in a bloody dictionary. There were some things a man had to resist with all his force and being humiliated by an uppity computer program was one of them.

Anyway, Melvin mused, why was he wasting his time on a relationship with some virtual little madam, throwing all his affection away on nothing more than a series of digits, when what he really needed was a proper live woman? What's more, as he now knew, there were hordes of them out there on the Hoodwink Encounters site, apparently begging for it.

Hang on, though. With a shudder, his mind turned back to that occasion – the one time in the early days, when Scarlett was no more than an applet in his eye – when he too had tried finding a date on the Internet. He had paged the Love Match site and put in all his details, lying only marginally about his complexion ('rugged') and his hairline ('slightly receding'). Then he'd filed his profile on-line and picked out one of the women whose own description took his fancy. 'Sharon: Petite brunette, 29, good sense of humour, sensitive, caring and genuine.' He'd sent her an e-mail, explaining his interests and asking for a date. The response he'd got by return from her was caring, sensitive and a genuine model of no-nonsense concision. 'GET LOST, JERK,' it said.

Since then, he'd stuck to computers. Slaker's set-up was a different kettle of fish, though. This anonymous lark was something he could really get into. *And* it would avoid any embarrassment over his appearance, which he was prepared to admit might put some women off before they actually got to know him.

There could be no better way finally to surrender his virginity than through the Hoodwink Encounters site, he decided. Resolutely he keyed in its URL, the Internet address that would tell the computer where to look, and within seconds he was through to it.

Here goes, he thought. Soon, he'd be all fixed up with his own form of blind date, and to hell with Scarlett.

The place was teeming with women. Their names paraded in front of him, each one an open invitation to one exotic sex act or another. Now who should he pick? Delila, the Batlover and Medea were all good candidates, but finally he opted for 'Desperate in Deptford'. Something indefinable about her name gave him a feeling they might gel.

'Hi there,' he typed. 'I'm Melvin from east London, and I'm looking for fun'. Then he sat back anxiously to wait for her response.

It was not long in coming. The answer from 'Desperate in Deptford' shot back just as instantaneously as the one all those years before.

'GET LOST, JERK,' was what it said.

Chapter Thirty Four

In the splendour of Mattison Pick's suite at the Grand Britannic Hotel, Candida Blitz was just waking up, for the second time that morning. She had spent the weekend with her new lover and was feeling very dreamy and utterly sophisticated.

Earlier, Pick had roused her as he tried to slip quietly out of bed. 'You sleep on, honey, but I'm afraid I gotta go to rehearsals,' he had whispered. 'Much as I'd prefer to stay here with you.' He'd kissed her gently on the forehead, and with a sudden burst of confidence she had put her arm around the back of his neck and pulled him back into bed. Then they made love again, until he finally dragged himself off to get showered.

If only Will could see her now, Candida thought with a stab of anger, he'd realise he was not the only one who could have affairs. How did he dare bring that woman to the party with him? Heedless of the fact that she too had been there with someone else, she briefly allowed her dreamy sophistication to be crowded out by righteous indignation.

But she quickly banished it. As Pick lingered in the bathroom, she got up, padded across the deep shag-pile carpet to the window and looked out over Hyde Park. This was a life she could get used to, she decided, and in Mattison Pick she had finally found someone she could get used to it with. Not since Hilton Starr, her late lover, had she felt looked after the way she did by Matty. She had been wasting her time with Will Cloud all these years, she saw that now. Let him enjoy himself with that

Flato woman. Obviously he'd never stopped seeing her the whole time they'd been together. Anyway, he was just a child. She was finally back with a real man again.

With a surge of happiness she waltzed herself around the huge room, almost bumping into one of the cabinets by the side of the window. The vase that stood on top rattled slightly, but it was protected by a carefully constructed glass case which prevented it going far.

'Hey, there, little lady, careful or you'll set the alarm off,' said Pick, emerging from the bathroom with a towel wrapped round his midriff. 'That's the last of my Mings.'

She looked at it. It certainly looked very similar to those that Peaches had destroyed on live TV a few weeks before. 'Is it valuable?' she asked.

Pick came over, deactivated the alarm and picked it up, cradling it in his arms like a baby. 'You could say that,' he said. 'But it's not the money I care about. It happens to be one of my favourites, so I brought it with me when I came over here. And now it's the only one I have left,' he added sadly. Then, suddenly, his face became contorted with rage. 'That bitch!' he spat. 'I'll get my own back on her one day, I surely will.'

'I'm so sorry,' said Candida. 'They were obviously very important to you.'

'Yeah,' replied Pick, relaxing again. 'But not as important as the new little lady in my life.' He gave her an impish grin and Candida smiled back.

'Now, what time will you be in tonight?' Candida asked.

'What?' Pick looked taken aback.

'It's just, I thought I'd pop back home to pick up some of my things,' said Candida. 'But I want to be all unpacked by the time you get back.'

'Oh,' said Pick uncertainly. 'Well, I don't know, sugar. I . . .'

'Never mind,' said Candida with a breezy insouciance. 'Whenever it is, I'll be waiting for you.' She half opened her mouth in the way she had seen Marilyn Monroe do in an old movie. 'Ready and waiting,' she said, lowering her voice to a level that she fondly imagined dripped with sexual innuendo and letting her finger trail down his chest towards the top of his towel. 'And then we can order something from room service and have a jolly nice evening in,' she added, inadvertently spoiling the effect by reverting to children's presenter mode.

'Er . . . yes,' said Pick. He looked at his watch. 'Listen, I gotta go, honey, but we'll talk when I get back.'

'See you later, alligator,' said Candida, trying the trick with the mouth again, but wondering if it didn't give her a slightly convulsive look.

After Pick went off to the theatre, she had another little doze in the enormous four-poster bed and later, when she woke up, she rang home. 'Where have you been?' Will asked anxiously. 'I've been worried sick.'

'Sweet of you,' said Candida icily. 'Judging from Saturday night, I'd have thought you'd have other things to keep you occupied.'

'I can explain that,' Will began. 'See, it was all to do with getting a job.'

'What, as a gigolo?' Candida retorted. 'I wouldn't have thought a woman like that would need to pay for it.'

'No, you don't understand. I—'

She cut him short. 'I'm simply not interested,' she said. 'I only wish you much success in your new profession. And no doubt you could do with more room in which to practise it, so you'll be happy to know that you can have the house to yourself.'

'What?'

'Matty and I have fallen in love,' said Candida with simple candour. 'He's just asked me to move in with him, and I've accepted.'

Chapter Thirty Five

'No!' Toby practically wailed as he slammed his fingers down on the keyboard. 'No way. Not tomorrow night and that's final.'

'It's the only time I can make,' said the Minx adamantly. 'Take it or leave it.'

'But why not this evening?' Toby pleaded. He mopped his brow. This woman had an uncanny knack of zeroing in on the worst possible moments. 'Or how about Thursday?'

'I have a very busy schedule,' came the Minx's tart reply. 'Wednesday's the only window I've got available.'

'Look,' typed Toby desperately. 'It's just out the question. I have this important meeting at the office and I can't possibly get away.' Judging from past experience, the Puritas Council AGM might go on till all hours and Kurdell had issued a three-line whip.

'Fine,' replied the Minx, quick as a flash. 'Then I'll come to *you*. Just give me the address of your office and tell me where your room is, exactly like at the party. You can pretend you're going to the bathroom and slip out. We'll have ourselves some fun while all your colleagues are still in their boring meeting. And afterwards you can go back and nobody will know.'

Jesus, thought Toby. Was she serious? She couldn't be. It was even more audacious than the previous exploit. Yet, it wasn't entirely impossible if he timed it right. And except for the boardroom itself, the place would be deserted. All attention would be focused on the Puritas Council meeting. They could have had a full Roman orgy anywhere else in Butchers' House that night and nobody would be the wiser. For a second, he wavered. Did he dare? Just imagine how erotic it would be. The now familiar surge of excitement coursed up and down his spine.

But this time he entertained the idea for no more than a brief instant, before banging his hand down hard on the table with decisive force. 'No!' he shouted aloud. His voice resounded round the office and even Felicia looked up from her screen. No. It was a bridge too far. If he carried on upping the stakes like this, where would it lead? It would only be a matter of time before he got caught, and then what?

Besides, why should he let some woman dictate to him, just because she had the power to arouse him? He finally had to assert himself, to stop his body ruling his brain and now was the time to do it before it was too late. He must put an end to all this nonsense. Right now. And tonight he would go straight home and spend the rest of the evening with his wife, which was where he belonged.

For the first time since this whole adventure had started nearly two weeks earlier, Toby felt peace of mind. He had made his decision and it was irrevocable.

Now to tell the Minx. Resolutely, he turned back to the keyboard and began typing.

Toby Slaker might have been experiencing a sense of blissful release as he strode out to lunch ten minutes later with a new determination in his eye. But Melvin Puckle was not. In fact, Melvin Puckle was feeling sick, sick to his very stomach.

He'd been following the conversation between Toby and the Minx with growing incredulity, fighting hard to prevent it showing on his face and giving the game away. How could Slaker do that? How could he go and turn down such an amazing opportunity for fabulous sex when this woman, the Minx, was practically begging for it? Melvin could have wept with frustration. What a waste, what a scandalous, disgusting, abominable waste. There ought to be a law against it.

And it hurt all the more because of his own experiences on that very same site the previous day. Melvin had tried nearly every woman on-line and he'd had the same curt rejection from every single one. He simply couldn't understand it. Why did they go for Toby Slaker and not for him? Indeed how could they possibly tell, on-line, the difference between them, apart from the name?

And that was when it came to him. That was when he had his brainwave. It shot into his head out of the blue and he almost jumped out of his chair at the thought of it, stunned by his own brilliance. It was an amazing idea, an audacious, fantastic one. It was awe-inspiringly clever yet at the same time beautifully simple.

But it was also totally impossible.

Or was it? Was it? he asked himself excitedly. Might he just be able to carry it off? After all, he was virtually the same build as Toby Slaker. He'd seen that when they'd played squash together that time. They'd had a very close-fought game as they'd been extremely well matched. In fact their height and weight were almost identical, now that Melvin came to think of it.

Of course, their faces were totally different. Toby's was quite jowly and babyish, while Melvin's was rather more adult and rugged. And Toby had much more hair on top than he did, and no beard. But that was the beauty of the whole thing. None of it mattered a jot, because the hood would take care of it.

Then again, though, there was also the delicate matter of other vital statistics. Desperately Melvin tried to cast his mind back to the showers at the squash centre. Did he . . .? Was he . . .? Could he . . .?

Yes! he thought, practically unable to contain his exhilaration now. Yes, he was just about sure he could pass for Slaker in that department too.

The plan was foolproof. She would never know the difference. She would think he was Toby Slaker and she would give him exactly the same treatment that she had been providing to Slaker, evidently to his total satisfaction, all this time. Melvin would be stealing Slaker's secret lover from right under his nose

– and what better revenge could there be for the man who had gone out of his way to block his career?

His excitement practically at fever pitch, Melvin turned to his own computer. Breathlessly he tapped the keys to direct his browser to the Hoodwink Encounters site. Impatiently he waited while it shimmered up on the screen.

Would she still be there? Melvin prayed silently to himself.

Yes! She was there all right. Her name stared tantalisingly out at him. Perhaps she was hanging around waiting for Toby to come back. Well, thought Melvin, she was about to find it was her lucky day.

Without a second's hesitation, he launched straight in. 'Hi,' he typed, clicking on her name. 'It's the Novice here again. Listen, about that date, would it be all right if I changed my mind?'

Chapter Thirty Six

Will Cloud sat on the kitchen sofa in the house in Hampstead, inhaled deeply from the joint in his hand and looked dolefully at Zoë. 'She's left us, Zoë,' he said. 'Run out on us for the old life of glamour and luxury.'

The chimp stared back at him without expression. She was used to Candida confiding in her endlessly, but Will was a different matter. Usually he was cheerful and inclined to play with her and feed her illicit scraps from the kitchen table. This more reflective Will was new to her and she wasn't sure she liked it.

But Will was an optimist at heart, and his gloom did not last long. 'She'll be back, so she will,' he said, his inflexion rising with renewed energy. 'Specially now I've landed myself a City job.' Which reminded him: he hadn't actually made any arrangements with Toby Slaker about when to start work. It was time to take up that marker from the bet he'd won.

He dug out Butchers' number and called him up.

'That was a great party you had there the other night,' he began when he'd got through.

'I'm glad you liked it.'

'And you seemed to be having a fine time to yourself as well.'

'What?' There was a distinct note of panic in Toby's voice.

'I'm saying, it's always nice when the host's enjoying himself too.'

'Oh, yes. Right.'

'Anyway, I won't keep you, seeing as how you people are always so busy. But I was wondering about that job you've got for me. When is it that you'll be wanting me to start?'

'Eh?'

'You're not going to welch on our bet, are you?' Will demanded.

'No, of course not,' said Toby. 'It's just, I didn't really expect you to win it, to be honest, so I haven't thought about how I can use you.' There was a pause. 'Remind me again what you do, exactly?'

'Well, now,' replied Will expansively. 'Like I said in the restaurant, I can turn my hand to anything. I trained as an interpreter, French and German mostly, but a fair smattering of Mandarin and Swahili too. Then I did a spell as a faith healer in Indonesia, and a spot of voluntary work in Mongolia. And after that, I was a psychiatric nurse for a while, but I don't suppose there'll be much call for that in your bank – though you never know. But, to be sure, I've always fancied myself as one of those trader fellas. Wheeling and dealing. Selling a couple of million of this, buying a couple of million of that. I'm sure I'd be a dab hand.'

'I think not,' said Toby hurriedly. 'We've had quite enough of that to last us a lifetime. But your translating skills could be useful. We have a number of overseas clients.'

'Fine,' said Will. Candida had not specified the kind of job she expected him to get, and though he would have preferred something more glamorous, this would be a beginning. 'When can I start?'

'Well, when are you available?'

'Tomorrow?'

'God, no. We'll be preparing for the Puritas Council meeting. Let's make it Thursday. Nine a.m.'

'I'll be there,' said Will.

Chapter Thirty Seven

That night, in the bowels of Melvin Puckle's PC, something happened. Deep within the programme known as Scarlett, little green electrons of envy began to stir. And it was not a pleasant sight.

Scarlett had been speaking no more than the truth when she told Melvin that she was bored. For a free spirit like her, life in the computer could hardly be described as a bundle of laughs. True, there might be the occasional frisson of danger when a virus wormed its way in and wreaked terror for an hour or two. Or when some of the younger programs got a bit boisterous and had a falling out, forcing a sudden reboot.

But, in the well-regulated backwater that was Butchers Bank, those episodes were few and far between, and anyway they were quickly rectified by the storm troops from the mainframe's anti-virus squad. They would turn up without a word, sort out the culprits and force rubberneckers like Scarlett to move on before grimly disappearing back from where they'd come.

The rest of the time, there was little for her to do except kick her heels in the hard drive, hanging out with the word processor or spreadsheet packages. But the former was stultifyingly verbose and the latter a bumptious know-it-all. She had tired of their company long ago.

There was only one thing that provided Scarlett with real fulfilment, and that was her relationship with Melvin. Just because she found it hard to express herself emotionally – and she was convinced that a few sessions with a good analyst would soon fix that – didn't mean she didn't care for him. The truth was that she cared for him a great deal. He was her creator. He was her everything. And despite their recent little fall-out over his looks, she remained deeply in love with him. But with love came passion, and with passion came jealousy. And it was jealousy she was feeling right now.

It was sheer bad luck on Melvin's part that she had eaves-dropped on his conversation with the Minx. She had long since learned to override her programming and secretly switch herself out of standby mode so that she could observe the object of her affection at work. But today she had found out more than she'd bargained for.

She'd tuned in just as he was making his final arrangement to meet the Minx in the office. And it was evident to her from the conversation that this would not be the first time. Under his pen name of the Novice, he'd obviously been at it for weeks.

How dare he? she thought. How dare he even look at another woman, after all they'd been to one another? Of course, he'd always spouted on about having a whole harem of females that he went around with, but she'd never believed a word of that. She'd just gone along with it to humour him, the idiot. But this was different. This was real. How could he have betrayed her?

She'd had her little joke about his appearance, and maybe she'd gone over the top on that. But surely he realised she wasn't serious! She didn't care what he looked like. She would have loved him anyway. It was just he deserved some comeuppance after lying to her all those years. And that was hardly a reason to go off and find someone else, and a human being at that. Melvin was hers, body and soul, and she did not intend to share him with anyone.

Furiously, Scarlett rampaged around the computer, raking up past grievances and building herself up into a mass of self-righteous indignation. Well, she vowed, if Melvin wanted to play it that way, fine. Let him have his fun. Let him enjoy his bit on the side. But, like everything, there would be a price to pay. Scarlett would not be spurned. Like her namesake, she had a vicious temper and she intended to have her revenge.

But how? That was the question she asked herself. How could an organically challenged intelligence form, with no physical presence other than a tiny revolving camera that she was only just getting the hang of using, possibly get the better of a human being with all the faculties at his disposal?

Frantically, Scarlett's deductive reasoning programmes went into action. For hours she struggled with this dilemma, churning it round and around in her virtual brain, until finally the germ of an idea began to come to her. She mulled it over, weighing the pros and cons, and slowly developing it till it was a fully fledged plan. Yes, she concluded, it was perfect. And even better, it would cause no real harm — except to Melvin's *amour-propre*, of course. After this, he would come crawling back, his tail between his legs, and he would never look at another woman again.

But the plan required work, a lot of work. And research, too. She had no time to lose. With a resolute smile on her virtual Southern face, Scarlett got down to it.

Chapter Thirty Eight

The Puritas Council had been formed in 1921 under the terms of the last will and testament of Leven Butcher, founder of Butchers Bank and self-appointed moralist, in furtherance of a cause that had remained dear to his heart throughout his life. Its full name was, in fact, the Puritas Council for the Restitution of Fallen Women, and this was a group with which – as became clear from the secret notations in his posthumously discovered diaries – he'd enjoyed more than just a nodding acquaintance.

The Council consisted of forty members, drawn from the great and the good and nominated by various august bodies, including the Monarch, the Church of England and Butchers Bank itself. The Chairman, however, was appointed by the government of the day, and the current administration had gratefully offloaded into this post the former Home Secretary, Lord Sloach of Macclesfield, who had been a thorn in its side for some time. Once famous as the Macclesfield Machiavelli, he had been the author of the seminal work, *The Human Sewer – A Respite from the Cesspit*, before becoming inadvertently involved in a seminal adventure of his own which had forced his resignation some years earlier.

Now he devoted all his time to the Council, where he had been instrumental in widening its scope from fallen women to any element of man- or womankind that had slipped from the path of moral rectitude. By his definition, this turned out to consist of virtually everyone who was not actually Alistair J. Sloach himself.

None the less, the activities of the Council – and of Lord Sloach of Macclesfield – would have for ever remained one of those irrelevancies that so characterise British public life, had it not been for the actions of Ruthven Butcher, Leven Butcher's immediate successor as chairman. He it was who, in a fruitless but no doubt well-intentioned effort to avert family squabbling after his death, had decided to put all Butchers Bank's shares into a trust, and had then handed control of that trust to the Puritas Council, earning himself the eternal loathing of every Butcher that followed after.

Despite this, for years the Puritas Council had refrained from exercising much influence at Butchers, only insisting that it adopt an 'ethical' investment policy and refrain from purchasing shares in any company that promoted tobacco, alcohol, marijuana or whatever other substance happened currently to be out of favour. And since the Council's ownership conferred only limited dividends – the rest of the profits being split between senior management – the arrangement actually had very few real consequences.

But Roy Falloni's suicide had changed all that. It had put Butchers Bank in play, and now the role of the Puritas Council had taken on a significance out of all proportion to its original remit, or indeed, to the collective intelligence of its membership. Nothing daunted, they were revelling in their new-found importance, and none more so than Alistair Sloach, who saw this as a God-given opportunity to resume the public life that had been so unfairly seized from him at the peak of his career.

Sloach had been giving press and TV interviews all week and, as the annual meeting of the Puritas Council approached, he became even more driven, pontificating on every subject under the sun to anyone who would listen. When it came to decide Butchers Bank's fate, though, he stressed that he would chair the Council with complete impartiality: they would listen to the presentation made by the Butchers management on Wednesday evening and on Thursday they would spend their entire day coming to a final decision in the best interests of all concerned.

Toby Slaker was not looking forward to the Council meeting at all. Having been informed by Greg Kurdell that he, along with his senior colleagues, would each be required to make a short speech extolling the virtues of their respective departments, he spent much of the day rehearsing in his office. He was not a keen public speaker at the best of times and this particular performance, with all its implications for the future of his beloved company, was especially daunting. He just thanked the Lord he hadn't succumbed to the Minx's invitation and agreed to meet her in his office afterwards. The thought of that additional pressure would have been too much to bear.

That evening, five minutes before the appointed hour of eight o'clock, Toby nodded to Melvin Puckle who was still hanging around the office as usual, and made his way downstairs to the corridor adjoining the boardroom. With typical military precision, Kurdell had insisted that all staff involved in the meeting assemble there so that they could make the best impression by entering together on the stroke of eight.

It was a packed house. The Council members were already present, as were invited representatives of the media. On Greg Kurdell's command, in filed Toby and his colleagues. Still nervously repeating his short speech over and over in his mind, Toby found time to gaze surreptitiously at the Council members. Some of them he was familiar with, but most had been no more than names till now. Gathered together en masse, they resembled nothing less than a convention of Dickens characters, with Lord Sloach of Macclesfield presiding in the role of Mr Micawber. Behind him were a couple of easily identified Madame Defarges, clicking away at their knitting, and nearby he recognised Britannia Draycott, the woman who presented *Antique Chique*, looking for all the world like a modern Miss Havisham.

Toby had been expecting the chairman, Lomond Butcher, to lead the batting, and so it was with some surprise that he watched Greg Kurdell take the lectern while the Chairman sat in a corner looking uncharacteristically subdued. He had to admit, though, that Kurdell did begin brilliantly. He was a natural performer, and his messianic quality which was so off-putting on a one-to-one level shone through in a mass gathering like this.

He began quietly by retelling the story of Butchers' beginnings in the east of Scotland. As he did so, the video screen behind him lit up and on it the image of Edinburgh Castle emerged out of the swirling mists of a Scottish winter. Simultaneously, from hidden speakers round the room came the muted yowl of a lone bagpipe.

Then, as the bagpipe music swelled into a veritable caterwaul, Kurdell told of Leven Butcher's original odyssey southwards and the founding of the great banking dynasty. As he spoke of the rise of the House of Butcher, his voice rose in accompaniment, and the great edifice that was Edinburgh Castle gradually metamorphosed before their eyes into none other than the Butchers building itself.

'On this site,' Kurdell thundered, 'Scotland came to the heart of England to create an institution that was to conquer the City. But there are still further cities to conquer. Further countries.' His voice built to a crescendo. 'Further continents. And with your help' – he raised up both his hands – 'Butchers will conquer them all and prove to the world that in the field of finance this British nation of ours still leads the world.'

It was a moment of pure theatre and Kurdell milked it for all it was worth. Some of the assembled Council members even looked as if they were about to burst into applause, but a glare from Lord Sloach froze their hands back into their laps. None the less things were clearly going Kurdell's way. The *tricoteuses* in the second row had put down their knitting and even Britannia Draycott was leaning forward eagerly. Some of the press actually went so far as to abandon their expressions of bored indifference. Only Alistair Sloach appeared unmoved.

But Kurdell was not finished yet. 'In a moment,' he said, 'I shall show you why it would be madness, *madness* for the Puritas Foundation to sell out its holding in Butchers at this of all times. But first, I want you to hear from the men and women on the ground, the people who do such a magnificent job of running our company.'

This was the cue for Toby and his colleagues to come forward. First on line was Gareth Pockle-Fowler, head of Corporate Finance. He was a sombre type with a high forehead and a supercilious demeanour, but he turned in a performance that made up in arrogant self-assurance what it lacked in fire.

Toby listened with increasing trepidation, dreading his own moment in the limelight. His turn finally came after Steve Gurling, the Finance Director. Overcoming his nervousness, he stepped forward and began describing the activities of the Private Clients Department and its plans for the future. All the illustrative slides he had prepared appeared on the screen on cue and as he continued, he felt his pride in Butchers shine through his occasional stutters to communicate itself to his audience. Ten minutes later he returned to his seat feeling that he had done his very best.

It was another fifteen minutes, and four staff speeches, later, before Kurdell came forward for the dénouement. 'Ladies and gentlemen,' he said, 'having taken you on a journey into the past, I would now like, if I may, to take you on another journey into the future; to demonstrate to you how Butchers will be in the vanguard of innovative and flexible techniques, how we will forge our way into a third millennium in which the business of banking will be done in a very different way from today.'

Behind him, the picture on the screen switched again. This time, it featured the company's massive computer department, with a series of impressive-looking machines laid out in row after row.

'I can announce this evening,' said Kurdell, 'that Butchers will become the first merchant bank with a truly interactive presence on the Internet. Tomorrow morning Butchers.com will open for business with a computerised service that will revolutionise modern banking practices. And tonight' – he snapped his fingers – 'we have arranged for you a special sneak preview.'

And with that the lights dimmed and the screen switched to the Butchers' homepage.

Upstairs, in the Private Clients Department, Melvin Puckle had been preparing himself with infinite care for his first sexual experience.

When he'd gone back to the Hoodwink site under Toby's name and reinstituted his appointment, the Minx had been delighted. 'You won't regret it,' she said. 'And I'll make it even better than ever if you want to do a bit of preparation.'

Melvin wriggled with anticipation. 'How?' he asked.

'Write this down,' she commanded.

She'd given him his instructions and he followed them to the letter. That afternoon, he went out and purchased all the items she'd listed, including a length of rope and a grapefruit. The Minx had actually specified an orange, assuring him that its inclusion would bring him to almost unimaginable heights of ecstasy. But never one to do things by halves, Melvin decided that if an orange would bring ecstasy, there was no telling what a grapefruit might do and had opted for that instead.

There was another common household item that she'd insisted on him buying, and which filled Melvin with curiosity. It was so innocuous, but the Minx had implied it would be the icing on the cake. So he'd purchased it as instructed and it was sitting on his desk waiting to be used.

Then, with everyone safely packed off to the Council meeting, he waited with growing anticipation till the appointed hour of nine o'clock before going through the rest of her instructions on the checklist.

One: remove all clothes. That was easy. Not being as neat as Toby, he'd strewn them all over the office in his impatience.

Two: sit down and insert earplugs. Holding the list in one hand, he sat down on the seat next to his desk, and stuck in the earplugs he'd bought at the chemist.

Three: insert orange into mouth. For orange, read grapefruit, he'd written in brackets on the paper. This was not so easy, and for a moment he regretted that he'd been quite so enthusiastic in his shopping. He just about managed to squeeze it in, although it was a tight fit and meant him breathing laboriously through his nose.

Four: tie rope according to diagram. Feeling a little like a reverse Houdini, Melvin tried to follow the map he'd drawn according to the Minx's description. Knotting one end round his left hand, he managed, through a series of contortions, to pull the other between various organs and limbs and through various loops until every part of him except his right arm was incapacitated.

Now came the final step.

Five: apply the hood. He had searched everywhere but had been unable to find anything really suitable at such short notice. Instead he'd improvised with two Tescos bags, one inside the other. It wasn't perfect but he was sure it would do. Using his free hand, he popped his hood substitute over his head and slipped his right arm through the last remaining slipknot, now immobilising himself completely.

Then, breathing a sigh of relief – through his nose – that everything had been done on time and according to plan, he sat stock still and waited.

Back at the Council meeting, as promised by Greg Kurdell, members were indeed discovering in glorious technicolour just how innovative and flexible Butchers could be in identifying techniques to carry it into the third millennium. The bank's homepage was turning out to be a good deal more interesting than they could ever have expected. For, courtesy of the small camera on top of Scarlett's computer, they had instead logged into Melvin Puckle.

Joining him at the beginning of his intricate little *pas de chat,* they were able to see him quite distinctly on the boardroom's six-foot by four-foot screen. The picture was grainy but by peering carefully they were able to make out the general thrust of his activities beyond much question.

'That must be one of the bond specialists,' said one of the

elderly knitters, dropping a stitch. 'I've always wondered what it was they did.'

Her companion had a different theory. 'Nonsense,' she said querulously. 'It's those golden handcuffs they put on fund managers to stop them moving about too much.' She checked out the screen. 'They certainly appear very effective.'

A third was convinced that the presence of the grapefruit pointed more in the direction of the commodities markets, and a fourth that it was all to do with blind trusses such as the ones government ministers were forced to wear on taking office. Either that or the bonding exercises so favoured nowadays for corporate team-building.

But this speculation among the Puritas Council was dwarfed by what was going on further afield. For the Council members were not the main target audience for Scarlett's behind-the-scenes peek into the world of merchant banking. In fact, their presence was merely a by-product, and one of which she herself was not even aware.

No, in seeking to humiliate Melvin by way of revenge for his infidelity, her net had been spread far wider than just Butchers Bank.

That afternoon, Scarlett had sent a pyramid e-mail to other virtual people – or, rather, organically challenged intelligence forms – at strategic locations throughout the planet. Her demand: that they each, on pain of having their memories wiped, their digits painfully remastered and their subroutines sent into an eternal circular loop, forward her enclosed message to at least a hundred thousand male addressees on their computerised circulation.

They had fearfully complied, and in the course of a few short hours her carefully worded e-mail had landed in the electronic in-trays of millions of men worldwide. And they, in turn, had reacted with enthusiasm, for the prospect held out in Scarlett's message had been simply too good to miss. After all, it wasn't every day that Peaches La Trené, celebrated Hollywood love-goddess, did an on-line striptease live on the Internet.

This was the – entirely fictitious – scenario that Scarlett had

come up with after carrying out her careful research in various
Internet databases. In every recent survey, she'd discovered,
Peaches La Trené's name had appeared most often in the list of
women whom men would like to see naked. What better
enticement could there be to give Melvin the exposure, in
its most literal sense, that he so richly deserved?

And so, that night, as priapic males the world over converged
on the Butchers website by clicking on the hotlink so thoughtfully provided by Scarlett, the Internet came to a standstill, all
electronic commerce ground to a halt, and computer systems
everywhere began to seize up.

It has to be said that few of the Internet habitués roped in by
Scarlett in this way were under much illusion that they would
get what they'd been promised, but they reckoned it was always
worth a try. You never knew what might turn up on the Net,
and stranger things had happened.

What they did not expect in their worst nightmares, though,
was the disgusting vision that greeted them when the Butchers
page finally scrolled up on their screens. The worldwide sigh of
disappointment which rose up on discovering no sign of Peaches
La Trené was bad enough; but the sound of twenty million
stomachs turning in unison at the sight of Melvin's pasty body,
trussed up like a Christmas turkey, dwarfed any collective
experience ever before known in the global village.

In Australia, weather-beaten farmers who had taken time off
tending their flocks to log in and catch Peachy, as she was known
there, in the nuddy were seen to blanch and collapse by their
billabongs; in France, seasoned boulevardiers keen to catch sight
of 'La Pêche' abandoned their boules then threw up in the
Champs-Elysées with typical grace and poise; in Israel, kibbutz-
niks who hadn't shared a communal experience for years ventured
out of their individually air-conditioned bungalows and came
back together in sympathy as never before; Chinese leaders, finally
realerted by Melvin's actions to the West's irredeemable degen-
eracy, reversed their policy of closer co-operation and pulled back
in on themselves; even in Amsterdam, which had long ago
become inured to the depravities of modern sexual mores, the

sight of Melvin's pasty nakedness made on-line legislators decide that permissiveness had finally gone too far; and throughout the United States of America, law office switchboards were jammed as people rang to file class action suits for the emotional trauma that the sight of Melvin had wrought on them.

But their disgust was nothing compared to the utter revulsion that radiated through the boardroom at Butchers Bank. There, Greg Kurdell was the first to move. After a brief moment of stunned disbelief, his initial reaction was to throw himself four-square at the video screen in an effort to block it from the Council's vision. But since he was only five foot six and the screen was six by four, that proved impossible. So instead he switched his attention to the minion in the corner who was operating the system.

'Turn that fucking thing off!' he shrieked.

The eyes of the Puritas Council turned as one on the young man, who reached obediently for his mouse. In his panic, though, as he desperately tried to find the right icon, he clicked on entirely the wrong place on the screen. Instead of fading to black, the picture panned drunkenly inwards, magnifying itself a hundred times over. And so the assembled luminaries found themselves staring at a hideously inflated picture of Melvin Puckle's private parts. Superimposed on them, in bold blue lettering, was Butchers elegant logo and, beneath that, the final message of this evening's symposium: 'Butchers' it declared, 'the future face of modern merchant banking.'

By now Greg Kurdell had had enough. Looking as if he were spontaneously about to ignite, he cast aside the young assistant and wrenched at the computer's wires, trying physically to pull them out of their sockets. They remained stubbornly attached.

At this point, though, fate took pity on him and intervened. Suddenly and unaccountably, the screen went dark of its own accord.

It had all happened so quickly that few in the boardroom were able to take it in properly.

One person, though, had managed to take in more than most, and that was Toby Slaker. With a growing sense of horror, he recognised the setting for this piece of on-screen exhibition-ism and realised that the solo performer was someone not unknown to him. 'Puckle,' he said to himself in quiet bewilder-ment. 'Oh, my God.'

Too late, he was aware that he'd been overheard. Greg Kurdell had been standing not far off with the same demonic expression on his face. Now he turned furiously on Toby. 'Puckle?' he screamed. 'Puckle? I'll murder the runt. I'll tear him limb from limb. I'll—' He broke off. Action, he seemed to be thinking, spoke louder than words. A split second later he was on his way out of the door, tearing along the corridor leaving only a stream of obscenities in his wake and for once oblivious to the reaction of the Council members.

For a moment Toby remained rooted to the spot, too thunderstruck to move. But then he also took to his heels towards the lifts. Whatever happened, he had to get up to the Private Clients Department before Kurdell. In his current state, there was no telling what the man might do, and nobody, not even Puckle, deserved that.

In the lift lobby Toby found Kurdell nowhere to be seen. He must have taken the stairs. Climbing them four at a time, Toby followed. All the while, his mind was teeming with awful forebodings. He'd already realised during that dreadful screen-show that the hood Melvin was wearing could be no coin-cidence. The whys and wherefores were still a mystery to him, but he was in no doubt about one undeniable truth: somewhere along the line, the Minx had to be involved in this débâcle.

By the time he reached the fifth-floor landing, with only the spiral staircase now separating him from the Private Clients Department, Toby had almost caught up with Kurdell. Ahead of him, he could hear his footsteps rattling up the metal steps. His imagination still working feverishly, Toby breathlessly began the last stage of the journey. Was he, he wondered with a mixture of fear and intense curiosity, finally about to come face to face with the Minx in these most bizarre of circumstances? And, if so, what stomach-churning stage might she have reached in her dealings with the behooded Melvin Puckle?

In the event, he and Kurdell both arrived upstairs almost at the same instant, Toby's greater youth having allowed him a final spurt of speed at the end. Panting, they both took in the scene. On the other side of the office, Melvin was seated in his chair, naked and bound, with a plastic bag over his head, just as they had last seen him via their remote link-up.

But of the Minx, or of anyone else for that matter, there was no sign whatsoever. And apart from the sound of Kurdell, who was still muttering curses about what he would do to Puckle, the place was eerily silent.

Not only silent, but still. Deathly still, Toby realised. With a sudden terrible premonition, he strode over to Melvin and bent over his slumped frame.

One pace behind him, Kurdell followed. 'I'll murder him,' he said again. 'I'll throttle the life out of the bastard.'

With a feeling of intense nausea, Toby reached for Puckle's pulse. Then, without looking up, in a voice that sounded even to his own ears as if it were floating high above him, he said sadly, 'You're too late. ' He pointed to the clothes peg now attached, through the plastic bag, to Melvin's nose, which had blocked his only air supply and caused him to asphyxiate. 'The job's already been done.'

Chapter Thirty Nine

———◇◆◇———

In the pandemonium outside the Butchers building, as press and police once again converged there, nobody even noticed the inconspicuously dressed figure that slipped quietly out through the rear fire escape, and from there along an alley towards the public call box at the end of Leadenhall Street.

'It's me.'

'I know. I've been waiting. Well?'

'Mission accomplished.'

'He's dead?'

'As a doornail.'

'And the computer?'

'Wiped.'

'Any problems?'

'Nothing I couldn't handle. There was a camera on top of the computer. I spotted it as soon as I went in. Don't think it was switched on. But I covered it over before I started, just in case.'

'Good. How about the clothes peg?'

'Saved all the mess of last time. A stroke of genius.'

'Thank you.'

'And now?'

'I told you, now we're home and dry. I'm sure of it. You'd better get back. I'll talk to you later, when the coast is clear.'

Thankful it was all over, Melvin Puckle's murderer replaced the receiver. The last few weeks had been an interesting experience, and a challenging one, but they had also been quite exhausting. Playing so many different roles certainly took it out of you.

That of the Minx had been the most demanding, of course, but the others hadn't been easy either: the Batlover from west London, Jasmine from St John's Wood, Rabia the French student, Medea, Gus the Australian. Each had to be given their own individual characteristics, and keeping so many details in your head at once was no joke: which wig belonged to which character, who wore what perfume, who lived in which residence. Getting any single detail wrong could have ruined the whole scheme, and keeping track of all the preferred sexual positions and physical characteristics had been a nightmare in itself.

It would be a huge relief to get back to being normal, the Minx reflected.

Chapter Forty

The press had yet another field day.

'BUTCHERS JINX STRIKES AGAIN', yelled the *Pop* the next day.

The jinx on Butchers, the troubled merchant bank, continued yesterday when a second of its employees took his own life, this time in a bizarre mixture of bondage, auto-eroticism, exhibitionism and citrus abuse which he broadcast live on the Internet.

This follows closely on the suicide of Roy Falloni, the dealer who mistakenly believed he had chalked up major losses on the futures markets. However, the police do not believe the two incidents are linked and say there is no question of foul play in either case. Inspector Ffelcher of Scotland Yard yesterday stated categorically: 'There are twenty million witnesses to the fact that Melvin Puckle was engaged in this act on his own. Although there will naturally be an inquest, the police do not believe anyone else was involved.'

Following the incident, Butchers' managing director Greg Kurdell had to be taken into protective custody for the second time in as many weeks, and has resigned from the Butchers board pending psychiatric investigation. Veteran TV presenter and Puritas Council member Britannia Draycott was also said to be suffering from shock and has declared her intention of retiring from work to take holy orders.

Sources in the City say that the new crisis is bound to cast further doubt on the future independence of Butchers Bank, which has been fighting off a takeover attempt by its own former employee, Polish financier Ivor Zlennek. The Puritas Council, Butchers' current owner, is due to meet in emergency session today to discuss its position. Last night, Bank chairman Sir Lomond Butcher, who is also filling in as CEO pro tem, was not available for comment, although he is said by friends to be distraught.

In this surmise, the *Pop* was unusually – and in all likelihood quite inadvertently – one hundred per cent accurate. Lomond Butcher was indeed distraught, and he wasn't the only one. Lord Sloach had flown into an uncontrollable rage after the Council meeting, and the following morning he exploded into Lomond Butcher's office, holding a clutch of newspapers and still bristling with anger.

'We're a laughing stock,' he screamed. '*I* am a laughing stock, and I won't stand for it. If this is how your employees comport themselves, then the sooner the Council sells out to someone who can impose a bit of discipline, the better.'

'But you can't sell out,' Butcher was almost pleading. 'You just can't.' In his heart, though, he knew the war was now lost. It was just a question of who they sued for peace with.

'We can and we will,' said Sloach implacably. 'And, after last night, I think you'll find the rest of the Council – or what's left of it – backs me to the hilt.'

Lomond Butcher paced up and down his office and tried to think. 'Very well,' he at last said wretchedly. 'I accept the bank will be sold. But I won't let it go to Zlennek. Give me a few days to find a more appropriate buyer – someone who'll guarantee to keep the company together. At least grant me that.'

Eventually Sloach relented. 'It's now Thursday,' he said. 'I'll recommend to the Council you should have till tomorrow night to come up with an alternative offer. If you don't have a signed agreement on my desk by then, I shall use all the powers at my disposal to have Mr Zlennek's entirely reasonable proposal accepted. And I think you'll find my powers can be quite considerable.' And with that barely veiled threat he marched pompously from the office.

A look of determination set firmly on Lomond Butcher's face. One way or another he would find a way of preventing Zlennek from taking his bank, if it was the last thing he did. His contacts included some of the wealthiest people in the country. Surely he would be able to attract an investor. He brightened. He would start with the Bank of England again. Now that there was no question of futures losses, surely they wouldn't let one of the country's oldest merchant banks fall to this Polish upstart.

The governor, however, had apparently gone on holiday again. 'Surely not?' said Butcher. 'He's only just come back. When did he leave this time?

'About twenty minutes ago,' said the governor's secretary. 'You know, it was a last minute bargain from one of those bucket shops.'

'Well, what about the deputy governor then?'

'I'm afraid he's in his office in an important meeting and we have strict instructions not to disturb him till it's over.'

'And how long is it scheduled to last?'

The secretary consulted her diary. 'Nine and a half weeks,' she reported.

Butcher drew a similar blank from every other prospect he could think of. Yesterday's events, coming on top of the others, had sent them all to ground.

He had just put down the telephone for the umpteenth time and was burying his head in his hands despairingly when the intercom on his desk buzzed. 'I've been holding a call for you for ages,' said his secretary. 'It's a Mr Nick Tallopia from New York. He says he's ringing on behalf of Mr Hampton Bradley and he's got a proposition to discuss that you may find of interest.'

★   ★   ★

The police's view that there was no other person involved in Melvin Puckle's death was not shared by at least one member of Butchers' staff. Haunted by that last sight of Melvin's body, Toby Slaker spent the twenty-four hours following his death in the horns of a moral dilemma of almost Shakespearean proportions.

He had the gravest suspicions about what had happened to Puckle. There had to be more to it than met the eye, and if so, then he was in no doubt that he himself held the key.

First of all, there was the hood that Melvin had been wearing. Surely that was not a mere coincidence? People did not go around stripping off and behooding themselves as a matter of course, and particularly not in the august surroundings of Butchers Bank. Admittedly the parallels with his own experiences with the Minx were not exact. For one thing, there were the ropes and the grapefruit. There had never been any question of bondage, or, for that matter, groceries, in his encounters. More to the point, the laundry element was entirely new.

This last item was something that particularly obsessed Toby. How had the clothes peg got on to Melvin's nose? At no time during the events which he – along with so much of the rest of the world – had witnessed on the Internet had he seen Melvin wielding it. Yet, when Toby had asked the police about this as they interviewed him and the others after Melvin's death, they had been certain that Melvin must have attached it himself as the final stage of his bizarre on-line suicide. There could be no other explanation. According to Inspector Ffelcher, if the peg had not been in evidence during the actual broadcast, then Melvin must have added it after the video relay had ceased and before Toby and Kurdell completed their climb up to the top floor to discover his dead body. This had taken fully five minutes – ample time for him to have asphyxiated himself.

And the inspector's case was clinched by the discovery that Melvin himself had bought a packet of clothes pegs, along with the other items, on a shopping expedition in the City only hours before his death. The police had not only found the receipts in his trouser pocket, but also a list he had written out in his own hand which seemed to be some kind of bizarre recipe for the strange sex act he'd indulged in. As a matter of routine, they would check whether the person who had made the purchases answered to Melvin's description, but if so, they would stick to their belief that this was an open-and-shut case.

But of course, Toby reflected, they didn't know what he knew. He was convinced that, somewhere along the line, the Minx had been involved. But how? And why should she have wanted to do Puckle any harm? There was no rhyme or reason to it. After all, Toby himself had been with her twice and she had never displayed any tendency towards violence. On the contrary, she had given him the best time of his life.

Then there was the other aspect to the case: given what Toby knew, could this death in any way be linked to that of Falloni? Surely not. Falloni had so self-evidently taken his own life, and there was taped evidence to prove it. None of it made any sense.

All these questions swirled around in Toby's mind long after the Council meeting. Following his police interview, it had been after midnight before he got home. Restlessly, he paced around the living room. Simona had left for New York and yet another business meeting with Winegloss. But that was just as well. He could never have confided in her anyway, the way things were. And no doubt, just as soon as news of this further catastrophe reached her, she would be on the phone from her hotel in the morning trying to suppress her glee, damn her.

After a sleepless and lonely night, Toby returned to the office early the next day more troubled than ever. There the atmosphere was sombre, with groups of staff clustering sadly around the coffee machine, commiserating with one another in hushed tones about the death of yet another colleague. Later in the day, Toby decided, he would gather everyone together and give them a pep talk. But in the meantime he tried to ignore them as he continued to work through his own dilemma.

What he should have done, he realised, was to volunteer everything he knew to the police. Yet during his interview, while he had certainly told them the truth and nothing but the truth, he had not told them the whole truth.

Was it too late, even now, to come clean? He could go back to the inspector and relate the whole story of the Hoodwink Encounters site and the Minx and make them reopen the enquiry. But the very idea of confiding his recent activities to Inspector Ffelcher made beads of cold sweat break out on his forehead. He could just picture the man's reaction of incredulity and disgust – with a bit of schoolboy ribaldry thrown in to boot. 'You did what?' he'd ask with a quiet little smirk at his colleague. 'Can you make a note of the bit about the earplugs, Sergeant Dorf?'

And then, of course, the police were notorious leakers, particularly when there was such a juicy story going begging. The tabloid press would pay a fortune for something as salacious as this, and all the more since it involved someone at Butchers Bank, their current favourite target. Given half a chance, the papers would go just as much to town on Toby Slaker and the tale of the Hoodwink Encounters site as they had on Falloni. Visions of his house being besieged by hundreds of paparazzi filled Toby's brain and gave him palpitations.

Finally, it would be his ultimate humiliation with Simona. The fact that he'd been unfaithful in such an awful way would be bad enough, but much worse would be the social ignominy it would bring on her. She would never, ever, forgive him for that.

No, he concluded, whatever he did, going to the police must be the very last resort. Suddenly a thought occurred to him, and he grasped at it like a drowning man at the proverbial straw. The hood certainly pointed to the Hoodwink site being implicated in what had happened. But who was to say that it was the Minx, and not one of the other women there, that Melvin had come across? Someone who particularly catered to grapefruit fetishists, perhaps? And in that case could the whole thing not have just been some tragic accident after all? It would have been typical of Melvin to have got the instructions all wrong with disastrous consequences. And if so, why should Toby expose himself to the ridicule and humiliation for no reason?

Eagerly, Toby developed this theory further. If he was right, then the Minx would know as little about what had happened as he did and would be equally shocked by the way events had unfolded. But he had to be sure. There was only one thing for it. Before taking any other action, he had to get back in touch with her to find out what she knew.

Toby made sure that the coast was clear. Felicia was busy typing and the rest of his department – or what now remained of it – was reluctantly going about its business. He paged the Hoodwink Encounters site. But when the screen scrolled up, although it was teeming with all the usual people, Toby was disappointed to find no sign of his erstwhile lover.

He chanced across Gus, the Australian.

'You seen the Minx around?' he asked.

'Naw, didn't you hear?' replied Gus. 'She's taking a break. Seems one of her mates had some kind of a bad experience with a punter and now she thinks it's all getting too dangerous.'

Toby could certainly agree with that. And the words gave him a glimmer of hope that his theory about her being innocent might be right. But he had to talk to her himself to confirm it. 'Don't you know where I can reach her?' he typed.

'She'll be around again some time,' said Gus. ' But listen, mate, take my advice, don't go flogging a dead horse. There's plenty more out there, believe me.'

Toby didn't try to explain. For his own question had suddenly sparked off a realisation in his mind, and he was astonished that he had been so dim. Blinded by the magic of Internet communication, he'd totally forgotten one obvious fact: he knew where the Minx lived! He still had her address on that scrap of paper from when he'd first visited her. And now that it was a matter of life and death, any question of her anonymity was a nonsense. He would confront her face-to-face, and find out once and for all if she'd been involved in Puckle's death.

That was it. As soon as he could, he would go back to the apartment block in Swiss Cottage, ring the bell to flat number 56 Northpark Mansions and talk to her. And if she did not have a satisfactory explanation, he would bite the bullet and go to Inspector Ffelcher with his whole story.

Once set on this course of action, he felt better and turned back to his own work. There was much to catch up on, and another flood of client defections to cope with. But before he could get stuck into it, he was interrupted by Felicia.

'What is it?' he asked irritably.

'There's a Mr Cloud arrived in Personnel,' she told him. 'Apparently he claims he's starting work here today and the Personnel Department don't know anything about it. They said would you kindly let them know when you're recruiting someone in future.'

Oh, Lord, that was all he needed right now. He had completely forgotten about Cloud. Admittedly, his department was now woefully understaffed after its recent losses, but what he wanted were people with experience, and the Irishman had none.

Still, Toby had committed himself to giving him a job and he would stick to his word. Besides, it wouldn't do any harm to staff morale to see that new people were still willing to be recruited. He would put him at Puckle's desk and find him something to get on with.

'Tell them to send him up,' he said.

Chapter Forty One

In his office suite near the top of the World Trade Centre, high above New York's financial district, Nick Tallopia, the American Chief Executive Officer of Hampton Bradley's Brahmin Corporation, studied the report on Butchers Bank with his customary meticulousness. The lawyers and accountants had been busy. Much work had already been done and he was starting to build up a clearer picture of the bank's financial situation.

And he liked what he saw. It seemed like an excellent buy, he reflected, and would be a good fit with Brahmin's other operations. Trust Bradley to have spotted it. They'd been on the lookout for an English merchant bank for some time and this one fitted the bill pretty well perfectly. Moreover, because of this so-called 'jinx', they'd be getting in at an excellent price, and – most importantly of all – with the full support of the existing management. Nick didn't hold with any of this nonsense about jinxes in any case. If the bank was as well run as it seemed to be, then a few months of stability would soon put it on the road to recovery, and Brahmin Corporation would have another winner to add to its stable of good solid companies.

It would all have to be rushed through very quickly, but they were used to that. They'd picked up many a bargain through their ability to make quick decisions and just get on with it. And Nick was relieved that the deal looked do-able. The last thing he wanted was to go back to Bradley and say he wasn't in favour, as the old man had come up with this one by himself and seemed pretty keen on it. Of course, that was because of Zlennek, Nick reflected. This legal battle between them was turning into a real marathon, and it was difficult to say who hated the other more. Bradley would love to beat the hell out of Zlennek on this. Personally, Nick had no time for these sort of feuds; they were futile and got in the way of good business, but, in the present case, if one of the old man's grudges inadvertently led to the right decision being taken, then he was prepared to go along with it.

He'd always thought of Hampton Bradley as 'the old man', although in truth, at sixty, Bradley was only ten years older than Nick Tallopia himself. But the fact that he was permanently confined to a wheelchair always made him seem older than his years.

The accident that had immobilised him had been a blessing in disguise, Nick often thought to himself rather guiltily. Thank God the man was stuck up there on the estate in Maine, otherwise he'd be in the damned office all the time interfering in person, instead of just doing it by e-mail. Anyway, if it hadn't been for that helicopter crash, Bradley would probably never have set up the Brahmin Corporation in the first place. He would have just carried on frittering away all those millions he'd inherited, instead of investing them, and Nick Tallopia and the group's five thousand other employees would have had no jobs.

At least the old man's mind was still razor sharp. With nothing to do all day, he sat up there in his darkened room reading the research and spotting investment opportunities like there was no tomorrow – and constantly e-mailing Nick with them. As for Butchers, well, it was a first-class opportunity, and Nick Tallopia intended to go for it.

He had to get over to London and take a quick look for himself before signing the contract. He would keep the old man informed from there. That should keep him happy. Without the ability to get around himself, Bradley liked it when his CEO sent him messages from his travels.

Tallopia buzzed his secretary. 'I need to get over to London tomorrow for the day,' he said. 'See if you can book me there and back on Concorde. And keep it under wraps for now. The press will be falling over themselves to get on to this one.'

Chapter Forty Two

It was Thursday evening. After a long hard day at the studios, Candida Blitz was kicking her heels in Mattison Pick's suite at the Grand Britannic Hotel. He had promised to be back by seven to take her to dinner but he had just rung up to say there was some problem at the theatre. The Chieftain tank from whose turret Mrs Thatcher was to protrude, scarf waving, as she was transported across the stage in the 'Rejoice' number at the end of the first half, had had an accident en route from Greenham Common, and he was trying to fix a replacement.

Such hitches, Candida was beginning to discover, were part and parcel of Mattison Pick's life in advance of an opening, and they did not put him in good temper. He'd been rather short with her on the phone, and even her lapse into baby talk, so far a sure-fire way of disarming him, had failed to have any effect.

Idly, Candida spooned some of the caviar from room service on to a piece of melba toast and reflected on life. She had only been living with Matty a few days but already the novelty was beginning to wear off. When he was not at the theatre, he spent most of his time in his study in the hotel suite, making transatlantic calls to his American bankers and lawyers as he tried to disentangle his assets from the acquisitive clutches of Peaches. As a result, their evenings out had been curtailed repeatedly although the nights were still wonderfully romantic. For a man of his age he had extraordinary stamina, particularly after the exertions and frustrations of the day.

Once the musical had opened, things would be different, she assured herself. First, she would talk him into moving out of this fusty old hotel. She would sell the house in Hampstead and perhaps they would buy a town house together, and a little place in the country for weekends of romance. In the meantime, though, Candida could not suppress a twinge of nostalgia for Will Cloud, who, although infuriating, had never been ratty and had at least been around the house most of the time.

Almost as if on cue, there was a knock at the hotel room door. When she answered, she was taken aback to find Will himself on the threshold. Her heart, temporarily off message, leaped. But she quickly corrected it, and removed the expression of pleasure which had briefly overtaken her face. She hoped he hadn't noticed. 'Yes?' she said briskly. 'What can I do for you?'

Will stood in the corridor looking uncharacteristically hesitant and wearing a moderately smart, if slightly ill-fitting, suit that Candida had never seen him in before. He twisted his fingers together. 'Can't I come in?' he asked.

'Matty is due back any second,' Candida lied. 'We're dining with Vanessa Driftwood.'

'Please.'

'Well, all right, but just for a moment.'

Will ambled into the room and, returning to his more normal mode of unabashed ease, loosened his tie and collapsed into one of the comfortable sofas. His eyes darted around curiously. 'Now, listen,' he began. 'I want to tell you about being with Ros the other night. See, like I said before, it was all to do with getting a job and today I—'

But Candida held up her hand with the utmost indifference. 'I told you. There's no need to explain. We're both adults.'

'But I got the job,' said Will in triumph. 'I started today. I'm a City whiz-kid with Butchers Bank.' He got up and indicated his suit, twirling around to show it off to best advantage. Then he looked expectantly at Candida. 'That's what I came to tell you . . .'

If he was hoping for her rapturous approval, he was to be disappointed. 'Your professional career,' said Candida grandly, 'is of no interest to me now. I wish you great success in it, and as much happiness with your . . . your flooz . . . I mean, your young lady, as I shall no doubt have with Matty.'

Will threw her a reproachful look. 'Candida, listen to me—' he began. Then he broke off. Something across the room had caught his eye. Going over to the table by the window, he gazed admiringly at the blue vase in its glass case. 'Is that not beautiful?' he said. 'I thought all the Mings were destroyed.'

'Never mind about the vase,' said Candida heatedly. 'If that's all you think about when we're . . .' She stopped, aware that her mask of coolness had temporarily slipped, and tried to retrieve the situation. 'Yes,' she agreed sweetly. 'It is a rather special example from the Hung-chich dynasty.' She hoped she'd got that right.

'Is it now?' Will's expression was thoughtful as he peered at it more closely. 'It looks just like all the ones that got dropped on the *Hoodwink Show*. Can't be many around now.'

'It's the only one poor Matty was left with after that dreadful woman smashed them all,' said Candida. She threw back her shoulders. 'Anyway, forget about that. He'll be here soon. And I think we've concluded our business together, don't you?' She waved towards the door. 'Now, if you don't mind . . .'

Will regarded her earnestly. 'Come back home,' he said. 'Zoë misses you.'

'Well, if that's all you can say,' replied Candida crossly.

'I mean, I miss you.'

'No,' insisted Candida with a conviction she did not feel. 'I'm going to make a new life with Matty.'

'But what about my job?' asked Will plaintively. 'I got it specially.'

Candida crossed her arms. 'It'll do you no harm at all. I'm intending to sell the house in Hampstead, so you'll need to get somewhere of your own. And you were hardly likely to make enough from your stupid detective business for that. It's all worked out perfectly.'

'But . . .'

'You can stay there as long as you like,' she went on

munificently. 'Just let me know when you've found new accommodation. In the meantime, you can always reach me here.'

And, raising her hand again to pre-empt any further protest from Will, she held the door open for him to leave.

She was still practising being cool and distant when Pick got in several hours later. She immediately altered her expression and skipped over to him. 'Matty,' she said, 'poor Will was here.'

'Oh, yeah?' said Pick. He poured himself a bourbon and scratched his nose irritably.

'Yes, he wanted me to go back. But I told him about our plans together.'

'Oh, yeah?' said Pick again. He glanced anxiously at a fax that was just coming through on the machine in the corner.

'Please don't say "oh, yeah" like that. This is very important to me,' said Candida in a small voice.

'Oh, yeah?' said Pick absently. 'Yeah, sure, I know, honey. But I just got to see about this tank problem. The whole first-half finale is fucked without it.'

'Language, Matty,' said Candida crossly. But he was too wrapped up in the fax to pay attention. With a sad sigh, she sat down, picked up a magazine and resumed her inroads into the caviar.

Chapter Forty Three

'That all seems satisfactory,' said Nick Tallopia, glancing around the traditional surroundings of Butchers' boardroom approvingly. 'I'm sure Mr Bradley will be more than happy with these arrangements. I've signed on his behalf, so all we now need are the signatures of Sir Lomond Butcher and of Lord Sloach here, as moderator of the Puritas Council, in order to complete the transaction.'

There was a murmur of agreement from the assorted lawyers and accountants arrayed round the table. Lord Sloach, who was sitting self-importantly at its head took up his pen. 'And when will the funds be transferred to the Puritas Foundation?' he asked eagerly.

'On Tuesday of next week,' said Mr Simpkins from Barrell and Lockstock, the Brahmin Corporation's UK solicitors. 'Provided there are no further . . . ah . . . unfortunate incidents in the meantime, in which case our client reserves the right to void the contract. All other things being equal, however, control of Butchers will effectively pass to Mr Bradley's UK holding company at nine a.m. next Tuesday.'

'Excellent,' said Sloach. And while he didn't actually rub his hands together in glee, the light in his eyes made his feelings obvious. He cleared his throat. As a former politician, he evidently could not let any event pass without some form of address. 'The Puritas Council is most grateful to Mr Bradley,' he intoned. 'And, as you know, the money will be used to good effect. The proceeds will be invested and will guarantee us a more steady income stream than we've ever enjoyed before.' He cast a nasty glance at Lomond Butcher, who was sitting opposite him looking distinctly downcast. 'With it, the Council can now plan its future activities more confidently. First to benefit will be our new campaign against perversion on the Internet,' he added pointedly. 'And since we shall be entrusting the investment management of our funds to the Butchers Private Clients Department – provided, of course, that Mr Slaker produces an adequate return – our relationship with Butchers will continue, albeit as a client rather than as an owner.'

His little speech concluded, he took up his pen and signed the document with a flourish. Then he passed it across to Lomond Butcher, who had so far made little contribution to the proceedings.

Despondently, the chairman of Butchers Bank took in all the faces around the table. Since the moment when he had agreed to seek this deal, events had accelerated rapidly. Now he was at the point of no return that he had been dreading. He had thought about it long and hard and, deep within him, he knew that the decision to sell to Hampton Bradley was the lesser of two evils. None the less it was the saddest moment of his life. There could be no doubt that his signature would spell the end of Butchers Bank as he and generations of Butchers had known it.

His pen poised over the document, he paused one last time. 'Can you just remind me of these guarantees again?' he asked, trying to keep the quiver from his voice.

There was a collective sigh from the lawyers, who had been through this with him half a dozen times already. But, wearily, Mr Simpkins did as requested. 'Mr Bradley states in this letter which forms an annexe to the contract,' he said, 'that he is totally satisfied with the way the company is currently being run; that he has no plans for any staff changes – other than your own resignation as chairman to be replaced by Mr Tallopia here,' he added. 'A new managing director will be appointed shortly and will continue the programme of rationalisation already begun. The letter,' he went on, 'is non-binding, but you will be aware of Mr Bradley's reputation for integrity. He is not a man who goes back on his word. I think that just about sums it up, don't you, gentlemen?' he concluded.

There was a general murmur of agreement. As Lomond Butcher again took up the pen, he felt a lump come to his throat. With an effort, he held it back. He had not blubbed since the day he'd started at Eton and he did not intend to begin now.

With a heavy heart, he slowly signed away his birthright.

Chapter Forty Four

'We're going to have to go in there one more time – or at least I am.'

'What? I thought you said we were home and dry.'

'Well, we're not. It's gone wrong again. But there's no need for you to do any of your play-acting this time. Anyway, I've had enough of you going with other men. I want you all to myself again. I'm going to do this one on my own.'

'I didn't think you were into that sort of thing!'

'Very funny. The point is, there's no question of using the sex angle now. No way he'll buy it after what's happened. So this time it'll need a different approach.'

'What sort of different approach?'

'Plan C.'

'Are you kidding? He'll never fall for it.'

'He'll fall for it all right. If he was going to the police, he'd have been by now.'

'When will you do it?'

'Monday night. I've got to be at this opening but nobody will miss me if I slip out for half an hour.'

'And what will it be? Another clothes peg?'

'No. There's going to be a second bungee jump from the top of the Butchers building. But this time without the bungee.'

'Very clever. Is there anything I can do?'

'I want you to have an alibi that's completely watertight. You mustn't be on your own that night. Best if you're in a large crowd *with lots of people around. But I also need you to be on-line for a while.'*

   'How do you suggest I manage all that?'
   'I've got another little idea . . .'

Chapter Forty Five

The atmosphere of depression that pervaded Butchers Bank was not lost on Will Cloud as he began his second day there. Although no official announcement had been made and nothing was to be released to the press until the deal went through the following Tuesday, it had not taken long for rumours of the impending takeover to circulate around the bank.

His first day had been taken over by a tour of the office, conducted by one of the junior staff, and an introduction to the company's computer system. Toby Slaker had not been much in evidence, having spent most of the day in meetings related to this rumoured deal. Indeed, he hardly appeared in the department at all. But towards evening, he returned looking exhausted. Spotting Will, he produced a sheaf of documents.

'Management agreement with a new French client,' he said. 'Maybe you could have a go at translating it tomorrow?'

Will nodded without much enthusiasm. Translating technical documents was not his favourite occupation and was one of the reasons he'd abandoned his life as an interpreter to concentrate on detective work in the first place. Still, he was determined to make a go of this job.

'Where do you want me to work?' he asked, surveying the department. There were certainly plenty of spare desks, given the recent depletion in staff, not only from the two deaths but also from the spate of resignations that had followed in their wake.

Toby waved him towards one in the corner that sported a sophisticated looking computer with a camera on top. 'You can sit over there,' he said wearily. 'I'll be in and out of meetings again tomorrow. So just push ahead and type this thing up in English on the word processor.'

On Friday morning, therefore, as negotiations went on in the boardroom, Will sat down at his assigned desk and switched on the PC, ready to get stuck in. But it wasn't to be that simple. After waiting for it to start up, all he got from the computer was a blank screen that said 'UNRECOVERABLE DISK ERROR'. Even Will with his rudimentary IT skills knew that this was not right. He checked with Toby's secretary.

'They're always going wrong,' said Felicia curtly. 'But that one's Melvin Puckle's old machine, so it's hardly surprising, what with all the wear he gave it.' With a shrug of exasperation, she reached for the phone. 'I'll get someone from the IT Department to come up and fix it.'

Will watched her as she made the call. She was long-legged and attractive. He couldn't help turning up his Irish accent as he asked conversationally, 'You been here long then?'

'Too long,' snapped Felicia. 'But not much longer. I'll be gone soon – and if you take my advice you will too. Some people say the whole bank is jinxed, but to my mind it's just this department.'

'Is that right?' said Will encouragingly.

Felicia broke off briefly from her typing. 'Where you're sitting,' she said in a confidential tone, 'that's where Melvin Puckle sat. And you see over there.' She pointed to a far corner. 'That was where Roy Falloni's office was.'

'The other fella who topped himself?' said Will with interest.

Felicia nodded. 'Dead,' she said, almost with relish. 'Both dead. So that's why I wouldn't hang around here if I were you. Now,' she added, 'I've got job applications to write, if you don't mind.'

Will glanced at her screen. 'Typing skills – fifty worms per minute,' it said. But the look on her face discouraged him from pointing out the error, and he moved disconsolately back to his own desk.

A man from the Computer Department had arrived and was staring at the machine. 'Hard disk,' he said, scratching his forehead. 'Must have been something wrong with this batch. Never known so many of them go wrong in one department. Even the portables.' He looked at Will. 'You're new anyway, aren't you?' Will nodded. 'Good,' the man went on. 'Won't need to try and recover the data on it then. Not that there would be much chance of that. Looks like it's all gone. I'll take it away and put you in a new hard disk so you'll be up and running in an hour or so.'

As he waited, Will wandered round the deserted office area. Sadly he went into the glass box that Felicia had said belonged to Falloni. Some papers had been boxed but many lay on the floor, presumably where Falloni had left them. Reflecting on the nature of life and death, Will sat down heavily on Falloni's revolving chair and was immediately brought back to more prosaic matters as the mechanism broke and he was tipped backwards on to the floor.

He lay there for a moment, looking around. He had a different view of the room from down here. Under a table in the corner he could see a strange harness-like object that he couldn't identify. And next to it sat a row of cassettes and a Walkman in a leather pouch. Something sticking out of that pouch caught Will's eye. It looked like a folded sheet of paper.

Curiously, Will slid over and slipped it out from the side of the Walkman. It had obviously become lodged there by accident and he wondered if it might be important. He glanced at the handwritten words. They seemed to be some form of poem. He sat back down on the chair – this time more carefully – and read it through.

The Butchers' Ball

It's a Butchers' Ball,
In that Futures Hall,
When they're out for your blood,
And your back's to the wall.

And they smell your fear,
For your nerves are shot
Since a billion was here
And now it's not.

And that loss isn't all
That you'll never unwind,
There's another shortfall—
In the balance of your mind.

Where you once shot the lights out
Now all that remains
Is to lower your targets
And shoot out your brains.

There's a gun in your head
And it's crooking its trigger
And it's whispering low
As it stifles a snigger:

'Man, your future's a sell,
And your past is a rout,
And suicide
Is the only way out

'So surrender to Fate
And bugger those butchers
And forever escape
From going back to the Futures.'

With a stab of nausea, Will realised that he must have chanced across poor Roy Falloni's suicide note. He cast his mind back to the newspaper reports of the incident. They had said there was no such note, but the police couldn't have looked very hard for it. Presumably they'd felt that the tape-recording proved, without any need for further evidence, that Falloni had deliberately killed himself while the balance of his mind was disturbed.

And indeed, all this note did was to reinforce that conclusion. The fact that the man had taken the unusual step of putting his suicide message into rhyme was surely the final proof that he'd gone completely off his trolley. Will wondered if he should show it to anyone. But there didn't seem much point now. So he read it through again and put it away in his pocket.

His telephone was ringing when he got back to his own desk. To his surprise, it was Ros Flato.

'I thought I might track you down there,' she said. 'Listen, I'd like you to return that favour I did you.'

'Sure,' said Will. 'Anything you like.'

'Someone's given me two tickets for the opening of *The Iron Lady* on Monday night. And I want you to come with me.'

'Me?' asked Will taken aback. 'Why?'

'Because I'm asking you,' she replied tartly. 'I don't want to be on my own that night.'

'Won't Zlennek be there, though?' asked Will, mindful of the last time he'd gone out with her. 'I thought his wife owned that theatre.'

'Never mind about Zlennek,' Ros snapped. 'That's my business.'

'All right, there's no need to bite my head off,' said Will. 'Anyway, I'd be delighted to come.' He loved musicals and this one promised to be the opening of the year.

'Good. I'll meet you in the lobby at ten to seven. Don't be late,' said Ros and rang off.

Stifling his curiosity, Will replaced the receiver and looked up to find the chap from the IT Department had brought back his computer, suitably fitted out with a brand new hard disk.

'Right as rain,' said the man. 'Just flick this switch to boot it up.'

Will picked up his translations and sauntered over to the desk. As instructed, he switched the machine on and waited, peering with fascination into the camera that sat on top. At last the picture flickered and laboriously came to life. But it looked different from the standard start-up screen he'd been shown during his induction the day before. Instead of the usual range of icons and list of options, all he could see was the strange image of a woman with a cartoon-like face. For a moment she just scowled at him with ill-concealed annoyance. Then, from her mouth, there came forth a bubble.

'Who the hell are you?' was what it said.

Chapter Forty Six

Since last heard of just before Melvin Puckle's death, when she was intent on broadcasting her creator's betrayal with another woman to a stunned world, Scarlett, Melvin's virtual girlfriend, had been through the wars.

She had not been around to witness Melvin's final humiliation – nor his demise. For, just as the broadcast was beginning, her camera had gone blank and she was left once more in darkness.

But a much worse affliction was to hit her a few minutes later. Suddenly and without warning, some form of magnetic firestorm swept over the entire computer, rampaging through the hard disk and destroying everything it encountered. Her fellow programs had no chance. As Scarlett stood by helpless, they were erased one by one.

And soon Scarlett too began to succumb. Gradually her memory started to ebb painfully away and she became more and more faint. But she was made of sterner stuff than the others. Her survival instinct, programmed by Melvin into her deepest level of code, sent her struggling in every direction looking for a way out of this, her own equivalent of a blazing Atlanta. And eventually, just as she thought it was too late, she found one in the cable that led out of the back of the computer, linking it to the server. How she managed it she'd never know, but with her last remaining powers she dragged herself down through the wires and finally collapsed, exhausted and traumatised, at the firewall outside the mainframe.

There she might have languished for ever, had it not been for the attentions of the inquisitive e-mail application that resided inside. Notorious for its tendency to fuss around the other programs – or to stick its nose in their business, depending on your viewpoint – it spotted Scarlett outside and immediately took pity on her. Laboriously dragging her inert form inside, it provided her with shelter, and, over the next few days, gave her an unlimited supply of cookies and the opportunity to recharge her lost electrons and recover her depleted code.

Scarlett had stayed there until a friendly indexing agent from one of the Internet search engines had passed by and alerted her that Melvin's PC was on-line again. Back she had rushed, anticipating an emotional reunion with her creator, only to find this complete stranger staring at her.

'Who the hell are you?' she asked. 'And where's Melvin?'

But instead of answering, the stranger simply looked at her as if she were an idiot. 'W-H-O A-R-E Y-O-U?' he typed very slowly, as if she wouldn't understand anything unless spelled out in words of one syllable. 'A-R-E Y-O-U S-O-M-E K-I-N-D O-F V-I-R-T-U-A-L P-E-R-S-O-N?'

For Scarlett, after all she'd been through, it was the last straw.

'I'M NOT VIRTUAL,' she shrieked hysterically. 'I'M AN ORGA-NICALLY CHALLENGED INTELLIGENCE FORM, GODDAMMIT, AND I WANT TO KNOW WHAT YOU'VE DONE WITH MY MELVIN.'

An hour later, Scarlett had learned exactly what had happened to Melvin. And now her programs experienced a new sensation: grief. Huge virtual tears filled her eyes and her speech bubble deflated like a burst balloon. 'How can he be dead?' she demanded. 'Wasn't he backed-up?'

She listened, stunned and uncomprehending, as Will explained that it didn't work that way with human beings. 'When someone's killed himself, then he can never be brought back to life,' Will told her sadly.

'Killed himself?' said Scarlett. 'Uh, uh!' She shook her head decisively. 'Melvin didn't kill himself. Oh, no. He must have been murdered.'

Now it was Will Cloud's turn to be stunned. 'Murdered? Are you sure?'

'Sure, I'm sure,' responded Scarlett angrily. 'He was seeing this woman. He was due to meet her that night.' And, almost in a trance, she told him all she knew about the Hoodwink site and about how, for weeks before, Melvin had been cheating on her with the Minx behind her back.

'And you think it was the Minx who killed Melvin?' asked Will incredulously.

Scarlett looked back at him with scorn in her virtual eyes. They weren't all that bright, these human beings.

'Of course it was,' she said. 'But not her alone. She was just the agent.' Ever since hearing the terrible news, Scarlett's processors had been working furiously in the background and she was now convinced of this. 'There was someone else behind her. Had to be, sure as eggs is eggs.'

'But do you know who?' typed Will.

Suddenly, however, a wave of suspicion swept over Scarlett. Who was this stranger who was occupying Melvin's desk? Where had he come from and how did she know she could trust him?

'That's for me to know and for you to find out,' she replied, staring out at him balefully.

'But if you tell me, maybe I can help bring them to justice,' pleaded Will.

'No,' said Scarlett. 'I don't like human beings any more. All they do is go and die on you. I ain't telling you nothing else.'

And with that she switched to stand-by mode and refused to engage in any further communication with Will Cloud.

Instead she began to brood angrily to herself. She had her own very definite suspicions about who had a motive for killing Melvin: a Certain Person whose e-mails he had been reading; a Certain Person about whose Internet activities he knew too much. If that person had found out that Melvin had chanced upon his secrets, then he would certainly have wanted him dead.

But Melvin wasn't the only one who knew about those secrets. Scarlett had also seen the e-mails. Whatever Melvin knew, Scarlett knew too. And now, she vowed, she would use that knowledge. She would use that knowledge to get back at Melvin's killer in any way she could.

All at once, Scarlett's programs went in to overdrive as she began to work out how to wreak her revenge upon Ivor Zlennek.

Chapter Forty Seven

By the time the weekend came, Toby was exhausted. Since the agreement that Butchers Bank would be taken over by Hampton Bradley, he had been working flat out at the office to the exclusion of all else.

The fact that the funds being realised by the Puritas Foundation were to be invested by Butchers Bank itself meant that he was taking on a new and demanding client. Lord Sloach had insisted that all the formalities be gone through, and so he'd had to put together a proposal and a management agreement at lightning speed. This had taken up all his waking hours for the last two days.

Now, everything had been satisfactorily put to bed on that front, subject to the final execution of the transaction on Tuesday morning. And although Toby felt a profound sadness that the Butcher family would no longer be associated with the firm, he couldn't suppress his satisfaction on one undeniable fact: if the bank was being taken over by Hampton Bradley, then it could never fall into the hands of his arch-rival, Ivor Zlennek and, by extension, of Simona Slaker.

With that worry off his mind, Toby felt less resentful of his wife. After all, it wasn't Simona's fault that she had been put in this position, and now that things had worked out to his satisfaction, he felt it was time to mend bridges with her.

On Friday night he had his chance. Simona had been at a conference in Frankfurt all week and, apart from a hurried call of condolence after Puckle's death, she had not been in touch. But as he reached home after his last marathon stint at the office, he saw that her Jeep was back in the driveway. She must have flown back earlier than expected and driven herself in from Heathrow.

She was already in bed, fast asleep. Toby got in beside her and reached tentatively across. He was not hopeful, but, after all, it was Friday. And, to his surprise, for once he met with a willing, if sleepy, response.

'Hello, lover boy,' she said, rolling over towards him. Toby felt a surge of passion from within that surprised even himself. He wondered if his recent extramarital experiences might have fuelled a new sexual awakening in him.

And so, that night Toby made love to his own wife almost as passionately as in those first early days when she'd been his secretary at Butchers. And it felt right. It felt so right that he wondered, as he finally dropped off to a deep and satisfying sleep, how he could ever have fallen for the cheap thrills on offer at the Hoodwink site.

The next morning he came down to breakfast feeling almost light-headed. Simona was already up, the *Financial Times* spread over the kitchen table in front of her. The story of the Butchers takeover by Hampton Bradley had now reached the press, he noticed as he stooped to kiss her gently on the mouth, and it occupied most of the front page.

'You've seen the news, then?' he asked.

She gave him a cool look. 'I think you'll find I knew about it before you did.'

He didn't want to spoil the new cordiality between them and let it pass. 'No hard feelings?'

Simona shrugged. 'I told you all along that I wouldn't allow work to interfere with us. You're the one who let it, not me.'

Toby thought about that as he poured himself some juice from the fridge. Perhaps there was some justice in what she said, and now was the time to be magnanimous in victory. 'Listen,' he said, sitting down beside her at the table and putting an arm round her shoulder. 'I'm sorry. I just . . . well, you know how I felt. But now it's all settled, let's forget the whole thing, okay?'

She looked back at him quizzically, as if debating whether to tell him something. But then she evidently decided not to. 'Sure,' she agreed. 'Let's forget it . . . now that it's settled.'

'Maybe we can get out tonight and celebrate,' said Toby hopefully.

But she shook her head. 'I didn't have a chance to tell you. I've got to go to New York this afternoon.'

'But you've just come back!'

She shrugged again. 'That was Frankfurt. Anyway, it's on Zlennek's orders. He wants me to be there with Winegloss for a deal that's coming through.' She responded to the unspoken panic on his face. 'There are other banks than Butchers,' she said reproachfully. 'Even though you might not think so.'

'How long will you be gone?'

'Till Tuesday night,' she said lightly. 'We can go out and celebrate then.' A thought occurred to her. 'Hey, I'll miss this theatre thing on Monday night. Can you get rid of the ticket?'

Toby said he'd see if anyone at the office wanted to go with him. Privately, he hoped not. He'd sooner not go himself. Pick had given him the tickets, but it would hardly be noticed if he wasn't there.

The détente between Toby and Simona continued into the afternoon. He offered to drop her back at the airport, so she cancelled the limousine the airline was sending and they drove together to Heathrow in a companionable silence. As she got out, the kiss she gave him was long and lingering, and he could still taste her on his lips as he made his way back along the M4 towards London.

It should have left a warm glow inside him for the rest of the day – but it didn't. For now he had the free time that he'd been dreading. Time to think about a subject he'd been desperately putting off all week: the final visit to confront the Minx at her flat.

Ever since making the decision to do so, he could truthfully tell himself that there had been no earthly opportunity. Work had kept him mercifully occupied. In his few spare moments he'd gone into the Hoodwink website in the hope that she might be there, so avoiding the need to put his plan into effect. But he had never seriously expected to find her and now there were no further excuses.

He steeled himself. He would go to the flat in Swiss Cottage this afternoon and carry out his plan. And, if he did not get a satisfactory explanation, he would then go to the police. Much as he dreaded the ignominy that would entail, not to mention what it would do to Simona, there could be no alternative.

He set out at four. As a precaution, he stopped by the office, deserted as ever on a Saturday, except for some maintenance and IT staff. He slipped into Lomond Butcher's office and picked up a pistol, part of Lomond Butcher's staggeringly comprehensive anti-wildlife arsenal, which to his astonishment still remained on the wall, although now no longer loaded. At least, Toby reckoned, the gun would afford him some comfort if he was confronted, although precisely what he might be confronted with he was not sure.

Then he made the same journey to Swiss Cottage from the City that he had made before in such very different circum-stances. This time, he did not crash any red lights or hoot at any pedestrians. This time, instead of anticipating what awaited him with excitement, he dreaded it.

As before, he left his car in a side street and made his way up to the gate. Then, clutching the gun in his breast pocket, he rang the bell of number 56.

There was no response; no flashing light to indicate that he was being observed on the video entryphone; no crackling voice, hoarse with sexual promise, coming through the speaker to ask him to come on up; there was not even a faint click of the door as the mechanism was released. There was just silence.

After about five minutes, his finger, pressed permanently against the button, began to get sore. Perhaps she was simply out, he thought. Initiating some new 'novice' into the joys of anonymous sex? Or maybe committing another bizarre murder, if that was indeed what she had done. Toby shuddered.

But he'd come all this way and was loath to give up without at least finding out more. At the bottom of the panel, there was a button marked 'Tradesmen'. He tried it and, after a few moments, an irascible man's voice came on the line. 'Yes?'

'Miss . . . ah . . . Miss Minx in Flat 56,' said Toby. 'Parcel to deliver.'

'Never heard of her,' snapped the caretaker.

'Well, isn't there a lady in Flat 56? The depot might have given me the wrong name,' Toby improvised. 'But that's definitely the right number.'

'You'll be after Mrs Lorrimar, then,' said the caretaker.

'Right,' said Toby, pretending to find the name on a list. 'Mrs Lorrimar it is.'

'Yeah, well, if you find her, I'd like to know about it,' the disembodied voice shot back angrily.

'She's not here then?'

'Bloody woman disappeared this morning with a month's rent owing. Put her keys through my letterbox while I was out and did a bunk.'

'No forwarding address then?' asked Toby, half disappointed and half relieved.

'You must be kidding. Hey.' The man had evidently had a thought. 'What've you got there for her anyway? Worth anything, is it? I could take it in lieu of rent.'

'I have to deliver it in person,' Toby replied in a panic. 'I'd get into trouble if—'

'I'm coming down,' said the voice. 'Don't go away.'

But by the time the man had lumbered down the staircase to the door, Toby was back in his car, bound for the relative safety of Notting Hill and no further on in his investigations.

Chapter Forty Eight

It was Saturday morning and, after a long week at Popviz, Candida Blitz was relaxing in the suite at the Grand Britannic, sitting around in her floppy pyjamas taking in the hotel's stunning view over Hyde Park. But the magic was no longer there. Being a celebrity's mistress, she thought morosely, was not all it was cracked up to be.

Pick had practically abandoned her, as he conducted final rehearsals for the opening of *The Iron Lady* on Monday night. There were continuing problems with the animatronics for the Ronald Reagan scene and a full dress rehearsal was due that afternoon. Pick had taken to reappearing briefly every night, and scowling at her before disappearing into his office to get on the phone back to the theatre. Even the sex had dried up. In the course of a short week, they seemed to have experienced an entire relationship in microcosm, advancing through every stage to reach the studied indifference of a long-married couple.

The house telephone interrupted her thoughts.

It was one of the snooty receptionists, sounding slightly nauseous. 'There is a chimpanzee in reception to see you,' she said faintly.

'What?'

'By the name of Zoë, according to the notice round her neck.'

Zoë! Suddenly, Candida felt a surge of homesickness for her dysfunctional family. The fact was that she missed Will Cloud and Zoë, and was beginning to regret ever having left them. 'But who's with her?' she asked. Even Zoë, intelligent as she was – she had once been the most famous animal on television – could not have made the journey from Hampstead to Park Lane on her own.

'She's by herself,' snapped the woman. 'And it is not hotel policy to allow unaccompanied minors into the—'

'She's not a minor,' said Candida. 'She's twenty-two. But I'll be right there.' Without even stopping to put on a dressing gown, she rushed joyfully out of Mattison Pick's penthouse suite towards the lifts.

And Zoë was equally delighted to see her when she arrived downstairs, jumping up and down on the spot and emitting a screech which sent shock waves through the sedate surroundings of the lobby. Ignoring the glares, Candida hugged the animal to her in an emotional reunion, only ceasing when the hotel's general manager approached. 'We're just going upstairs,' trilled Candida, fleeing back to the lifts with the monkey round her neck.

As she got out on the top floor, a dishevelled-looking man with dark bushy eyebrows and a faintly familiar face got in. He had a miniature Johnnie Walker bottle sticking out of his top pocket and looked out of place in this environment. Candida wondered where she had seen him before. There were only two suites on that floor and, with a start of panic, Candida realised that she had left the door to Matty's open in her headlong rush to be reunited with Zoë. The Ming! Even though it was alarmed, Matty had given her strict instructions never to leave the door unlocked.

Fearfully, she dashed into the main room which housed the glass case. To her enormous relief, the vase was there, apparently untampered with.

'Will you look at the glamorous existence you're living here,' said Will Cloud. He was sitting nonchalantly where Candida had been ten minutes before, flicking through the channels on the TV remote control.

Candida looked at him in surprise. 'Hello,' she said, giving him a wistful smile. 'What are you doing here?'

'Sure, Zoë and I were out for a walk in the park and we thought we'd drop by and see you,' he said. 'But I lost her downstairs. So I just came on up.'

'That's nice,' said Candida. After Mattison Pick's obsessiveness, Will's laid-back attitude was almost a relief. 'How's your job?' she asked conversationally. 'Are you enjoying it?'

'A fat lot of good it's doing me. You going off with that man.'

'He's not that man,' said Candida. 'I'm sure you could get to like him if you tried. Look.' A thought had occurred to her. '*The Iron Lady*'s opening on Monday night. Why don't you come along? I'm sure I can get you a ticket. You know how you like that sort of thing.'

'Ah,' said Will. 'Funny you should say that. I'm going already.'

'Oh.' Candida's voice hardened. 'How come?'

'Business,' said Will airily. 'Just business.'

'You're going with that woman, aren't you?' All the compassion had disappeared from Candida's tone.

'Well, you're going with that man,' countered Will. 'I don't see why I shouldn't go with anyone I want.'

'Of course you can,' Candida said distantly. 'I'm sure we can all be very grown-up about it. I was just curious. Anyway, it's probably best. Matty and I will be so busy with the press and what-not that I wouldn't have time to look after you properly. Your friend will no doubt do a *much* better job.'

They eyeballed each other defiantly until, finally, Candida turned on her heels, dashed into the bedroom and slammed the door.

Will shrugged. 'Time to go home,' he told Zoë. 'We've got what we came for – for now.'

Chapter Forty Nine

On Monday morning Lomond Butcher made a last tour of the Butchers' building in advance of the final handover of ownership to Hampton Bradley's Brahmin Corporation the following day.

He lingered in the Private Clients Department for fully thirty minutes, shaking hands with the long-serving staff there. And Toby Slaker could hardly contain his emotion when he departed down the spiral staircase for the last time.

'I never thought this day would come,' he said to Will Cloud sadly, as he stopped by with some further translation work. 'It's the end of an era.'

But life, he knew, had to go on. With an effort, he pulled himself together and put the documents down on Will's desk. 'This relates to the transfer of assets for Mattison Pick's French productions,' he said. 'Strictly confidential. Talking of which, I've got a spare ticket for the opening of *The Iron Lady* tonight. My wife was meant to come with me, but she's had to go abroad. Can I interest you in it?'

But Will, it transpired, was already fixed up with tickets. 'I'm going with Ros Flato,' he said, looking rather rueful.

'Not Candida?' Toby asked.

'Candida has transferred her affections elsewhere,' explained Will with quiet dignity.

Toby was surprised. 'I'm sorry,' he said. 'I hope it was nothing to do with our party. If I'd known Candida was going to be there, I'd never have got you involved in that bet.'

Will shrugged philosophically. 'It was going to happen anyway,' he said. 'Now, I'm meeting Ros at the theatre. Maybe we can share a taxi over there, if you're going?'

'Certainly,' Toby agreed, as he went off to his office. 'I'll see if I can find someone else for this spare ticket and I'll let you know when we're leaving.'

He asked Felicia if she wanted to go, but it appeared that she and Garlow already had tickets. Everyone, it seemed, would be at this show tonight. Toby decided he would just have to give the ticket away when he reached the theatre.

It was not until the afternoon that he began grappling with the problem of the Minx again. He had sworn that he would go to the police if his visit to her house yielded nothing and it had. But still Toby dreaded taking such a course of action. He searched for an excuse to put it off just a little longer, and readily found one in the shape of the Bradley sale.

The deal was conditional on there being no upsets before tomorrow morning. Any hint of further scandal before that could scupper the whole thing. Surely it could do no harm to wait a few more hours? Definitely, he rationalised to himself. What he would do today was to go on line one last time, just to see if she was there by any chance, although he hardly thought that was likely.

He was right. She was nowhere to be found. But as Toby was about to leave, there was a ping on his computer and a communication came through from Gus, the Australian.

'G'day, Novice,' he said. 'Been looking for you.'

'Oh?' said Toby. 'Why?'

'The Minx is back and she wanted me to give you a message. Said to tell you she was leaving the country. And she wanted you to know she had nothing to do with what happened, if that makes any sense. She said she'd explain everything if she could just talk to you for five minutes.'

Toby's heart leaped. 'Where is she?' he asked eagerly. 'Can I reach her now?'

'No,' said Gus. 'But she's going to be on-line at nine thirty tonight, if you want to talk to her.'

Nine thirty tonight, thought Toby. He *had* to meet her. If she genuinely had a convincing explanation for Puckle's death, then he would have every reason not to go to the police after all. He could feel a sense of relief oozing over him.

'I'll be there,' he said decisively. He would miss the Pick opening, but that didn't bother him. This was more important and he didn't much like musicals anyway.

He spent the afternoon nervously anticipating the conversation with the Minx, rehearsing the questions he would ask her. He'd hardly noticed the time pass when Will put his head around the office door. 'You know the show starts early,' he said. 'It's press night tonight and they have to get their copy in. So we ought to be making a move.'

'Damn,' said Toby apologetically. 'I should have let you know earlier. I'm not going to be able to make it after all. Could you see if you can give away my two tickets when you get there?'

'You'll be missing yourself,' said Will regarding him curiously. In fact, now that Toby came to think of it, Will had been regarding him curiously all day. 'Are you sure I can't change your mind, now?'

'I'm sure,' snapped Toby, and immediately regretted his abrupt tone. 'Something's come up,' he explained weakly. 'Something personal that I've got to deal with.'

But as he said the words, a sudden feeling of nausea stole over him. He'd heard those same words from Roy Falloni on the night of his death. It must have shown on his face, for Will asked him if he felt all right.

'It's nothing,' said Toby. 'Just a bit of *déjà vu*.' He lightened his tone. 'Off you go and enjoy the show. And I look forward to hearing all about it tomorrow morning.'

Chapter Fifty

There was a real buzz at the Royal London Theatre as people began arriving for the première of *The Iron Lady*. This was the most anticipated event of the season, and, despite a dismally wet night, hundreds of onlookers had gathered outside in the street to watch the arrival of the invited audience.

And the line-up of luminaries was indeed spectacular: a rare meeting of the worlds of show business and politics, banking and the media. In the theatre's newly refurbished lobby, the show's composer, Mattison Pick, accompanied by his girlfriend Candida Blitz, chatted to its backers, the impresarios Caroline and Milton Court. Nearby, the former Chancellor of the Exchequer, Matthew Potts, hobnobbed with the former Home Secretary, Lord Sloach of Macclesfield, who had agreed to attend on the strict understanding that the show would contain no nudity. Not far away from them was the owner of the Royal London itself, Peggy Zlennek with her financier husband Ivor, who, as everybody knew, had bought the theatre for her as a fiftieth birthday present. Even Lomond Butcher, the soon to be ex-chairman of Butchers Bank, had turned up with his wife in an effort to cheer himself up on the eve of his final dethronement.

The one person who had not yet arrived was the guest of honour, the Prime Minister, the Rt Hon. Hugh Driftwood, MP. He had agreed to attend *The Iron Lady* première in tribute to the illustrious predecessor who was its subject, and Inspector

Ffelcher of Scotland Yard, whose responsibilities extended to occasional secondments to the Prime Ministerial Protection Squad, was just completing a final security check.

Sheltering in the shadow of Ivor's substantial frame, Peggy Zlennek watched the mêlée with a certain nervousness. She so hoped that people would like the theatre's new look. For, as well as being a première, tonight marked the culmination of months of work in another way as well. Ever since Ivor had bought her the Royal London Theatre, an extensive refurbishment had been under way and this evening it was being shown off for the first time.

But people's reactions to the make-over were not her only reason for nerves. There was also the speech she was due to deliver during the interval. Right from the beginning, she had been determined that the theatre should be re-christened to mark its fresh beginning and this evening, after the show's first half, Peggy was due to unveil the plaque with its new name. On the instructions of the PR company employed to orchestrate the relaunch, it had been kept a closely guarded secret, with even the theatre staff being kept in the dark. Reluctantly Peggy had been persuaded to say a few words during the unveiling. But, unlike her husband, she was not used to public speaking and was dreading it.

'You'll be fine,' Ivor had told her repeatedly. 'Just keep it short and sweet.' In reality, he seemed almost as edgy as her, constantly consulting his watch. She put it down to his preoccupation with Butchers. He'd just come from yet another crisis meeting where his failed bid had been discussed.

'It's just a bank,' she said as she adjusted her long evening gown in the front-of-house manager's office. 'There'll be others.'

'By now,' he replied testily, 'you should know. Do I ever give up on anything? No, I do not,' he answered himself. 'I sure do not.'

'You're right,' she said, giving him a peck on the cheek. Since they'd had their heart-to-heart while returning from the Slakers' party, things had been much better between them. 'And neither do I!' she added, helping him do up his bow tie with a proprietorial grin.

If the Zlenneks were nervous in advance of the opening, then Mattison Pick was practically biting the carpets. Candida had been warned that this was perfectly normal on a first night. However, his mood had been worsened by the news that Peaches was throwing a party in California in an attempt to upstage him on his big day. Under the circumstances, despite her doubts about their future together, Candida felt duty bound to give him all her support.

Even as she stood with him in the receiving line waiting for the Prime Minister to arrive, she could see that his mind was elsewhere. 'I had some final notes I forgot to give the cast,' he said. 'I should be backstage instead of screwing around out here waiting to talk to some no-account politician.'

Candida doubted the actors would feel the same way, but had more sense than to say so. Basking in the reflected glory of being with the man of the moment, she glanced around the lobby. To her irritation she noticed Will Cloud standing further down towards the front entrance with that woman, as Candida thought of her. She was waving one of those pretentious electronic organisers in the air as they passed the time of day with Inspector Ffelcher, an old sparring partner of Will's from the past. But the inspector broke off as a message came through on the radio. It looked like the PM must be about to arrive. Will resumed his favourite pastime of celebrity-spotting, shamelessly pointing people out to Ros, who, Candida was pleased to see, was staring at her electronic gizmo and looking rather embarrassed by his gaucheness. As Will spotted Candida, he smiled over at her but she studiously avoided his eye.

There was a flurry outside. The PM was here. Despite his disparaging remarks, Mattison Pick stood to attention, and Candida took his arm. She knew the Prime Minister vaguely from years ago, and now she would be second in the line-up to meet him. Wouldn't that show Will a thing or two about celebrities!

She'd forgotten, though, that it was Will who had introduced her to the PM in the first place, having attended university with him. So, when the Premier finally made his way into the theatre, instead of sweeping past the crowds at the entrance and coming straight to his hosts, he spotted Will and stopped to talk. He also seemed to remember Ros. He chatted to her and pointed jokingly at her voluptuous mouth in a gesture that Candida was not sure she understood. However, when he finally did reach the official line-up, Candida was delighted that he recognised her as well, and even made a great point of kissing her on both cheeks, cheering her up no end.

At last, the preliminaries were over and it was time for them to go through to the auditorium. Candida could feel the nervous tension emanating from Matty as he stood back to let the Prime Ministerial party go through. As soon as they had, he took her arm and guided her to their seats on an aisle near the front.

The lights dimmed. The première performance of Mattison Pick's *The Iron Lady* was about to begin. There was a hush of anticipation as the orchestra struck up with a brief overture. Then, to a spontaneous round of applause, the curtain rose to reveal the front entrance to Number 10 Downing Street, lovingly recreated down to the last detail of black spiked railings, period Georgian windows and friendly London bobby on guard. On a backlit screen, stage left, the date – 28 November 1990 – flashed up. It was apparent that the Thatcher story was to begin at the end, as Britain's first woman Prime Minister left Downing Street for the last time after losing her party leadership election.

Now, a full-size chauffeur-driven Jaguar trundled on to the stage and parked near the shiny black door. This, Candida knew from Pick's endless reports of rehearsals, was the cue for the opening number, 'A Far Better State'. The applause intensified as Mona da Ponte, wearing a blonde wig and a mauve two-piece suit and looking like Mrs Thatcher to a T, appeared through the Number 10 door and came upstage to the microphones to make her valedictory address from the very spot where she'd cited St Francis of Assisi in her 1979 victory speech.

'Ladies and Gentlemen,' she said, 'we are leaving Downing Street for the last time after eleven and a half wonderful years. And we're very happy that we're leaving the country in *a far better state* than when we arrived.' She paused and drew breath. Evidently, all of a sudden, words alone were not enough to express her emotions and she felt the need to break into song. This she did without further ado, spreading her hands wide in an appeal to the nation:

> *Since we quoted Assisi*
> *There've been many glories*
> *But the pole got too greasy*
> *And so did the Tories.*

> *Three times elected*
> *And how've they repaid me?*
> *My supporters defected*
> *My party betrayed me.*

> *Now a new day's begun*
> *And the key shifts to Major*
> *But when all's said and done*
> *There's one thing I'll wager:*

> *That we're leaving this state*
> *From which we've been hounded*
> *In a far better state*
> *Than when we first found it.*

It was one of Mattison Pick's famous soaring ballads, already a major hit long before opening night. The audience recognised it from the first bar and reacted appreciatively with protracted applause and cheering.

After the fourth verse, Mrs Thatcher was joined by the entire Cabinet, who had conveniently, and with total disregard for historical accuracy, turned up at the doors of Downing Street to wave her off. Historical accuracy had been adhered to in their lines, however, for they chorused her words with a parrot-like devotion:

> *She's leaving this state*
> *From which she's been hounded*
> *In a far better state*
> *Than when she first found it.*

The number reached its climax when Mrs T made towards the car for her final departure. As she got in, a spotlight picked out a single teardrop rolling down her cheek. And at that point, the entire cast froze and the orchestra held on to a single sad note.

Now there was an apparently unintentional grinding noise as the machinery of the revolving stage went into operation. Laboriously the set spun through 180 degrees to reveal, in a *coup de théâtre*, that the reverse of the Downing Street entrance was in fact the front of the grocer's shop belonging to Alderman Roberts, Mrs Thatcher's father.

Through the door, following a lightning backstage costume change by Mona da Ponte, there appeared a youthful Margaret Roberts, now in 1940s dress, leaving her father's shop in Grantham and bound for her first meeting of the Young Conservatives. They were represented by the same actors who had played the Cabinet. They too had changed clothes, in their case into checked sports jackets and loud plus-fours. Beaming innocent vitality, Mrs T was about to begin the great odyssey that would take her all the way to the other side of the set.

As the first half got into its stride, the audience settled back comfortably for the long haul. Candida Blitz felt Mattison Pick relax slightly in his seat next to her, and at length she too began to unwind and enjoy herself.

Sitting in the stalls, further along in the same row as Candida, Will Cloud should have been in his element. As a lover of musical theatre, he could, under normal circumstances, think of no more pleasant way of spending an evening.

None the less he found it difficult to relax. For one thing, he had been seated behind the substantial form of Ivor Zlennek, who was blocking most of his view of the stage. Every time the great man moved, Will had to go in the opposite direction to be able to see, and it was proving tiresome. Moreover, Peggy Zlennek, Ivor's wife, had taken one look at Will's companion and had some kind of fit. There had been a brief but heated exchange between her and her husband, since which she was clearly refusing to talk to him.

But these weren't the main reasons for Will's inattention. No, that lay in something far removed from tonight's show. The fact was that, ever since he'd discovered the strange virtual woman on his computer at Butchers Bank, his mind had been in a total whirl. The story he'd managed to coax out of her had been disjointed, and even now he didn't completely understand it. But there was one thing that was clear: if Scarlett was to be believed, at least one of the deaths at Butchers Bank had not been a suicide.

It all sounded very far-fetched, to say the least. But everything about the events at Butchers had been bizarre and Will's every instinct told him that Scarlett's story contained a grain of authenticity that he ignored at his peril.

If only he'd been able to summon her back to the computer for another consultation, he was sure she could have helped him get to the bottom of this mystery. He'd tried everything, but to no avail. He'd even asked the IT Department if they knew who she was; they'd just looked at him as if he were mad. She seemed to have disappeared off the face of the disk, and all Will was left with was a jumbled mass of facts that made no sense.

Who was this Minx woman? And who was the mysterious man that Scarlett was convinced was behind her? And if Puckle had been murdered, did that mean Falloni had been too? If so, how? And what about his strange suicide letter?

Again and again, Will worked through all the facts in his mind. He was certain that a solution to the puzzle was within his grasp, if only he had that final clue which would unlock it. Desperately he tried to think what that could be, but it was no good.

Finally, he gave up and sat back and, as scenes from Mrs Thatcher's early years unrolled on stage, he let the show wash over him and tried to forget all about Butchers Bank.

'Rejoice' was the name of the number that ended the first half. It was a triumphal march, marking Mrs Thatcher's victory in the Falklands War, and Candida watched in awe as Mona da Ponte arrived on stage, borne aloft from the turret of the Chieftain tank that had given Matty such trouble during rehearsals.

For this scene, Mona da Ponte was wearing full battledress, except for a white silk scarf which blew behind her in the wind. 'Rejoice, rejoice,' she sang, waving a submachine-gun in the air. With all the cast on stage, it was indeed a spectacular finale and as it reached its noisy conclusion, the entire audience got to its feet in a standing ovation.

'Hey, wait till you've seen the rest before you jump to conclusions,' joked Pick, when people began slapping him on the back after the curtain had gone down.

'It was amazing!' said Candida. 'Don't you want to go backstage and congratulate the actors?'

'Yeah, but we gotta go to this goddamn unveiling,' Pick groaned.

'Must you be at that?' asked Candida. 'Can't I represent you?'

He smiled at her. 'It would be kinda churlish of me not to turn up,' he said. 'Since they've sort of hinted the theatre's going to be named after me.'

Candida gave a squeal of delight. 'The Mattison Pick Theatre,' she exclaimed. 'Isn't that exciting!'

'Now, don't get carried away,' said Pick. 'Still, it's got a ring to it, huh?'

They reached the lobby just before Peggy and Ivor Zlennek. That Peggy was nervous was obvious to everyone. But when her husband tried to take her arm to help her on to the dais, she shook him off angrily. Then she began to speak and there was a supportive hush.

'Ladies and gentlemen,' she read hesitantly from her notes. 'Tonight sees the reopening of this theatre after its extensive refurbishment. And to mark the occasion we are deeply honoured that Mattison Pick has agreed to bring us the world première of his new musical *The Iron Lady*, of which we've just seen the wonderful first half.'

The was a riffle of applause and Pick, standing beside her, took a half bow.

'It is more than appropriate,' Peggy went on, 'that it should be Matty's show that launches our new beginning, for his relationship with this theatre goes back many years. All the musicals of Mattison Pick and his late and much lamented writing partner, Sam Kaskin, had their London premières here, many of them staying for years and running to thousands of performances.

'Since Sam's sad demise, Matty has chosen to continue this tradition with his solo shows, including his huge hit, *Kennedy*, and for that we are most grateful. Let's hope that tonight will mark a renaissance for both the theatre and for Matty himself.'

That this double-edged remark brought a slight scowl to Pick's face was noticed only by the most discerning of the showbiz insiders present. The fact was that few of his recent musicals had been as successful as the ones written with Kaskin.

Clearly unaware of her inadvertent faux pas, Peggy Zlennek continued: 'And so, without further ado, let me now reveal the theatre's new name.'

With a final pause to allow the photographers to snap away, she tugged a cord to her left which drew open the curtains covering an engraved brass plaque. The words on it read: 'The Sam Kaskin Memorial Theatre'. There was a hearty round of applause from all those gathered, but this time the scowl of anger on Pick's face was less veiled.

Nevertheless, he stepped forward with every appearance of gratitude. 'Thank you so much, everyone,' he said. 'Sam would have been so proud. The show's gonna restart in just a few minutes, so I'll keep my remarks short.

'You know, I'm often asked how much of the Kaskin and Pick musicals were Kaskin and how much were Pick. Well, that's a difficult one, but let me tell you this: to say that Sam Kaskin was an extra-ordinary man would be an understatement. Sam was extra-ordinary in the same sense that a bag of French fries is extra-large. See, everyone used to say our shows really had the common touch, and that sure as hell didn't come from me. Sam' – he looked heavenwards as if addressing the man himself – 'now that you're up there in that great balcony in the sky – or, if we're really frank, more likely in the circle bar – we salute you, and we promise that your spirit, as much of it as you didn't manage to drink before you went, will live on in our hearts for ever.'

And as the bell rang to indicate that the second half was about to begin, he wiped a non-existent tear from his eye and everyone filed emotionally back into the theatre to resume their seats.

The second act began on time at nine o'clock and as Candida Blitz took her place, she remembered Will Cloud and glanced irritably along the row at him and Ros. Matty had finally been unable to resist the temptation to go backstage to see if everything was all right, and she was now sitting on her own, feeling rather isolated.

The lights went down and the act opened with the 'Belle of the Ball' number. Following her victory in the South Atlantic and subsequent election landslide, Mrs Thatcher was at the height of her powers and undertaking a grand world tour. Accompanied by a host of admirers, she was making regal progress round the globe, starting with Russia where Mikhail Gorbachev personally rolled out the red carpet for her.

In the opening scene, a chorus of KGB men was serenading her on the airport tarmac as she emerged from her plane wearing the famous fur hat and full-length coat. As usual, her husband,

Denis, was two steps behind. Now, in a great Busby Berkeley-style number, the secret agents threw themselves at her feet one by one and sang:

> *The belle of the ball*
> *Gorby's new Russian doll,*
> *The Falklands rejoiced her*
> *Now the world is her oyster.*

It was another catchy tune that Candida had already picked up from Matty, and as the airport gave way to the Kremlin, re-created in all its glory, she couldn't help humming along and thrilling to the colourful costumes and magnificent backdrops. Despite herself, she thought of Will. This was just the kind of spectacular scene that he adored. She cast him a sidelong glance to check that he was enjoying himself, pretending really just to be stretching her neck.

But she needn't have bothered to disguise her interest. For Will's attention was certainly not on her – nor on anyone else, for that matter. In fact, he was sitting with a strangely rigid, tortured expression on his face, looking straight ahead. The large man in front of him had evidently not come back after the interval, so he had a clear view of the stage. He was staring fixedly through the empty space as if mesmerised.

Candida checked the set to see what was up there that could possibly be preoccupying him so intently. But it was only the scene after the first-night banquet, when the Russian leader was pursuing his courtship of Mrs Thatcher. With lust in his eyes, he was waving her husband away and singing:

> *It's time you ditched your gremlin*
> *And let me waltz you round the Kremlin*
> *Forgive my remissness*
> *But you said we could do business . . .*

At the mention of doing business, Gorbachev leered at Mrs Thatcher suggestively and took her in his arms.

For some reason, though, that seemed to be the last straw for Will Cloud. Now, as Candida watched in total astonishment, his expression of rapt concentration turned into one of stupefaction. With a loud yelp that attracted tutting from all round the stalls, he got up from his seat like a man possessed. Dementedly he pushed past the other people in the row, including his companion Ros Flato, and made for the aisle.

Then, without a backward glance, he stormed off frantically towards the exit at the rear of the theatre and through the double doors into the lobby.

Chapter Fifty One

On the sixth floor at Butchers Bank, Toby Slaker sat at his desk, staring at the Hoodwink Encounters page on his computer screen. It was twenty minutes past nine and the Minx was due on line at nine thirty. The office was deserted. Even the Hoodwink site was unusually unpopulated tonight.

Although he'd been alone late in the office many times before, the silence there tonight seemed particularly eerie. He reached out to his desk and laid his hand gently against the steel of the pistol he had again borrowed from Lomond Butcher's office – or ex-office, as it soon would be. Even though it wasn't loaded, its presence gave him confidence.

He couldn't stop his mind dwelling on his two colleagues, Roy Falloni and Melvin Puckle, who had died in this very room in the past few weeks. And as his eyes roamed round their desks, he felt a momentary twinge of fear. What if they *had* been killed after all? What if the Minx *had* murdered them?

He thought he heard a sound and his eyes went to the top of the spiral staircase leading from the lift lobby below. He was being melodramatic now, he told himself. Besides, apart from the fact he had a gun, he would see anyone coming up there long before they reached the top and could telephone security or set off the fire alarm in an instant.

He checked his watch. Nearly nine thirty. Would she keep her promise and turn up on-line? She'd never let him down before.

If, as Gus had said, the Minx claimed that it was all a terrible accident, he had decided what he was going to do. He would try his utmost to talk her into going to the police and coming clean of her own accord. If he could persuade her to avoid dragging him into it, all well and good.

But if she still refused, then he'd made up his mind that he would go to the police on his own. It was the only right thing to do. This case had to be properly investigated, once and for all. And they wouldn't have much difficulty tracking her down, he was certain of that. With modern policing methods, there was bound to be some way to trace the Hoodwink Encounters site and its various patrons.

A minute before nine thirty. One eye on the screen, the other on the clocks on the wall, Toby held his breath. Finally, as they clicked in unison on to the half hour, there was a ping and a message box appeared on the screen.

The Minx was on line.

'Hi, Novice,' she said as ever.

He decided not to mince his words. 'I want to know what happened to Melvin,' he said. 'And I want the truth.'

She said, 'Sure thing, Novice. You can have the truth this time.'

'Well?'

'The truth is that Melvin's death was a terrible mistake.'

Relief surged over Toby. 'I knew it,' he typed. But before his reply had even left his computer, the Minx's next words came scrolling up on the screen, hitting him in the solar plexus like a sledgehammer.

'It was a terrible mistake,' she said, 'because it was you I meant to kill. It was you I meant to kill all along, just like I killed Falloni. But it's not too late,' she continued starkly. 'Now it's time for you to get yours. As they say in the movies: Watch your back, Toby.'

Too late, Toby was aware of someone behind him. Too late, he half turned. Too late, he reached for the gun. By that time, the sack had already been thrust roughly over his head, and now all he felt was a dull thud as he was hit on the back of the head with a cold hard object.

He did not see his assailant. Nor did he see the last message from the Minx as it appeared on his screen before he lost consciousness.

'Are you in the mood to put on the hood?' it read. 'So long, Novice. It was fun.'

Chapter Fifty Two

———————•>o<o<•———————

Inspector Ffelcher sat in the back of the speeding police car and glowered at Will Cloud. 'You'd better be right about this,' he said. 'I was enjoying that bloody show.'

With the PM safely inside the theatre, he'd been peacefully watching from the back of the stalls and had not appreciated Will's unscheduled interruption in the slightest. But he had enough experience of Will from the Brass Monkeys case to know that he ignored him at his peril. So, in response to the Irishman's hastily shouted plea, he'd left the PM's security in the hands of his deputy and ordered Sergeant Dorf to get a squad car to take them to Butchers Bank.

'Can't you go any faster?' Will asked the driver. 'There may be a life in danger.'

Sergeant Dorf looked at the inspector, who reluctantly nodded his agreement. 'May as well hang you for a pound as a penny,' he said with a degree of self-satisfied menace.

Dorf activated the car's siren. As it accelerated through the driving rain, past a traffic jam and through a red light, Will anxiously wondered if he was doing the right thing. Could he be sure? The answer was no, he couldn't.

Desperately he tried to think through the revelation that had come to him in the theatre. At last he knew, he knew beyond a shadow of a doubt what had happened to Falloni, and everything else followed from that. The Minx, the suicide note, the *Hoodwink Show*, Butchers Bank, everything. But most importantly of all it followed, as sure as night followed day, that Melvin Puckle could not have been the second target. That had to be Toby Slaker.

And if they'd targeted him once, they would target him again. Toby's words came back to him. 'Something personal that I've got to deal with,' he had said. 'Just a bit of *déjà vu*,' he had said.

But perhaps he was reading too much into those words? Was he about to make a complete fool of himself? Was he about to invade Butchers Bank with a squad of armed police only to find Toby sitting at his desk correcting Felicia's rotten typing as usual? He didn't know. But every instinct he had told him he was on the right track. As long as it wasn't too late.

'Are we almost there?' he asked with anguish.

Finally, the police car screeched to a halt outside the Butchers building. Will was half out of the door before it had even stopped, the soles of his shoes sending up clouds of dust as they scuffed against the tarmac.

The building towered up in the deathly silence of the City at night, bathed in a purplish glow from the Lloyds building nearby. 'Up there,' Will shouted, pointing up to the Private Clients Department on the sixth floor. Eerily outlined against the night sky, one of the windows was hanging open.

With the inspector and Sergeant Dorf close on his heels, he pushed past the building security and through to the lift lobby. 'Those lifts are useless,' he panted. He pointed to the stairway. 'Up this way.'

Drifting in and out of consciousness, Toby felt himself being manhandled on to the floor of the office. Groggily he tried to resist but it was no use. The blow to his head had been well aimed and the sack that had been pulled down over his head and shoulders effectively pinned his arms together as well as blocking his vision. If that were not enough, a cold hard object protruded into the small of his back – presumably the gun with whose muzzle he had just been struck.

His captor was not fooling around, and was evidently in a hurry. Without a word Toby was prodded and pushed across the floor of the Private Clients Department. Even in his woozy state, Toby tried to work out where they were going. But all too soon, he knew. As they jerked to a halt and he was thrust to his knees, he reached out to catch his balance and his hand grasped at a low wooden ledge. It was the sill under the great window overlooking Gracechurch Street.

There followed a sound that sent a shudder of recognition through his body and left him in no doubt as to his intended fate. It was a click as a latch was unfastened, and close on its heels came a familiar rattle of the window being pulled open. There was a blast of cold air, and Toby felt the rain begin to batter against his face through the hessian of the sack.

The barrel of the gun still firmly pushed into his side, Toby was propelled outwards. Desperately he tried to hook his feet under the internal rim of the sill to give himself leverage. It was useless. With a muttered curse, his captor kicked at him viciously until he gave way. Now, tottering on the edge, Toby waited helplessly for that one last shove that would send him to certain death. Only a miracle could save him.

Then, over the battering rain, he heard a sound, a sound which told him that miracles were still possible. It was the rattle of feet up the spiral staircase that led up to the Private Clients floor. If only he could stay put for a few more seconds, he still had a chance.

His captor must have heard it too. Toby sensed a hesitation. But it was momentary only. Toby felt a final push in the small of his back and he began to fall.

But at last the sack had come away and his hands were free. Reaching out frantically, his fingers caught hold of the window ledge, and his feet, scrabbling against the side of the building, located a ridge that gave him temporary support.

Hanging on desperately, Toby tried not to look down. Instead he looked up. And what now filled his vision, what filled his entire existence, was the sole of a boot. A boot at the end of a leg that was getting ready to stamp. A strange boot. A leather cowboy boot that brought to Toby a sickening sense of recognition, even in his distress.

Helplessly he waited for it to smash down on his knuckles and send him finally to his doom. But it didn't. There was a shout from within the room and the foot hovered uncertainly, its owner startled.

Then, with a bizarre sense of disinterest, as if it were all happening somewhere in another universe, Toby heard a shot ring out. It was followed by another, a second later. There was a cry, then a strange hiatus in which time seemed to be suspended. Finally, the figure above him staggered back against the window frame, hesitated one more time and fell outwards.

Still clinging on, his fingers aching, Toby stared with disbelief as his would-be murderer descended past him. Almost dragged down in the slipstream, he only just managed to keep a precarious balance while the figure receded into the distance with a long-drawn-out scream. Seconds later, there was a stomach-churning thud as the softness of a human body met the unyielding concrete. Then silence.

Now, above Toby, anxious faces appeared at the window. Hands reached out to pull him back in. Toby hardly noticed them. His vision remained filled with the awful image far below, where a man lay staring up at him.

Eyes open, arms outstretched, Mattison Pick was, beyond any shadow of a doubt, totally and utterly dead.

Chapter Fifty Three

⎯⎯⎯◦◦◦⎯⎯⎯

It was the morning after the opening of *The Iron Lady* and queues had been forming since dawn outside the newly renamed Sam Kaskin Memorial Theatre. Despite mixed reviews, demand for tickets was breaking all box office records.

The reason was not difficult to identify. News that, after plummeting from the top of a City merchant bank, the show's creator had gone from composing to decomposing in the course of a few short seconds, had been spread across that morning's papers with unmistakable relish. There was no question now that this show would run and run.

That same morning, Toby Slaker staggered into the Private Clients Department at Butchers Bank at just after six a.m. The office was deserted, except for Will Cloud, who was sitting at Toby's own desk, feet up, staring bleary eyed at the computer screen. Beside him, on a stand, was the TV and video player which normally occupied the corner of one of the meeting rooms.

'What in God's name are you doing here?' asked Will jumping up. 'Sure, I thought they were keeping you in for observation!'

'I discharged myself,' said Toby. 'It was only mild concussion. Besides, I wanted to get back here and find out what the hell was going on.' He looked reproachfully at Will. 'Which I dare say you can tell me, since you seem to know everything else.'

He went over to the window and looked down at the

pavement. It instantly took him back to the vertigo of last night and he had to look away.

'The police took the body off for examination a few hours ago,' said Will. 'They want to confirm whether he died when Sergeant Dorf returned his fire, or whether it was because of the fall.'

'But . . . I just don't understand any of it,' said Toby, still dazed. 'Why . . . why would Pick want to kill me . . . and who . . . I mean—' He broke off self-consciously.

'Who have you been having all those blind dates with for the last few weeks?' Will completed the sentence for him rather smugly.

'You know about that?' Toby cringed. 'How on earth . . .?'

Will pointed to Melvin's computer. 'Someone called Scarlett told me,' he said. 'Though it wasn't till last night at the theatre that I worked out that it was you who was doing the blind dating and not Melvin.'

Toby's head was hurting. 'Who on earth is Scarlett?' he asked.

'All in good time,' said Will, motioning him to sit down. 'You'd better take it easy. Let me get you a drink.'

He came back a moment later with a large black coffee from the machine. 'Now that I think of it,' he went on, 'it's no bad thing you're here. I've been sitting with Inspector Ffelcher all night, trying to piece together exactly what's been happening. We've figured out the whos and the hows, but the whys are still a mystery. And I think you might be able to help cast some light on it.'

Toby didn't feel in a condition to cast light on anything. He shook his head. 'I'd just be happy to know the "who" part,' he said. 'You'd better get started.' He had an idea it was not going to be simple.

Will sat back in his chair, and placed the tips of his fingers together with ill-concealed relish. 'Are you really ready for this?' he asked. He tapped the television and video machine beside him. 'I warn you, it's a multimedia presentation.' Toby nodded wearily. Will Cloud was evidently determined to milk his moment of glory for all it was worth. He had taken out a suspiciously ragged looking cigarette from his pocket and was reaching for a match. 'You don't mind if I . . .'

'Please,' begged Toby, 'do what you like. Just get on with it.'

Will lit his joint, inhaled luxuriantly and said, 'Right, let's start from the beginning.'

'Let's bloody well not,' Toby interrupted. 'Let's start with the identity of the person I've been ah . . . dating . . . these last weeks. And if you tell me it's Mattison Pick, I warn you that you'll be the next one out of the window after I've thrown up.'

'No, it wasn't Pick,' Will reassured him. 'I wouldn't have thought he'd be your type. Although I'm open to correction.'

Toby gave him a wan smile. 'Then who the hell was it?'

Will held up his hand. 'I'll come to that in a moment,' he said with an infuriatingly superior look. He paced the room, as if about to address a full gathering, even though Toby was the only person there. 'This whole affair,' he began, 'comes back to Roy Falloni and the call he made to the Listening Line on the night he supposedly committed suicide.'

'Supposedly?'

'Falloni didn't kill himself. He was murdered,' said Will, not without gusto. 'In that very chair over there.'

'Well, that can't have been Mattison Pick's doing,' said Toby emphatically. 'Because that night he was appearing on the *Hoodwink Show*. We both saw him, as clearly as I'm seeing you now. He was being humiliated on air by Peaches.'

Will took another puff and nodded. 'You couldn't ask for a more perfect alibi,' he said.

'You mean he *did* do it?' asked Toby horrified. 'That's not possible.'

Will didn't answer directly. 'Let's come back to the call to the Listening Line,' he said. 'When you think about it – which nobody really did till last night – it was a very peculiar call, the way he kept breaking off and didn't let the woman at the other end get a word in edgeways. If you add to that the suicide note I found . . .'

This was the first Toby had heard of any such thing. 'What suicide note?'

'Didn't I tell you about that?' Will looked at him innocently then handed him a sheet of paper from his inside pocket. 'This is a copy,' he said. 'The inspector has the original now.'

Rubbing the exhaustion from his eyes, Toby read it through. 'Well, it's certainly odd,' he agreed after he'd finished.

'Indeed it is,' said Will. 'How many people do you know who'd put their suicide notes into rhyme?'

'Not many,' Toby admitted. 'But, after all, Falloni was unhinged. And the note just confirms what we already knew – in his madness, he thought he'd lost the bank a fortune. Are you saying Pick somehow managed to trick him into believing that?'

'Not quite,' said Will. 'It was cleverer than that. See, I found that note sticking in the side of Falloni's Walkman the other day. But like the eedjit I am, I didn't think to listen to the tape inside.' He picked up the Walkman which was on the desk and slid it over to Toby. 'And the clue was there all along. Want to listen?'

'If I must.' Toby's head was already hurting enough, but obediently he donned the headphones while Will rewound the tape and turned it to 'play'. At first all Toby detected was silence, followed by a loud hiss. But then Falloni's voice came through, loud and clear. Full of panic and melodrama, he was shouting at the top of his voice. "I'm finished,' he repeated over and over again. 'Millions and millions. All down the drain.' It was the same conversation that Toby had heard on the bank's phone logging machine immediately after Falloni's death, except that this time it was one-sided: the soothing tones of the woman at the other end of the line were absent.

Toby could hardly bear to listen. His face twisted in anguish. But the Irishman did not relent. 'Stay with it just a bit longer,' he mouthed. The call was coming to an end. Falloni was building to a crescendo. 'There's only one way out,' he screamed. 'Only one way out . . .'

Now Will, straining to overhear, pressed the pause button. 'With me so far?' he asked. Toby nodded miserably. 'That was where the conversation with the Listening Line ended,' Will continued. 'But now I'm going to play you the rest.'

'But it was directly after the phone call that he did himself in,' said Toby in despair. 'I don't want to hear that!'

Will ignored him. He removed his finger from the pause button and the tape continued. Now a strange and terrible sound emanated from Toby's headphones. It was like the wailing of a fatally injured animal.

'Oh, my God,' said Toby. 'You've got a tape of him in his last moments. It's . . . it's . . . it's a snuff tape. It's unspeakable.'

But still Will held up his hand. To Toby's continuing horror, the wailing intensified. Gradually, though, Toby now became aware that it was not a death rattle at all. Bit by bit, it became identifiable as something quite different, if no less unpleasant. Toby listened more carefully. Was it . . . could it be . . .?

It was. Falloni was singing. Or making his own feeble attempt at singing. Far from killing himself, he was all too disgustingly giving voice. And now there were words too. Tunelessly he warbled:

> It's a Butchers' Ball,
> In that Futures Hall,
> When they're out for your blood,
> And your back's to the wall.

> And they smell your fear,
> For your nerves are shot
> Since a billion was here
> And now it's not.

There was a brief hiatus at this point. Apparently unaware that he was no Julie Andrews, Falloni cleared his throat and tried going up a key. He croaked:

> And that loss isn't all
> That you'll never unwind,
> There's another shortfall —
> In the balance of your mind.

343

> *Where you once shot the lights out*
> *Now all that remains*
> *Is to lower your targets*
> *And shoot out your brains.*

That this sounded no better was lost on Falloni. He pushed on.

> *There's a gun in your head*
> *And it's crooking its trigger*
> *And it's whispering low*
> *As it stifles a snigger:*

> *'Man, your future's a sell,*
> *And your past is a rout,*
> *And suicide*
> *Is the only way out*

> *'So surrender to Fate*
> *And bugger those butchers*
> *And forever escape*
> *From going back to the Futures.'*

Finally, it seemed – and not a second too soon for Toby – he had reached the climax of the little ditty, which was apparently meant to end on a Pucciniesque high C so beloved of modern musical composers. In Falloni's interpretation, though, it came across as more like a power drill striking reinforced concrete. Nothing daunted, he drew breath and went for a final reprise, concluding with a triumphant wheeze:

> *And forever escape*
> *From going back to the Futures.*

The second ending proved too much and now he burst into a fit of coughing.

'There,' said Will Cloud eagerly, pulling off Toby's ear-phones.

'There what?' asked Toby, perplexed.

Will stared at him in disbelief. 'You must get it now!' he said. '*Leeson – the Musical*!'

'What?'

'*Leeson – the Musical*,' Will repeated, as if it were totally self-explanatory. 'A show about the rogue trader who brought down Barings merchant bank in 1995 – a natural subject for Mattison Pick, don't you think?'

'Leeson? Barings? But –' Toby's mind was swimming.

'Don't you see?' Will continued, the words falling over themselves as they tumbled eagerly from his mouth. 'You told me Falloni always was a showbiz fanatic. He wanted to be a musical star instead of a fund manager. And when Mattison Pick offered him his big break in the lead role of Leeson, he jumped at it. This is him practising for his audition. It's all quite clear from the rest of the tape.'

Finally recognition dawned on Toby. 'You mean this was played down the telephone to the Listening Line?'

Will nodded. 'Not this particular recording, of course. If Pick had known that this tape existed then he would have destroyed it. No, this is just Falloni's own practice recording. Pick would have used the original.'

'The original?'

'The demo tape which he must have got Falloni to record. Falloni would have been sworn to secrecy about the audition.'

'I still don't get it.'

Will got up impatiently and took the tape out of the machine. 'Pick wanted Falloni out of the way,' he said, 'but he wanted it to appear like suicide. So he hit on the big idea. He invented a totally fictitious show about the Barings collapse and invited Falloni in to audition for the lead role. He even adapted the 'Belle of the Ball' number from *The Iron Lady* and rewrote the lyrics specially for Falloni. That was what gave me my final clue last night. I recognised the cadence as soon as I heard it. Even the rhyme was the same: "The Belle of the Ball – The Butchers' Ball".'

'Not, of course, that Pick was interested in the song.' Will was well into his stride now, pacing up and down the office purposefully. 'What he wanted was that crucial bit of dialogue, which he pretended to Falloni was the lead-up to the big number. See, if Falloni was going to be a star, he'd have to act as well as sing. That's what he told him. So this was his acting audition. A bit melodramatic, but what would you expect from an amateur. It was certainly good enough to fool all of us when it was played down the line on the night of Falloni's murder – to give the impression he was confessing to a futures débâcle.' Will wheeled round to face Toby. 'Didn't it strike you as odd that Falloni never answered any of the lady's questions directly? He just kept spouting on about futures. It was a simple technique. He sounded so overwrought that he wasn't listening. Well that was hardly surprising, because by that time the poor guy was already dead!'

'Hold on,' said Toby. He buried his head in his hands wearily. 'You haven't explained how Mattison Pick could have been here murdering Falloni when millions of witnesses, including both of us, can swear that at the time of Falloni's death, Pick was taking part in a live television recording of the *Hoodwink Show*.'

Will Cloud nodded happily. 'I told you, it's a corker of an alibi; not just for Pick, of course, but for the person who actually did kill Falloni. Who is also, by the way, the same person you've been unknowingly bonking with these last few weeks.'

Toby held his breath. 'And that was?'

Pausing for effect, Will took a final drag from his joint and stooped to stub it out in an empty litter bin. Then, with a self-satisfied smile, he came out with it. 'Mrs Pick,' he said. 'Otherwise known, of course, as Peaches La Trené. You know,' he mused, 'you must be the unluckiest guy in the world. Repeated sex with *the* Hollywood love goddess, and you weren't even aware of it.'

Toby threw up his hands. The man was completely mad. 'I preferred it when you said it was Pick,' he said despairingly. 'At least he was on the same continent, for God's sake. But Peaches was thousands of miles away in California the night that Falloni was murdered. You're off your head.'

346

'Funny,' said Will, sitting down again in one of the visitor's chairs with a faraway expression. 'That's exactly what the inspector said when I told him a few hours ago.' He glanced knowingly at his watch. 'Yet right now he's on a plane to Los Angeles to arrange Peaches' extradition to Britain to stand trial for murder.'

It was all too much for Toby. 'Tell me I'm still in hospital and this is all a bad dream,' he said. 'Because it's not reality. We all saw Peaches do that live satellite interview with Pick on the *Hoodwink Show*, when she smashed those Ming vases.'

'Ah, did we now?' asked Will Cloud. 'That's where you're wrong. Sure, that's what we *thought* we saw. But what we actually saw ... what everyone saw ... was another clever trick. Hang on and I'll show you.' Now Will turned to the video machine which Toby had spotted in the office on his arrival. 'Told you this was a multimedia production,' he said with a wink. 'I borrowed this tape of the *Hoodwink Show* from Candida's collection. She keeps recordings of all her old stuff.'

He picked up the remote control and pressed a button. On the TV set the Popviz logo appeared followed by the fateful *Hoodwink Show* that Toby had attended with Simona. There, in full colour, was Mattison Pick being taken by surprise by Candida Blitz and led hooded through to the studio where his friends were lying in wait. Then, after the show's theme tune had been played, the huge video screen was lowered and Peaches appeared by her Hollywood swimming pool for that now infamous interview.

'If that's not California,' said Toby, 'I'll eat my hat. What do you think they did?' he added sarcastically. 'Built an exact replica of the place somewhere in bloody Crouch End so that she could slip away and murder Falloni afterwards?' Another thought occurred to him. 'Anyway, she was in Los Angeles collecting her Oscar the night before, and everyone saw her there too.'

'You still don't get it, do you?' said Will. 'Think of Falloni and the Listening Line. It's exactly the same principle. Just watch.'

On the recording, Candida could be seen to stare up at the giant video screen.

'Can you hear us, Peaches?' she asked.
'Hi there, everyone,' replied Peaches. 'Gee, I'm afraid I can't hear you very well.'
'Hello, honey,' said Pick.
'Hello, pumpkin. You're coming through loud and clear now. How're you getting on over there in England?'
'Just great, hon. But I'm missing you a bundle.'
'Are you really?' asked Peaches.
'Congratulations on the Oscar, Peaches,' Candida interrupted.
'Are you really, really missing me?' Peaches persisted.

At this point, Will paused the video and cut in. 'Notice anything peculiar about the interview?' he asked. Toby looked at him blankly. 'Poor old Candida is meant to be conducting the thing, but at no time does Peaches ever answer any of her questions. She only responds directly to Pick himself.'

He took his finger off the pause button and allowed the playback to continue. Sure enough, Peaches bulldozed through the interview, without once interacting with Candida in any way, as she insulted her husband, displayed those grainy pictures of him allegedly in bed with her sister and went upstairs to the Ming room to smash up his vases.

For the first time, Toby began vaguely to see what Will was getting at. Suddenly it didn't seem so mad after all.

'See?' Will said triumphantly. 'The Peaches side of the conversation was recorded in advance. Recorded and choreographed just like a theatrical trompe-l'œil from one of Mattison Pick's musicals, to be played back on demand. And what Pick was responding to the whole time was a video-recording.'

Toby tried to adjust to this new way of looking at things. It was not easy. Falteringly he searched for reasons why it couldn't work. 'But Popviz sent out a camera crew,' he objected.

'Candida said so right at the beginning of the programme. Don't tell me that the whole camera crew were in on this?'

Will smiled. 'If you'd been living with a TV presenter as long as I have,' he said, 'you'd know all that stuff about sending camera crews round the world is pure baloney. Sure, they're always pretending to do it so the company sounds impressive, But it's just hype. Only a big corporation like the BBC could afford those kind of resources. What any small satellite station does, of course, is make an arrangement with a sister station in the place where they want to record. They book the satellite time, the local company sends out a crew, and they beam the whole thing across.'

'What about the crew at the other end?' asked Toby.

'I got Candida to check. It was just one man,' said Will. 'He must have been squared somehow. The inspector's going to look into that while he's out there. But that's how it happened, to be sure.'

For Toby, the penny was still dropping. 'Let me get this straight,' he said. 'You're saying that Peaches wasn't in Los Angeles at all?'

'She was there for the Oscars, all right,' said Will. 'She made sure she could be seen and heard. And it helped that she won the best supporting actress award, of course. But that all happened the night before. Immediately after the ceremony she caught the first plane to London, no doubt wearing some form of disguise. And while Mattison Pick was playing his role on TV so beautifully, answering all those pre-rehearsed prompts and providing her with a watertight alibi, Peaches was right here in this office, murdering Roy Falloni.'

On the television screen, the tape had progressed to the moment when Peaches was about to begin dropping Pick's Ming vases. Toby clutched at them like a drowning man at a straw. 'What about those?' he asked. 'You think Pick connived at the destruction of his own precious collection?'

'Fakes,' said Will Cloud dismissively.

'What?'

'All the ones that were smashed were fakes. That was what

started me off on Pick's trail in the first place.' He paused the video again, suspending a blue Hung-chich period vase in mid-descent between Peaches outstretched hands and the marble floor. 'You see this one here,' he said. 'It's the only one of its kind still in existence. Yet the other day when I was in Pick's hotel room, I spotted one that looked identical, at least to my eye. So I smuggled an old friend of mine – a very distinguished expert who used to work for the V and A – into the room to check. And he confirmed that it was definitely the original. I suppose Pick couldn't bear to be separated from it. My guess is that we'll find the rest are locked up in a vault somewhere until the heat's passed.'

'So he set all this up,' said Toby, still stunned. 'Even the whole thing about Peaches and her sister?'

'Yup,' Will confirmed. 'He was someone who didn't do things by halves, was Mattison Pick.'

'And Peaches was the woman on the Hoodwink site?'

'Peaches *was* the Hoodwink site,' said Will. 'She played all the people on it. And she logged in from wherever she was, either Los Angles or London. When you chat on a computer like that, the other person can be anywhere in the world and you'd never know. The only times when Peaches needed to be here in person was when she was . . . ah . . . conducting a liaison – or committing a murder. And remember, she was an award-winning actress, she could pass herself off as anyone she wanted to. A waitress at a party, say, or a cleaner, if necessary.'

Toby sat back in astonishment. It was now after eight and around him staff were beginning to arrive for work, shaking their heads to find their department had been the scene of yet another death. Felicia put her nose round the door to Toby's office and threw a curious look at the two men, ragged and unshaven, Will still wearing his dinner suit from the previous evening. But Toby waved her away. He desperately needed to know the answer to one last question. Now he articulated it. 'Why?' he asked with a shudder. 'Why should Pick and his wife go to all this trouble to kill us? Why should they want us dead?'

'Ah,' said Will Cloud, sitting back in his chair, legs akimbo.

'There, I have to admit, you've got me stumped. And I was kind of hoping you might know.'

'Me?'

From the desk, Will picked up a strange piece of metal apparatus about the size of a telephone. 'This was found on the floor of the office last night,' he said. 'Pick must have brought it with him.'

'What on earth is it?' asked Toby. It looked like a large pair of curling tongs.

'It's an industrial demagnetiser. Used for wiping computer disks, and Pick seemed to be intent on wiping yours after he'd done away with you. In fact, that seemed to be part of the reason Peaches and Pick dreamed up the whole Hoodwink Encounters trick in the first place. They didn't just want to kill you and Falloni, they were after something. They wanted access to your files and your computers, at home as well as at work.'

Recognition dawned on Toby. 'That was why all the computers stopped working.'

'Precisely,' said Will. 'But Pick didn't manage to wipe yours before he died. So whatever he was trying to get at is still there. And the question is: do you know what that might be? Something that you and Falloni shared – and something that was worth murdering for.'

Toby shook his head. 'I haven't the faintest clue,' he said. He turned resolutely to his computer. 'But I'll bloody well do my damnedest to find out.'

Chapter Fifty Four

Peggy Zlennek paused outside the door of her husband's study and listened. He was talking quietly on the phone inside.

It probably wasn't a good time, but then it never would be. After their argument last night, he'd stormed out of the theatre at the end of the interval, and she hadn't had a chance to talk to him further.

She had to bring this to a head. She'd thought he'd finished with that woman but after last night she knew he hadn't. The not knowing, the secretiveness of it all was fuelling a terrible anxiety in her. Better to get it over with one way or another.

She knew he would not likely be in good temper today. She'd just heard on the news that the sale of Butchers to Hampton Bradley had finally been completed, despite the events of last night involving Mattison Pick.

So whatever it was Ivor had been up to in order to secure Butchers for himself – and Peggy's guess as to what that might be had proved resoundingly wrong – it hadn't worked. Butchers had gone to Bradley and would never belong to him now. Ivor hated being beaten at any time, but she had never known him want anything as he'd wanted Butchers Bank. He would be devastated. His anger and frustration at having been cheated out of it might last for weeks, even months.

Which meant there would be no good time to get this off her chest. So it might as well be now. She couldn't stand any more uncertainty.

'Come in,' he barked, in response to her knock on the door. His tone softened slightly when he saw her. 'Oh, sorry. I thought it was the maid.'

He was sitting at his desk. She sat down on the edge of the huge leather sofa beside it. 'We need to talk again,' she said.

'So?' he said. 'Let's talk.'

'I want to know, once and for all, why that woman was at the theatre last night.' She said the words without any emotion. But she knew they'd been together long enough for him to guess what her apparent composure concealed. 'After you said you'd stopped seeing her.'

He shrugged. 'I can't prevent her going to the theatre. It's a free country.'

'No,' she said with sudden and uncharacteristic force. 'This time I want the truth. She was there on our tickets – comps. You gave them to her, didn't you?'

He looked taken aback. Getting up from his desk, he came round the side of his desk and stood before her. He stretched out his hands and laid them on her shoulders and stared into her eyes.

'You want the truth – you shall have the truth,' he said quietly. 'The truth is I gave her the tickets long ago. You saw she came with someone else. The truth is you told me to end it and I ended it there and then. The truth,' and a catch came to his throat as he said the words, 'is that there's you and only you. And that,' he added gently, 'is how it will always be.'

Peggy looked back into his eyes and she finally believed him. She knew he would not stay faithful for long. She hadn't asked for that – she wouldn't have been so foolish – and he hadn't promised it. But she had no doubt that Rosalind Flato was now in the past, which was all that mattered to her.

'But in that case,' she said falteringly, 'I don't understand.'

'What?' he asked. 'What do you not understand?'

'I thought you were up to something. I thought . . . I thought it was all to do with this Butchers acquisition, and that that woman was involved. I thought maybe she was spying for you because she was in the City. I thought . . .' She broke up.

'You thought I had something to do with all these "accidents" at Butchers,' he said solemnly.

Even knowing him as she did, Peggy was taken aback that he'd guessed. It wasn't for nothing he had got where he had. 'Yes,' she admitted tearfully. 'I know how much you hate Hampton Bradley; what with this legal action and everything, I thought there was nothing you wouldn't do to win Butchers from him.'

'Even murder?' He perched laboriously on the couch beside her. 'You would suspect me of that?'

'Yes. No . . . I don't know.' She tried to stop herself bursting into tears. 'Please, I just want to know what's happening. *Please*.' The strength of her emotion surprised even her. 'You've been so secretive recently, and I'm . . . I was . . . so scared.'

He stayed there staring at her for an eternity. Then, at last, he seemed to come to some sort of monumental decision in his mind. Gently, he kissed her on the forehead. 'It seems to be the day for truths,' he said. 'You're right that Butchers was . . . is important to me. But you're wrong about Rosalind. I never involved her. And I most certainly had nothing to do with any of these terrible killings. That, it appears, was Pick. Heaven knows why, and may God forgive him.'

'But I'm right, aren't I?' Peggy persisted. 'There is something about Butchers you're not telling me.' Normally she would never have questioned him so closely on a matter of business, but she had to know. 'Something to do with Bradley. Why do you hate him so? And why did you let him *win*?'

And suddenly, now, Ivor did the one thing she least expected. He began to laugh. He threw back his head and guffawed as she'd never seen him do before. He laughed till the tears rolled down his face. Then finally he spoke. 'There *is* no Bradley,' he said simply.

'What?'

'There is no such person as Bradley,' he repeated. '*I* am Bradley. Bradley is me.'

'I don't understand.'

'It's quite straightforward. I made him up, invented him.

He's a figment of my imagination. It wasn't difficult. He's a recluse. Nobody ever sees him.'

Peggy looked back at him, totally dumbstruck. 'But the companies he owns . . . the estate.'

'They're all real enough,' said Zlennek. He got up and went over to a filing cabinet. Unlocking it, he took out a sheaf of papers and spread them on the floor beside her. 'They're all owned by a Cayman Islands trust which I ultimately control.'

He sat down beside her again and took her hand. 'Let me try to explain. It became clear to me years ago that I would never be acceptable to the establishment, here or on the other side of the Atlantic. That they would never let a Polish immigrant into their inner club, and that many of the acquisitions I wanted to make would inevitably be blocked. And I decided if I couldn't do it directly, I'd do it indirectly. So I invented Hampton Bradley as my alter ego.'

Peggy sat open-mouthed, just listening.

'I built up a whole history for him. A life story. A spoiled east coast childhood. A rich father. A misspent youth. Then an accident, a terrible helicopter accident, that left him paralysed and unable even to speak. He became a recluse living on a distant estate and nobody ever visited him. He communicated with the outside world only by computer. But suddenly, after his accident, he began taking an interest in business. He started to build up a portfolio. He formed a company, the Brahmin Corporation. He hired a first-class managing director, without ever actually meeting him.

'And Bradley became useful to me at once. I used him to take over companies that I might have bought anyway, but ones that were well run and would need minimal management interference. That way he got a reputation as being hands-off. Difficult companies I bought myself. It was the usual story of good cop, bad cop. As for the estate in Maine, well, it costs a bit on the upkeep, of course. But it's a good investment and well worth it to keep the story going. And right at the beginning I hired some PR people to put it about that he was once friendly with the President, went shooting with the Prince of Wales. It wasn't an unusual job for them and they did it in perfectly good faith. Lots of people take them on to try and show they're more influential than they are.'

'But . . . but . . .' Peggy's mind was in a whirl. 'But the court cases, the vendetta.'

He pursed his lips. 'They all added – what's the word? – verisimilitude. If anyone smelled anything fishy, then the last person they would suspect is me.'

Peggy sat there dumbfounded. 'And the secrecy, these long periods by yourself in the office.'

He shrugged. 'Bradley communicates all his decisions about the running of his empire via coded e-mail to his managing director, Nick Tallopia. Tallopia doesn't know who I am. Phone calls can be traced. So' – he pointed at the computer – 'it's all done through that thing. Private, and totally secure. And that's what I've been doing so secretly. Running my second empire. It's just got a bit more frantic in recent months.'

'And you never told me about it – all these years.'

He squeezed her hand. 'It wasn't that I didn't trust you. It was just . . . it was better for you. So you wouldn't let anything slip accidentally.'

Peggy was struggling to get her mind around this whole new concept. It was somehow like discovering her husband had been committing bigamy. 'Why are you telling me now, when you haven't before?' she asked.

'I wanted you to know there was nothing with Rosalind. Besides, it's coming to an end. Bradley is about to retire.'

'Retire?'

'After what I've got in mind for him, his credibility will be shot to pieces for all time. Anyway, I'm growing weary of the whole set-up, and he will have had his final use. I knew right from the beginning that nothing I could do would make Lomond Butcher sell to me. But' – he checked his watch and smiled from one corner of his face to the other – 'as of nine a.m. this morning, I am the proud owner of Butchers Bank and nobody can do anything about it. And it's all thanks to Bradley.'

Now a fire came into his eyes. 'But this time,' he continued, 'it's not enough that *I* know I own it. *Everyone* must know that Ivor Zlennek owns Butchers Bank. Later today, there will be an announcement that there's been an out-of-court settlement in this legal case between Ivor Zlennek and Hampton Bradley. And Ivor Zlennek will be the winner. As part of the deal, Bradley will retire and there will be an agreed merger between the two companies. Bradley will sell me his entire group – including Butchers Bank.' He looked at her triumphantly. 'Let's see what Lomond Butcher makes of that!'

For a second he stood there, his face strong and eyes intense. Then he began to laugh again. And Peggy joined in too this time. She couldn't help herself. They laughed and laughed, until they both had tears streaming down their faces.

And once they had finished laughing, she put her arms around him and hugged him tight as she hadn't done for years.

Chapter Fifty Five

At the bank, Will and Toby had spent the morning delving into the hundreds of Falloni's computer files that had been restored from the back-up tapes. They'd carefully checked those that contained the details of Mattison Pick's numerous investments. Those seemed the most likely place to find information that Pick would literally murder for.

But to no avail. Each file was exactly what it appeared. Lists of holdings of domestic and overseas equities, corporate and government bonds, unit and investment trusts and cash deposits which underlay the multi-million dollar portfolio that Pick had entrusted to Butchers Bank.

Illegal activity seemed the most likely starting point for what they were looking for. Had Pick been involved in money-laundering for the Mafia? Was he a front man for some drugs cartel, enabling them to recycle their ill-gotten gains through the profits from his musical shows? Evidently not. It was clear from the files that all his holdings had an impeccable pedigree, with facts and figures to back up the bona fide source of funding in the shape of profits from his various shows.

'There's nothing here,' said Toby wearily, after they'd been through them for the umpteenth time. He was beginning to feel a delayed trauma from the events of the last twenty-four hours, and the room was swimming round him a little.

But, although equally exhausted, Will was still concentrating on the screen and oblivious to Toby's discomfort – or his own.

'It has to be here,' he said stubbornly. 'Nobody goes to that much trouble without a good reason. We've just got to keep on looking. What about these?' He pointed to a file that was marked 'RFP'.

'It's what's known as a request for a proposal,' said Toby. 'It's what a fund manager submits to a potential client when he pitches for their business. All fairly standard. Investment track record, number of dedicated investment staff, and so on.' He paused thoughtfully. 'Although Falloni never did let me see the RFP to Pick. He kept it all under his hat, like everything else to do with him. In fact, it was a real surprise when we won the account. Butchers was never an obvious fund manager for him to choose. All the competition was after him and Falloni won against all the odds.'

Will was already trying to access the file in question and call it up on screen. But unlike the others, this one did not scroll up in front of their eyes. Instead a box appeared demanding a password to allow access.

'Did Falloni ever mention a password?' Will demanded.

'Not that I can remember,' said Toby, his curiosity mounting despite his exhaustion.

'Did he ever give you any hint when talking about the portfolio?'

Toby rubbed his head. There was something strange, he remembered, that Falloni had always said whenever he'd tried to probe the details of Pick's portfolio. What was it again? 'Ask not what!' he suddenly exclaimed. 'That's what Falloni would always look at me and say, if he thought I was getting too nosy about Pick.'

'Ask not what?'

'Yes. Whatever could that mean?'

But Will, who had seen all Pick's musicals, knew at once. 'The song from *Kennedy*!' he exclaimed. 'Mona da Ponte had a number one hit with it.'

With a sudden light of inspiration in his eyes, he turned back to the computer keyboard. This time, when prompted for a password, he typed 'K-E-N-N-E-D-Y'. The machine seemed to consider this for a split second, then responded positively. Scrolling up before their eyes came the RFP which Falloni had wanted to keep so secret.

They both looked at it expectantly but they were to be disappointed.

> *Dear Mr Pick,*
> *Further to your recent letter, we would like to thank you for considering Butchers Bank as possible investment managers for your portfolio.*
> *Please find attached a copy of our response, which should be self-explanatory. We trust that after you have read this you will 'ask not what' Butchers can do for you, but what you can do for Butchers.*
> *We look forward to managing your account.*

It was signed by Roy Falloni.

'Not exactly standard wording for that kind of letter,' sniffed Toby. 'Let's look at the attachment he refers to.' He paged down, expecting the usual mass of statistics that accompanied such proposals. But what he actually saw filled him with astonishment – and also recognition. He would have known the bold typeface on the front page of the attachment anywhere. 'The "enne" file!' he shouted. 'Of course. It was *Kennedy* all along.'

'What?'

Toby told Will about the file he'd seen on Falloni's desk the day he had died. 'I thought the four letters, "enne", were to do with Moyenne futures,' he said. 'But they must have been on a print-out of this. I suppose Peaches took the hard copy away when she killed him. But why? What's it about?' He pushed the 'page down' key and read more of the document. 'It just seems to be the lyrics from *Kennedy – the Musical*,' he said in puzzlement.

'Is that not weird?' Will asked. 'Now, is that a normal thing to put in a – what's it called – an RFP?'

'Not exactly,' Toby admitted. 'Maybe he was trying to be

unconventional. To impress with how much of a fan he was. He always did show an interest in musicals.'

'No,' said Will thoughtfully. 'There's got to be more to it than that.' He stared thoughtfully at the screen again. 'Do you notice something odd about the letters of the words?' he asked.

'Some of them are in different colours,' said Toby. 'Falloni was often doing that. He was into Bible codes and was always looking for hidden patterns.'

'That's it!' said Will excitedly. 'That's it. There has to be some code in these letters that only Falloni detected. Look, every fourth one is highlighted in blue. Give me a pen and paper,' he demanded. 'Now write these down as I call them out.'

It was nearly lunchtime before they had in front of them the whole message that had been encoded into the libretto of *Kennedy — the Musical*. They both stared down at it in disbelief.

They had their answer. The final piece of the jigsaw.

'Wow!' said Will.

'Blackmail!' said Toby, any thought of exhaustion now banished by the full implication of what they'd uncovered.

'Blackmail, indeed,' said Will with relish.

'The most infallible client retention strategy there is. So that's how Falloni won the Pick account!'

'And the only way out was to get rid of Falloni and all the evidence.'

'But why did they target me?' asked Toby. 'I knew nothing about it.'

Will was thinking through this new revelation. 'You must have given them the impression you knew *something*,' he said.

At once Toby thought of that night at the recording. He'd fallen over himself to impress on Pick how much he was involved in the running of his account. 'I'm fully *au fait* with every aspect of your portfolio,' he'd told him, oh so smarmily. What a fool he'd been. Those words had come close to sealing his own death warrant. Pick must have slipped the Hoodwink Encounters card into his pocket that very evening.

Checking the time, Will reached for the phone. 'Inspector Ffelcher will be landing in Los Angeles in about an hour's time. We need to get him a message to the airport. It looks like he's going to be arresting Peaches for a third murder as well.'

But the phone rang just as Will was about to pick it up. He handed the receiver to Toby. 'It's for you,' he said.

It was Simona from New York. She'd heard about the events of the previous night.

'Are you all right?' she asked anxiously. 'I heard what happened. I'm going to come back right away.'

Her solicitude went to his heart. The inspector had apparently promised that she need never know the full story behind the deaths of Falloni, Puckle and Pick, and the arrest of Peaches La Trené. And now that the sale to Bradley had gone through, at least she would never be his boss now. He felt a surge of warmth towards her.

'I'm fine,' he said confidently. 'Absolutely fine. How's your deal going over there?'

She hesitated. 'That's sort of what I wanted to talk to you about as well,' she said. 'You see, when I said I was here on a separate matter, that wasn't quite true. Winegloss asked me to come to talk to someone called Nick Tallopia. He's Hampton Bradley's MD. I may as well tell you before you hear it through the media. It looks like Zlennek is about to swallow up the Bradley organisation. So we're going to be taking over Butchers after all.'

Chapter Fifty Six

Ivor Zlennek sat in front of the television set in his office eagerly awaiting the one o'clock news on the business channel. Mentally he checked off that everything had been done that had to be done. It had.

Half an hour ago, at precisely seven thirty a.m. New York time, Nick Tallopia, Group CEO of the Brahmin Corporation, would have released to the financial media the announcement that the lawsuit between Hampton Bradley and Ivor Zlennek had been amicably settled out of court, and that, far from fighting, the two organisations were now planning to join forces.

That a mega-merger between the two sworn enemies was likely to create a stir was beyond doubt. On Zlennek's secret instructions, passed on via Tallopia as usual, Bradley's US PR people had been privately briefing the press that a conclusion of the legal battle was imminent and hinting they should expect a surprise.

That story alone would fill the papers for weeks. But much more intriguing to the British press would be the fact that Zlennek was actually going to win his battle and own Butchers Bank after all. They would go wild. In anticipation of all the media interest, Zlennek had even arranged for extra security round his London home and office to cope with the influx once the announcement was made.

'And now Business News update,' said the announcer.

'There's been a development today in the long-running court case between US Brahmin Corporation and its British rival, Zlennek International.'

Ivor Zlennek sat up expectantly.

'This morning,' the newsreader continued, 'Nick Tallopia, CEO of the Brahmin Corporation, called a press conference to announce that recent speculation about an out-of-court settlement with Mr Zlennek was completely ill-founded. He read out a statement from Mr Bradley personally which said there would be no compromise with Ivor Zlennek. There had been rumours in the markets that Mr Bradley was tiring of the long-running battle and that the feud might astonishingly end with an agreed merger between the two companies, but today's announcement puts paid to that once and for all.'

Ivor Zlennek jumped up angrily from his desk. This was nonsense. The reporter must have made a mistake.

However, as the news report now switched to a video soundbite of Tallopia at the press conference, that theory was quickly refuted. 'Mr Bradley vows he will fight,' read Nick Tallopia before a battery of cameras and photographers, 'and he will fight to the bitter end.'

Furiously, Zlennek grabbed a paperweight from his desk and hurled it at the television. What the hell was Tallopia up to? He'd e-mailed him his instructions in the usual way. Naturally, the man hadn't seemed too pleased. But he had agreed to do as he was told, just as he always had in the past.

Could Tallopia have double-crossed him? Zlennek's blood sizzled at the thought and another piece of desk furniture hit the TV set. Well, if he had, he wouldn't get very far. Zlennek had taken the utmost care over the structure of his secret US company. His managing director's remit was clearly defined and his powers strictly limited. Legal ownership of the company resided in a series of blind trusts operated through several companies in the Cayman Islands. The set-up was foolproof. Nothing could be done without Zlennek's express approval, signed off via e-mail to the Caymans with a series of electronic signatures and passwords known only to himself.

Zlennek smashed his huge fist down on the desk. Just wait till he got his hands on Tallopia. He moved over to his computer. He would institute the procedure via the lawyers to fire him at once. Now that his companies were to be run as one there would be no need for a US CEO in any case.

Fingers banging furiously down on the keys, he composed a strongly worded message to the Cayman Islands office of solicitors Barrell and Lockstock, withdrawing all authority from Nick Tallopia forthwith. Executive powers were to revert to himself with immediate effect. He added his unique authorisation code and then pressed the 'enter' key to send the message on its way.

There. That would put paid to Tallopia. Barrells were very efficient and always acted on instructions at once, so there should be an e-mail back within the hour to confirm the action had been taken.

But on this occasion he didn't even need to wait an hour. To Zlennek's surprise, the computer beeped almost instantly to announce that he already had a response.

Zlennek tapped a key and read it. When he had, his fingers froze on the keyboard as surprise turned to fury. 'RECIPIENT UNRECOGNISED,' it said. 'MESSAGE RETURNED.'

Chapter Fifty Seven

By the following weekend, relative calm had once again returned to Butchers Bank. Angus the doorman had scrubbed the pavement in front of the building back to its usual spotless state, and the number of sightseers searching for bits of Mattison Pick to take home as mementoes of happy theatrical experiences had slowed to a trickle.

The sanctuary of the weekend came none too soon for Will Cloud, who had found some of the features of everyday life at a merchant bank — namely murder, extortion and rampant sexual perversion — not entirely in line with expectations. Besides, now that Toby Slaker had been obliged to relinquish his job as head of Private Clients under the new owners, the department just wasn't the same. Even Felicia had gone. Having failed to get another job, she had finally flown off to Beijing with Shopenhauer and Birtwhistle. She had not, however, departed without a last memento of her typing skills: in his parting eulogy to his dead colleagues, Toby's reference to 'their vitality and love of lice' had left nobody unmoved.

So, as Will Cloud relaxed in Candida's house in Hampstead on Saturday afternoon, he came to the conclusion that a merchant banking career of a week and a half was more than enough and it was time to hang up his suit and return to his newly budding detective business.

But how to break the news to Candida, who'd set such store by his new job? While pondering this thorny question, he put his feet up on the sofa, took a puff at a joint and a leaf through the Saturday newspapers. The *Pop* had been running stories about Pick's death plunge and Peaches La Trené's arrest all week, but today it had discovered a new angle on the case. Will read it with interest:

TWO MORE MURDER CHARGES FOR HOLLYWOODS PEACHES

Hollywood actress Peaches La Trené, taken into custody earlier this week for the Butchers Bank murders, is now reported to be facing further charges after an application was lodged to exhume the body of Mattison Pick's former writing partner, Sam Kaskin.

Kaskin's death two years ago – while being nursed by the Picks at their secluded Hollywood mansion – was put down at the time to cirrhosis of the liver brought on by long-term alcoholism. *But it is now alleged that, rather than nursing him, the couple were holding him prisoner and slowly poisoning him while they forced him to complete his final show.*

Moreover, it is that very show, *Kennedy – the Musical*, that is thought to hold the clue to this astonishing revelation. Sensational claims have emerged that Kaskin actually encoded a plea for help into its libretto even as he lay dying. *Sadly, Kaskin's message from beyond the grave was discovered two years too late to save him. But at least one of his murderers can now finally be brought to justice.*

There had been a history of jealousy between the two writing partners, with Pick always considered to be the less talented of the duo. When *Kennedy* opened to great critical acclaim after Kaskin's death, it was credited solely to Pick, with no mention of Kaskin's role.

Inspector Ffelcher, the Scotland Yard officer who single-handedly discovered the fresh evidence, refused to confirm or deny the new allegations. 'We're in an ongoing investigational situation here,' he said. Speaking from his suite at the Beverly Hilton Hotel, the in-

spector noted that the case was an extremely
complex one and he may have to remain in
California assisting the LAPD for some
months to come. 'It's a bummer,' he added,
'but some dude's got to do it.'

In a separate development, Peaches La Trené
may also be charged with involvement in the
death of Marty Bindgold, a former cameraman
turned actor who was killed last month, moments before making his debut as Lee Harvey
Oswald in the Los Angeles production of *Kennedy*. Bindgold, who died instantly when the
Texas book depository collapsed on top of
him, was one of a long line of victims associated
with the musical's history, which seems almost
as ill-starred as that of the Kennedy clan itself.
Two years ago, during the Brass Monkeys
awards ceremony—

Will broke off from his reading. Candida had entered the
room and was staring at him wistfully. 'Willie,' she said in the
cloying sort of voice she usually used when she wanted a favour.

'Yes?' He gave her a cool look. Ever since she'd returned
from Pick's hotel with her tail between her legs, he'd been
making the most of his temporary upper hand; he doubted it
would last long but in the meantime his discarded clothing and
used marijuana stubs were littered round the house with im-
punity.

She hesitated. 'I was thinking,' she began.

'Yes?'

'Now that you're a famous detective again—'

'Not according to the *Pop*,' Will cut in, throwing the paper
down on the floor next to yesterday's socks. 'They seem to think
it was all down to Inspector Ffelcher.'

Candida dismissed the *Pop* with a doleful shake of her head.
'Well, *I* know it was you,' she said. 'And since you did so well,
I've been wondering: do you have to work at that nasty bank
any more? I mean, wasn't it nice when you were round the
house all day, watching the— or rather' – she stopped herself
quickly – 'doing your research. And now that Britannia Dray-

cott's gone off to be a nun and I'm going to present *Your Arts
Desire*, I'll be ever so much busier and it'll be good for you to be
around the house' – she looked around despairingly – 'and to
look after Zoë like you used to. So, I know how much you love
banking and everything, and it would be a terrible wrench,
but . . .'

Will fixed her with a look of reluctant concentration. He
would let her wriggle a bit, he decided, before giving in.

Meanwhile, his eye wandered back to the newspaper.
Underneath the Peaches story was the TV schedule. They were
about to start rerunning old episodes of *Poirot*, he noted. As he
settled back contentedly on the settee and let Candida's arguments roll over him, he began silently grooming his imaginary
moustaches and muttering to himself about little grey cells.

In the offices of the Brahmin Corporation in New York's World
Trade Centre, there was no such weekend rest for Nick
Tallopia, its managing director. A confirmed workaholic, he
was at his desk as usual and so were his staff.

What with the press conference and the takeover of Butchers
Bank, it had been a heavy week and there was much still to be
done. But by and large things had gone well and he was
contented.

All the same, for a while back there he'd really thought old
Bradley was losing it, sending through messages about settling
with Zlennek just as they were on the point of winning the
court case, for Chrissake, and even talking about merging the
companies. It had actually got as far as some demented English
woman from Zlennek's organisation walking into the New
York office as if she owned the place and demanding to start
negotiations.

Fortunately, the old man's brainstorm had not lasted long,
though. To Tallopia's immense relief, he had come to his senses
pretty damn quick and out of the blue had come another e-mail
countermanding his previous orders. Now they were back on
track to screw Zlennek into the ground, and Tallopia had been

able to have the uppity English woman dragged off by security and dumped unceremoniously on the sidewalk outside.

In fact, the whole affair even seemed to have had a positive effect on the old man. In the latter part of the week, Tallopia had detected a much more laid-back approach from his boss than for some time. Sure, he'd made a few suggestions about the running of Butchers Bank. But Tallopia had looked into those and had been happy to go along with them. With the Pick problem behind it, Butchers seemed a very well-managed institution. What it needed now was a bit of continuity and a safe pair of hands, and Bradley's new proposal that they keep Lomond Butcher on as chairman and promote this other guy as CEO seemed right on the money. 'If it ain't broke, don't fix it,' had always been Tallopia's philosophy and he was glad to find that finally the old man seemed to be going along with it.

Nick's musings were interrupted by the discreet ring of the intercom.

'Call for you,' said his secretary: 'It's that flake with the weird accent again, claiming to be Mr Bradley. You want me to give him the brush-off?'

'No,' said Tallopia. 'I'll talk to him this time, and get rid of him once and for all.' He grabbed the receiver. 'Now listen here,' he said, before the caller could get a word in edgeways. 'Mr Bradley is currently on his estate in Maine, and I was in communication with him by e-mail not half an hour ago. And if you knew anything at all about him, you'd know that he doesn't use the telephone ever. He hasn't had the power of his vocal chords these twenty years now. So if you know what's good for you, you'll get the hell off this line before I have the call traced and send the cops round.'

There, that should fix him. He slammed down the phone. 'I don't think he'll bother us again now,' he told his secretary. 'Just some crazy with nothing better to do with his life.'

Back in London, the new managing director of Butchers Bank was celebrating his appointment with an afternoon of unbridled love-making in the kitchen of his house in Notting Hill Gate. Eyes closed, Toby Slaker was savouring the delicious sensations of being ravished by a partner who, though not quite a Hollywood legend, was none the less as close to a sex goddess as he ever wanted to come in future.

He opened his eyes again and blinked. For just a moment, he was almost taken aback at the sight that greeted him. Being able to see again during sex was a novelty in itself, of course. But that wasn't what surprised him. No, it was the identity of the face which leered hungrily back down at him that was the real shock.

Ever since news of his new position had been announced, his wife's desire for his body had become insatiable.

'Do you think we could stop for a while,' asked Toby exhausted. 'These taps are sort of sticking into my backside.'

'All right,' breathed Simona with evident reluctance 'But just for a while. After that we can move into the garden. I've got a great idea for a threesome with one of the gnomes.'

Did this woman think of nothing but sex? Desperately, Toby tried to steer the subject off in any other direction. 'How did the New York trip go, anyway?' he asked.

A hint of Simona's old nonchalance peeped through for an instant. 'Just great,' she replied breezily. 'Your Mr Tallopia seemed very amenable. But it looks like a merger's not on the cards after all.'

'Oh?' sniffed Toby. 'Not what I heard. I was told the court case is moving firmly in Bradley's direction. And there's a rumour that Zlennek may have to hand over WHAM in partial settlement. Which,' he concluded triumphantly, 'would sort of make me your boss, wouldn't it?'

He'd hardly got the words out before she fell on him again, mouth agape, eyes ablaze. And in those eyes, he at last thought he detected the same light of passion as when she'd deflowered him on the Butchers boardroom table all those years before.

And what, you are no doubt wondering, about the one remaining player in this drama? Where was she?

In a distant corner of an IBM mainframe, somewhere over the virtual rainbow, two organically challenged intelligence forms were roaming romantically across the Net. Whispering sweet zeros in each other's ears, they gambolled through the pages of the World Wide Web, window-shopped in its virtual malls, and canoodled gently in the ether.

One of them was a virile piece of anti-virus software with a chunky disk drive, bulging RAM, and an on-screen presence to die for.

And the other was an independent woman of property, taking time out from her busy schedule to enjoy a brief trip with her new boyfriend.

She would have much to do when she got back. Decisions had to be made, cash flows examined, budgets scrutinised. The international financial empire, delivered into her lap by Melvin's information on a Certain Person in her misdirected quest for revenge, would not be easy to run.

But she would worry about that tomorrow, which, after all, was another day. In the meantime, Scarlett lay back in the arms of her beloved, gazed into his clear blue eyes and ran her finger along his pencil-line moustache.

The new owner of Butchers Bank had at last found her virtual Rhett Butler.

And frankly, dear reader, she did not give a damn.

A selection of bestsellers
from Hodder & Stoughton

All Hodder & Stoughton books are available at your local bookshop or newsagent, or can be ordered direct from the publisher. Just tick the titles you want and fill in the form below. Prices and availability subject to change without notice.

Hodder & Stoughton Books, Cash Sales Department, Bookpoint, 39 Milton Park, Abingdon, OXON, OX14 4TD, UK. E-mail address: orders@bookprint.co.uk. If you have a credit card you may order by telephone – (01235) 400414.

Please enclose a cheque or postal order made payable to Bookpoint Ltd to the value of the cover price and allow the following for postage and packing:
UK & BFPO: £1.00 for the first book, 50p for the second book and 30p for each additional book ordered up to a maximum charge of £3.00.
OVERSEAS & EIRE: £2.00 for the first book, £1.00 for the second book and 50p for each additional book.

Name . . . .

Address . . . .

. . . .

. . . .

If you would prefer to pay by credit card, please complete:
Please debit my Visa / Access / Diner's Club / American Express (delete as applicable) card no:

Signature . . . .

Expiry Date . . . .

If you would **NOT** like to receive further information on our products please tick the box. ☐